RESCUED

FINDING PROVIDENCE - BOOK 1

JILL BURRELL

Cover Design © 2021 Brennylou Design at Blue Valley Author Services.
Edits by Michelle Henrie

First edition: May 2021
Library of Congress Control Number: 2021908016

ISBN: 978-1-955507-02-8 (eBook)
ISBN: 978-1-955507-03-5 (pbk)

To my father,
who taught me what to look for in a man
by the way he treated my mother. I miss you dad.

This story was originally his idea.

CHAPTER 1

*A*my needed help.

She approached the modest brick home, hoping the light coming through the window meant Celeste was still awake. It was late, but Celeste was her oldest and dearest friend, and Amy desperately needed to vent.

Thank goodness Celeste is a night owl.

Crickets chirped from somewhere deep inside the dappled willow trees forming a privacy hedge between Amy's friends and the neighbors. The scent of freshly mowed grass hung in the air.

A cat screeched somewhere down the street, and a shiver raced through Amy despite the pleasant August night. She chalked her reaction up to the disturbing events from earlier.

How did my life fall apart in a matter of hours?

Fighting the urge to give in to the tears that had been threatening for the past hour, she knocked on Celeste's door. Amy was not a crier. She'd learned at a young age crying solved nothing.

The porch light came on, blinding Amy, and the door opened a crack. She couldn't fault Celeste's caution. This Portland neighborhood was much nicer than the one Amy lived in, but it still left something to be desired. Especially at midnight.

"Amy? What's wrong? What are you doing here?" Celeste rarely minced words.

Rightfully so, since Celeste usually tended Amy's daughter, Kallie, through the night.

Celeste had come to Amy's rescue six months ago when Amy's new boss, Dennis, moved her to the night shift. Now Kallie spent the nights Amy worked at Aunt Celeste's.

Celeste swung the door wide, and Amy pressed a hand to her stomach quelling the churning sensation.

What am I going to do?

Amy kicked off her shoes and made herself comfortable on the overstuffed couch in the family room. She hugged a throw pillow to her chest and chewed on her bottom lip. Pages with colorful sketches in various stages of completion for Celeste's next children's book littered the coffee table.

Celeste sat at the other end of the couch, cradling her hands around her seven-month baby bump. "Okay, spill. I can tell by the way you're gnawing on your lip something bad has happened."

Trust Celeste to perceive in a matter of seconds how messed up Amy's life was.

"I left work early tonight—"

"Why?"

Amy let out a heavy sigh. "Because I quit."

"What? Why?" Celeste's left eyebrow shot up.

"Dennis gave me an ultimatum." A shiver of disgust swept over Amy as she remembered how he'd backed her into a corner of the storage room.

Celeste scowled. "What kind of ultimatum?"

"If I want my job as day manager back, I have to make it worth his while." Amy didn't even attempt to hide the disgust in her voice.

"Worth his while? As in...?"

"Sleep with him." Amy filled in the blank.

"That louse! Isn't he married?"

Amy winced at Celeste's volume as she nodded. She glanced at the door to the master bedroom where Celeste's husband, Grant, slept.

"Doesn't he realize you're in a... relationship with Lance?"

Celeste's hesitation before saying *relationship* reminded Amy, her friend didn't have a high opinion of Amy's boyfriend and Kallie's father. If Celeste knew what Amy walked in on less than an hour ago her hesitation would have been much longer.

The knot in Amy's stomach tightened, and a crawling sensation pricked her skin.

Someone should have reminded Lance *he* was in a relationship. Not only did he have a sexy voice—a perfect mix of mellow and gravelly—he was gorgeous too. So, it never surprised her when girls showered him with attention. Problem was Lance never discouraged it.

"Dennis knows I was with Lance." Before Celeste could pick up on Amy's use of the past tense, she hurried on. "He said it didn't matter. He doesn't want a relationship. He..." Bile rose in her throat as she made air quotes with her fingers. "Just wanted some workplace perks."

Celeste gasped. "What a scumbag!"

The bedroom door to Amy's right flew open, and Grant darted out wearing boxers, hands balled into fists. "What's wrong?"

Celeste sprang to her feet and pushed her wide-eyed husband back into the bedroom. "Nothing. Sorry, honey. I'm talking to Amy."

"Oh." His mumbled acknowledgment proved Celeste often got excited when Amy was around.

Celeste often got excitable, period. With her, it was all or nothing. She never did anything halfway.

Amy wished she was more outgoing, like her friend. *No time like the present.* She needed to get far away from Lance and Dennis.

After a few muffled words and the unmistakable smack of a kiss, Celeste returned to the family room. A grin split her face. "He'll be so embarrassed if he remembers this tomorrow."

Amy's face heated. She'd seen plenty of her mother's boyfriends wander around the apartment in their boxers when she was young, but Grant was her best friend's attractive husband. A few months ago, she accidentally told him, "You make me hot." When what she meant to say was, "You make me mad." A slip he wouldn't let her live down.

3

Every time Grant got within five feet of Amy, he asked, "Am I making you hot?"

"Even if he doesn't remember flashing me, I'll never let *him* live it down." Amy grinned.

"You shouldn't." Celeste's smile faded. "Seriously though, A, what're you going to do without a job?"

"There's more," Amy whispered.

"More what?" Celeste leaned forward, brow furrowed.

"I went home early after quitting my job. Figured I'd get Kallie in the morning like I usually do." A dull pounding resonated in Amy's head. *I should have eaten something tonight.* But she'd been too busy trying to avoid her lecherous boss. She sucked in a deep breath and forced herself to tell her friend the worst part of the night. "Lance wasn't alone when I got home."

"Did he take the band home for an after-party again?" Celeste rolled her eyes. "When will he realize his weekend gig at Charlie's Bar and Grill isn't the same as being on tour?"

"He wasn't with the band." Amy squeezed her eyes shut and took a slow steadying breath to fight the nausea from the memory of Lance in her bed with a long-legged brunette. The same one that had ogled him all night at the bar.

She'd already spent fifteen minutes dry-heaving at the realization that while she'd been working nights, Lance had had plenty of opportunities to entertain other women in her bed.

"Oh." Celeste put a hand on Amy's knee. "I'm so sorry." The absence of Celeste's usual animation told Amy her friend was not surprised.

Amy planted her elbows on her knees. She rubbed her temples with trembling fingers. Apparently, she wasn't the only one who suspected Lance was cheating on her again. Or was it still?

He'd made such a fool of Amy for who knows how long. That's why she'd planned on leaving him.

Lance had never made her any promises. He'd made no commitment to her, except to act like he was doing her a favor by moving in with her. He'd sucked her in with his good looks and charm, and she'd let him walk all over her, knowing he'd never commit.

I'm such an idiot.

"If I had the money I'd been saving, Kallie and I would be okay for a while, but…"

Celeste let out a low growl. "Lance had no right to blow your hard-earned money on another guitar."

Amy had told Celeste about the money, because her friend insisted on knowing how she'd gotten the black eye last week. She hadn't told her she'd been saving the money so she could leave Lance and make a fresh start somewhere.

She didn't want to admit Lance didn't love her anymore.

Am I really that hard to love? The thought came unbidden.

Amy recalled the determination she'd experienced as she packed her bags before walking out on Lance. "I'm leaving, C."

"Darn right, you're leaving that loser. It's about time."

"No, I'm leaving Portland."

"What?" Celeste shrieked.

Amy shushed her, casting a glance at the bedroom door.

Celeste lowered her voice and said, "You and Kallie can stay here as long as you need. You don't have to leave Portland."

Warmth flooded Amy's chest. Celeste and Grant didn't have much room, so the invitation meant a lot to her. With Grant's younger siblings living with them and a baby of their own on the way, they didn't need Amy and Kallie underfoot.

"That means the world to me, C, but that isn't necessary." Amy squared her shoulders and raised her chin. "I have to leave. If I stay here, I'll end up letting Lance talk me into coming back." As disgusted as she was with Lance, her resolve always weakened when he turned on the charm. It made her sick to realize how easily he played her.

"Over my dead body. I'll make Grant go beat up Lance tomorrow and threaten him if he ever comes near you."

Her best friend since fifth grade would do anything for her, and Grant, who was hopelessly in love with his wife, would do whatever

5

she asked. But the last thing Amy wanted was Celeste coming to her rescue, again.

No, I need to do this by myself.

"It's just as well I quit my job," Amy said, getting to her feet. "This way I can leave without any ties. Without regrets."

Except she had regrets. The last three years were full of them.

"That doesn't mean you have to leave the city." Celeste stood too.

Amy opened the door to the partially finished nursery where her daughter slept and studied Kallie's peaceful, angelic face. *When did my baby get so big?*

Kallie was the best thing that ever happened to Amy. She'd taught Amy what it meant to love, wholly and unconditionally. Amy could never regret or resent that like her mother had resented her.

My mother.

"I turned out like my mother," Amy said in a strained whisper.

"No, you are nothing like her. You're ten times the woman she was."

Oh, how she wanted to believe Celeste, but Amy's actions betrayed her. "I'm taking my child out of bed in the middle of the night to leave an abusive, cheating boyfriend—exactly like my mother did on more than one occasion."

Celeste's gaze dropped to the floor.

Amy lifted Kallie from the crib and cradled the toddler in her arms, drawing comfort from the powerful surge of love flowing through her. She buried her nose in Kallie's soft curls and inhaled her daughter's clean, innocent scent. It wouldn't stay that way. Life had a way of stealing innocence.

Not if I can help it.

She'd protect Kallie as long as she could. Starting by getting as far away from Lance as possible.

"Where will you go?" Celeste followed her to the front door.

Fear and uncertainty tightened Amy's chest. "I don't know, but my next job won't be in a bar. And I swear, I'm done with men."

"Come on, Amy, just because Lance was a jerk, doesn't mean all men are."

After the day she'd had, Amy couldn't disagree more, but she didn't want to argue with her best friend.

Celeste had been as jaded as Amy, but she'd found happiness a year ago with Grant, and ever since, she'd been an advocate for love. That's partly why Celeste had never liked Lance—he was self-centered and not at all concerned about Amy's happiness.

As Lance's true colors had shown themselves, Amy had been too proud to leave because it meant she'd turned out like her mother.

"I'll call you tomorrow and let you know where I end up."

"You better." Celeste's voice grew husky. "Drive safe and take care of my sweet Kallie."

"I will." Amy blinked back tears and gave her friend a one-armed hug before leaving.

"Amy, wait. I know you need time to heal from this but promise me you won't lock your heart too tightly. Who knows, you might find love when you least expect it."

Celeste had almost lost out on love because of stubbornness, but this wasn't a promise Amy could make. She wouldn't give her heart to a man unless she was sure he was committed to her. Since she couldn't see that ever happening, she said the only thing she could.

"Bye, C. Love you."

PROVIDENCE, *2 miles.*

After four hours of mindless driving on the interstate with no clear destination in mind, Amy needed a break. She peered into the dark, seeing no lights, no signs of life.

Do I dare stop?

The caffeine she'd purchased when she gassed up had long since worn off. Her anger had dissipated about an hour ago when she crossed into southeastern Washington, leaving her physically and emotionally depleted. The hopelessness of her situation sunk in, and fear coiled like a snake in her gut. She'd been grateful for the cover of darkness while driving. The last thing she wanted was to see how aptly the barren landscape matched her circumstances.

How will I provide for Kallie without a job?

If she made it another hour and a half to Spokane, maybe she could find a women's shelter to stay at until she got on her feet. Shoving a stick of gum in her mouth, she turned up the cool air and pressed harder on the gas pedal.

Her car stuttered and lost speed. Her gaze flew to the gas gauge. She still had a quarter tank. She pressed harder on the gas, but the car lurched and clanked. Her stomach lurched right along with the car. Gripping the wheel, she veered to the Providence exit.

Her shoulders knotted as her car continued to hesitate and decelerate, despite pressure on the gas.

Amy spotted lights in the distance. "Come on, just a little farther."

She clenched her jaw and tightened her grip on the steering wheel, as she crept down a dark main street. She didn't dare stop without the prospect of help.

A sign for Knight's Auto Repair shone like a beacon. She heaved a sigh as she pulled into the parking lot. Her car clanked again as it rolled to a stop under the Knight's sign. Cringing, she released a groan and flexed her fingers.

Stifling a scream, Amy rested her forehead against the steering wheel. She couldn't afford car problems. She couldn't even buy food and diapers for her daughter.

She squeezed her eyes closed to stop the tears that threatened to fall, again. She already had a massive headache, besides more crying wouldn't change anything.

What am I going to do?

"MEL!" Ben shot up in bed, gasping for air. The still air in the dark room lay heavy in his chest.

Heart racing, he dragged his hands over his face where tears mingled with beads of sweat. He'd almost touched them this time.

Once again, he'd raced through a bizarre, ever-changing maze, repeatedly glimpsing his wife and daughter. They were so beautiful. So perfect.

Melanie often whispered his name in the nightmares, and sometimes Cassey giggled. No matter how hard he tried to reach them, they always disappeared, leaving him in despair.

He'd followed them into the void many times, but the darkness consumed him. Suffocated him. Every time, he woke up gasping for air.

He scowled at the bottle of sleeping pills on the nightstand. He didn't take them often, but yesterday was Melanie's birthday. He rarely had the nightmares when he took them, but they hadn't worked this time.

Picking up the bottle, he hurled it at the wall.

He fell back and stared at the ceiling. No use trying to go back to sleep now. Without checking the clock, he knew it was almost five a.m. These dreams always occurred around the same time, and his overwhelming grief always made it impossible to find sleep again.

A flash of light streaked through his window, followed by a metallic clank. A car had pulled into the gas station and repair shop below his apartment, and judging by the sound, it had serious problems.

The slamming of a car door brought him from his bed. He pulled back the curtain in time to see a slim figure with blond hair slip into the backseat of an older model Ford Focus.

Yawning, he turned away from the window and dressed in his running clothes. Running was the best way to dispel the heaviness that clung to him after the nightmares.

The driver of the car would have to wait for the repair shop to open. He should be more concerned about the blond's misfortune, but he didn't care about much of anything lately.

CHAPTER 2

*a*my awoke to an unfamiliar rattling noise. She lifted her head, her stiff neck protesting, and turned to see a garage door roll up. Rubbing tired eyes with one hand, she stretched her cramped limbs, trying not to awaken her daughter.

Kallie pushed herself upright in Amy's arms and looked around, bright-eyed.

Holding Kallie close, Amy climbed out of the car.

A man stood in the large, open doorway of the first bay of the garage, watching her. With the sun in her eyes, she couldn't see his face, but she could tell he was tall and broad-shouldered. He turned and walked back into the repair shop.

Heat warmed her cheeks, and she raked her fingers through her hair. *Great. He caught me sleeping in my car.*

Swallowing her pride, she slung Kallie's diaper bag over her shoulder and approached the garage. Despite the tidy appearance of the inside of the shop, the odor of grease and oil hung in the air. Shiny tools hung in organized rows against the back wall.

Amy stopped a few feet behind the mechanic and cleared her throat.

He turned, and she sucked in a sharp breath. He had the most striking, sapphire-blue eyes. With eyes like that, Amy would consider him handsome if it wasn't for the full beard covering his face and the sandy-brown hair hanging past the collar of his blue shirt. The distant way he regarded her and lack of a welcoming smile gave him an intense, brooding appearance.

"Can I help you?" His low, firm voice was not as gruff as she expected.

"Um… I need… some help with my car." She gave herself a mental shake. He was probably a nice man, even if he looked like he belonged on a Harley.

Before he could respond, Kallie cried and squirmed in Amy's arms. His eyes shifted to her daughter. A flash of unreadable emotion crossed his face. His gaze remained on Kallie while Amy explained what happened with her car.

"How old is she?"

"What?"

"How old is your daughter?"

Surprised by the question, Amy hesitated before responding. "Sixteen months."

"What's her name?" he asked, his voice huskier now.

Kallie frequently drew people's attention, but it was usually women, not men. Was this an attempt to be friendly? *Maybe he should try smiling.*

The mechanic's gaze never left Kallie's face, and Amy's chest grew tight. Something about his eyes made her look closer. The bleakness she'd read as distant seemed more like sorrow.

Unnerved, Amy stepped back, rotating Kallie away from him. "Kallie, spelled with a K."

His eyes narrowed, and he sucked in a sharp breath before turning away, his hands balled into fists.

What's his deal? Her brow furrowed as she stared at his back.

After a long moment, with his back to her, he cleared his throat. "Would you like me to check out at your car now?" The husky quality of his deep voice sent a shiver of awareness through her. His voice sounded every bit as sexy as Lance's.

11

She contemplated going to a different garage, but this was the only one she'd seen when coaxing her car through town last night. Besides, she'd barely made it here, it's not like she could drive her car somewhere else.

Perplexed, she pulled her keys from the diaper bag and extended them toward him. "Yes, please. Is there a restroom where we can freshen up?" Kallie needed a diaper change, and for reasons she couldn't explain, she needed to put some distance between her daughter and the mechanic with the most beautiful and saddest eyes she had ever seen.

BEN TURNED, took the keys, and motioned inside the convenience store, his gaze once again on the baby.

He watched the woman walk away with the blond, blue-eyed toddler in her arms. The woman looked nothing like Melanie, but the baby… even her name was similar. Pain gripped his chest, and he fought to catch his breath for the second time this morning. The first had been when she climbed from her car; the sun reflected off her platinum blond, creating a halo around her head.

Something happened inside him at that moment. Something foreign and powerful—a complete contrast to the emptiness and darkness that had filled him for so long. He'd retreated into the garage, trying to analyze the feeling. He didn't think it was physical attraction, although she was certainly pretty with her curly, blond hair, sky-blue eyes, and slender, but-with-an-appealing-amount-of-curves figure.

Forget about the woman and do your job.

But that baby…

Twenty minutes later, Ben stepped inside the convenience store as the woman and her daughter exited the restroom. He knew what was wrong with her car the moment he put it into gear and it made the same clanking sound he'd heard early this morning. She wouldn't like the prognosis.

Don't look at the baby. Just talk to the mom.

"Hi, ma'am, I apologize for not introducing myself earlier. I'm Ben Young." Thankfully, his voice held steady. He extended his hand, then caught sight of the smudge of grease across his knuckles and jerked it back. He pulled a rag from his pocket and rubbed the offending spot.

"Amy Lawson." The woman extended her hand and waited for him to take it.

Her grip was not as steady as her voice. She gave him a shaky smile. *Is she afraid of me? Or does she fear all men?*

Fear was not what he usually saw in people's faces when they looked at him.

He released her hand and dropped his gaze. This would be easier if he didn't look at her or the baby. Especially the baby. "Well, Ms. Lawson—"

"Call me Amy, please."

"Amy, I'm afraid I have—"

"Oh Ben, I'm so glad I caught you." A busty redhead in red high heels and a snug, low-cut jumpsuit stepped between him and Amy.

Ben bit back a groan and moved back. Debbie Wheeler was out of bed early for a Saturday.

"My car is making a funny noise. I brought it in for you to look at." Debbie leaned toward him, exposing her cleavage.

Ben lifted his eyes to somewhere above her head and let his aggravation out in a controlled sigh. "I'm sure your car is fine, Debbie. I'm busy today, but Scott can check it for you."

She pouted and pressed a red fingernail to his chest. "But Ben, you know you're the only one I trust with my baby."

He repressed a shudder. That was the problem. Debbie didn't even trust her own brother, who was an excellent mechanic, to touch her Porsche. She came in almost weekly, insisting Ben check her car while she hovered near.

Behind Debbie, a smirk formed on Amy's pretty face. Ben bit back a smile of his own. Judging by the broadening of Amy's smile, he wasn't as successful at keeping his eyes from rolling. Even this stranger could see how phony Debbie was.

13

"Later, Debbie. I'm busy today."

He stepped around Debbie and took Amy by the arm, guiding her to the door of the repair shop. Before they walked through, he shifted his hand from Amy's arm to the small of her back. He shouldn't use a stranger like this, but he was fed up with Debbie and her expensive foreign sports car. Maybe if he acted interested in Amy, Debbie would get a clue.

If only I could be so lucky.

Amy shot him a sideways glance, eyebrows raised. Keeping his touch light, he hurried her through the door to the sound of Debbie's heels clacking as she exited the gas station. As soon as they stepped into the repair shop, he dropped his hand and stepped away from her.

Amy took an additional step back.

"Sorry about that." Hopefully, she'd realize the apology was as much for touching her as it was for Debbie's interruption.

She gave him a tight smile. "If you're too busy today to fix my car, maybe you could recommend someone else here in town."

An unexpected sense of desperation seized him at the thought of her leaving. "I'm not busy. I said that because... well, never mind." He raked his fingers through his hair. He couldn't let her leave. "I'm working on your car today."

Relief filled her face.

"But I'm afraid I have some bad news." He grimaced, hoping to soften the blow. "And some worse news."

Amy's brow creased. Bouncing the fussy toddler on her hip, she closed her eyes for a long moment and took a deep breath. "Okay, let me have it."

"You have a cracked gear in your transmission."

"Transmission?" Her eyes widened, and her chin dropped. "Isn't that expensive to replace?"

"Yes, but I can rebuild it for much less than what a new transmission costs." He gave her a ballpark figure.

She sucked in a sharp breath and cringed.

"Unfortunately, I don't have the parts for a rebuild in stock. I'll need to order them from a dealer in Kennewick. The earliest I can have it delivered will be Monday. Then it will take another few days to get your car running again." Ben always hated giving this kind of news.

She turned her head away, but not before tears filled her eyes.

An odd pang filled his chest again. The same one he experienced when the sun haloed around her head. His heart felt like it was trying to expand.

Sensing the air of defeat surrounding Amy, he studied her. Why had she been driving in the middle of the night? And how long had she been on the road? The red polo with *Charlie's* written on the left breast and black slacks suggested she'd started driving after work.

Amy swiped at her cheek and took a deep breath. She turned back to face him but didn't make eye contact.

"Listen, I'm going to be honest with you..." her voice faltered, and she bit her bottom lip. "I... um... don't have the money right now to fix my car and I can't... afford a motel."

Ben studied Amy. She'd pulled her hair back in a ponytail, but several strands broke free and curled around her face. The mascara smudges he'd seen earlier were gone, but dark shadows ringed her red eyes. Redness caused by crying, he guessed, and shadows from lack of sleep. Despite the obvious fatigue, she was attractive.

What had she been through?

He hooked his thumbs in his pockets as a desire to help Amy and her daughter crashed over him like a wave of warm water. Instead of talking himself out of it, he shifted his gaze to the fussy toddler. Her blond curls had been pulled into a small ponytail. His chest tightened and a strange tingling filled his extremities. If he didn't help Amy, who would? Could she care for her daughter without help? He couldn't protect and care for his own daughter, but he could make sure hers was safe and provided for.

He put a hand on her shoulder. "It sounds like you're in a tight spot. Don't worry. I'm sure we can work something out. I don't need money from you." He paused, letting his words sink in. "I can take care of you if you'll let me."

Amy's eyes widened, and she jerked away from him, taking a step back.

Okay. The lady doesn't like to be touched.

She retreated and bumped into a workbench, knocking off a wrench. It clattered to the floor with a harsh metallic clang. Amy jumped.

Ben shot her a concerned glance as he bent to pick up the wrench. *What's wrong with the lady?*

She side-stepped as though desperate to maintain her distance.

"I can't... um... I won't..." she blurted, then taking a deep breath, she chewed on her bottom lip as she focused on the fussy toddler.

She was clearly uncomfortable here with him, but he had to wonder if she was unwell. Why was she driving in the middle of the night?

"Is there someone you can call? Do you have relatives or friends here in Providence?"

"No." The single word squeaked out.

"Where were you heading? Maybe I could arrange a ride for you until your car is fixed."

"I don't know where—" Tears filled her eyes again, and she ducked her head. "I just... needed to leave."

Who or what was she running from? An abusive husband? His gaze jumped to her left hand. No ring. Boyfriend maybe?

Fighting the urge to step closer, he said, "Please, let me help you."

Amy licked her lips and rubbed her forehead with a shaky hand.

Ben held his breath. Would she accept his offer? He glanced at the toddler in her arms and prayed she would.

"I won't deny I'm in a tight spot right now... and I need help." She grimaced as though the words tasted bitter. "But I need to make it clear that I won't trade any... um... favors... in lieu of payment."

Ben's eyebrows shot up, and he gave an uncomfortable cough. He stepped back and raised his hands, palms out. "Whoa. That's not what I had in mind. I'm sorry if I gave you that impression. I only meant I could arrange a place for you to stay."

"A *place* to stay? Not... with you?"

"Not with me."

Amy let out a shaky laugh, but her posture remained stiff. "I'm sorry for assuming—"

"Don't worry about it. I should have been clearer about what I meant."

His attention turned to the fussy baby again, and his brow furrowed. "I don't mean to pry, but is your baby okay? She seems really fussy."

"She's hungry."

Hunger. He could do something about that.

"I'll bet you're starving too. Come with me." Careful to keep his distance, he motioned for her to follow him. He led her out of the garage and across the street.

What am I doing? The thought echoed in his head with each step.

THE MOST AMAZING smells assaulted Amy when they entered the quaint diner: coffee, bacon, maple syrup, and a hint of cinnamon. Her stomach growled in anticipation.

The heads of the dozen customers seated at tables and booths turned their direction, and all chatter ceased. Everyone studied Ben in surprise, then greeted him by name when he passed. Ben nodded in return and grabbed a highchair for Kallie, leading them to a table near the window.

"Ben, my dear, you've finally come for breakfast?" A petite, slender woman with shoulder-length, honey-colored hair approached them, her face split in a wide grin.

"Hi, Aunt Charity." Ben kissed the woman's cheek. "Nothing for me, thanks, but I would like you to give Amy and her daughter whatever they want. Put it on my tab."

Amy expected his aunt to eye her, questioning who she was and why Ben would buy her breakfast. But the aunt's eyes widened and remained on Ben. Amy glanced over her shoulder at the rest of the customers in the diner. Everyone stared at Ben with the same surprised expression.

"Absolutely, I'll take good care of them. But you know I'll never let you carry a tab."

Ben pulled out his wallet.

"Put that away! Your money's no good here. Now, why don't you sit down and join them? I'll bring you one of my big ol' cinnamon rolls." Charity tried to nudge him into a chair, but he resisted.

"Sounds tempting, but I've already eaten."

"Nonsense. That toast you eat isn't a fit breakfast for a hard-working man."

"I'm fine." He turned to Amy. "Order anything you want, okay?"

He stared at Kallie for a long moment, his hand lifting. Then, inches from Kallie's head, he curled his fingers into a fist. His eyes filled with pain before he turned and walked away.

Amy frowned as a knot formed in her stomach. *Have I made a mistake accepting his help?*

She didn't have a choice, though. When she told Ben, she had no one to call, she meant it. No one to turn to and nowhere to go. Celeste and Grant would help her in a heartbeat, but they didn't have the extra resources, nor did Lance. She wouldn't call *him* even if he did.

The same customers who greeted Ben a few moments ago gave him encouraging smiles as he left the restaurant. His aunt's gaze followed him, a mixture of concern and affection on her face. He couldn't be *that* bad could he, if everyone smiled at him?

Ben's aunt turned her bright smile back to Amy. "Welcome to Providence. I'm Charity. What's your name?"

"Amy."

"And what about this little angel?" Charity rested her hand on Kallie's head.

"Her name is Kallie."

"Oh, I see." The older woman's eyes widened, and she stared out the window at Ben crossing the street.

Amy's gaze followed hers. *See what?*

~

AMY SHOVED a last bite of the delicious cinnamon roll in her mouth and pushed the rest away. She'd barely made a dent in all the food Charity had brought. Amy was stuffed.

No longer hungry, Kallie played with her spoon and straw.

Amy's full stomach churned as she realized how little money she had. Thirty-seven dollars. Lance must have taken her tip money from her wallet again, and she'd almost drained her checking account paying for gas last night.

Thanks to Lance, she didn't even have an emergency credit card anymore. Instead of increasing her limit, like he'd insisted after he maxed it out last month, she'd cut it up. She'd paid for it that night when Lance came home. His drunken rages had become more frequent over the past year.

She attempted to pay for breakfast from her meager funds, but Charity refused. "Honey, it's on the house. Any woman who can get Ben out of the garage eats for free."

What's that supposed to mean? He didn't even stay to eat with her.

Thank goodness. She would've lost her appetite if he'd been across the table from her. Especially if he continued to stare at Kallie with those intense blue eyes.

Having worked for years as a waitress, she'd met all kinds of people, and she'd become good at reading them. She couldn't seem to figure Ben out. He seemed to be filled with sorrow, and everyone around him reflected that sadness.

With a full stomach, and no longer trying to quiet a fussy toddler, Amy focused on her dilemma. *Now what?* She was destitute and broken down in the middle of nowhere. She should have thought this through before she left in such a hurry last night.

Memories of Lance in her bed with the brunette brought the sting of tears to her eyes again. She blinked them away before they could spill over. *What's wrong with me? I am not a crier. Besides, he doesn't deserve more tears.*

True. This was not how she expected things to turn out, but she was better off getting out now instead of waiting until Lance's next fling or drunken rage. One thing she was certain of, Lance would never change.

Ben offered her help but at what cost? She needed to do what was best for Kallie. Getting herself into another bad situation was a terrible idea.

Can I trust him? Despite his bushy beard and brooding eyes, he didn't appear dangerous. She'd known plenty of dangerous men in her life, but she hadn't seen that lecherous make-her-skin-crawl-look in his eyes like she had seen in theirs. His eyes held pain and sorrow.

Of course, Lance hadn't appeared dangerous when she first met him. She couldn't trust anyone right now. Trusting people gave them power to hurt her.

A few minutes later, Ben slid into the seat across from her. Amy's breath caught as every muscle in her body tensed. He both frightened and intrigued her. It didn't help that she'd felt an undeniable warmth against her low back earlier when he'd touched her. The sensation had been so powerful, her senses were still on high alert.

"Did you enjoy your breakfast?"

"Immensely. Your aunt brought us a little of everything." She motioned to the plates of partially eaten food. "Including her famous 'Big Ol' Cinnamon Roll'." She set the plate that held half the pastry in front of him. "I think it would please Charity if you helped me with this."

He stared at the plate, and one corner of his mouth briefly raised in a half-smile before dropping again. "She's a fantastic cook, isn't she?" He broke off a piece and put it in his mouth. His eyes closed, and a look of pleasure softened his features.

Amy's gaze lingered on his face. *Is he smiling?* Judging by his brooding nature, she had a feeling it didn't happen very often.

Ben opened his eyes and caught her staring at him. He held her gaze for a long moment before lowering his eyes.

He pulled a paper from his shirt pocket and put it in front of her. Light reflected off the gold band on his left hand. *He's married.* She felt like an even bigger fool for thinking he'd suggested an intimate relationship as payment for his help. Of course, that hadn't stopped Dennis from propositioning her.

What made Ben any different? And what had she agreed to by accepting his help?

"Here's my parent's address. They've agreed to let you stay with them." His voice was confident, assertive.

His parents. Amy breathed a sigh of relief, then hesitated. "I don't want to inconvenience anyone."

"You won't. My father's a doctor and my mother's the high school principal. Neither is home much."

And he's a mechanic? That must have been a source of contention with his parents.

"They have a large house and plenty of room for you and..." His gaze rested on her daughter. "Kallie."

Was it her imagination, or did his voice hitch when he said Kallie's name? Amy lifted her daughter from the highchair and held her protectively. Why did pain fill his eyes every time he looked at her?

"Why are you helping me?" Amy asked.

He twisted the wedding band on his finger as his gaze dropped to the cinnamon roll.

Amy doubted he actually saw it.

He cleared his throat. "My life... would be very different right now... if someone had helped my..." His Adam's apple bobbed. "The ones I loved."

CHAPTER 3

*T*hirty minutes later, Amy pushed Kallie's stroller into a cul-de-sac after passing quaint shops and homes with white picket fences.

Ben offered to drive them to his parents' house, but the thought of riding in such close confines with him tied her stomach in knots. So, she'd insisted on getting Kallie's stroller from the trunk of her car and walking. But the pain she'd seen in his eyes when he said his life would be different if someone had helped the ones he loved haunted her the whole way.

Two large homes stood on either side of the cul-de-sac with an empty lot between them. She checked the homes for the correct address. There, above the garage of the red-brick, rambler, hung the numbers she sought. She pushed the stroller up the driveway, taking in the wide covered porch with white pillars.

Ben hadn't been kidding when he said his parents owned a big home. The house screamed wealth.

Amy sucked in a deep breath through a suddenly tight throat. She was out of her element in this neighborhood. The manicured lawns and colorful flower beds—complete with buzzing bees—were a far cry from the apartment building she'd lived in where she'd struggled to keep flowers alive in a pot on her tiny patio.

Amy lifted Kallie from the stroller and approached the front door. What would she say to Ben's parents? *"Hi, I'm homeless, and my life's a wreck. I'm so tired, I might burst into tears if you don't take me in?"*

The door swung open before she could knock. There stood Ben's aunt from the diner.

Taken aback, Amy froze. How had Charity gotten here and changed clothes so quickly?

The woman smiled. "Hello, you must be Amy. We've been expecting you." She motioned Amy into the house.

Amy stumbled on the threshold, her confusion manifesting itself in her clumsiness. "Yes... I'm Amy," she stammered. "I'm sorry... is this Mr. and Mrs. Young's house?"

"It is. I'm Ben's mother, Hope."

Hope? She and Charity must be twins.

Before Amy could respond, Hope pulled her deeper into the house. She led her past the sitting room to an immaculate spacious family room decorated in shades of dusty rose and ivory. A fireplace filled one wall, and a large, flat screen TV occupied another.

A tall, distinguished gentleman entered the room through a side door at the same time they did. He offered his hand. "I'm Dr. Young. You may call me James."

"Nice to meet you." Amy shook his hand, then turned back to Ben's mother.

"You looked so much like Charity; it threw me."

Hope's eyes widened. "You've met Charity?" At Amy's nod, she said, "Yes, Charity and I are sisters—not identical, but we do look alike."

"I take it you've been to the diner?" James asked.

"Yes, Ben took us there for breakfast."

"He did?" they said in unison, exchanging surprised glances.

"Ben has been very kind." The words were true, despite the unease she couldn't shake concerning him.

Kallie babbled something unintelligible, drawing the couple's attention.

Hope reached out and took Kallie's hand. "She's a cutie. Such beautiful, blue eyes and curly blond hair." Her eyes misted, and she looked up at her husband.

James studied Kallie's face. "What a beautiful little angel." His eyes glistened.

"How old is she?" Hope asked.

"She's sixteen months." Again, Ben's parents exchanged a surprised glance. "Her name is Kallie," Amy said.

Hope gasped and turned away, but not before Amy saw the sheen of tears in her eyes.

"Would you excuse us for a moment?" James said in a husky voice. He ushered Hope into the room he had come out of only moments before.

The door didn't close tight behind them, and Hope's muffled cry reached Amy.

She frowned. *Did I say something wrong?*

Kallie strained to get down, diverting Amy's attention. She fished toys from the diaper bag as her gaze roamed the room filled with brown-leather furniture and mahogany shelves, full of glass and porcelain figurines. This house not only screamed wealth, it was not childproof.

What was it about Kallie everyone found so fascinating, and why did it make them emotional?

Hope's voice from behind the door interrupted Amy's thoughts. "Does Ben think it's her? Is that why he wants them to stay here?"

Her? Her who? A crowd of marathon runners raced through Amy's chest.

The Youngs were upset about something, and it had to do with Kallie; she was sure of it. She picked up James' lower voice but couldn't make out his words.

Perhaps staying here wasn't a good idea. She wracked her brain for other options.

When Ben's parents returned to the family room, they both wore smiles and apologized for their rudeness.

Hope sat beside her, and James sat in a nearby chair.

Amy sucked in slow, steady breaths, trying to ease the tightness in her chest.

"Tell us a little about yourself, Amy," James said. His tone of voice, though not harsh, sounded like he expected compliance.

She wasn't ready to share her life story, but if these people were willing to let them stay in their home, they deserved to know why she was in her current predicament.

Amy cleared her throat. "I'm from Portland, and I was traveling on the interstate when my car broke down. I barely made it to Knight's Repair Shop."

"You broke down this morning?" James asked.

Amy nodded. "Around five."

"Why were you traveling in the middle of the night?" Hope asked. "Were you expected somewhere this morning?"

Amy lowered her gaze to hide her discomfort. "No, I don't have anywhere to go." She cringed at her choice of words. She'd never spoken truer words.

"Where were you headed?" Hope asked in a gentle voice.

"I don't know." Amy shrugged. "I know it seems irresponsible of me as a mother to take off in the middle of the night with no money, and a car that apparently had problems, but I needed to leave. I needed to get away... from him," she finished, barely louder than a whisper.

Hope gasped and put a hand on Amy's arm. "Did he hurt you? Are you in danger?"

Amy bit her bottom lip and shook her head. She wasn't ready to share with these people all the ways Lance had hurt her.

"Please don't feel like we're judging you, dear." Hope leaned closer. "We're simply concerned for you and your daughter. We'd like to help you in any way we can. You're welcome to stay here as long as you'd like."

The sincerity in Hope's words stole Amy's breath. She looked at

James. He smiled and nodded, seconding his wife's words. Unable to speak around the lump in her throat, Amy gave a quick nod. She could see where Ben got his generosity.

Hope took her on a tour of the house, showing her a spacious, state-of-the-art kitchen with granite counter tops and stainless-steel appliances was Amy's dream kitchen. And the guest bedroom with a walk-in closet and adjoining bathroom was almost as big as Amy's entire apartment.

"Would you like to put Kallie in a separate room or keep her in here with you?"

"With me will be fine." Amy wasn't about to let Kallie out of her sight. Not with the way everyone acted around her.

"I have a playpen stored away somewhere in the basement. I'll set it up and make sure it's clean."

"I don't want you to go to any trouble. She can sleep on the bed with me."

Hope waved a hand. "No trouble at all. Besides, I've slept with babies in my bed before, and it can hardly be called sleeping."

When they rejoined James in the family room, he asked, "So Amy, do you have any plans? Have you considered staying in Providence for a while? Until you get back on your feet, at least."

She'd planned to stay only until her car was fixed. *But then what?*

"Well..." Amy hedged. "I don't have any specific plans. I wouldn't mind sticking around, but I'd need to find a job and a babysitter." She smiled down at Kallie, who played contentedly with her toys. She was such a good-natured baby.

Hope put a hand on Amy's arm. "Providence is a good place for a fresh start." She and James shared a smile that said there was a story there.

"I might know of an opening," James said. "Excuse me for a minute while I make a phone call." He crossed the room and entered what Amy assumed was his study.

After he left, Hope asked about her luggage.

"I only have a couple bags. Ben said he'd bring them over after work."

Hope's face lit up. "Maybe he'll stay for dinner. I'll have to make his favorite."

James returned a short time later, saying he'd arranged for Amy to have an interview. "The dispatcher and secretary at the Sheriff's Office will have a baby soon, and the sheriff hasn't found anyone to cover her maternity leave. Sheriff Winters said he'll be in the office all morning, barring any emergencies, and you're welcome to drop in anytime."

A rush of excitement bubbled up in Amy. Maybe she could make a fresh start here. Getting a job would be the first step. *But what about Kallie?*

Bringing a baby to a job interview wouldn't make a good impression. She couldn't leave her with the Youngs, though. That was asking too much. They were generous to open their home to her and Kallie, but she wasn't sure she trusted them with her baby, yet. She picked Kallie up and held her on her lap.

"You can leave her here if you'd like," Hope said, reading Amy's concern.

Amy didn't answer, instead, she held Kallie a little closer.

James gave Hope a pointed look. "I'm sure Robert wouldn't mind if she brought the baby along. She seems well behaved. I'm sure she'll be fine."

What message was the doctor trying to convey to his wife?

"Is the Sheriff's Office close enough to walk to?"

Hope chuckled. "Pretty much everything in this town is close enough to walk to." She took Amy to the kitchen, where she grabbed a pencil and paper and drew a map to the Sheriff's office. Hope walked Amy to the front door and watched her settle Kallie in the stroller.

Amy's thoughts spun as fast as the stroller wheels while she walked to the Sheriff's Office. First Ben's, then Charity's, and now the Young's strange reactions to Kallie left her with a multitude of unanswered questions.

She talked to Kallie as they walked. "What's the deal, Kallie Bug? Why do you upset everyone we meet? And who does Hope think you are?"

Forcing the confusing thoughts from her mind, she focused on the quaint, small-town scenery. What a beautiful oasis in this desert landscape.

Amy had never believed in fate or destiny. She'd been on own her since she was seventeen. Yes, she'd made some poor choices, Lance being the biggest, but that's why she'd left. So things could be different, and she wouldn't repeat her mistakes.

Celeste would tell Amy her car breaking down was destiny. Usually, Amy would argue with her, but she couldn't deny her car had worked fine until the exit for Providence.

Why this small town?

Despite Ben's broodiness, she was fortunate to encounter a mechanic who was willing to help her.

Amy spoke aloud again. "I don't think we would've gotten such compassion from a mechanic in a big city. And we wouldn't have found people as generous as Ben's parents." After meeting them, she felt better about accepting Ben's help. But she wished she understood what is was about Kallie that upset everyone.

"If this job works out, Kallie Bug, I might have to admit fate may be playing a part in our lives after all. Breaking down might turn out to be a good thing."

I hope.

"TELL ME, MS. LAWSON," Sheriff Winters said, "What brings you to Providence?"

Amy crossed her legs and took her time answering, hoping to give off a relaxed air of confidence. She wasn't sure what she'd expected a small-town Sheriff's Office to look like, but the building was even smaller than she'd expected. The reception area couldn't have been more than fifteen square feet, but the wall of windows, letting in plenty of light, made the room—crowded with chairs, a coffee table, and an L-shaped desk—feel bigger than it was.

The sheriff looked nothing like Amy expected. She'd pictured the sheriff as a middle-age man with a receding hairline, graying side-burns, and a belly that came from years spent behind a desk. Sheriff Robert Winters, at roughly thirty years old, was none of these things. He epitomized the description tall, dark, and handsome and had the most gorgeous brown eyes—surrounded by the longest lashes—Amy had ever seen.

"Please, call me Amy." She cleared her throat and told him a brief version of her car breaking down and how she found herself in a difficult position financially. When she mentioned Ben taking her to the diner for breakfast, the sheriff's eyebrows shot up.

"He ate breakfast with you?"

Taking a stranger to the diner was obviously not normal behavior for Ben. *Rightly so, since he's married.* Which made all the diners' encouraging smiles that much more confusing.

"Not *with* me, no. But he paid for my meal." Despite Charity's generosity, Ben had dropped some money on the table on their way out.

"Still…" the sheriff said, a grin splitting his handsome face.

Amy wasn't sure what to make of his comment, so she remained silent.

"And you're staying with the Youngs?"

"Yes." She thought about Hope's desire for Ben to stay for dinner. "I get the feeling they'd do anything for Ben."

"We'd *all* do anything for Ben," he said with a fierceness that surprised her. Then he cleared his throat and changed the subject. "Tell me, what type of previous work experience do you have?"

Could she leave out the last six months without raising the sheriff's suspicions? Amy pasted on a smile. "I've worked in the same restaurant and bar since I was fifteen. Initially, busing tables, then as a hostess. I've waited tables for the past seven, and I was the day manager for a year."

"Do you have any experience with computers?"

Kallie made sing-song noises in the stroller beside her, and the sheriff's gaze shifted to her. When Amy first arrived, she'd apologized for bringing a baby with her, but he'd brushed it off like it was no big deal.

As the interview continued, his gaze repeatedly returned to Kallie. After a few more minutes of conversation, the sheriff leaned forward and planted his elbows on the desk. "I'd like to give you the job."

The knot of tension in Amy's shoulders released, leaving her feeling light and hopeful. She fought the urge to pump her fist in the air. "Great! I can start right away." Then her spirits sank as quickly as they had risen. "But I need to find a babysitter."

He rubbed his jaw for a moment, deep in thought. "I might know someone who could watch her. Give me a few minutes to make a phone call." As he led her to the foyer, he handed her an application. "It's merely a formality, but I do need references. And I'll need to do a background check. That won't be a problem, will it?"

She had plenty of skeletons in her closet, but nothing that would show up on a background check. Who should she list as a reference?

"No, but the restaurant where I worked was sold six months ago, and I didn't exactly get along with the new owner. Is it okay if I list the previous owner as a reference?"

Sheriff Winter's brown eyes remained on her face. "That's fine, but did your issues with your most recent boss have to do with your work ethic."

"More like his work ethic," Amy said, hoping he'd let it go.

The sheriff scratched his jaw. "List him as a reference and I'll be sure to take anything he says with a grain of salt."

Before returning to his office, the sheriff played with Kallie. He studied her face for a long moment.

A ripple of unease shot through Amy, making her stomach churn. *What is it with people in this town and my daughter?*

ADRENALIN TIGHTENED Sheriff Winters chest as he returned to his office. Amy seemed nice, but before he officially hired Amy, he needed to make sure she wasn't a kidnapper.

He pulled a file from his desk. He'd retrieved it after Uncle James called. He didn't need the file in front of him—he had every detail of this particular case memorized. Turning to his computer, he opened the age-progression software and uploaded the image of the missing baby from the file.

He held his breath as hope surged in him. *Will I finally be able to close this case once and for all?*

He studied the result.

Stomach sinking, he let out the breath he'd been holding. The baby in the photo, despite the blue eyes and curly, blond hair, was not the one out in the foyer. He let out a deep sigh, pulled out his cell phone, and texted Uncle James.

The baby is not Cassey.

CHAPTER 4

*A*fter another enjoyable walk, following the sheriff's instructions this time, Amy stood on Miss Faith's front porch. Though not as large as the Youngs' house, it was a beautiful home in another nice neighborhood.

Does Providence even have any undesirable neighborhoods?

Like the Youngs' house, colorful flower beds lined the front walk. For some reason, the sight made Amy long for a normal family in a normal home—something she'd never had—in a normal small town. Ignoring the tightness in her chest, she rang the doorbell and waited with Kallie on her hip.

The door opened to reveal a petite, slender, familiar woman with a welcoming smile. Doing a double take, Amy stepped back and stared at the house, then at the woman again.

"Um… I'm looking for… Faith?" It sounded odd stammering her words out as a question, but Amy couldn't hide her confusion. The woman in the doorway looked exactly like Ben's aunt and mother.

"I'm Faith." The woman took Amy's hand and pulled her through the door before letting go. "You must be Amy, and that would make this little angel, Kallie." She stroked Kallie's cheek. "You're every bit as beautiful as everyone said."

"Excuse me?" Amy asked, trying to put things together in her mind. Charity and Hope weren't twins as she'd earlier supposed, but rather Faith, Hope, and Charity were triplets. Why hadn't Hope mentioned she had another sister?

Not only did her daughter have a strange effect on people in this town, they were also not entirely forthcoming about their relationships to one another. Did they enjoy seeing outsiders' confusion as they struggled to unravel the mystery of three different women who looked the same?

"Charity called to tell me Ben had brought a pretty woman and her daughter into the diner for breakfast, which surprised us all, of course. Then later, Hope called and told me you would be staying with them and how beautiful your daughter is." Faith sucked in a quick breath before continuing. "You must think we're such gossips, but that's not the case. We're just so happy."

Amy's brain struggled to keep up with Faith's ramblings. The man was married. Why was everyone so pleased he had taken her to the diner? Amy wanted to ask Faith, but the woman rambled on as she led them to a sunny kitchen where sandwiches, soup, and fruit lay on the oak table.

Amy protested, but Faith insisted they sit down and eat.

"It's lunchtime. Besides, it's always easiest to get to know one another over a meal, especially with little ones." She motioned to a booster seat strapped to a dining chair.

Amy attempted to eat, though she was still full from breakfast. They talked as they ate. Gratefully, Faith did most of the talking while Amy listened, relieved Faith didn't ask questions she didn't want to answer.

"This house actually belongs to Charity. I moved in with her after her husband, Richard, died from a heart attack six months ago. I've been a widow for almost two years myself, and I didn't want Charity to be alone. She has three sons, but none of them live at home anymore. The oldest two, from Richard's first marriage, live here in Providence with their wives and children. Steven has two children, ages four and two, and Matt has a three-year-old. Charity and

33

Richard's youngest son, Damon, is in the military and currently stationed at Fort Bragg in North Carolina."

The steady stream of information coming from Faith left Amy reeling.

Faith continued to share random details about her family and the town of Providence. Occasionally, she asked Amy a question about herself and Kallie. Amy kept her answers brief, offering what little information she deemed necessary. If Faith noticed Amy's reticence to talk, she didn't show it.

Their conversation eventually turned to Amy's new job and her need for a babysitter.

"Sheriff Winters said you're the best babysitter in town." Amy picked up her glass and took a drink of water.

"He'd better say that," Faith chuckled. "I'm his mother."

Amy choked on her water, trying not to spit it all over the table. That meant the sheriff was Ben's cousin. She hadn't seen the resemblance other than both men were tall. They certainly didn't get that attribute from their petite mothers. Was Ben as good looking under that beard as his cousin? She pictured a younger version of the distinguished Dr. Young and suspected he might be.

Faith laughed at Amy's surprise. "Robert can be a tease. He probably thought he was being funny by not telling you he'd sent you to his mother."

"So, do you tend other children?" Amy asked, pushing away thoughts of Ben. She'd expected Miss Faith to be running a daycare if she was the best babysitter in town.

"I watch Charity's grandchildren occasionally, but I don't tend any children on a regular basis. Everyone in town knows how much I love babies, since I spend most of my free time volunteering in the nursery at the hospital. Robert knows I'd never forgive him if he didn't send you my way. My own children haven't seen fit to give me any grandchildren, so I have to find them anywhere I can."

Did Faith have any idea what she was getting herself into? A fondness for children and rocking sleeping newborns didn't qualify a person to care for a toddler for eight hours a day, even a toddler as well-behaved as Kallie.

Faith smiled. "You see, I'm a nurse, or at least I used to be. I retired a few years ago to take care of my husband when he had a stroke. After he passed away, I didn't feel like going back to nursing full-time. But I miss the babies, so I volunteer whenever I get the chance. In a small town like this, the nursery isn't exactly crowded, so I find projects to keep me busy." She smiled at Kallie and stroked her cheek. "This little angel will no doubt give me some distraction and entertainment."

Amy's reservations about Faith caring for Kallie dissipated. "How much do you charge?" Amy asked, then rushed to clarify, "I won't get a paycheck for two or three weeks."

Faith waved a hand. "Don't you worry about that. If I need money, I'd have gone back to nursing."

"I wouldn't feel right about letting you take care of Kallie without paying you."

"Well, I'll think about it, but don't stress over it."

Because Faith was so friendly, Amy decided to do a little probing.

"Can you tell me why everyone seems sad when they meet Kallie?"

"You're referring to Ben and his parents?"

"And Charity, although her sadness seemed to be for Ben."

"We're *all* sad for Ben." Faith let out a deep sigh and grew quiet.

Amy thought the talkative woman wasn't going to say anything more.

Then Faith spoke through a watery smile. "Kallie reminds us, and especially Ben, of what he lost." She paused again and fiddled with her napkin.

Amy's chest grew tight. *What had Ben lost?*

"He lost his wife and daughter in a car accident almost a year ago. His little Cassie had beautiful blue eyes and blond curls, just like your Kallie."

Heaviness filled Amy's chest, stealing her breath. Tears blurred her vision. *That poor man.*

~

BEN STRAINED to loosen a stubborn bolt on the engine of Amy's car. Without warning, the wrench slipped, and his hand slammed against the sharp metal edge of the car's frame. He swore under his breath as the wrench clattered to the floor with a loud, metallic clang and blood oozed through the hole in his rubber work glove.

"Stupid gloves."

They kept the oil and grease from soaking into every crack and crevice of his hands, but they also affected his grip. Stripping off the gloves, he picked up the wrench and tossed it on the workbench. Casting Amy's car a final glance, he shrugged. He'd done all he could until the new parts arrived, so he may as well stop torturing himself.

He rarely took a lunch break, but he'd taken one today to take Amy's luggage to his parent's house. If he saw her and Kallie and assured himself they were okay, then he'd be able to stop worrying and focus. But they hadn't been there, so he'd jumped at his mom's dinner invitation.

Why am I so anxious to see them again?

What had he been thinking when he'd promised to take care of them? True, he'd never been able to walk away from someone in need, but he'd done a good job this past year of ignoring other people's needs. Why did he have to start today?

Because they need me.

No. They needed help, but they didn't need him. Except to fix their cars, no one had needed him in a long time. The surprise on everyone's face in the diner proved that. Or maybe they were surprised to see a pretty stranger in town.

"I'm calling it a day," he called to Scott as he headed for the door. "Lock up, will you?"

He let himself into his apartment. Small and sparsely furnished, it could hardly be called cozy, but it had served him fine for the past five months. Small and sparsely furnished, the one-bedroom apartment felt especially dark and quiet today.

He washed his hands in the bathroom sink and inspected the cut on his finger. Good. Not as bad as he'd first thought. His gaze shifted to the mirror, where he studied his reflection. *I look like a mountain man with this thick beard and shaggy hair.* No wonder Amy was reluctant to accept his help.

He couldn't remember the last time he shaved or got a haircut. With no one to impress anymore, and no desire to draw attention to himself, he hid behind his beard. It'd become his way of telling people to keep their distance.

It worked with most people. Too bad it wasn't more effective on Debbie Wheeler.

He ran his hands through his hair. *Maybe I should visit the barber.* Amy was dealing with enough, she didn't need to be frightened of him.

Amy stood in front of the fireplace in the Young's family room, studying the photos spread across the mantle. She'd offered to help with dinner, but Hope shooed her out of the kitchen and told her to relax. Relaxation was slow in coming, however.

This morning, Amy had felt helpless, but now, she felt hopeful. Having a safe place to stay and a job, not to mention a nap and shower, had changed her perspective. An uneasiness settled over her, though. Despite feeling grateful for the Young's generosity, she felt like she didn't belong here. Amy had never known such luxury. When she'd called Celeste earlier, she'd told her she was safe and comfortable, but comfortable felt like an understatement. Even the expensive soaps and hair products in the bathroom screamed wealth.

That wasn't the only thing making her tense; she was uneasy about seeing the bearded mechanic again. Trust never came easily to Amy, so why had she trusted him?

His eyes.

Now that she understood the source of Ben's pain, his fascination with Kallie didn't bother her so much. He and his parents undoubtedly saw the resemblance between Kallie and Ben's daughter, Cassey.

Even their names were similar. Her heart hurt for them. She couldn't imagine losing Kallie.

She studied a picture of the Young family on the mantle. To the right of Hope stood a pretty girl she assumed was Ben's younger sister. On James' left stood a younger, beardless Ben. *So that's what he looks like when he smiles.*

"Nice," she murmured. "He *is* handsome under all that facial hair."

Realizing she'd spoken aloud, she checked over her shoulder to see if anyone had heard. She was alone, except for Kallie, who played on the floor with toys that hadn't been there this morning. Kallie was used to hearing her mom talk to herself.

She stared at Ben's picture again. His full beard hid strong cheekbones, a chiseled jaw, and a dimple in his left cheek.

A wedding photo of Ben and his wife caught her attention. "What a beautiful couple." Not only was he handsome, his wife looked like she'd walked off the cover of a magazine, with beautiful brown eyes, and long, blond hair hanging in loose curls. The Ben she met today looked so different from the happy groom in the picture.

"Poor Ben. He lost everything in that accident."

Tearing her eyes away from the wedding photo, she studied a picture of Ben's little family. His wife held a beautiful baby girl about six months old, with fluffy blond curls, and her father's sapphire-blue eyes. *How adorable.* No wonder everyone grew emotional when they saw Kallie. The baby in the picture resembled Kallie at that age.

Amy studied the next photo, a close-up of the baby's smiling face. She looked familiar. *Is it because she has her father's blue eyes?*

Hearing the front door open, Amy stepped away from the photos not wanting Ben to catch her snooping.

He entered the family room and smiled. "I hope you've settled in."

Amy's heart stalled, and a smile pulled at her lips when she took in Ben's appearance. Was this the same man she met this morning?

He'd cut his hair and trimmed his beard down to the jawline. His cheekbones, now more pronounced, emphasized his slenderness. *No wonder everyone wants to feed him.*

Despite his lean build, prominent biceps showed below his sleeves. The blue of his t-shirt emphasized the intensity of his eyes.

Amy had never seen eyes so blue. *Nor had she ever seen eyes so full of pain.*

"Yes, we have, thank you."

"And Kallie is adjusting okay?" His face filled with longing as his gaze rested on Kallie.

"I think so. She's such a good-natured baby, it takes a lot to upset her."

"As long as her tummy is full, right?" Ben gave a slight smile.

Amy laughed. "Yes, she's not happy when she's 'hangry'." Pointing toward his head, she said, "You look different, I mean... nice."

Ben dipped his head and scratched his jaw. "Thanks."

Amy soon found herself seated across from Ben at a gleaming cherry wood dining table. Kallie sat in a highchair beside her. Hope must have had it stored away in the basement with the playpen and baby toys. Had they been for Ben's baby? Would seeing Kallie in this highchair be a painful reminder of what he'd lost?

Throughout dinner, Amy felt Ben's gaze on her and Kallie. Of course, her eyes were often drawn to him too. She'd never been a fan of beards, but she couldn't deny Ben was hot.

What's wrong with me? She'd left one attractive man last night and now was ogling the next one to come along? *Boy, am I messed up.*

"Amy got a job at the Sheriff's Office," James told Ben. "She'll cover for Janice's maternity leave.

Ben's eyebrows arched. "You're sticking around? That's... that's great."

Was the stumble in his words caused by surprise, or didn't he like the idea of her staying with his parents indefinitely?

"And Faith's going to tend Kallie," Hope added.

"Why am I not surprised?" Again, a half-smile lit his face.

Amy saw a glimpse of the dimple in his cheek at the edge of his newly trimmed beard. The sight of it caused a funny flutter to race through her stomach.

"Amy, why don't you tell us about your family?" James said.

Tension coiled in Amy's shoulders. She hated talking about her life, which was so different from most people, especially people as affluent as the Youngs. But they deserved her honesty.

Fighting the urge to squirm in her seat, she put her fork down and balled her napkin in her fist. "Well, I pretty much spent my whole life living in one apartment or another in Portland. It was me and my mom until I was eighteen."

Actually, it had rarely been just the two of them, and Amy moved out at seventeen, but they didn't need to know that. They would want to know why, and Amy didn't share that with anyone. Only Celeste knew what happened that day. Nor did the Youngs need to know she hadn't spoken to her mother since the day she walked out.

"What about your father?" Hope asked.

"He was never a part of my life. He refused to marry my mom when she got pregnant at seventeen."

"That must have been hard for her. Did she have a supportive family?"

"No, her father kicked her out after she got pregnant."

"That's horrible." Disapproval filled Hope's voice.

Amy shrugged, trying to appear indifferent as she talked about her mother. "Her father was abusive, so it was probably for the best. My mom stayed with a friend until she found a place of her own. She got married shortly after I turned three." She swallowed the lump that filled her throat every time she thought about her stepfather, Bruce. "But it only lasted a few years. She married two other times, but both were brief and ended badly. After her third divorce, she didn't bother getting married anymore. She kept a steady string of boyfriends after that."

Amy bit her bottom lip to shut herself up. Could they hear the bitterness in her voice? She didn't usually share this part of her life with others, because talking about her mother's lifestyle reminded Amy her mother didn't love her.

"I bet you found that difficult." James' voice held none of the disapproval she expected. Instead, it was full of compassion.

Amy shrugged again. "I learned at a young age to take care of myself and stay out of the way."

She'd been successful most of the time.

Amy propped her elbows on the table and rubbed the back of her neck, forming a shield in front of her. If only the action could block the unpleasant memories. She had no desire to share with these strangers, her struggles to avoid drunk, abusive men and their unwanted advances.

An uncomfortable silence settled around the table, and Amy glanced up to find Ben watching her. She lowered her arms and looked away from his penetrating gaze.

Kallie blew raspberries against her spoon at that moment, attracting everyone's attention, and Amy wanted to hug her.

CHAPTER 5

*B*en couldn't keep his eyes off Kallie. Everything about her fascinated him, including her developing fine-motor skills as she fed herself, and the way she wrinkled her nose when she smiled.

Is this what Cassey would be like if she were here?

"Tell us about Kallie's father. What's he like?" His father's serious tone pulled Ben from his musings.

"Dad." Ben's tone held a warning.

His father, known for his excellent bedside manner, could come across as brusque when he used that tone. Though Ben was curious to find out what or whom Amy was running from, he didn't want her to feel defensive.

Her body language a moment ago suggested there were things in her past she'd rather not talk about. Was Kallie's father one of them?

"It's okay, Ben." She smiled but didn't meet his gaze. "Since I pretty much admitted to running away this morning, your father is probably worried about an abusive husband showing up on his doorstep." She smiled at James. "There's no husband, just a... boyfriend, and he's only abusive when he's drunk, which is often. But I doubt he'll come after me." Amy's gaze dropped to her plate.

Ben could tell she struggled to keep the hurt from her voice. What kind of man lets his girlfriend and daughter walk away?

Not a gentleman. Not if he beat her.

He continued to watch Amy. Faint shadows still rimmed her eyes, though not as dark as this morning. She wore little make-up. She didn't need it. Her curly blond hair, sky-blue eyes, and rosy lips were enough to attract any man's attention.

Whoa! Where did that come from?

Amy sucked in her bottom lip, which was fuller than the top, and chewed on it for a moment before speaking. "I've worked at Charlie's Bar and Grill since I was fifteen. A few years ago, Charlie hired the Lance Haye's band to play on the weekends. That's when I first met Lance. The band was pretty good, and I became something of a groupie, since I always worked weekends. Lance was charming and charismatic. We got serious and eventually... I got pregnant. I wanted to get married, but he wanted to wait until his career took off, since they had a record label interested in signing them. About ten months ago, the band finally put out an album and went on a three-month tour of the west coast with other artists." Amy tucked a lock of hair behind her ear and fiddled with the handle of her knife.

Lasagna forgotten, Ben studied her face. He had a feeling she didn't want to share what came next. The emotion evident in her pretty eyes mirrored the pain he saw every time he looked in the mirror. This woman had been hurt deeply, and he had a feeling it wasn't just physically.

"I started suspecting he was sleeping around while he was on tour earlier this year. When I confronted him about it, he got angry, telling me I didn't understand how demanding and stressful being on tour was."

Jerk!

"When he finished the tour, he promised it wouldn't happen again. I wanted to believe him, but deep down I knew I couldn't. So, I started saving money, hoping to make a fresh start... somewhere."

Her expression remained passive, but her voice rose in pitch. If she was trying to hide how badly Lance's actions hurt her, she wasn't doing a very good job. Her inner turmoil manifested itself in the way she twisted her napkin.

Amy let out a heavy sigh then said, "He went from introducing me as his girlfriend to calling me 'just a friend.' A friend and her baby, that's all we were to him. He didn't want to claim Kallie as his daughter because he thought it would hurt his career."

Ben's grip on his fork tightened as pain sliced through his chest. *The man didn't want to claim his own daughter?* Ben would give anything to be able to hold his daughter again.

"I'd saved almost two thousand dollars and planned to leave soon because I knew he was sleeping around. But Lance found the money last week and got angry with me for holding out on him." She rubbed absently at her temple, and Ben had the feeling Lance had taken his anger out on her. "He blew the money on a new guitar. I planned to start over, but last night, I decided I couldn't stay any longer." Amy's voice caught, and she sucked in a deep breath.

"What happened, dear?" His mother squeezed Amy's arm.

"I um... I quit my job last night and came home early. When I walked into..." Amy bit her lip, and Ben watched the emotions play across her face, as though struggling to decide how much she wanted to share. "He was... with another woman." Amy's eyes dropped to her lap. No doubt trying to hide the pain Lance's actions caused her.

Lance was an idiot! Ben bit his tongue to keep from calling Amy's ex a much worse name aloud. He balled his fists under the table. Lance had to know Amy would be coming home. Had he planned to get the woman out of there? Or had he wanted Amy to catch him, hoping it would drive her away?

It worked. But at what cost? Amy was better off without the loser, but to suffer that kind of rejection... not only on her behalf but her daughter's too?

The urge to gather both of them in his arms and keep them safe took his breath away. *Where did this sudden hero complex come from?*

"And while he was caring for the baby." His mother's disapproval rang clear.

"Lance never took care of Kallie. My friend, Celeste, did. I've been

44

stuck working nights for the past six months and don't usually get home until after midnight, so Kallie stayed at Celeste's house."

"I'm sorry for everything you've been through, Amy, but why did you quit your job last night?" There was his father's gentle bedside manner.

Ben's mom always joked that his dad could charm the appendix from ladies, young and old. It was a personal joke since his dad had to perform an emergency appendectomy on his mom the night they were supposed to go on their first date.

Amy's cheeks turned red as she pushed the food around her plate. "Charlie, my boss for the past ten years, was ready to retire, so he sold the restaurant to his nephew about six months ago. Dennis basically demoted everybody and told us we had to work our way up. Those that kissed up to him got their choice of shifts."

"The fact you were stuck with the night shift tells me you didn't think very highly of your new boss," his mom said with a knowing look.

"I did not." Amy's hand trembled as she raised her water glass and gulped down half of it. "Last night... Dennis offered to give me my job as day manager back... for a price."

Ben's eyes stayed glued to Amy's face. *What was she saying? Dennis wanted her to pay to work there?*

"I take it the position came at a price you weren't willing to pay?" his dad said.

His dad's meaning hit Ben square in the gut and disgust turned his stomach. He pushed his nearly empty plate away.

The color in Amy's cheeks deepened. "Exactly."

No wonder she'd been so uneasy at the garage this morning. Her dad was a deadbeat, her boss a scumbag, and her boyfriend a jerk. Amy probably didn't hold the male species in very high esteem.

Amy let out a tight chuckle. "There you have it. I quit my job, packed my bags, and Kallie and I left. I intended to get as far away from Lance and the bar as I could, but we ended up broken down here four hours later."

His mom leaned over and put a hand on Amy's shoulder. "Sounds like you're due for a fresh start. Providence is a good place for that."

After dinner, Ben hesitated in the doorway where the dining room joined the living room. He usually made a quick getaway after eating with his parents but tonight, he had no desire to leave.

Following Amy and Kallie into the family room, he sat across from them in an armchair. Once again, his gaze rested on Kallie as she sat on the floor near her mom playing with a basket of toys. They looked a lot like the toys his daughter had played with an eternity ago. He forced thoughts of Cassey from his mind. He couldn't handle that kind of pain right now.

Looking up, he locked gazes with Amy. Hers darted away. This wasn't the first time she'd caught him watching her and Kallie. Something about her intrigued him, but he couldn't understand what. Nor could he understand why. He was grieving for his wife. He wasn't interested in another woman. Kallie fascinated him, though.

Amy was likely still wary of him, and he didn't blame her. He wasn't sure how to set her at ease. He didn't understand why it mattered what she thought about him. But it did.

Kallie picked up a toy and toddled over to him. Ben froze, unsure how to respond. She stood in front of him, holding out the rattle.

"She wants you to take it." Amy's voice came to him from far away.

He took the rattle and gave the toddler a small smile. *What do I do with it?*

Encouraged, Kallie returned to Amy, who handed her another toy. She turned and brought it to Ben. She repeated the process until the entire contents of the basket sat on his lap.

He stole a glance at Amy. She smiled at Kallie then at him. A one-eighty from her behavior this morning. An emptiness settled in the pit of his stomach.

She knows.

Amy had heard what happened to Melanie and Cassey. That's why she encouraged Kallie to interact with him.

This is a small town. Of course, she was bound to find out.

Would she pity him too, like everyone else?

Kallie yawned and rubbed her eyes.

"You're tired aren't you, sweetheart?" Amy stood and picked Kallie up. "Tell Ben night-night."

Kallie gave him a shy smile and waved at him.

His heart twisted.

"Excuse me." Amy gave him a brief smile before leaving the room.

Amy and Kallie had barely left when Ben's dad stepped out of his office. "Can I have a word with you, son?"

About what? His dad's ominous tone sent a chill racing down Ben's back.

AFTER TUCKING KALLIE IN BED, Amy returned to the family room, hoping to find Ben still here. She needed to thank him for his help. It terrified her to think how things might have turned out if she'd broken down farther along the freeway.

Ben sat in the same armchair he had before, wearing a scowl. He masked his expression and rose. "Can I have a word with you outside?" Not waiting for a response, he left the room.

Outside?

Unease swept over Amy. They were already alone in the family room. Couldn't he say what he wanted to say here? She shot a desperate glance at James' closed office door, behind which came Hope's muffled voice. She sounded upset.

After a lengthy hesitation, she followed Ben. *He's in pain. Surely, he won't hurt me.*

Her stomach hardened as she took in his rigid posture. Had she or Kallie said or done something to upset him? Would he ask them to leave? She had nowhere to go. Memories of being a young girl, living out of their car for a short time twisted her stomach into knots. She couldn't even take her car and park in some out of the way spot.

What would the handsome sheriff do if he found her sleeping in her car right there on Main Street?

Ben opened the front door and waited for her to walk through.

The knots in her stomach tightened as she stepped out onto the porch.

After pulling the door closed behind him, he stepped away from her and raked both hands through his hair, making his waves unruly.

Amy stepped away, taking advantage of the wide front porch. A cricket chirped from somewhere in the red roses, but Amy couldn't appreciate their beauty or aroma. Despite the warm evening, she wrapped her arms around herself and studied Ben standing at the edge of the light, hands deep in his pockets.

"Is something wrong?"

"I owe you an apology." His voice sounded tight.

"For what?"

"For my father's and my cousin's actions." Her confusion must have been apparent, because he added, "I'm sure you've heard my wife was killed in a car accident almost a year ago."

Amy's heart twisted at the pain on Ben's face. She wanted to reach out to him. Comfort him, somehow. Squeezing her arms tighter around herself, she fought the urge.

"Yes. Faith told me you lost your wife and daughter in a car accident. I'm so sorry for your loss. I can't imagine—" Amy's voice caught. Swallowing the lump in her throat, she said, "How difficult that must have been for you."

"I lost them both, but my wife was the only one who died that night." Ben's voice grew more strained with each word.

"I don't understand. What happened to your daughter?"

"She was taken from the car," he choked out. "Kidnapped."

Kidnapped! Amy's lungs seized, and an icy chill radiated through her body. She rubbed her trembling hands against the cold chills on her upper arms. *Ben had no idea where his daughter was? Or if she was even alive. How horrible!*

Wait. His wife died in the accident and someone took his daughter? As the familiar story registered, Amy realized why the picture on the mantle looked familiar. She'd seen it in the news and plastered everywhere after the baby's disappearance last year.

Close to the same age, the blond-haired, blue-eyed baby had

reminded her of Kallie. For months after the baby's disappearance, Amy had slept in the same room as her daughter, otherwise, she couldn't sleep.

Babies could just disappear. Even in this small town.

"You're the one...? That was you?"

"The past year has been a living hell." The pain in his eyes matched the gruffness of his voice.

Again, she resisted the urge to reach out to him; it wasn't her place. The man was still a stranger to her. Besides, what could she say or do to ease his pain?

"I want you to know when I offered to help you and Kallie this morning, I never once thought she could be my daughter or suspected you to be a kidnapper."

Kidnapper? Amy's stomach plummeted as his words sank in. She took a step back, then another. His mother's words *'Does Ben think it's her?'* rang in her head. She remembered the way the sheriff studied Kallie's face. Did they really suspect her of kidnapping his daughter?

Then another thought crashed in on her like a giant weight. Could they take Kallie away from her? To try to prove she was Ben's missing daughter. Would someone question her competence as a mother, because of her current situation?

Gray spots filled her vision, blurring Ben's face. Her legs weakened, and she feared they might give out. She reached out to steady herself against the cool brick of the house, pressing her free hand to her chest.

Staying at the Young's house no longer mattered. She wanted to rip Kallie from her bed and run for the second time in twenty-four hours. But she couldn't leave town without a car.

Ben must have read the fear on her face because he stepped closer. "It's okay. I've no doubt Kallie is your daughter. She's got your sky-blue eyes and platinum-blond hair. My Cassey had... has deep-blue eyes, like mine, and golden-blond hair. I haven't seen her for almost a year, but I know I'd recognize her in a heartbeat if I ever saw her again." The words came out tight and tortured.

Amy heaved a sigh of relief, but she reeled from the insinuation someone suspected her of being a kidnapper. "But…"

"My parents thought I offered to help you because I thought Kallie might be my daughter."

"Your father insisted I take her to the Sheriff's Office with me, so he could check me and Kallie out." Amy started putting the pieces together and couldn't help taking offense.

"Yes, but Robert was certain Kallie is not my missing daughter. When he informed my dad, he asked for more proof. So, Robert called Charlie. He planned on calling him anyway, to check your references. But as he questioned Charlie about how long you'd worked there, he confirmed you'd been pregnant and raised your baby from birth."

Amy silently processed this information. She'd met one friendly person after another in this town, never once thinking they might suspect her of being a kidnapper. Were all people in small towns this suspicious of strangers? Or was it simply because of the magnitude of the loss they'd suffered?

"When you went to put Kallie to bed, Dad told me they'd verified Kallie wasn't my daughter. I told him I never thought she was." His voice was tight as he continued, "I'm sorry he was suspicious of you and went behind my back, instead of talking to me or you about it."

He's angry with his parents, not me. Amy lowered her hands to her sides. No one had asked her to leave. In fact, the sheriff had offered her a job.

Amy stared at the deep red roses surrounding the porch. The darkness made them appear almost black. Was that how Ben felt? Like darkness had overshadowed his life with no prospect of light. Ever.

How could he find any light, as long as his daughter was missing?

She considered all his parents had lost. A granddaughter, daughter-in-law, and in a way, even their son. Grief and pain caused people to act irrationally. If she'd been the one to lose her daughter, she was certain every blond-haired, blue-eyed toddler would remind her of Kallie and spark hope. They must carry the hope that someday Cassey would be found. Understanding this made it easy to forgive their actions.

Amy stepped closer to Ben, again fighting the urge to reach out to him. "They're concerned for you. They probably thought they could spare you more pain by doing what they did."

"I suppose you're right." He sighed and shoved his hands into his pockets again. "Unfortunately, one thing I've learned this past year is that no amount of good intentions from family and friends can take away the pain."

He was right. No matter what anyone said or did, they couldn't take away his pain. But the desire to comfort him was so strong, she touched his arm. He stared at her hand, and for a moment, Amy thought he might pull away.

He didn't.

"It's my own fault, I guess. I shut them out. I shut everyone out. They didn't dare talk to me about it for fear of driving me away again."

Again? Though curious about what he meant, Amy didn't feel it her place to press him for an explanation. She dropped her hand. "If my staying here with Kallie is a problem... I mean, if she's too much of a reminder... of what you've lost... I can find another place to stay."

"No. It's fine. It might be a little hard at times, but it will be good to have her around."

Is he trying to convince me, or himself?

He turned to leave, then abruptly turned back. "I almost forgot..." Pulling out his wallet, he took out a fifty-dollar bill and extended it toward her. "I'm glad you found a job, but I want to make sure you have enough to see you through until you get your first paycheck."

Amy held up her hand palm out and stepped back. "You've already done enough."

Ignoring her protest, he took her hand in his large, calloused one and pressed the folded bill into her palm. He closed her fingers around it, brushing the inside of her wrist. A tingle of warmth shot up her arm.

Wide-eyed, she pulled her hand back, still gripping the money. She rubbed her wrist against her hip willing the tingles to subside. *What is wrong with me? I hardly know the man.*

Ben's blue eyes bore into hers, and their intensity stole her breath. "I promised I'd take care of you and Kallie. Make sure she doesn't go without."

His concern for Kallie touched her. Lance had never shown such concern for his own daughter. Wanting Ben to know how grateful she was, she stepped forward and grabbed his hand. "You're a lifesaver, Ben. I can't thank you enough."

Less than a foot separated them, and the proximity stole her breath. Warmth emanated from him, and his earthy, spicy-with-a-touch-of-citrus scent filled her nose. She liked his smell.

Ben sucked in a sharp breath and she felt him stiffen.

She'd clearly surprised him. She'd shocked herself. This was not like her, and though her first inclination was to let go and retreat as fast as she could, she had a feeling Ben needed some human contact.

Ben's fingers curled around hers and his grip tightened.

Warmth radiated up her arm. Amy loosened her hold and stepped back into the shadows, hoping he couldn't see the flush that heated her cheeks. She'd enjoyed the brief contact more than she should have.

He smiled, the first real smile she'd seen since meeting him, and that dimple creased his cheek.

"You're welcome."

Then he was gone.

Amy drew in a deep breath, inhaling the scent of the roses—sweet, heady, and perfect. The scent provided a balm to her troubled soul. Everything was going to be okay.

BEN'S THOUGHTS lingered on Amy as he drove home. She'd surprised him when she grabbed his hand, but he'd enjoyed it, brief as it was. Not because she was an attractive female, but rather because of the sincerity of her gratitude. Being on the giving end—instead of the receiving end for a change—felt good.

From the things Amy said at dinner, she deserved a break. If he ever got the chance to meet Lance, he'd probably give him a well-deserved punch in the face.

Despite hearing about Amy's problems, Ben had enjoyed dinner. Usually, he dreaded time spent with his family. Their concern for him was stifling. He hated being the focus of their well-meaning intentions.

Just like he'd had good intentions when he'd lied to Amy.

Watching Kallie filled him with a painful longing for his Cassey. Who played with her and put her to bed each night? Did they sing to her and rock her to sleep like Melanie used to? Thinking about such things put him on a dangerous path and would only continue to drag out the pain he'd endured for almost a year, but his daughter was out there, somewhere.

He knew it.

Everyone was concerned about him. At times he was concerned about himself, but he couldn't bring himself to do anything different than what he'd done for the past year.

Which was to hide away with his pain.

Was that why it felt so good to help Amy and Kallie?

CHAPTER 6

"Would you like to go to church with us, Amy?" James asked the next morning when he and Hope walked into the family room. He wore a dark suit and looked handsome for an older gentleman. Hope wore a blue dress with a lace collar. Both of Ben's parents were attractive people. Amy could see where he got his good looks.

Amy licked her suddenly dry lips. "Um... I don't... I've never..." She bit her tongue to shut herself up. James' invitation not only took her by surprise, it bothered her.

Why did a simple invitation to go to church make her so uncomfortable?

Hope seemed to sense her discomfort. "Perhaps you'd like to join us another time."

"I think I'd like that."

Truth was, Amy had never been to church, ever. Not even for Christmas or Easter, since her mother had never been the church-going type. Amy usually worked late on Saturday nights, and consequently, spent Sundays sleeping. Church had been the farthest thing from her mind.

As much as she didn't want to be the kind of mother her mom had been, she'd become exactly that. Taking the child she had out of wedlock and leaving an abusive, cheating boyfriend in the middle of the night, was exactly the kind of thing her mother had done multiple times.

Maybe I should go to church. Would making religion a part of her and Kallie's lives help stop the cycle of poor parenting and bad relationships?

Amy continued to mull this over as she took Kallie for a walk. She had always worked hard, hoping to provide a better environment for her daughter than she'd had growing up. When she rented her latest, two-bedroom apartment—the nicest and most spacious apartment she had ever lived in—she'd experienced a level of pride she'd never known before.

Everything she was so proud of seemed cheap and shabby compared to the luxury the Youngs shared with her. Even the expensive bath towels she'd splurged on a few months ago didn't seem near as thick and soft as the ones the Youngs owned. And the satin sheets... She had no idea they could contribute to such a refreshing night's sleep. Or maybe it was the quality of the mattress she'd slept on.

After their walk, Amy rocked Kallie on her lap on the front porch. While she admired the brick and stucco home across the cul-de-sac, the garage door opened, and a candy-apple red Porsche backed out. Before it pulled away, Amy caught a glimpse of the redhead who had sought Ben's attention yesterday at the gas station.

"Nice car," Amy said in awe, bouncing Kallie on her knee. "And nice house. What do you think, Kallie Bug? I think Mommy's jealous."

Amy sucked in a deep breath, then slowly let it out as she studied her reflection. She had never worked anywhere but Chuck's Bar and Grill. The thought of working somewhere new both excited and terrified her.

The walk to Faith's, then on to the Sheriff's Office eased some tension. But all too soon, she sat next to Janice, the about-to-burst pregnant dispatcher, getting hands-on training. The more Amy learned, the more nervous she became.

"And this program is the 911 protocols." Janice clicked on an icon, opening a list of questions.

Amy's stomach tightened. Computers didn't scare her. As the day manager, she'd ordered supplies, processed receipts, and balanced the books. The programs here were different, but not complicated.

However, knowing her quick responses when someone called with an emergency could mean the difference between life and death terrified her.

"In a small town like this, we rarely have many emergencies," Janice said. "Unless there's an accident on the interstate. Most of the calls we get are from old ladies whose dogs escaped. And of course, Widow Wheeler always calls with one imagined emergency or another. But she only wants help if Robert is available."

"Who is Widow Wheeler? And why does she want Robert?"

"She's your neighbor."

At Amy's look of confusion, Janice clarified, "You're staying with the Youngs, right?" When Amy nodded, Janice said, "Debbie Wheeler lives in the other house in that cul-de-sac."

Amy pictured the driver of the red Porsche. "She's a widow?"

"Yep. She's about ten years older than me, so I don't know all the details, but I guess she married her high school sweetheart right after graduation. They both wanted to get out of this small town, so they moved away. To Seattle, I think. Anyway, they divorced after a few years. She came home for a year or two, but she didn't stick around long."

Janice sucked in a sharp breath and rubbed the side of her round belly.

"Are you having a contraction?" Amy asked in concern.

"Nah, just Braxton-Hicks. Been having them for weeks. Anyway, Debbie went back to the city and married a wealthy old man. He died a year or so later, and she inherited his fortune. She came back here to flaunt her wealth, telling everyone she was a widow. Which makes no sense, really, because she went back to her maiden name. But the name Widow Wheeler kind of stuck. Of course, we don't call her that to her face."

Amy's thoughts turned to the unexpected scene she'd witnessed last night when she went to close the drapes before putting Kallie to bed. Ben, who'd come for Sunday dinner and hardly spoken two words, crossed the cul-de-sac to the large brown house. Surprised, Amy had watched until the redhead opened the door and welcomed him in.

Ignoring the same odd pang of jealousy that tightened her chest last night, Amy turned her focus back to Janice. "Why does she only want Robert to answer her calls?"

"She's got all the money she needs now, so she's set her sights on Providence's most eligible bachelors. Which are Robert, his brother, Jake, who is every bit as handsome as Robert, and Ben. I'm not sure why she bothers with Ben. The poor man is so deep in his grief, I'm not sure he'll ever surface. But she finds one reason or another to take her car into the shop every week, so she can see him."

No wonder he seemed annoyed by Debbie on Saturday. Again, the question plagued Amy as it had last night—why would Ben go to Debbie's house so late in the evening? Did they have some sort of relationship? For some reason, Ben didn't strike her as the type to make late-night visits to a single woman's house, especially one he apparently didn't like.

"Why does she always call 911 to get a hold of Robert instead of calling him personally?"

"Because Robert is smart. He refuses to give her his cell number. And anyone in town who has his number knows better than to give it to her."

Amy's curiosity got the better of her. "What does she do to get to Jake?"

"Well, he owns a huge ranch outside of town and doesn't come into town often, so Debbie had to get creative there." Janice rolled her eyes. "She bought a horse and asked Jake to stable it for her. Apparently, she goes out to the ranch quite often, but doesn't actually bother to ride the horse much."

"How old are Ben and his cousins compared to Debbie?" The widow looked older than Robert and Ben.

"Let me see," Janice said, tapping a finger to her lips. "I can't remember if they were five or six years ahead of me in school, but Robert and Ben are around thirty and Jake is twenty-eight, I think. Widow Wheeler's probably mid-thirties. She's a little older than them, but in this town, there aren't a lot of choices of single men, or single women." She winked at Amy. "You'd better watch out."

"No way." Amy shook her head. "I'm done with men."

THE NEXT DAY, Amy found the front office empty when she arrived. Sitting in Janice's chair, she attempted to make herself comfortable as she gave herself a mental pep-talk.

Robert came out of his office and greeted her with a smile. "Good morning."

Nice smile. And those eyes... gorgeous. Though the color wasn't as striking as the length of his thick lashes.

"Wow... I mean, g-good morning." Amy resisted the urge to fan herself when heat rushed to her cheeks.

What's wrong with me? First, I'm attracted to Ben's beard and dimple and now my boss' eyes?

Robert pulled her from her musings. "I didn't get a chance to talk to you yesterday. How did your first day go?"

"Good. I have a lot to learn, but I'm looking forward to the challenge."

"Good, because we have a situation which poses a challenge. Janice went into labor early this morning and won't return to work for at least six weeks."

"Oh my." Amy's stomach tightened at the magnitude of responsibilities she'd taken on.

Janice was supposed to have spent this week teaching her the ropes. They had barely scratched the surface yesterday. Amy sucked in her bottom lip. The thought of answering emergency calls terrified her.

Robert must have read her concern. "Don't worry, we won't leave you alone until you're comfortable. My deputies and I will take turns, staying here in the office to help out."

Relieved, Amy relaxed in her chair. Just then, a young, red-headed man dressed in a deputy's uniform walked into the office. He looked like a teenager, but Amy guessed he was in his early twenties.

"Amy, I'd like you to meet, Rudy Wheeler," Robert said. "Rudy, this is Amy Lawson, she'll be filling in for Janice."

After the introductions, Robert returned to his office, leaving Amy alone with the young deputy.

"Wheeler, huh? Any relation to Wid—" Amy realized what she had almost said and shut her mouth.

Rudy laughed. "Yes, Debbie is my older sister. There are five children in my family. Debbie's the oldest, and I'm the youngest, with fifteen years between us. Despite her vanity and fascination with money, she's a good person." Rudy continued to talk about his family after dragging a chair over from the waiting area. He proved to be almost as talkative as Faith Winters.

Amy relaxed, no longer feeling overwhelmed. She had a feeling she would enjoy working with Rudy.

When Robert left the office that afternoon, Amy commented on how young the sheriff was, which started Rudy talking again.

"Yeah, he's pretty young, I guess, but he's a great sheriff." He shrugged. "I think folks elected him more for who he was rather than how long he'd worked in law enforcement."

"What do you mean?"

"Well, his family is one of the most influential families in town."

"Let me guess, the other influential families are the Knights and the Youngs?" It made sense that the three sisters, who were so generous, would have an impact on the small community.

"Bingo! I'd list a few other families too, but yes, we affectionately call Faith, Hope, and Charity the three matriarchs. Robert's father's family has lived in Providence for generations too. His uncle, Dawson

Winters, was the previous sheriff and groomed Robert to take his place. He retired from being sheriff to be the local justice of the peace."

"Did Faith, Hope, and Charity grow up in Providence?"

Exactly how closely is everyone related?

"No, they're transplants. I don't know all the details, but I think Dr. Young and Miss Faith worked at the same hospital in some big city, and when he decided to come back to Providence, she came too."

"Were they dating at the time?" Amy asked, curious. She remembered the smile Hope and James shared when Hope said *Providence was a good place for a fresh start.*

"I don't know. I think they were just friends. When Faith decided to stick around, her sisters came to visit, and they ended up staying too. Anyway, Robert had been sheriff less than a year when Melanie Young died in the car accident and her daughter disappeared. He did an amazing job, processing the scene of the accident meticulously. The sheriff worked harder than anyone to organize searches and get the baby's picture distributed to every law enforcement agency and media outlet throughout the nation. He personally followed up on every lead and refused to give up searching and doing everything possible to find Ben's daughter, even after the other agencies withdrew." Rudy paused for a moment before continuing, "I'm not sure he'll ever get over the fact he couldn't solve that case."

A now-familiar pain twisted Amy's heart every time she thought about all Ben had lost. Dealing with such a difficult case must have been hard for Robert. Being the sheriff in such a situation would have been stressful enough, but Cassey was his cousin's daughter.

Just like every other time she thought about Ben, Amy wished there was something she could do to help him.

BEN BROUGHT Amy's car to a stop in front of his parents' house as Amy unbuckled Kallie from the stroller. Today was Wednesday, and he hadn't seen them since Sunday evening. It had been all he could do to keep from dropping by to check on them every day. Instead, he'd spent long hours rebuilding her car's transmission, so he would have an excuse to come over.

He didn't understand the draw to be near them, but he was glad they seemed to be doing well.

Amy waited on the porch with a smile so big it reached her eyes while he walked up the driveway. *Is she happy to see me or her car?* A part of him hoped it was the former.

He dangled the keys in front of her. "All fixed."

In addition to rebuilding the transmission, he'd changed the oil, replaced the air filter, checked the tires, and topped off the fluids, including the gas tank. But she didn't need to know all that.

"Thank you, you're a lifesaver." Her fingers brushed his when she took her keys.

An electric jolt shot through his hand and up his arm. He jerked back and shrugged off her compliment. "It's a tough job, but someone's got to do it, I guess."

"Seriously, Ben. I could kiss you." Amy's eyes widened, and she slapped a hand over her mouth. Her cheeks turned crimson, making her even more attractive.

"Excuse me?"

She squeezed her eyes shut and groaned. "Sorry, I didn't… mean to say that. I tend to speak without thinking." She opened her eyes again but didn't meet his gaze. "I meant to say… I did a little research online about rebuilding transmissions, and I appreciate how hard you worked to fix my car… for me."

Last Saturday, she grabbed his hand when she expressed her gratitude and now she wanted to kiss him for the same reason?

It's just a figure of speech.

Of course, she didn't really want to kiss him. But the thought of kissing Amy sounded very appealing. His gaze dropped to her lips. He liked how her bottom lip was a little fuller than the top.

Ben shoved his fists in his pockets. *Why on earth am I thinking about kissing Amy?*

Kallie took the keys from Amy's hand and jiggled them, pulling him from his crazy thoughts.

Amy's brow furrowed. "How much do I owe you?"

Ben waved a hand. "Don't worry about it."

"I appreciate your help, but I have every intention of paying my bill in full. It'll probably take me months, but I'll pay every penny."

The woman's self-esteem may have taken a hit when she caught her boyfriend cheating, but she had spunk.

"Fine. I'll bring you a bill," he said with a smile of admiration.

Liar. He had no intention of letting her pay for her car repair.

Shuffling his feet, he studied his shoes. He'd done what he came to do, but he didn't want to leave yet. Following Amy into the house, they found his mom coming out of the kitchen.

"Look what the cat dragged in," Amy said.

"Perfect timing. Dinner is ready." His mom hugged him then pulled him toward the dining room. "Keep us company. Your father is working in the ER tonight."

Ben considered refusing, but the aroma coming from the kitchen smelled much more appealing than frozen pizza.

During dinner, his mom steered the conversation toward Ben's childhood, sharing stories about all the trouble he used to get into with Robert and Jake. Occasionally, he corrected her version of the stories, adding details his mom had never heard. Details, that had she known, would have resulted in serious punishment for him.

Ben wiped his mouth and tossed the napkin on the table. "We wouldn't have done half those things if it wasn't for Robert. He was always more adventurous than Jake and I. Makes sense he would pick the dangerous profession. Not that Providence has much crime."

Except for that one accident, almost a year ago, that shattered my life. And just like that, the pain he tried to ignore crashed over him.

After dinner, he told himself to go home, but still he lingered. His small apartment held no appeal compared to the warmth of his parents' house, especially with Amy and Kallie here. He'd avoided this house for the past eleven months, but now, he didn't want to leave.

He sat in the family room with his mom, Amy, and Kallie, who brought him toy after toy again. He wasn't sure how to react to the cute toddler, but he enjoyed being around her. She reminded him of his Cassey. Where was she? Was she happy and healthy? He might never know the answers to those questions, but he found himself drawn to Kallie and her sweet personality.

Kallie's pretty mother intrigued him too. Her spunk and determination to be a good mother impressed him.

When he walked home, his heart felt lighter than it had in forever. A slow smile crept to his lips. Kallie seemed to have that effect on him.

Or was it Amy?

CHAPTER 7

*R*obert leaned against the corner of Amy's desk and folded his arms across his chest. "So, how do you like the job, Amy?"

Her gaze lingered on the way the sleeve of his uniform stretched around his bicep. Averting her eyes, she cleared her throat. "I like it."

The more Amy worked at the Sheriff's Office, the more she enjoyed her job and this small town. She missed the hustle and bustle of waiting tables, but she didn't miss drunk or belligerent customers and their lewd comments. Dale and Brady, the other two deputies, who'd taken turns helping her the last two days, were both friendly, but not as talkative as Rudy. However, like Rudy, they both had a deep respect for Sheriff Winters, despite being older than him.

"Are you comfortable with everything?" Robert asked.

"I think so. I still get nervous every time the emergency line rings." She'd only answered half a dozen non-emergency calls all week. She dreaded the day a true emergency came through.

"We all get that feeling of dread at the possibility of an emergency. It's usually followed by a burst of adrenaline."

When Robert lingered, Amy realized he'd be taking his turn

hanging around the office to make sure she could handle anything that came up. She chewed her bottom lip. Would he be scrutinizing her performance?

It wouldn't be a big deal if she didn't find him so attractive. Tall, dark, and handsome. He was almost as attractive as Ben.

Oh brother, I'm as bad as my mom.

"Great. I look forward to it." Robert stood and walked to his office, calling over his shoulder, "Let me know if you need anything."

Amy let out a deep breath and brushed her hair back when he walked away. *Look forward to what?* She had a feeling she'd missed something Robert said before he walked away—while she was distracted by his biceps—but she was relieved to have him gone.

Four hours later, Amy greeted Rudy when he walked through the front door.

Robert stepped out of his office within seconds of Rudy's arrival and stared at Amy. "Are you ready?"

Ready? For what?

Rudy stood by her desk, waiting for her to vacate her chair. Then it dawned on her. It was lunchtime, and he was here to cover her lunch break. But what was Robert waiting for? Had she agreed to go out to lunch with him when she'd been distracted by his muscles?

Robert pulled his keys from his pocket and stared at her.

Apparently, she had. Pulling her purse from her desk drawer, she followed Robert out the door.

Five minutes later, she sat across from her boss at Charity's diner at the same table where she ate breakfast less than a week ago. This was awkward.

This isn't considered a date, is it? No. It can't be. She couldn't date. Not for a very long time. *We're just co-workers having lunch. That's all.*

Robert's charm and skill at making conversation set her at ease, and she laughed and shared snippets of information about herself she didn't easily share with people.

Her gaze repeatedly drifted to the repair shop across the street, hoping for a glimpse of Ben. When she went to pick up a few necessities after work yesterday, she noticed Ben had washed, vacuumed, and gassed up her car.

When he showed up after dinner last night to mow his parents' lawn, she'd watched for him to finish, so she could thank him. But he took the riding lawn mower to Debbie Wheeler's house to mow her lawn as well.

Did he mow for the widow to supplement his income? She had no clue how much mechanics earned, but she'd learned he lived in the apartment above the repair shop. His rent probably wasn't very high, since his aunt owned the apartment. The same aunt who refused to let him pay for his meals at the diner.

When the mower shut off, she glanced out the window to find Debbie handing him a glass of lemonade, which he accepted with a smile. Perhaps Janice was wrong. Ben did seem to be deep in his grief at times, but the Widow might get him to surface after all.

The thought made her stomach drop and her chest tighten. She was attracted to Ben, and it didn't help that thoughts of him and all he'd lost were never far from her mind. Her heart hurt for him.

Pulling her eyes, but not her thoughts, away from the repair shop, she turned back to Robert. "Rudy said you hadn't been sheriff long when... Ben's wife... died in the car accident. Was that difficult to deal with?"

Robert's eyes narrowed then clouded. He laid his fork on his plate and pushed it aside, His eyes remained on the table in front of him.

She'd caused him to lose his appetite. *Good thing he was almost done.*

All joviality disappeared from Robert's face. He cleared his throat. "At the police academy, they teach you how to be tough when dealing with criminals. Then they tell you to be compassionate when breaking the news to someone who has lost a loved one. But they never prepare you to have to break such news to your own family." His voice lowered as he spoke. "Telling my best friend his wife died in that car accident was hard but having to turn around and tell him his baby had vanished was the hardest thing I've ever done in my life."

A lump filled Amy's throat as she watched Robert's Adam's apple bob. The whole ordeal had been devastating for Ben, and for Robert as well. She wished she could say something to ease his pain, but words seemed inadequate, so she remained quiet.

Robert crumpled his paper napkin into a ball. "Melanie's cell phone rang while we investigated the accident. I found it on the floor of the car, but when I saw Ben's face on the screen..." He shook his head and cleared his throat again. "I couldn't... break that news to him over the phone."

"I can't imagine how difficult that must have been." She reached out and squeezed his hand—the one mangling the napkin.

He released the napkin and grasped her hand with a desperation that matched the emotion on his face. "They also cautioned us at the academy not to make promises to the victim's family. But when I saw Ben's pain, I forgot that caution. I promised him I would bring Cassey home."

"Oh, no." Amy's chest ached from the emotion rolling around inside her.

"Oh, yes," Robert said, his voice full of anguish. "I swear I tried to find his daughter. I memorized every single detail in that file, and I searched daily for new evidence that would give me some clue to her whereabouts. But the blue Suburban we searched for seemed to have vanished into thin air. Even after the FBI withdrew, I continued to drive around. I searched every backroad in this county and the neighboring counties. To this day, I still take long drives hoping to find that Suburban."

"I'm sure you did everything you possibly could."

He rubbed the back of his neck, as though trying to chase away a tension headache. "I did, but it wasn't enough. I didn't bring Ben's baby home. The only thing harder than telling Ben his daughter had disappeared, was having to tell him, the chances of finding her at all, let alone alive, were slim to none."

Tears filled Amy's eyes, blurring Robert's grim face. That must have been so difficult. The news surely devastated Ben. She released his hand and picked up her water glass, blinking away her tears while she sipped.

Charity approached the table at that moment. She must have heard what Robert's words, because she laid a hand on his shoulder and squeezed. "There's nothing more you could have done. You need to stop beating yourself up over it, and Ben needs to find a way to move on with his life." After a brief pause, she continued, her voice thick with emotion, eyes misty. "Moving on is hard, though."

Robert patted the hand resting on his shoulder. Charity had lost her husband not long ago. Her pain, though somewhat different, was as raw as Ben's.

Charity pasted on a smile. "Who's ready for some of my fresh peach pie?"

Amy groaned. "Sounds delicious, but I'm stuffed."

"Me too, but her peach pie is amazing. I'll take a piece to go."

Charity beamed. "That's my boy."

Amy and Robert both walked out of the diner with pie in hand. As they drove away, Amy caught a glimpse of Ben in the garage. After hearing Robert's struggle over the inability to bring Ben's daughter back, she wondered how Ben managed his grief and continued, day after day, serving others.

The desire to help Ben burned in her like a glowing ember, but she had no idea how.

~

"Amy, would you like to join Paige and me for lunch and shopping in Kennewick, this afternoon?" Hope's invitation Saturday morning took Amy by surprise.

Ben's sister, Paige, had arrived home last night from her summer job as a nanny on the east coast. Amy, and especially Kallie, had been drawn to the beautiful, bubbly girl, who wore a perpetual smile and talked with her hands. She frequently bounced up and down when her excitement grew.

Amy knew moms and daughters did things like lunch and shopping together, but she'd never had that kind of relationship with her mother. Her mom spent all her time working or with her current boyfriend. She couldn't be bothered with things like brushing her daughter's hair, let alone taking her shopping and to lunch.

"Thanks for the offer, but I've got a few things to take care of here." Amy hated lying, but she didn't want to intrude on their mother-daughter time. Hope and Paige needed their time together, since Paige would soon return to college. Besides, Amy couldn't afford to go shopping.

The invitation made Amy think about the one person who'd always been there for her. Celeste. Picking up the phone, she called her best friend.

"Amy!" The greeting came through the phone as a squeal. "I've missed you so much. How's my Kallie Girl?"

Amy laughed. She called Celeste every couple of days, so it's not like it had been that long since they talked to each other. "She's good."

"And how is my best friend?" The seriousness in Celeste's voice let Amy know her friend was concerned about more than Amy's physical well-being.

Amy took her time answering. Lance's infidelity still stung, and her mother's rejection still hurt. It probably always would, but Amy had come to accept that. Trying to maintain a positive attitude, Amy said, "I can't complain. I've told you about the nice house I'm staying at, and I don't receive a single drunken come-on at work anymore. Life's good."

"You poor thing," Celeste's voice held sarcasm. "And have you met any good-looking men?"

Ben's deep blue eyes filled Amy's mind. Her pulse kicked up a notch as she remembered the electric shock she'd felt on her wrist when Ben tucked the money into her hand a week ago.

"I've sworn off men, you know that."

"Just because you've sworn off men, doesn't mean there aren't any handsome ones around. Even if you're not interested, doesn't mean they aren't. Besides, there's no harm in looking."

Warming to Celeste's teasing, Amy played along. "Actually, you should see my boss, the sheriff."

"Ooh, tell me more, girl."

Amy told Celeste about Robert's long eyelashes and how nice he looked in a uniform, but thoughts of Ben's dimple and beard caused her voice to take on a breathless quality.

"You say you've sworn off men, but your voice says otherwise."

Amy grew quiet. Why did thinking about Ben excite her? And why didn't she want to tell her best friend about him? She told Celeste everything. The last time they'd talked, she did tell Celeste about Ben and what happened to his wife and daughter. But she didn't tell her about his sapphire-blue eyes or the jealous twinge she'd experienced when he accepted Debbie's lemonade with a smile.

Her attraction to the mechanic didn't sit well with her. Ben wasn't ready to move on with his life, and she refused to get involved with a man who couldn't commit to her.

"I will not get mixed up with the first man to come along. I think I want to go back to school." She'd been almost finished her associate degree at the community college and was ready to apply to culinary school when Lance sidetracked her life.

It would be a long time before she could afford culinary school, but she wanted to do more with her life than wait tables in a bar. She couldn't afford to get mixed up with the first man—or the second—to come along. Kallie deserved better. She deserved a mom who put her daughter first.

After she ended her call with Celeste, she took Kallie on another walk to explore more of Providence. Amy had yet to find anything undesirable about the quaint, all-American town that already felt like home.

A familiar red Porsche came to a crawl next to them as they entered the cul-de-sac, the engine humming a low purr.

Debbie lowered her window and sneered at Amy. "Still here, huh?"

"Excuse me?"

Debbie rolled her eyes. "I guess I can't blame you. I mean, you've got it pretty nice here."

Amy's hands tightened on the stroller. "I don't know what you're talking about." Except she did.

"Don't you? The Young's are very charitable, but I'd hate to see them taken advantage of."

Heat filled Amy's body. "They *are* very hospitable, but I assure you I have no intention of abusing their generosity." She'd offered to pay rent, but they'd refused. So, Amy had been diligent in helping with the cleaning and cooking, to try to assuage her own guilt.

Debbie studied Kallie. "She's cute. Too bad she's illegitimate." She turned hard eyes on Amy. "You may be living with Ben's parents and working with Robert but don't, for one minute, think either of them would be interested in a poor, little, cast-off, nobody like you. You don't belong here."

With a rev of the car's powerful engine, Debbie shot out of the cul-de-sac, leaving Amy feeling more out of place than ever.

She'd found something she didn't like about Providence.

Debbie.

~

"Book," Kallie said, not quite pronouncing the "K." She stood in front of Ben holding a small book, waiting for him to take it. Everyone else in the room waited as well, watching him.

Ben had joined his family for Sunday dinner, and since Paige was home but would be leaving soon, he'd attempted to connect with her. He'd mostly just teased her about her social life at college, but she'd seemed pleased with his effort. After he and his dad finished the dishes, they joined the women in the family room.

Now, Kallie stood in front of him.

"Yes, book." Ben took the book from Kallie and set it on his lap, expecting her to bring him other toys like she had the last two times he'd been here. But Kallie stood in front of him as though expecting something. She put her hand on his knee and stood on tip-toe, letting him know she wanted to be picked up.

Ben's breath caught in his chest. He hadn't held a child for almost a year, not since before Cassey disappeared. Kallie's blond hair and blue eyes reminded him so much of his daughter. The physical reminder was painful, but when Kallie smiled at him with sweet innocence like she did now, he couldn't help smiling back.

With tightness lingering in his chest, he picked her up, aware of four sets of eyes on him. Powerful sensations coursed through him as he held the friendly toddler on his lap. Her hand on his arm was the softest touch he'd felt in ages, and her curly blond hair smelled fresh, clean, and oh so familiar. Holding her felt both foreign and wonderful.

As always, when he saw this little angel, he wondered where his princess was. Who held her? Did they read her stories? Was she as vocal as this little girl, who repeated "Book, book"?

Ben cleared his throat, opened the book, and started reading to his demanding, pint-sized audience. A collective sigh from the others whispered across the room.

Kallie slid off his lap when he finished the book and returned seconds later with another. Ben picked her up again, but before he could open the next book, his father chuckled. "Careful son, don't let those puppy-dog eyes suck you in. You'll be reading to her for an hour and there are only four books."

When Kallie demanded a third book, and a fourth, he realized his parents had likely read these stories to Kallie many times. An odd burning sensation pulled at his midsection, leaving him puzzled. Was he jealous of the time his parents spent with Kallie? Or was it something else entirely.

Amy distracted Kallie with something else before she could demand he read the books again, and Paige sat on the floor to play with her. Kallie had only sat on his lap for a few minutes, but when she left and didn't return emptiness replaced the burning in his abdomen.

A jumble of emotions tumbled around inside him while he walked home. Holding Kallie was amazing; it filled him with loss, sadness, guilt. And a tiny spark of hope.

The more time he spent with Amy and her daughter, the more he smiled. He was beginning to feel things he hadn't felt for such a long time. He found Amy attractive, but he didn't think the desire to see her so often was triggered by attraction. He admired her honest, hard-working nature, and how she strived to be a good mother. Her love for Kallie was evident in everything she did.

Admiration. That's all it is.

And Kallie brought out his protective nature. Ever since he'd realized what a difficult situation they were in, he'd been concerned about making sure they were taken care of.

He was doing what anyone would do. *Right?*

CHAPTER 8

*A*my bit back a smile as she listened to Paige talk.

"We always get together at the ranch for a barbecue on Labor Day, Memorial Day, and the Fourth of July. Oh, for Thanksgiving and Christmas too." Paige sucked in a breath and waved her hand in the air as she talked. "Come to think of it, we spend most holidays and special occasions at the ranch. I guess it's because they have so much space and so many fun things to do." Paige's excitement about spending Labor Day at the ranch was apparent, not only in her words, but in the way she bounced in her seat as she talked.

Ben's sister had missed the ranch while she'd been away.

"You'll like the ranch, Amy" Paige said.

Amy nearly dropped her spoon. "I don't think... I should go." Ever since her brief run-in with Debbie two days ago, Amy had been conscientious about not taking advantage of Ben's family. Crashing a family party seemed to cross that line.

Everyone at the table responded at once.

"Why not?" Paige asked.

"Of course, you should come," Hope said.

"We'd love to have you," James said.

"I don't know... It seems like a family event."

She'd never spent time with a big family before. It had only ever been her and her mother.

It had taken Amy several days to feel comfortable with Ben's parents. She wasn't eager to face his extended family. She'd feel like an outsider looking in, liking what she saw but knowing she could never have anything like that.

"Well, as long as you're staying here, we'll treat you like family," Hope said. "Besides, you won't be the only one who's not related. There will be ranch hands and other friends."

"Please say you'll come," Paige pleaded. "I can't wait to show Kallie the horses, cows, and other animals."

Paige's enthusiasm was contagious. Amy wanted to raise Kallie differently than her own upbringing. This could be a good start. Growing up in the city, Amy had hardly ever seen a horse, let alone other animals. A day at the ranch might be fun.

"All right, we'll go."

Before she knew it, Amy found herself driving to the Double Diamond Ranch. The three women had spent the morning preparing food while Dr. Young did morning rounds at the hospital. She'd insisted on taking her own car in case she needed to bring Kallie home for a nap. Truthfully, Amy still felt uncomfortable with the idea of spending so much time with Ben's extended family.

Would he be there? From the concern she'd seen his family— immediate and extended—exhibit she didn't think Ben spent much time with them.

Paige talked the whole way about time spent on the ranch when she was young. Riding horses and four-wheelers with her cousin, Riley, and the ranch foreman's son, Daniel.

"My cousin Damon, Aunt Faith's son, sometimes joined us too. Damon and Daniel are two years older than Riley and me, but they were too young to keep up with our older brothers," Paige said, talking with her hands again. "Daniel hung out with us a lot. It's not like we were girly-girls or anything, though. I mean, we spent most of our time riding horses and four-wheelers. We liked it when he hung out with us because our parents were more lenient." With a chuckle, she added, "If they knew half the things we talked Daniel into letting us do, they wouldn't have let us hang out with him so much."

Shortly after they left the outskirts of town, Paige pointed out a white rail fence along the highway. "This is part of the ranch."

Amy's eyes widened.

The fence spanned miles. This was no small ranch. Robert's family appeared to be as affluent as Ben's. Amy wasn't sure why, but the knowledge made her uncomfortable.

Debbie's words, *you don't belong here,* echoed in her head, and Amy couldn't help but agree.

Following Paige's instructions, Amy drove through a large gate with the words Double Diamond Ranch written in wrought iron across the top, flanked on either end by interlocking diamonds. She followed the tree-lined lane to a sprawling, white ranch house with a wrap-around porch. If the expansive fence line hadn't convinced her of the ranch's success, the size of the house did, not to mention the massive stables and other outbuildings.

Amy climbed from the car and stretched, taking in the front lawn that blended right into the fenced pasture. A breeze stirred the branches of the massive oak trees, carrying the unmistakable scent of animals and hard work on the otherwise fresh air.

Paige unbuckled Kallie and began introducing Amy to the family. She would've been overwhelmed with all the names and faces if not for her years as a waitress. Faith's daughter, Riley, and Paige could almost have been twins, except Riley had darker hair and eyes. They were younger versions of their mothers.

When she met Robert's brother, Jake, she agreed with Janice. He was every bit as handsome as Robert, despite not having his brother's long eyelashes. Both stood roughly six feet tall, but Jake had broader shoulders.

She met Charity's two oldest sons, Steven and Matt, and their families and learned Steven managed Knight's Grocery, the only grocery store in town. Matt worked as the pharmacist inside the store. Not only did Charity own the diner, the gas station and repair shop, but Knight's Grocery was among the family-owned businesses as well.

Amid the introductions, Paige pointed out three ranch hands, who seemed to prefer to keep to themselves. So Paige didn't bother to introduce Amy to them.

Lastly, Paige introduced Amy to Zane Hamilton, who had been the ranch foreman for over thirty years. His wife Charlotte—known as Lottie—worked as the cook and housekeeper in the ranch house. Their son, Daniel, lifted Paige up off the ground in a hug before returning to Riley's side. If Paige hadn't told her what good friends they were, she would have mistaken Daniel and Riley for a couple.

DURING LUNCH, Amy couldn't help herself, she watched Ben and his cousins out of the corner of her eye. She pretended not to eavesdrop while Robert told Ben and Jake about how she'd handled Widow Wheeler's 911 call on Friday. The young widow insisted Robert come over to her house, because she'd heard noises in the basement.

Robert laughed as he finished with, "Then Debbie said, 'Stop calling me ma'am. I'm not that old.'"

Jake threw back his head and laughed. Ben, more reserved, only chuckled.

Ben had shown up shortly before lunch. Everyone acted happy to see him, if not a little surprised. Amy had sensed from many of the family members, they were never sure if he would come. Other than being his usual brooding self, he seemed to be having a good time.

Amy thought she'd feel like an outsider at the family gathering, but Ben's family had been friendly and inclusive of her and Kallie. In fact, she'd hardly seen her daughter all afternoon. Paige had kept her entertained, showing her the animals and taking her for a ride on a four-wheeler and a horse.

Robert insisted on taking Amy for a ride on a four-wheeler after lunch, which she would have enjoyed more if she hadn't found it so difficult to breathe. Sitting behind Robert with her arms around his waist was distracting. She kept reminding herself he was her boss. An attractive and very fit boss.

She'd just left a relationship and couldn't get involved with another man so soon.

Following their ride, Amy sat on a lawn chair under a massive oak tree and listened to Robert and Jake talk about growing up on the ranch. Robert did most of the talking. Jake seemed more serious and less talkative. Robert, on the other hand, took after his mother— chatty and cheerful, often joking around.

She enjoyed their company, but she couldn't keep her eyes from searching for Ben. She spotted him and Paige, sitting on the back-porch swing. They appeared to be having a serious conversation. Paige held Kallie, and it looked like Kallie might have fallen asleep.

Robert barely finished one story before starting another, and Amy got a glimpse of what it would have been like to have a brother or sister to get into trouble with? Her childhood had been anything but normal, but as an only child, she couldn't help feeling like she'd missed out on a lot.

Robert stopped in the middle of his story and cleared his throat. He gave his brother a pointed look. "Jake, why don't you take Amy on a tour of the stables?"

The sudden request struck Amy as odd. A quick glance at Jake's face told her he found it equally surprising. She caught the subtle nod Robert gave his brother. Looking in the direction of Robert's nod, she saw a red Porsche turning down the lane.

Ah. Widow Wheeler. Apparently, Robert wanted Debbie to see her and Jake together. She wasn't sure what he thought it would accomplish, but she didn't see and harm in playing along. Amy barely knew Jake, but she could pretend to be interested in him for a little while. She'd flirted with plenty of men at the restaurant and bar. Not because she enjoyed it, but because it brought in good tips.

Jake let out a groan, then smiled at Amy. "Would you like to see the stables and horses?"

She stood. "Sure."

It would serve Robert right, if Debbie, after seeing her with Jake, searched him out instead. His sheriff's vehicle was parked out front, Debbie would know he was here.

"I'm not much of an actress," Amy said to Jake as they crossed the back lawn. "But if you want, I can play up my attention toward you. For Debbie's benefit."

Color flooded Jake's, face and she laughed. "I've heard about her attempts to get at Providence's finest bachelors." She laughed again as the color in Jake's cheeks deepened. "Do you want mildly attentive or fall down and twist my ankle, so you can rescue me?"

Jake chuckled. "Maybe somewhere in the middle. Whatever you do, don't leave me alone with that woman."

A few moments later, they stood at a stall door petting the nose of Jake's best mare, when they heard, "Yoohoo, Ja-ake! I know it's a holiday but..." Debbie's words died off when she spotted Amy standing beside Jake. Her lips pressed together, and her eyes narrowed. "Oh, I thought you were alone."

"I'm showing Amy the horses." Jake placed his hand on the small of Amy's back. "You've met Amy, haven't you, Debbie?"

Debbie gave Amy a tight smile, her perfectly chiseled, heavily made-up features giving nothing away. But Amy didn't miss the flash of animosity in her eyes.

"Not formally, no."

Liar. True, they hadn't been formally introduced, but they'd spoken.

"Nice to meet you." Amy stepped forward and held out her hand.

Debbie shook her hand for the briefest of moments before pulling back. Her eyes roamed over Amy, then dismissing her with a look of disdain, she turned her attention to Jake.

Self-conscious, Amy smiled back at Debbie. Did she have any idea how out of place she looked in the stables, in her skin-tight leggings, and four-inch heels? As if that wasn't enough, she fairly glittered in gold and diamonds.

Who wears jewelry to ride horses?

Of course, Debbie wasn't here to ride, was she?

Despite feeling plain and poor next to Debbie, Amy held her smile.

The widow was a fake. From the top of her brassy-red hair and long fake fingernails down to the red toenails, peeking from her gold, high-heeled sandals.

Debbie stepped close to Jake's other side. Putting her hand on his arm, she turned him to face her and asked in a seductive voice, "How's my baby doing, Jake?"

Amy, not to be outdone, hooked her hand through Jake's other arm and leaned against him. "Jake has been telling me about your horse. We were about to go check on it, weren't we?" She smiled up at Jake.

It was a lie, but he played along.

"Yes, I was just telling Amy what a fine horse you have." He put his hand over Amy's hooked in his elbow, subtly disengaging his other arm from Debbie's grasp. He led the way toward a stall at the other end of the stable.

When they approached, a beautiful black horse put its head over the half-door and snorted.

"Hello, Lady." Debbie reached a trembling hand out to pet her horse.

Was Debbie afraid of her own horse? The woman was so desperate to get Jake's attention she'd bought a horse she was afraid of—and cost who knows how much—to have an excuse to see Jake.

Amy didn't know whether to laugh or feel sorry for Debbie. Surprised by the latter emotion, she brushed it off and gasped. "Oh, she's beautiful!"

Despite her own fear, Amy stroked the other side of the Lady's neck, hoping she appeared more confident than she felt.

"I don't know the slightest thing about horses. But you must be quite the horsewoman to have chosen yourself such a fine animal."

Debbie raised her chin. "Well I… I guess I know a thing or two."

Jake coughed to hide his laughter. He shot her a 'What are you doing?' look.

What am I doing? Amy was so far out of her element, she hoped she didn't make a fool of herself. And Jake.

Just keep his attention. Maybe Debbie will get tired of the competition and leave.

"I've never ridden a horse, but if I had a horse as beautiful as Lady, I'd want to ride her all the time."

"I do enjoy riding, but it's no fun riding alone." She batted her long eyelashes at Jake, her lips pouting.

Amy bit her tongue to keep from laughing. She leaned into Jake's side. "It's too bad Jake is so busy. With the size of this ranch, I doubt he gets much time for pleasure riding."

"No, I don't." Jake did a good job keeping his expression serious.

Amy gasped as though she'd had the best idea ever. "I'd love to ride with you sometime, Debbie. Of course, you'd have to teach me how. I'll bet you're good with horses. I'm sure Jake would let me borrow a horse, wouldn't you?" She poked him playfully in the stomach. Her eyes widened when her fingers met firm muscle behind the fabric of his shirt.

Jake made a small sound that sounded somewhere between a cough and a snort before clearing his throat. "Of course." He put his arm around Amy's shoulders and pulled her closer.

The other woman's lips tightened into a thin line, her gaze narrowing on Amy. Debbie definitely wouldn't become a friend anytime soon.

Wanting to keep Debbie off balance, literally, Amy smiled up at Jake. "Weren't you going to show me the other horses outside?"

Let's see how gracefully she traverses the uneven ground in her heels.

Jake kept his arm around Amy's shoulders while they walked outside, so she wrapped hers around his waist. He did it for Debbie's benefit, but Amy couldn't help thinking about how handsome and strong the man at her side was. And wow, did he smell good. Walking this close to him, his fresh, zesty scent almost blocked out the less-pleasant odors of horses and leather.

Good grief. Not only did she find Ben and Robert attractive in their own ways, she was attracted to Jake too? *I am one messed up woman!*

Good thing she'd sworn off men, because Ben and his cousins could easily tempt her to jump into another relationship.

She couldn't do that.

Jake led them to the fence of a large pasture where a dozen horses grazed. She wrinkled her nose. She appreciated the beauty of the magnificent animals much more than their smell.

Knowing Debbie wouldn't be able to in her heels, Amy climbed onto the middle rail of the fence, and swung her right leg over the top. Reaching a hand out to Jake's shoulder to steady herself, she watched Debbie shoot daggers at her.

If looks could kill...

Perched on the fence, Amy admired the horses that came near, occasionally reaching out to stroke their necks. She fired off question after question to Jake, monopolizing his attention.

"Is there a significance to the brand?" she asked, pointing at the interlocking diamonds on one horse's flank.

"My grandfather created the brand. The W is for Winters, and the inverted W that completes the diamonds is meant to represent future generations."

The story touched something deep inside Amy. She sensed Jake's pride in his forefathers, and judging by the ranch's apparent success, she figured they would be equally proud of him.

She wished she could provide a heritage like that for her daughter. Would Kallie ever look back at Amy's life and be proud of the life her mom had led? Maybe not to this point, but Amy was determined to change that.

Debbie's annoyance manifested itself in her stony silence and her glare aimed at Amy.

Amy did her best to ignore her. Eventually, her leg grew numb and the foot she'd hooked over the rail fell asleep. Deciding it was time to get down, she shifted her body and swung her leg back. Teetering, she grabbed Jake's shoulder for support.

He raised a hand to her waist in response.

Debbie gave an exasperated huff, spun on her spiked heels, and walked away.

Amy aimed a smile of triumph at Debbie's back as she lowered her numb, right foot to the bottom rail. Her smile faded when her well-worn tennis shoe slipped from the middle rail. Off-balance, she shrieked and flailed her arms as she went down.

Jake's other hand flew out to steady her, but it was too late. She barely managed to get her foot under her before hitting the ground. The toe of her right foot landed first, taking all her weight. Another cry burst from her lips as searing pain lanced through her big toe and into her foot. Helpless, she crumpled at Jake's feet.

Lying on the ground, Amy was vaguely aware of Debbie glancing back and giving a disgusted grunt before marching off. Amy rolled onto her back, half laughing at her clumsiness and half crying from the pain in her toe.

Laughter bubbled out of Jake as he dropped to one knee beside her. "Are you okay?"

"I don't think so." Still laughing, she wiped a tear from the corner of her eye.

"I have to say, your method is a little unorthodox, but effective." He watched as Debbie's shiny red Porsche roared to life and sped out of the yard.

"Okay. Time to be my knight in shining armor and rescue me from my clumsiness." She reached out hand for him to help her up. Once on her feet, pain shot through her toe again. She whimpered and grabbed Jake's arm for support.

"Are you hurt?"

She grimaced. "I think I broke my toe along with my pride."

Jake chuckled. "Seriously?"

"Seriously," Amy admitted, her cheeks growing hot. She squeaked as Jake swept her up in his arms and started toward the house.

"I can walk. I just need an arm for support."

He stopped walking and glared at her. "Stop squirming, or I'll drop you."

With a scowl, she shut her mouth and wrapped her arm around his shoulder. The subtle scent of his cologne hit her, and she forced herself to keep her arm loose, instead of pulling her face into his shoulder and inhaling.

Jake started walking again. "I take it falling from the fence wasn't part of your act?"

"Not at all. My right leg fell asleep, and my left foot slipped." She giggled again. "Did I look as clumsy as I felt?"

He chuckled. "Yeah."

"Man, Debbie missed the best part. Wouldn't she be upset to see you carrying me in your arms right now?"

Jake threw back his head and laughed.

She liked his laugh. And his scent.

Ben breathed in the fresh ranch air. He was alone at the moment on the back-porch swing, but he doubted it would last. It wouldn't be long before, another family member told him how glad they were to see him.

In the past year, he'd avoided many family get-togethers, preferring solitude to the well-meaning comments and pitying stares. His family meant well, but he found it hard to be around them. Every time he forced himself to come to one of these things, they took it as a sign he was doing better.

Their cheerful smiles and the same question, 'How are you doing?' again and again, had turned him into a liar. He couldn't tell them the truth. He couldn't tell them today was as hard as every day had been for the last eleven months. The loss, the pain, and loneliness were all still there. They'd become his constant companions. Sometimes, making it difficult to even breathe. He feared they'd never go away.

That's what scared him the most. Fear that the pain might never go away.

Paige dropped onto the swing with Kallie in her arms. "Hi." She let out a deep sigh, then remained silent while she rocked the toddler on her lap.

Something is wrong. Paige's never this quiet.

"You okay?"

"I'm fine," she said, as another sigh escaped.

"You want to talk about it?" He didn't want to press her, but she obviously needed to talk to someone. She never hid her feelings well, nor was she the type to hold things in.

"I found out Riley and Daniel have become a thing."

"A thing? As in, they're dating?" He'd noticed the two of them seemed especially close today. When had that happened? Maybe if he came around more often, he'd know these things. It looked like both Steven's and Matt's wives were expecting again. Isabella was beginning to show, and Maria looked like she had about a month left. His mother had probably told him, but he hadn't let it register. He didn't pay much attention to other people's happiness.

"When did this happen?" he asked.

"This summer, while I was away."

"Does their being together bother you?"

"I don't know, sort of, I guess." She played with Kallie's curls.

Ben curled his fingers into a fist, the urge to run his own fingers through the toddler's blond curls overwhelming. "You don't think they are right for each other?"

"Actually, they're perfect for each other. They seem happy."

"Why does it bother you so much then?"

"I don't know. They're kind of young. I mean, I know I'm not ready for a serious relationship."

"Are they talking marriage?" If they were, he would have to agree with Paige. Technically, they weren't too young, but marriage was a big deal. They should at least finish their schooling first.

"No, I don't think they're that serious. They've only dated for two months"

"They'll be going off to different colleges soon. I bet, once they face a long-distance relationship, it doesn't last."

"You're probably right. It's just weird how it happened, you know? I mean, the three of us have always been so close. And Damon too, but he didn't spend as much time at the ranch as I did. We've always done everything together, except when Daniel left for college two years before us. I feel left out, I guess. I went from being a three musketeer, to a third wheel."

Ben didn't know what to say. This was difficult for Paige. It had been a similar situation for him when he and Melanie moved back to Providence. He'd still enjoyed hanging out with Robert and Jake, but things had changed. Almost overnight, he'd somehow grown up and moved on without them. Not that Robert and Jake were immature, they weren't. But marriage had changed him, and they stayed the same. Besides, he'd preferred spending time with his wife.

"It's hard feeling like everyone has move on without you, you know?" she asked.

"I know," he said without hesitation.

Paige put a hand on his arm. "Oh Ben, I'm sorry. That was so insensitive of me. Of course, you do. Better than anyone."

They swung in silence for a moment, both watching the little angel who had fallen asleep in Paige's arms.

Despite the eight years difference between them, Ben and Paige had always been close. He'd always been the big brother she could turn to and rely on, especially with things she didn't want to discuss with their parents. And she'd been the little sister who could always read his mood and cheer him up or calm him down. She'd been at college last year when his world collapsed, but she'd taken a whole week off to stay with him. After she returned to school, she'd made it a point to come home every weekend to be there for him. He'd appreciated it. She never said the things everyone else did; 'I'm sure they'll find her' or 'It'll get easier'. She was simply there.

"Is it getting any easier?" Paige's quiet question pulled him from his musings.

He let out a sigh. "Most days, no."

"And other days?"

He took his time answering. "Last Saturday, when I recognized Amy needed help and I realized I could do something for her, that turned out to be a good day." It had been a hard day too, but Paige didn't need to know that.

"She's nice, Ben. I like her." She stroked Kallie's chubby leg. "And this little cutie has stolen my heart."

"She is a little angel, isn't she?" He gave into the urge to touch her soft curls. The ever-present tightness in his chest seemed to loosen at the feathery soft contact.

"Is it hard being around Kallie?"

"A little. It's painful, but I'm trying to think of it like rubbing a sore muscle. The deeper you rub, the more it hurts, but eventually the soreness starts to ease. She reminds me of what I've lost, but she makes me smile. I keep hoping if I can endure the discomfort, the pain will subside."

The muscle in question was his heart. Despite his words, he wasn't sure his heart could endure any more pain. Would he ever feel something other than the despair and emptiness that filled it now?

They lapsed into silence, each lost in their own thoughts. Ben watched Amy cross the back lawn with Jake, who laughed at something she said. Both Robert and Jake had stuck close to her all day. He'd seen Robert take Amy to lunch at the diner on Friday and for a ride on the four-wheeler today. Now, she walked to the stables alone with Jake.

He couldn't blame either of them for taking an interest in her. There weren't a lot of single women in Providence, and Amy was certainly pretty enough to warrant any man's attention. Was she making a play for one of them? She was by no means a Debbie Wheeler, but would she lead his cousins on for her own purposes?

She didn't strike him as that type, but desperation drove people to do crazy things. Despite his efforts to make sure she was comfortable, she probably felt desperate to provide stability for her daughter. Was she looking for a husband? She'd just left a relationship, surely, she wasn't ready for another one already. However, it didn't sound like much love was lost between her and the unfaithful musician.

He felt responsible for her in a way, but he wasn't sure what more he could do for her. So why did he think about her so often?

After quite some time, he heard the unmistakable sound of Debbie's Porsche. He hadn't heard her arrive—he must have either been in deep conversation or even deeper thought. Laughter caught his attention.

A smiling Jake carried a laughing Amy across the back lawn.

Who was flirting with whom now? Had Amy convinced Jake to carry her or was Jake showing off? This wasn't typical behavior for Jake. Robert maybe, but not Jake.

When Jake called, "Uncle James," Ben realized something must be wrong with Amy.

Paige elbowed him. "Go see what's wrong. I can't move." She motioned to the sleeping baby on her lap.

Ben approached the group gathering around Amy as Jake described how Amy had fallen off the fence.

Amy laughed. "Not very gracefully, I might add."

"Was that Wid—" Robert bit back a smile. "I mean Debbie's car I heard leaving?"

Jake nodded, not even trying to hide his grin.

Ben caught the glance his cousins shared, and suddenly things became clear. Jake had used Amy to drive Widow Wheeler away. Ben struggled to hide a smile of his own. He couldn't blame them, but to what lengths did Jake and Amy go to make Debbie mad enough to take off? In his experience, it wasn't that easy to get rid of her.

And why did he suddenly want to rip Jake's arms off?

CHAPTER 9

*a*my flinched again as Dr. Young poked and prodded at her toe. It was all she could do to hold back the tears. The last thing she wanted was to bawl in front of Ben's whole family.

"I think it's broken," he said. "We'd better get it x-rayed."

"I'll drive her to the hospital," Robert and Jake said in unison.

Dr. Young straightened from bending over Amy. "Ben can drive Amy to the hospital. I'll take my car, so I can stay and do my evening rounds. Amy, if you'll give your keys to Hope, she can bring Kallie and Paige home in your car."

Ben nodded and pulled the keys from his pocket, so Amy handed her keys over to Hope. Apparently, when Dr. Young spoke, everyone obeyed.

Robert scooped her up off the lounge chair where Jake had deposited her. She protested, but Robert ignored her and walked toward Ben's truck. He set her on the seat and smiled at Ben behind the wheel. In a dramatic whisper, knowing full well Amy could hear him, he said, "Hey, Ben, bring her around more often. She makes great widow repellent."

"Yes, and I provide comic relief while doing so," Amy said in the same whisper.

Robert laughed and stepped back.

Faith tucked an ice pack around her foot before closing the door.

Amy turned to see Ben smiling. It wasn't a big smile, but it was a nice smile. One that caused her heart to do a somersault.

The cab of the truck grew quiet as they drove, and Amy wracked her brain for something to say. Whenever she thought about Ben this past week, which had been more often than she'd like to admit, she couldn't help but think about everything he'd lost, and her heart hurt for him.

"You're lucky, Ben. I envy you." She cringed as soon as the words came out. That was not what she meant to say.

His eyes widened. "How so?"

"Sorry… that's not… that didn't come out right. I mean… I don't envy… what you've been through." She bit her tongue to make herself shut up.

"So, you envy me for my good looks, then?" A smile teased at his lips making his dimple play peek-a-boo.

"No. I mean, it's not that you're not good looking… you are… very good looking. I just…" She clamped her mouth shut again as heat burned her cheeks. She turned her head toward the window, hoping he couldn't see her face.

His deep, rich laughter filled the cab of the truck, surprising her. "Is it your verbal wit that makes you such good widow repellent?"

Amy let out a groan and hid her face in her hands. Ben's amusement pleased her, even if it came at her expense. He was usually so serious, and she liked his laugh. She lifted her face from her hands, gave him a flirty smile, and said, "My wit and my grace."

Ben chuckled again, and a lightness filled Amy's chest.

"So, what did you and Jake do to drive Debbie away? Stage a public display of affection?"

She gasped, feigning offense. "A PDA? I would never." Then she smiled, so he would know she was teasing. "Just some frequent flirting and monopolizing Jake's attention." She wasn't sure why, but she wanted Ben to know she wasn't the type of person to do such things with someone she hardly knew. She let out a dramatic sigh. "But

Debbie stormed off in a huff before my grand finale, where I threw myself at Jake's feet."

Ben laughed again. "I'm not sure I put a lot of stock in your verbal skills or your gracefulness. You must be quite the flirt. What exactly does that look like?"

She clapped a hand to her chest. "I'm crushed. If you can't tell, then I'm obviously not very good at that either."

"On the contrary," he said under his breath before clearing his throat.

But Amy heard him. She covered her smile of satisfaction. He wasn't too shabby himself.

They arrived at the hospital to find Dr. Young waiting near the entrance with a wheelchair. Ben insisted on lifting her out of the truck and into the chair. Amy was quickly learning it did no good to argue with the men in this family. As Dr. Young pushed her inside, leaving Ben to park his truck, she caught a glimpse of a smile on the good doctor's face out of the corner of her eye.

He'd insisted Ben be the one to drive her to the hospital. But why?

"YOU'VE GOT a hairline fracture in your big toe near the joint." Dr. Young said as he returned to the exam room. "The good news is it should heal in a few weeks as long as you're careful. But if you don't stay completely off it for the next two days, you'll make it worse. Then you'll be facing surgery."

Amy frowned at the seriousness of his tone. Two days? How was she supposed to take care of Kallie and go to work? A nurse walked in carrying a boot and crutches, and Amy groaned.

Fifteen minutes later, Ben insisted on lifting her into his truck. She wanted to argue, but she had a feeling he was every bit as stubborn as his cousins.

The short ride from the hospital back to Ben's parents' house passed quickly.

Moments before they arrived, Amy spoke up. "Ben, what I wanted to say earlier was… I envy you, your family. You have a wonderful family."

Ben pulled into his parent's driveway and shut the engine off. He sat still for a moment before speaking. "You're right, I do. They've helped me through some dark times, even when I didn't want their help. I think I take them for granted most of the time."

"I can tell they really care about you. I know you've been through a lot, but I hope you realize how lucky you are."

Amy reached to open her door to get out, and Ben glared at her, making him look like his father. "Stay put!" He climbed out and hurried around to her side.

"I'll use my crutches if you'll get them out of the back for me."

Scowling, he put his keys in her hand and lifted her out of the truck.

She let her breath out in a dramatic huff, then chuckled. "I wonder if Debbie is peeking out her window by any chance."

"Maybe you'd better lay your head on my shoulder, just in case."

She didn't dare look at his face—it was too close. But she could hear the smile in his voice. "I better be careful, I'll get a bad reputation in this town," she said before resting her head on his shoulder.

Ben carried her into the family room and laid her on the couch. With efficiency, he took off the boot, propped her foot on the ottoman, and found an ice pack.

"Now, how about something for the pain and inflammation?"

"I'll be fine. Your dad gave me a few pain pills, but I don't like taking anything that strong."

Ben walked out of the room, returning a few moments later with a glass of water and some ibuprofen. "Here."

"I'll be fine—"

"Take them already so we can relax and watch a movie."

Yes. He definitely looked like his father with that scowl.

She scowled at him before taking the glass and pills.

Ben was usually distant and withdrawn, but not tonight. She liked the change but couldn't help but wonder what had caused it.

~

INSTEAD OF TURNING on the television, Ben sat on the other end of the couch. He didn't want to watch TV; he wanted to talk to Amy. To get to know her better. Why, he didn't understand.

"Are you doing okay? Other than the broken toe, I mean. Do you and Kallie need anything?"

"No, Ben, we're fine. By the way, thanks for gassing up my car."

Ben waved away her thanks. Unsure of the best way to steer the conversation, he decided to jump right in. "So, have you heard from Lance?"

Amy scowled. "He called a couple days ago, to ask if I was coming back."

"Please tell me you told him no." The thought of Amy returning to that jerk made his insides churn.

"Emphatically." She lowered her eyes. "You know what bothers me the most? He didn't say he missed me, he didn't beg, didn't even demand I come back. I mean, we were together for three years, and we have a daughter together. And his only concern about me leaving is whether he's actually going to have to come up with the rent."

Ben reached out and squeezed her hand. It felt delicate and fragile in his, and warmth radiated up his arm. The urge to protect her from everyone and everything that could ever hurt her surged in him again. "I'm sorry, Amy. Any man who would look at another woman when he's got an amazing woman like you at home is a jerk. You're better off without him."

He hadn't intended to compliment her like that. The words just slipped out. But they were true. Amy *was* pretty and had a strength and determination about her that would attract any man's attention.

She'd earned his.

His chest tightened. He shouldn't be attracted to Amy. *I'm still mourning Melanie and will be for a long time.* Letting go of her hand, he pulled back.

Amy gave him a tight smile. "Lance *is* a jerk, and I *am* better off without him. I have to keep reminding myself of that."

"Was he always abusive?" He caught a glimpse of sorrow in her eyes before she lowered them, and he hated himself for being so blunt. "Sorry, that's none of my business. You don't have to answer."

"It's okay." Amy tucked a strand of hair behind her ear. "He was actually very charismatic, but he was an angry drunk. He didn't drink heavily when things were good. But... when Kallie was about six months old... his drummer, who was kind of flaky, missed a Friday night gig. If the band didn't play, they didn't get paid." Amy picked at her fingernails. "Lance got very drunk that night. When I took him home from the bar, he got angry over nothing and hit me. The next morning, when he realized he was the one who gave me the black eye, he felt horrible. He bought me flowers, chocolates, and a beautiful gold necklace. I honestly thought it would never happen again, but the next night... the drummer didn't show again. Things were pretty rocky for a while. But they eventually got a new drummer, and things got better. Until he started sinking in debt."

Ben curled his hand into a fist to prevent himself from reaching out to her again. "I'm sorry you had to deal with that, Amy."

She stared at him, eyes full of sadness. "Do you want to know the worst part about it all?" Without waiting for an answer, she said, "I turned out like my mother."

Her words twisted his heart. It wasn't sadness that filled her eyes. It was self-loathing.

Heat coursed through Amy's body. She couldn't believe she'd told Ben her fear of turning out like her mother had come true. Her horrible habit of speaking before thinking often got her in trouble. This was one of those times when she wished she could take back her words.

"How so?"

So much for hoping he'd ignore her comment. Amy didn't want to tell Ben how neglectful and selfish her mom had been, so she gave a weak smile. "You know, dating unfaithful, abusive jerks."

"So, the men your mom dated were abusive too?"

Did she really want to tell Ben about her childhood? She met his gaze. A sincerity filled his blue eyes that opened her mouth. "Some of them. I remember a couple times her pulling me out of bed in the middle of the night to leave." She dropped her eyes to her lap, knowing how incriminating the evidence was that she was as bad as her mom.

"Hey." Ben enclosed her hand in both of his strong ones, warming a frozen part deep inside her heart. "From the little you've mentioned about your mother, I'm guessing you don't have a lot of respect for her. I can't say I do either, but just because you found yourself involved with a man who turned out to be a jerk, doesn't mean you are anything like her. You said yourself, Lance was charming. You couldn't have known things would turn out like they did."

Amy weighed his words as warmth crept up her arm. "Maybe not, but I knew he was a player. With all the women he had hanging around, it surprised me when he took an interest in me."

"It doesn't surprise me. You're beautiful, Amy."

Amy's gaze jumped to his. *Does he mean it?*

Sincerity filled his eyes, along with some other emotion. Something that made her heart race and her mouth go dry. Attraction? Desire?

Ben's phone buzzed, but his eyes lingered on Amy for a long moment before he pulled his gaze away and released her hand.

Shocked by the powerful attraction arcing between them, Amy sucked in a deep breath. She turned her head away when he pulled out his phone. From the corner of her eye, she saw him scowl at the text message.

Who it was from and why it made him upset she didn't ask. She was just grateful the moment that seemed to be building between them had ended. She couldn't get involved with another man. Her focus needed to be on becoming the mother Kallie deserved.

Before either of them could say anything, the front door opened, and a flurry of activity ensued when Paige, Hope, and Kallie entered.

"Mommy." Kallie ran to Amy.

Amy pulled Kallie onto her lap, spotting the smile on Hope's face when she saw Ben sitting beside her.

In what appeared to be a burst of nervous energy, Ben bolted to his feet and rubbed his palms down his jeans. He almost acted guilty. Maybe the guilt wasn't because his mother caught him sitting by Amy, but rather because he felt guilty, period. He was still grieving his wife. Surely, he hadn't intended to tell her she was beautiful, and if he'd felt the same attraction she did, it probably confused him.

"How are you doing?" Paige sat in the spot Ben had vacated. "Was it broken?"

As Amy told Paige the prognosis, she heard Hope ask Ben to carry something in from the car. The next thing she knew he was gone, and her crutches leaned against the couch. Her spirits drooped even as she bit back a smile. Something had changed between her and Ben tonight.

She wasn't sure what, but she'd enjoyed talking to him. Even if it meant telling him what a mess she'd made of her life.

Paige whisked Kallie off for a bath and bedtime stories, and a short time later, Amy headed to bed. As she stepped to the window to close the drapes, she spotted Ben's truck in front of Debbie's house.

Her stomach plummeted.

He didn't seem to like the widow any more than his cousins, so why did he always go over there, and so late in the evening?

CHAPTER 10

*A*my groaned in frustration the next morning when, despite doctor's orders, she tried to put weight on her booted-foot. A sharp pain sliced through her toe, making her grateful she'd accepted Paige's offer last night to tend Kallie today. Although Kallie could walk, she wasn't sure how she'd manage the crutches and the toddler.

She'd just kissed Kallie goodbye when Ben walked through the door. He smiled and gave a slight bow. "Your ride is here."

"Wha— I'm fine... I can..." Why did she always stammer around him?

He grinned, eyebrows raised.

Focusing, she tried again. "I'm perfectly capable of driving myself to work, thank you very much."

"Seriously? You have a huge boot on your right foot and unless you're ambidextrous, driving with your left is harder than you think."

"You sound like you speak from experience."

A tinge of pink filled Ben's face. "I do."

"You're not going to elaborate?"

Ben turned away. "Nope."

Paige laughed. "That's because he's embarrassed."

Ben snatched up a pillow off the couch and threw it at Paige, causing her to laugh again, but neither of them explained.

Amy debated whether to press the issue but decided against it. She'd get Paige to tell her later. Instead, she glared at Ben.

"Hey, this is Robert's idea, not mine. He wants to make sure his dispatcher arrives in one piece. No offense, but I'm more afraid of Robert than I am of you."

Amy rolled her eyes and growled. She pointed one crutch at his chest. "Fine, but if you even so much as try to carry me, I'll hit you over the head with this."

Thankfully, the ride to the Sheriff's Office passed quickly, providing little opportunity for the electricity that had built between them last night to return. When they got to the office, Ben held the door open for her, then moved a chair from the foyer for her to prop her foot up on.

When it looked like he might linger and hover, she pointed at the door and smiled. "Thank you. Now, don't you have to get to work?"

❧

AFTER SHARING the embarrassing story of how she fell off the fence and broke her toe, for the third time, Amy wanted to crawl in a hole. Of course, she'd left out the part about flirting with Jake.

During the few quiet moments she had to herself, Amy's curiosity about Ben's wife's accident and his daughter's disappearance piqued. She browsed the Internet and read every article she could find. The picture of the beautiful baby girl from the Young's mantle, popped up again and again—the same picture she'd seen plastered everywhere last October.

Amy knew firsthand bad things happened all the time, but she'd had a hard time believing someone could be so callous as to walk away with Ben's baby. Now, having met him and seen the depth of his pain, her heart hurt for him.

She came across a later article that mentioned the blue Suburban Robert mentioned. She didn't remember hearing anything about it last October, but she had problems of her own with Lance around the same time. That was when he'd started drinking heavily.

Reading about the accident and pondering on the negative turn of events her life took around the same time, put her in a bad mood. She tried to shake it but couldn't. Not being able to move freely didn't help.

She'd never been so eager to leave work as she was when Robert announced he'd be driving her home.

When he pulled into the Young's driveway, he glanced toward Debbie's house before getting out of his Tahoe. He followed close behind as she crutched her way to the house. Amy hated to admit that after her clumsiness yesterday, Robert was right to be concerned.

Amy hoped helping with dinner would provide the distraction she needed, but Hope refused to let her in the kitchen. "Go put your foot up."

Wishing she could take Kallie for a walk, Amy took her out on the back patio instead to read stories. She hoped the fresh air would improve her mood.

Paige joined them after a few minutes. "I took Kallie for a walk to the park this morning. Then, after lunch, we made cookies." Paige continued to talk about their day, then switched seamlessly to ramble on about college, and how strange she found it that Riley and Daniel were dating.

If Amy didn't know better, she'd have thought Paige was Faith's daughter. They were both so talkative. Could Riley and Paige have been switched at birth? Not likely, since she remembered Paige mentioning she was exactly one month older than Riley.

"I'm so glad you're staying here." Paige said, abruptly changing the subject again.

"Me too. I'm grateful for your family's generosity."

"I know your job at the Sheriff's Office is temporary, but I hope you can find something permanent, and stay in Providence."

"I'd like to stay." Goosebumps covered Amy's skin as she said the words. She meant what she said. She wanted her fresh start to be in Providence.

"You have to stay. There aren't near enough single women in this small town for my handsome brother and cousins."

Amy sucked in a sharp breath, inhaling her saliva. She coughed as heat flooded her cheeks. *What do I say to that?* Ben and his cousins were handsome. She'd said as much to Ben last night. Strong too. Each of them had carried with ease. Their attention gave her bruised ego a boost.

"Listen Paige, I don't think you should get your hopes up about Ben being able to move on anytime soon."

Paige let out a sigh. "I know. But you're good for him."

"Me?" Amy gasped. "I'm not... I don't... I could never... do... or say—"

"Stammering again?" Ben stepped onto the patio, approaching from somewhere in the backyard. His sapphire-blue eyes twinkled with amusement.

Another wave of heat hit Amy's face. Where did he come from? Had he heard them talking about him?

"By the way, Amy, I insisted Ben come for dinner, since I'm leaving tomorrow." Paige stood and handed Kallie to her brother. "Go, wash her up, please." Paige sat back down after Ben left. "I don't expect any miracles, but you and Kallie have helped him. I've seen him smile more in the last few days than he's in the last eleven months. I know it's because of you."

"But I can't... I don't—"

Paige put a hand on Amy's arm. "Just be yourself. It's enough." She went into the house, leaving Amy alone.

The problem was Amy didn't feel like herself when Ben was around. She was normally confident and outgoing, but it seemed every time he was around, she became a bumbling idiot.

Was it because she felt bad for all he'd lost or because she was so attracted to him?

"Ben, wait. Can I talk to you for a minute?" Paige followed him out the back door.

Ben froze and bit back a groan. He was trying to make a quick escape after dinner, but Paige wasn't having it. Every time he'd looked at Amy across the table during dinner, he'd remembered how delicate her hand had felt in his. He'd wanted so badly to pull her into his arms and comfort her last night. To assure her she was a good person, despite her circumstances.

Good thing his mom and Paige had come home when they did. If Ben had pulled Amy into his arms, there's no telling what might have happened. And he couldn't let anything happen between him and Amy, or any woman for that matter. He wasn't ready to move on. He doubted he'd ever be ready.

It would be wrong of him to lead a woman on, especially someone as fragile as Amy was right now.

Ben leaned against the support pillar and shoved his hands into his pockets. "What is it, Paige?"

Paige wrapped her arms around herself. "I thought a lot about what you said—about rubbing a sore muscle."

Ben's eyes narrowed. Paige's face held a mixture of concern and caution. She was afraid he might push her away as he'd done with his family in the past. Part of him longed to do exactly that. Unfortunately, doing so hadn't helped him in the long run.

Paige stepped closer. "Sometimes, the best way to ease the soreness in a muscle is to exercise it."

Ben scowled. "What are you saying?"

"You've lost so much, Ben." Her voice grew husky. "You've suffered more than any of us can comprehend. I'm not saying you need to move on, because I know without closure that's almost impossible."

He clenched his jaw as heat rushed through his body. How could his own sister rip open these wounds?

"Sometimes, when it hurts to use a muscle, we compensate by not using it." Paige paused and waited for him to meet her eyes. "That's what you've been doing. You're not living, Ben. You're simply existing and your muscles are atrophying. I know you're still grieving, and that's going to take time, but I'm afraid if you don't get up and move, you'll waste away, and we'll lose you."

Swallowing the lump that clogged his throat, Ben looked away, into the shadows of the backyard. Shadows as dark as those that had taken over his life. Paige's words stung, but they were true. It had taken monumental effort to make himself go to the ranch yesterday, and despite the connection he'd felt with Amy last night, he'd found it equally hard to make himself come be with his family tonight.

Would it always be this hard? Why does living take so much effort?

"I'm not sure I know how." The words came out as a strangled whisper.

Paige hugged him, and he returned the embrace, clinging to her.

Gradually, he loosened his hold, and Paige stepped back. "The hardest part is always the first step. You've already done that. Helping Amy and Kallie was a good first step. Now, find something to follow it up with. Get outside. Go for a walk. Enjoy a sunset. When was the last time you went to the ranch and rode a horse or a four-wheeler?"

Ben didn't respond. He didn't need to. Paige knew the answer. He hadn't done a single one of those things since the accident. He went running most mornings, but he rarely took the opportunity to enjoy the sunrise.

Paige got in his face. "It will be hard. And it'll definitely be painful. I'm sure you'll encounter a lot of memories, but hopefully, they'll be mostly good ones. You need to cherish them, but don't let them keep you from exercising your most important muscle." She poked his chest near his heart.

"Paige, I can't... simply decide..." Ben choked on his words.

"Just move, Ben. Open the door and enjoy the fresh air. If it hurts too much to get this muscle involved..." She poked his chest again. "Then use your other muscles. Focus on things that don't affect your heart, yet."

Ben studied his little sister. When had she become a woman?

He wrapped an arm around her shoulders. "When did you get so smart?"

She made it sound so easy, but Ben had a feeling learning to live again was going to be the hardest thing he'd ever done.

~

"I'm sorry you came all this way, Jake, but I can drive myself to work." Amy had been about to herd Kallie to the car when Jake and Riley walked through the door.

Riley had come to pick up Paige to head off to their final year of college, and Jake was there to drive Amy to work.

Jake chuckled. "Ben said you'd say that. I'll put Kallie's car seat in my truck." Then he was gone.

Amy stamped her booted-foot. Despite Jake's stubbornness, she planned to argue her point, but she couldn't do that when she had no one to argue with.

When it came time to drop Kallie off at Faith's, Amy was glad Jake had driven her. Faith followed Jake out with Kallie on her hip, talking nonstop while he removed Kallie's car seat.

After he helped her settle behind her desk, he apologized. "I'm sorry about the broken toe, Amy,"

Tired of so much attention over a stupid broken toe, Amy bit back a groan. "It's not your fault. I've never been very graceful." Besides, the way she saw it, it served her right for trying to upstage Debbie Wheeler.

Despite being incapacitated, Amy kept busier than usual. Amid the projects Robert gave her to work on, she answered three calls on the 911 line. Only one was an actual emergency—an older woman had fallen and couldn't get up.

When Rudy hung around the office again after her lunch break, her curiosity got the better of her. "Will you tell me about the accident?" she asked. "The one Ben's wife died in."

He let out a dismal sigh. "It was bad. I don't mean bad as in gruesome and bloody. Of course, there was blood, but we've seen a lot worse accidents on the interstate. I mean, it was hard, because they were two of our own." He snapped his fingers. "Just like that, Melanie was dead, and her baby gone. With no clues."

A cold chill swept over Amy, leaving her feeling empty inside. "What happened?"

"The accident occurred out near the county line where State Road 22 intersects Highway 15. The nearest we could tell, a blue Suburban failed to stop at the intersection. Whether due to wet roads, distracted driving, or what, we're not sure, but it T-boned Melanie."

Amy grimaced. "That does sound bad. How do they know the other vehicle was a blue Suburban?"

"I'll go get the file and show you the forensic evidence we gathered." He went to the record's room and returned a minute later carrying a thick file folder. Opening it, he hesitated. "Maybe this isn't such a good idea."

"Why?"

"This isn't as bad as some accidents we've dealt with, but for someone who isn't used to seeing these kinds of pictures… it might be tough to handle."

"I'm sure I've seen worse on TV," Amy said with false bravado, unsure of whether she really wanted to see the contents of the file, spreading out several photographs. The pictures hit Amy harder than she expected. The crumpled driver's side of the car looked horrific. She had seen worse on TV, where it was all fake. Everything was staged or made-up, but this was Ben's wife.

The picture in the file didn't look like the beautiful, smiling blond from the Young's mantle. Blood covered the left side of Melanie's hair and face, but the lifeless brown eyes hit Amy the hardest. She bit back a gasp and blinked away the tears that filled her vision.

How horrible it must have been for Robert to arrive at the accident and recognize the driver. Then to have to tell Ben.

She pulled her gaze away from Melanie's image and forced herself to focus on the other photographs. There were multiple images of each view from different angles. When Amy saw the photo of the backseat with nothing but an empty car seat base, acute sadness filled her. What a terrible discovery for Robert to make.

What a terrible loss of life.

Amy's eyes burned and her throat itched. She blinked and cleared her throat. "So, what type of evidence did you gather?"

For the next thirty minutes, Rudy showed her pictures of skid marks, boot prints, and tire tracks. Then he showed her close-up photos of the dents and dark blue paint scrapings they'd taken from Melanie's red car. In one photo, he pointed out the dent pattern in the metal of Melanie's car, caused by a grill guard.

"What's a grill guard?" It should have been self-explanatory, but Amy couldn't visualize it.

He leaned over to her computer and did a quick Internet search. When the results popped up, Rudy clicked on an image. "It looks something like this. It didn't cover the whole front of the vehicle, just the grill."

Amy studied the picture where the guard covered the radiator area of a truck, leaving the headlights exposed. She tried to picture it on the front of a blue Suburban, but she wasn't sure she knew what a Suburban even looked like. She knew it was an SUV, but didn't all SUVs look the same?

"We sent all the evidence to the state crime lab because we don't have the high-tech equipment here to process any of it. They identified the paint as Atlantic Blue Metallic, used specifically on 1996 Chevrolet Suburbans. We couldn't get a single fingerprint off the car that didn't belong to Melanie or Ben, suggesting whoever hit her and took the baby, either wore gloves or was especially careful. The sad thing is, if Melanie had gotten medical attention right away, she might have survived."

A fist tightened around Amy's heart, and she blinked away more tears. How could anyone leave someone to die?

Considering what a close-knit community this was, and how many relatives Ben had in Providence, Melanie's death and Cassey's disappearance must have shaken the entire town.

After Rudy returned the file to the records room and returned to work, Amy opened a new tab on her computer and did a search for blue Suburbans. As images filled the screen, she clicked back to the picture of a grill guard, mentally putting the two together.

A dark blue Suburban with a grill guard.

The image in Amy's mind seemed familiar. Like she'd seen such a vehicle before. But she couldn't for the life of her figure out where.

Out of nowhere, came the unmistakable impression she'd broken down in Providence for a reason.

~

ROBERT WALKED out of his office a few minutes after five. "Amy, are you ready to go home?"

Amy nodded. Learning about the accident and viewing the photos and reports had given Amy a headache and left her feeling melancholy. She wanted to lock herself in her room and have a good cry. Her heart ached for Ben and his family, and all the officers who had worked this case.

The feeling she'd broken down in Providence for a reason stuck with her and gave her a sense of urgency she didn't understand.

When they pulled into the Young's driveway after picking up Kallie, Amy caught sight of Debbie sunbathing on her front porch in a bikini. It almost appeared as though Debbie expected Robert.

He jumped out of the truck and hurried to open Amy's door before unbuckling Kallie from her car seat. Robert walked unnecessarily close to Amy as she made her way into the house. At one point, she felt his hand on the small of her back.

It suddenly became crystal clear why Robert insisted he, Jake, and Ben take turns driving her. *They're using me.* She gripped the handles of her crutches tighter as heat filled her.

Jake's words rang in her head. *'Whatever you do, don't leave me alone with that woman.'* Debbie had no doubt earned Ben and his cousins' disdain, but that didn't excuse Robert from taking advantage of her injury.

She waited until they were in the house and Robert had put Kallie down in the family room before she let him have it.

"How dare you?" She accused as she dropped onto the couch.

Robert's gaze jumped to her, eyes questioning. "What?"

She pointed her finger at him. "Don't you 'what?' me. You used me!"

"What are you talking about?" Robert feigned innocence, but his inability to meet her gaze screamed *guilty*.

"Shame on you for taking advantage of a poor, innocent, injured female." She bit back a smile. Pretending to be offended was harder than she thought it would be.

He scratched the back of his neck. "When Ben said you needed a boot and crutches, Jake felt bad, and I sort of felt responsible too."

Good.

"It's nobody's fault but my own. I climbed that fence. My clumsiness got me into this mess."

Robert looked relieved as he sat near her.

She pointed a finger at him. "But that doesn't excuse you from using me to send a message to Debbie."

Robert flinched. "We were only trying to help."

"Right. And *you* purposefully volunteered to bring me home in the afternoons, I bet."

"Well... my schedule is the most flexible. Ben and Jake have no idea when their work will wrap up every day."

"Are you sure it doesn't have anything to do with the fact Debbie is rarely out of bed before ten?"

"I swear." He raised his right hand, but Amy could tell he bit his lip to keep from smiling.

She groaned. "I'm going to get a bad reputation in this town, thanks to the three of you." She glared at him. "I swear, if one of you shows up tomorrow to drive me to work, your deputies will have a homicide to investigate."

He laughed and raised his hands in surrender. "Okay."

"I mean it, Robert." She pinned him with her gaze.

"Fine, I'll call off the chauffeur squad right now."

He pulled out his phone and typed in a text. As he hit send, Kallie demanded his attention. He set his phone beside him, screen up.

Amy read the text he'd sent before the screen went black.

Cat's out of the bag. You should have seen the fireworks! Amy's cute when she gets mad!

She gasped. This was all a big joke to him. She picked up the decorative throw pillow beside her and threw it at him. "I'll show you fireworks!"

CHAPTER 11

$\mathcal{T}$he lawn mower in the Young's garage started as Amy finished the dinner dishes. Curious, she watched out the window, hoping to catch a glimpse of Ben. Tonight, he mowed Debbie's lawn first.

Baffled, she made a mental note to make a payment on her car repair as soon as she got paid. A repair she hadn't received a bill for. She needed to talk to Ben about that.

Amy bathed Kallie earlier than usual, and when Ben mowed his parent's yard, she took Kallie out to the back patio, hoping her actions didn't look calculated. They watched Ben, enjoying the scent of fresh-cut grass.

Each time he drove the lawn mower in their direction, Kallie bounced up and down, excitedly waving at him. And each time, Amy hung onto Kallie to keep her from falling off the swing.

Ben smiled and returned the wave, again and again.

By the time he finished mowing, the sun was setting. It was past Kallie's bedtime, but Amy lingered, enjoying what promised to be a beautiful sunset. She'd drop by the garage tomorrow to discuss her repair bill with Ben.

A few minutes later, she looked up in surprise as he stepped out of the house.

"Mind if I join you?" he asked, settling into a nearby wicker chair.

Amy's pulse kicked up a notch. Glad he'd chosen to sit in the chair rather than on the swing with her, she smiled at him. "Not at all. I think it's going to be a beautiful sunset."

He grinned at Kallie, who smiled back, then hid her face against Amy's chest.

"How's the toe?"

"A little better each day. And I didn't cause a single accident while driving today."

Ben chuckled. "Good."

They made small talk for a few minutes before lapsing into a comfortable silence. Despite her desire to discuss the bill for her car repair, she decided to wait. She had a feeling Ben would argue with her about it, and she didn't want to disturb the tranquility of the sunset. Besides, every time she opened her mouth around him, she said something she regretted.

They watched the golden rays streaking through the scattered clouds turn from pink to a fiery red, then deeper still, until streaks of crimson lit the sky. Finally, the colors faded, and darkness fell.

Amy shivered. The sun had taken its warmth with it. The weight of Kallie's sleeping body lay heavy on her arm.

"Would you like me to carry her to her bed for you?" Ben's low voice broke the silence as he rose from his chair.

"I can do it, but thanks for offering."

"You're likely to wake her up with your uneven gait." He nodded to her booted-foot.

"Good point."

Ben bent over her, his gaze locking with hers. He sucked in a sharp breath and straightened.

Reading his hesitation as discomfort with the forced proximity to her, Amy lifted Kallie's limp body away from her own, so Ben could get his arms under her.

Once he'd taken Kallie, he couldn't seem to step away fast enough. He followed her into her bedroom where she lifted Kallie's blanket from the playpen and laid it over the edge before stepping aside. Ben laid Kallie down and covered her. He stood upright and turned directly into Amy.

They stood frozen, mere inches apart, Ben's breath caressing her cheek. His body radiated warmth, and his heady, masculine scent, mixed with fresh-mowed grass, teased her nose. His eyes filled with an intense emotion she couldn't read in the dim light.

Her gaze dropped to his parted lips, and an insane urge to kiss him raced through her.

Without warning, Ben closed the gap between them and encircled his arms around her waist, his strong hands pulling her against his chest. A small groan escaped him as he pressed his lips to hers.

Stunned by the sudden flood of desire that swept over her, Amy yielded to the pressure of his kiss. The soft tickling sensation of his beard against her face heightened the rush of desire flowing through her. Amy's pulse raced, and a warmth ignited in her chest, spreading outward.

The pressure of his mouth against hers increased, and a sigh escaped as her lips parted, allowing him to deepen the kiss. Her mouth moved with his, simultaneously giving and taking. She wrapped her arms around his neck, needing to pull him closer, if that was possible.

Then she caught herself. *What am I doing?*

She barely knew this man. She should feel repulsed or threatened by his uninvited advances, but she wasn't. She was attracted and wanted more. She felt none of the things she should have, and all the things she shouldn't.

She had no intention of getting mixed up with a man again, even a man as handsome and nice as Ben. So, why was she kissing him with such abandon?

She shifted her hands to his shoulders, intending to push him away, but Ben tensed before she could push. He gasped, releasing her so abruptly she fell back a step. In the brief moment before he fled the room, she saw a flash of something in his eyes. The passion in his gaze instantly replaced by something dark.

Anger?

Was he angry with her? Trying to catch her breath, she followed him from the room. She'd wanted to talk to him about something, though at the moment, she couldn't remember what.

In the hallway, Ben turned to face her so suddenly she nearly collided with him.

"Amy, I'm sorry. That was so barbaric of me. I never should have… It's just that…" Ben raked both hands through his hair. "I shouldn't have done that. I'm sorry." Turning, he walked straight to the front door and disappeared before she could say anything.

She followed him, but he obviously didn't want to talk to her right now, so she let him go. What was she supposed to say, anyway? *Don't worry about it. I enjoyed it.*

It had been less than two weeks since she'd left Lance, and now she'd nearly lost herself in a kiss from the first man to come along.

Her mother had never taken long to replace a boyfriend, but Amy may have her beat. Bile rose in her throat.

No! Ben is not a new boyfriend. He can't be.

She stepped into the dark front room and stared out the window at Ben sitting in his truck.

Why didn't he drive away?

He was obviously upset with himself for kissing her. So why had he done it?

And why did I let him?

BEN SAT IN HIS TRUCK, forehead pressed to knuckles that gripped the steering wheel.

This was all Paige's fault. She'd told him to watch the sunset.

She didn't say you had to do it with Amy. That was all on you. She also told you to go for a walk. That's what you should have done. But he hadn't been able to resist spending a few minutes with Amy and Kallie.

Analyzing exactly what had happened, he remembered how Amy's perfume teased him when he bent to take Kallie. Flowery and feminine. A perfect fit for her. Fighting the wave of longing that swept over him, he'd stepped away from her as soon as he had Kallie in his arms. But the scent of Kallie's freshly washed body, and her soft, silky hair against his cheek invoked another type of longing. He'd held her closer than necessary, relishing the feel of her in his arms, inhaling her sweet, innocent scent.

He'd planned on making a quick escape after laying Kallie down, hoping to outrun the memories that had surfaced, but he'd found himself face to face with Amy instead. Her perfume had invaded his senses a second time as memories he tried to block overwhelmed him.

He laid Cassey in her bed and covered her, smiling at her soft sigh. Could there be anything more beautiful and perfect? Turning to find Melanie close behind him, he answered his own question. Yes. Pulling his wife into his arms, he kissed her passionately, before picking her up, and carrying her to their bedroom.

Realizing he was kissing Amy while remembering the intimacy he'd shared with his wife, riddled him with guilt. He'd kissed her for another long moment before he'd found the strength to release her. Kissing her had felt so good. So right.

Pain and anger had risen in him so sharply, he'd had to leave. Fast.

Amy would think him rude, but he didn't care. He was a jerk for taking advantage of her like that. He had no right to kiss her. He'd told her he had no intention of a physical relationship with her. That's why he'd arranged for her to stay with his parents, where she'd feel safe.

And he'd accosted her in her own bedroom.

It wasn't supposed to be like that. He wasn't supposed to find comfort by kissing another woman. His arms ached to hold Melanie again.

Ben groaned. This is what Paige and everyone didn't understand. When he allowed himself to remember and got his heart involved, the pain overwhelmed him. Knowing he'd never again tuck his daughter into bed, and never again have his wife return his embrace, was more than he could bear most days.

He functioned better if he didn't allow himself to remember, and if he didn't associate with people. He couldn't even handle being alone in a dimly lit room with a beautiful woman after viewing the sunset, for Pete's sake.

Ben pounded the steering wheel with the heel of his hand, then started his truck.

Stick to cars, man.

Though it wasn't that late when he entered his dark apartment, he headed straight to the bottle of pills on his nightstand. He longed to sleep, where he wouldn't remember and wouldn't feel the pain of losing Melanie and Cassey.

And hopefully, he'd forget, for a few hours anyway, how amazing it felt to hold and kiss Amy.

"Earth to Amy." Robert stood over her desk, looking down at her.

"I'm sorry, what did you say?" Amy hadn't slept well last night and consequently had trouble focusing.

"Can I take you to lunch again?"

Considering how attractive Robert was, lunch was probably not a good idea, but maybe it would provide the distraction she needed to forget the incredible kiss she'd shared with Ben.

"Um... sure. That sounds fun."

Robert kept her entertained during lunch by telling her about Providence's most eccentric and bizarre people. "Then there's Debbie Wheeler. That woman is creative. She's found more reasons to call the Sheriff's Office than I knew existed." Mimicking a woman's high-pitched voice, he said, "My dog keeps barking at the basement door. I think there might be someone down there. It's not safe for a single woman to live *all* alone. I'd feel so much better if you'd come check it out for me."

Amy laughed at his impression of Debbie.

"She can be so annoying. She acts like she's doing this town a favor by spending money. Don't get me wrong, she's donated generously to a lot of causes, but she likes to make sure everyone knows she donated the most."

Amy's eyes drifted toward the repair shop, hoping to catch a glimpse of Ben when they left the diner. She couldn't get that kiss out of her head. Nor could she forget how her body responded. She spotted booted feet and blue clad legs sticking out from under a car, but she didn't know if it was Ben or one of the other mechanics.

Why was she always watching for him, anyway? Sure, he was attractive, but was she attracted to him?

Yes. That kiss proved it.

The man sitting beside her was equally attractive. If she didn't see Robert every day, would she feel the need to watch for him every chance she got? If Robert had been the one to kiss her, would she have responded the same way?

Stop it! This is your chance to turn your life around. You cannot get mixed up with the first guy to come along, or the second. No matter how attractive they are.

She had to find a way to get thoughts of Ben and that kiss out of her head.

CHAPTER 12

"You have no idea how grateful I am, Faith. Please let me pay you for taking such good care of Kallie."

Amy hadn't expected to get paid for another week, so Robert surprised her when he dropped an envelope, containing her first paycheck, on her desk that afternoon. She'd cashed it and was anxious to pay her debts and start planning for the future. Her first goal was to save enough money for a deposit on an apartment. She didn't want to have to rely on the Youngs' generosity any longer than necessary.

"I neither want, nor do I need your money. I do it because I love little ones." Faith planted a kiss on Kallie's cheek.

"There must be something I can do to show my appreciation."

"Give back to the community, dear."

This took Amy by surprise. She loved this community. Was that what made it such a wonderful place to live? Everyone gave back.

"I would love to give to the community. How do I donate? Do I go to the city offices?"

Faith laughed. "I suppose you could. But I had something else in mind."

Amy's eyes narrowed. "What?"

"Every year, on the first Saturday in November, Providence holds the Fall Festival," Faith said. "It draws a large crowd, not only from Providence but also from neighboring counties. We serve a spaghetti dinner, with carnival games, raffles, and prize drawings. We work all year long, making crafts to sell and quilts to auction." She explained how the money raised funded improvement projects for the hospital, the schools, and community. "It would be wonderful if you'd help make quilts and other crafts."

"I'd love to help, but I don't sew, and I know nothing about quilting."

"There's plenty to do besides sewing. We're having a planning meeting tomorrow. Please say you'll come and help. You can bring Kallie along."

"Sure, I'll come." Amy hoped she wasn't volunteering for something she couldn't handle.

"It's lots of fun, but also a lot of work."

Amy left full of excitement and trepidation. *Do I really have any skills to contribute?*

Before going home, she stopped at the repair shop, hoping to catch Ben, so she could pay on her car repair. As she unbuckled Kallie from her car seat, she caught sight of Debbie driving away in her Porsche, a smug look on her face.

She walked into the open service bay and spotted a mechanic named Scott, according to the tag on his shirt, who looked like an older version of Rudy.

"Is Ben here?"

Scott motioned over his shoulder to a door at the back of the garage. Obviously, not talkative like Rudy.

Amy stepped to the door and paused, shifting Kallie on her hip. She was probably the last person Ben wanted to see right now, except perhaps Debbie Wheeler.

Making a payment had sounded like a good idea a few minutes ago, but as Amy stood a few feet from Ben's office, her palms grew damp, and her heart raced as she recalled the kiss they shared last night. Would those few incredible moments change the easy cama-raderie they'd developed?

Yes. Kissing changes everything.

She wanted that easy-going Ben back, not the one who'd sat in his truck, no doubt berating himself. And though she'd like to forget the kiss ever happened, she had a feeling that would be impossible.

~

BEN SAT with his elbows propped on his tidy desk, rubbing his temples. This office and his apartment upstairs were the two areas of his life where he hadn't totally lost control. Chaos reigned everywhere else.

For the first time ever, he'd welcome Debbie's intrusion, hoping it would force him to think about something other than Amy. But Debbie had flirted incessantly, sitting on the corner of his desk with her plunging neckline at his eye level, leaning toward him, and rubbing her hand up his arm.

A shudder rippled through him. She must feel threatened by Amy's presence at his parent's house, because she'd doubled her efforts to get his attention.

The woman would not take 'no' for an answer. It's bad enough she brought her car in almost weekly, but the level of maintenance needed at the house lately annoyed him. Debbie must go around with a screwdriver and wrench loosening screws and pipes and shaking light bulbs. Her creativity in getting him to come to the house drove him crazy. He was tempted to hire a handyman to take care of her problems.

He raised his head at a soft knock.

Amy and Kallie stepped in, sweeping the air from his lungs. Amy wore a pale-pink t-shirt, jeans, and tennis shoes. Nothing fancy. So why did she look so darn sexy?

"Are you okay?"

He rolled his shoulders to ease the tension. He'd hoped not to have to face her again until Sunday. He spoke through clenched teeth. "I'm fine, it's just… that woman…" He'd rather Amy think Debbie was the source of his tension, instead of her.

This is all your own fault. Debbie, Amy, all of it.

Why had he kissed her last night?

"Let me guess, her car is 'making a funny noise'?" Amy mimicked Debbie.

Was she trying to lighten the mood? *If we pretend we didn't share an amazing kiss last night, will this situation be less awkward?*

Not likely, but it was worth a try.

"*Again.* I keep assuring her the car is fine, but she's willing to pay the service fee." He shrugged.

"Can you blame her? You're an attractive man." Amy's cheeks turned rosy as she realized what she'd said. "I mean… you're a… a great mechanic. And a woman like her…" Amy clamped her mouth shut and suddenly became very interested in Kallie's shoe.

This was the second time she'd accidentally admitted she found him attractive. He found her embarrassment refreshing, especially after Debbie's overt advances. He liked the rosy glow in her cheeks.

She's cute when she's flustered.

Laughter bubbled up in him, the emotion almost foreign. "Is it just me, or are you like this with all men?"

Her face registered surprise, then her lips curved into a reluctant smile.

He leaned back in his chair, arms folded, waiting for an answer.

"I've come to make a payment on my car repair," she said, ignoring his question.

"I told you not to worry about it."

"And I told you I don't want your charity. What is it with people in this town refusing to accept money for their services? How do any of you make a living?"

"What do you mean? Who else is refusing to accept your money?"

"Faith refuses to let me pay her for babysitting. She said she'd rather have me give back to the community by helping with the Fall Festival."

"If you ask me, Faith is getting the better end of that deal. The festival is a big deal around here. It's a lot of work." He watched Kallie play with one of Amy's ringlets. He itched to hold the toddler almost as much as he itched to tangle his fingers in Amy's curls. He gripped the arms of his chair with both hands. These two females were going to be the death of him.

"I'm happy to help with the festival *and* pay for babysitting, but apparently my money isn't as good as Debbie's." She pretended to look hurt, her lips forming a pout.

What a lousy actress.

Ben chuckled. "You need to bat your eyes a little more."

Amy's lips pinched together as though she tried to keep from smiling. But her blue eyes sparkled, giving away her mirth. She batted her eyelashes and jutted her hip out. Placing her hand on her hip, she said, "Please take my money, Ben."

The seductive tone of her voice sent a shiver of warmth down his spine. He wasn't sure exactly what she was trying to do, but ignoring his body's reaction, he acknowledged how ridiculous she looked.

He threw back his head and laughed.

Amy joined him.

Was she flirting with him?

No, of course not. She's just trying to make me laugh.

It worked. He couldn't remember the last time he'd laughed like that. Amy always made him laugh and smile.

It feels good.

His laughter faded as he remembered seeing Robert and Amy leaving the diner again this afternoon. His cousin seemed to be staking a claim. Was she as interested in Robert as he was in her?

It doesn't matter. Ben wasn't interested in Amy. So why had he felt like a drowning man coming up for air when he kissed her?

He cleared his throat. "Okay, I'll take your money, but please don't hurt yourself. I'd hate to have you drop Kallie or throw your hip out or something."

Amy dropped the charade. "Right. We both know I'm not that graceful."

She may not be very coordinated, but she had plenty of other admirable qualities. *Stop it!* Ben located a folder on his desk and took out an invoice for the parts for her car.

Amy stepped closer to his desk. "How much was the labor?"

He shrugged. "I don't remember how much time I spent working on it."

"Is it just me, or are you like this with all women?" Amy asked, using his words from earlier.

Ben stared at her, his eyes drawn to her lips. His mouth went dry as he remembered their kiss. "L-like what?"

Color flooded her cheeks, and he knew her mind followed the same train of thought as his.

Amy cleared her throat. "If any other woman in town brought her car in for repairs, I bet you'd let her pay parts plus labor." Her voice rose as she expressed her frustration. "But because you know I was in a difficult position, financially, you're trying to give me a break by not making me pay my full obligation. I got paid today, and though I can't afford to pay the full amount right now, I assure you I will pay every penny I owe you."

He gave plenty of women a break on their car repairs, but he'd never seen one get this feisty for not charging enough.

Ben's lips curved in admiration. "Fine." He grabbed a pen and a blank service invoice and began to write. "Robert's right. You're cute when you're riled up."

Amy let out a dramatic huff and stomped her booted-foot. Judging by the fire in her eyes, it's a good thing she was holding Kallie, or she might have found something to throw at him.

The scent of Amy's perfume surrounded Ben as he filled out the invoice. His grip on the pen tightened, and he tried to block out how amazing it felt to hold and kiss her. A palpable tension filled the room.

He dropped his pen and cleared his throat. "Listen, Amy, I'm sorry for… what happened… last night."

"Ben, it—"

"No, let me finish." He raised a hand, cutting her off. "I shouldn't have… attacked you like that."

"I appreciate the apology, but you hardly attacked me. Besides, it didn't really mean anything, did it? I mean... we were just caught up in the moment, after the sunset and all..."

Caught up in the moment. Did that mean she enjoyed it as much as he did? She'd definitely responded.

He resisted the urge to stick out his chest as a sense of pride swelled in him. *Stop it.*

"I thought..." Ben struggled to find the words to explain his behavior as memories of his wife filled his head. "I wanted..." He blew out his breath in a frustrated sigh. He didn't have an explanation. He'd made a huge mistake. "I don't know what came over me. You're right, it didn't mean anything. It was a mistake. One, I promise won't happen again. Can we please forget it?"

She gave him an impish smile. "Forget what?"

Ben breathed a sigh of relief, then cringed as a fresh wave of guilt swept over him. Problem was, he wasn't sure he could forget, nor could he forgive himself as easily. Especially since he wanted a repeat.

AMY LET her gaze roam Ben's office, trying to find something to focus on besides him. Being near him raised the temperature in the cramped office, add in the lingering effects of last night's kiss, and Amy felt the need to fan herself.

A photo on Ben's desk caught her attention. She stared at the picture of Ben's daughter—there was so mistaking Cassey's blue eyes —in a puffy, pink snowsuit.

Goose bumps covered Amy's arms, despite the warmth of the small room. Ignoring the proximity to Ben, she picked up the picture.

She felt him tense beside her, but she couldn't take her eyes off the photo. She'd seen this picture before. That wasn't possible though, was it?

This wasn't the picture that had been all over the news for the past year.

Ben cleared his throat. "That uh... was the last picture taken of... my daughter."

Amy's brow furrowed as though trying to make sense of his words.

"Melanie sent it to me the day... of the accident. She'd took her sister to Kennewick to go shopping for her birthday. It was rainy and cold that day, so Melanie bought Cassey a snowsuit for winter. She sent me this picture right before she... headed home."

"Sh-She's adorable," Amy said. "Did you give this picture to the police or news people?"

Ben's voice was wary when he spoke. "I showed it to them, but they wanted a picture that showed more of her face and hair."

Ben was the only one with this picture. So, why did it look so familiar?

She squeezed her eyes shut, concentrating. She had seen, those deep blue eyes and blond tuft of hair framed by the fuzzy, pink hood, somewhere. She was sure of it.

But, where?

She studied the picture again. Had Cassey's deep blue eyes, so like her father's, become that common to her?

No. Amy's skin tingled. The pink hood framing Cassey's face was familiar, too.

"Are you okay?" Ben asked.

"Y-yeah." Amy shook her head and handed the picture back to him. "I had a déjà-vu moment."

Why had she lied? This wasn't déjà-vu. She had seen a baby with deep blue eyes and blond hair dressed exactly like this somewhere, but she couldn't remember where. Or even when. She just knew she'd seen this baby.

CHAPTER 13

$\mathcal{P}$rovidence's community center turned out to be bigger than Amy expected. With a large gym, several small meeting rooms, and a large kitchen, Amy wasn't surprised to learn it was used for all kinds of activities. From weddings, to dances, to Friday night youth activities designed, to give the kids someplace to go and keep them out of trouble. The ping-pong and pool tables had been pushed aside for today's meeting.

Amy found the number of people—mostly women—in attendance impressive. Many of them introduced themselves to Amy before the meeting started, making her feel welcome.

The meeting was well organized. A woman named Naomi talked about the purpose of the festival and the projects they hoped to raise money for, including new computers for the school and park improvements. They discussed how much money the festival brought in last year.

Amy was good with math, and her calculations of what they expected to bring in fell far short of what they needed to raise.

As the women threw out new fund-raising ideas, Amy wracked her brain for something that could bring in large amounts of money. She recalled Robert telling her how generous Debbie was, and how she liked to make it known how much she contributed. How could they capitalize on Debbie's generous donations? What did she want most?

An idea struck Amy. Ben probably wouldn't participate, and Robert and Jake would hate her for it. But if they realized it was for a good cause, maybe they'd be willing to go along.

Biting her bottom lip, she raised her hand.

"Amy, do you have something to add?" Charity asked.

"I might have an idea. I'm new here… and I don't want to offend anyone. If you don't think this is a good idea, I understand."

"What's your idea?" Hope asked.

"What about a bachelor auction?"

Two women gasped. Three ladies clapped. Then pandemonium broke out as women spoke one right after another.

"What a great idea!"

"How would it work? Would we make the women bid to go on a date planned and paid for by the bachelor?"

"We'll need the bachelor's permission to auction them off."

"We'd have to set ground rules for the date. We wouldn't want anything inappropriate happening." This from an older woman.

"We should make the minimum bid a hundred dollars since the guys will have to pay for the date."

"Ladies," called out Naomi, the one who seemed to be in charge. "We're getting ahead of ourselves. Someone needs to make a mo—"

A woman's hand popped up. "I make a motion that we include a bachelor auction as part of fundraising for the Fall Festival."

"I second it," said the women on either side of her.

Then the chaos ensued as women called out names of bachelors, and the woman beside Naomi wrote frantically to keep up. Robert's and Jake's names landed at the top of the list, of course, followed by Rudy and his brother, Scott, and another half dozen names Amy didn't recognize. Women also threw out ideas for ground rules. The date needed to be at least two hours, and had to include a meal, and should take place within two weeks of the Festival.

"I'd pay to go out with Robert or Jake," said a woman who appeared to be in her early thirties.

"So would I," an elderly woman echoed. "Sorry Faith, but your sons..." She let out a breathy sigh and fanned herself.

A chuckle rippled through the crowd.

"Can you imagine how much money Debbie would pay to have Robert or Jake take her out?" another woman asked.

"Should we set a rule you can only buy one bachelor? Because she would get them both if she could. You know she would."

"Do you think Ben would do it, Hope?" asked an older lady.

"I don't know." Hope's voice was quiet, and she shot Amy a hopeful glance.

Why did she look at her like that? Did she think Amy could talk him into participating?

No way. She'd put her foot in her mouth plenty of times where Ben was concerned, but she wouldn't touch this with a ten-foot pole.

Her thoughts turned to Ben and his daughter as they had a thousand time since she saw the picture on his desk yesterday.

She kept asking herself if it was possible that she'd seen the person who kidnapped Cassey? Her heart raced again at the thought.

Surely, more than one blue eyed baby with a pink snowsuit lived in the Portland area. But the little girl's eyes had been so like Ben's. If she could remember the deep blue eyes, why was it so difficult to remember where she had seen the infant? She couldn't make the image fit with the restaurant or any of the other places she went regularly before moving to Providence.

The discussion continued around her, and Amy pulled her mind back.

"We should advertise the auction on the posters and fliers, that way women can come prepared."

Women volunteered to talk to various bachelors to see if they would agree to be auctioned off. When it came to Robert's and Jake's names, no one volunteered because everyone knew Debbie would be the high bidder there. And no one wanted to have to talk them into going out with her.

Amy turned to Faith. "Do you think…"

"Oh, leave me out of this, dear." Faith raised her hands in surrender. "A mother knows there are times when you simply don't butt into your children's lives."

Charity smiled at Amy. "It was your idea. Maybe you should talk to the two of them."

Amy nodded, swallowing hard. "I'll do it."

A knot formed in her stomach. *What have I gotten myself into?*

"AMY, it's good to see you," Naomi said.

Amy took a deep breath and returned Naomi's smile. She'd barely stepped into the church, and already she feared her breakfast might come up. She'd finally accepted the Young's invitation. Thinking she'd like to attend church and actually going were two very different things.

What if she said or did something wrong? Something that let everyone know she'd never been to church before. Would people judge her for showing up to church with an illegitimate child?

Another woman whose name she didn't recall greeted her, followed by Robert and Jake. Before long, she found herself surrounded by friendly faces.

Maybe this won't be so bad.

The message about having charity set Amy at ease and made her want to do more to help others around her. She'd expected to feel guilty for the way she'd lived her life in the past, but she didn't feel like anyone judged or condemned her. In fact, she couldn't have felt more welcome. From now on, she planned to make church attendance a part of her life.

That evening, Amy grinned as she tied on one of Hope's aprons. Friday, after getting paid, she'd tried to pay the Youngs for room and board, but like Ben and Faith, they'd refused. Amy had anticipated that, so she'd insisted on buying groceries and doing the cooking. To her relief, Hope had agreed. Knowing Ben would be coming for dinner created a flutter in her stomach that stuck with her until she sat at the table with Ben and his parents.

"This is delicious," James said, after sampling the sirloin stroganoff Amy made. "I thought you waited tables in a bar. How did you learn to cook so well?"

"I've always enjoyed cooking, even when I was young. But I learned a lot from occasionally helping in the kitchen at the restaurant." Once she'd figured out the recipes, she'd tweaked them, making them even better. Of course, she never dared admit as much to Charlie. "As the day manager, I spent most of my shift in the restaurant. That changed when Dennis moved me to nights." Amy couldn't hide her distaste for the bar and for her former boss.

"Did you have to deal with a lot of unwanted advances from drunk men in the bar?" Hope asked.

Amy shrugged. "I got them all the time, but they didn't bother me. I knew it was the alcohol talking. And I was rarely alone, so I never felt threatened. It was the ones who were sober and not in a public place that I had to worry about."

Instantly, she regretted speaking so freely. Instinctively, she propped both elbows on the table and put her hands on either side of her neck, as she fought unwanted memories, both from her childhood and her more recent experiences with Dennis.

A flash of guilt crossed Ben's face, then his eyes narrowed as he studied her. She forced herself to lower her arms and look away from his probing stare.

After dinner, Hope insisted on doing the dishes since Amy cooked, and James stayed in the kitchen to help.

Amy left the kitchen amid compliments for the meal and found herself in the family room with Ben and Kallie. Warmth stole over Amy as she remembered the kiss they shared a few days ago.

Blocking it from her mind, she sat on the floor to play with her daughter, where she coaxed Kallie to roll a ball to her. The toddler smiled every time Amy rolled it back.

Ben sat across the room, his usual handsome, brooding self, and

Amy wracked her brain for something to talk about. "I went to church with your parents today."

Ben's eyebrows rose. "You did? How did you like it?"

"I liked it. I thought I'd feel out of place, but everyone was so nice."

"There are a lot of good people in this town, and the best of them can usually be found in church on Sundays."

She hadn't seen him at church. She was certain he'd been raised attending church.

"I didn't see you there. I mean, you're one of the most charitable people in town." Her voice dropped, and she glanced away. She sounded like Debbie. When he didn't respond, she glanced up at him.

Ben twisted his wedding band as he stared at Melanie's picture on the mantle.

She shouldn't have brought up church. It was obviously a touchy subject for Ben.

He cleared his throat. "I haven't gone since the funeral."

She gave him a look of understanding even though she had no idea what he was going through.

He surprised her when he spoke again. "I can't bear to see the pity in everyone's eyes." Then his voice dropped. "And church is the last place I belong while I'm angry with God."

"I take it you're angry at him for taking your wife?" When Ben gave the slightest nod, she went on. "I guess, I understand why you feel like that, but I'm not sure I see it that way."

"What do you mean?" Ben's brow wrinkled, and he studied her like she'd lost her mind.

Maybe she had. What did she know about God?

"I've always believed God existed, but I've never had enough of a relationship with him to blame or credit him for the things that have happened in my life. I felt like He never played much of a role." She shrugged. "I've had plenty of bad things happen, but I never felt the need to blame God for them. I always knew who was at fault. Sometimes, the fault was mine." Most of the time, though, it had been her mother.

"Yeah, well, I don't know who's at fault. If I did, I'd have my daughter back." Pain laced his words, and Amy's heart twisted.

"You're right. I'm sorry, I shouldn't have said anything. I just never thought much about God until I came here."

"What made you start thinking about Him now?" Ben leaned forward in his seat as though genuinely curious to hear her answer.

She shrugged, unsure how to express all the little things she'd experienced since coming to Providence that told her she wasn't in control of her life. Would he laugh if she told him she felt like she was meant to break down here? Telling him she knew she was supposed to somehow find his daughter would not only sound crazy, it would cause him more pain.

She gave him a half-smile. "I always thought if something good happened to me, it was because I worked hard and earned it. And of course, I knew where to place the blame for the bad things." She didn't want to think about the bad things. "But, from the time my car broke down, which seemed like a bad thing, I've felt like someone or something meant for me to be here, in Providence. And good things—that I can't take credit for—keep happening."

"Breaking your toe was a good thing?" Ben asked, attempting to suppress a smile.

"No. That was bad, and totally my fault. I mean you... or rather your help, your parents' generosity, and the job that fell in my lap. I don't feel like I can take credit for any of it. Is it crazy to think a god I barely believe in is guiding the little details of my life?"

"I used to think God cared about every little detail of my life, but..."

Amy didn't know what to say. Ben was hurting. She shouldn't have brought up God. She wanted to tell him God still loved him even though he'd lost his wife and daughter, but she couldn't. Surely a god, who loved his children, wouldn't stand by and watch a good man like Ben suffer.

Kallie got to her feet and ran after the ball that rolled toward Ben.

"When did she learn to crawl?" Ben asked, changing the subject.

Amy silently thanked him. She'd gotten in way over her head talking about God.

"She started with the army crawl around eight months and by nine months she was up on all fours and unstoppable."

"Cassey had learned to roll and had started sitting up on her own when…"

Emotion tightened Amy's throat, making it difficult to breathe. "I'm so sorry, Ben." The words sounded trite, considering the depth of his pain.

He cleared his throat. "Tell me more about Kallie, when did she start walking?"

"She walked around things by eleven months, then on her first birthday she let go. She never crawled again after that, no matter how many times she fell. It was like she knew it was a special occasion and decided she wanted to be a big girl."

"When did she start talking? What were her first words?"

Amy wondered whether sharing all the things Kallie did that he would never experience with his daughter was a good idea, but she couldn't bear not to share when he asked. Especially when he seemed so interested. She would do anything to ease his pain.

"Well, she started with the 'mama', 'dada' stuff around a year. In the past few months, she started saying 'uh-oh' and 'tsat' for what's that? I said 'uh-oh' a lot when she became more mobile and got into things."

"When's her birthday?" Ben's voice was tight.

"April fourth."

"She's exactly two weeks older than my Cassey."

Ben's parents walked into the room, and Kallie jumped up and went to Hope.

Hope picked Kallie up and planted a kiss on her cheek as she sat on the couch.

Amy glanced at Ben out of the corner of her eye, trying to read his stoic expression. He sat with his elbow propped on the arm of the chair. His chin rested in the curve of his thumb and index finger, stroking the left side of his beard. What did he think about Kallie's relationship with his mom? Was it hard for him to know his Cassey would never know her grandparents?

Her heart ached as she remembered the picture of the empty car seat base in the backseat of Melanie's car. These people had shown her and Kallie such kindness, she wished she could somehow ease their pain. She thought again about the picture on Ben's desk.

Amy couldn't let go of the thought that she'd seen Cassy after she was kidnapped.

Kallie slid off Hope's lap, picked up an activity book with flaps, and stood in front of Ben. She seemed to sense somber mood and wanted to cheer him up.

He swiped at the corner of his eye before pasting on a smile and lifting Kallie onto his lap.

Hope brought up the Fall Festival and all the work that went into it, and Amy shifted her attention.

"The women meet every Wednesday evening from seven until ten to work on the projects. Amy, you should come help so you can get to know more people."

"I'd love to help, but I'm about as talented as I am coordinated." Amy pointed at her booted-foot.

"Don't worry, there will be plenty of things you can do."

"I'm not sure what to do with Kallie." Crafting areas with scissors, pins, needles, and hot glue guns was no place for a busy toddler.

"We have some teenage girls who babysit every Wednesday."

Amy cringed as she remembered the two harried teenagers who had cared for twelve children under the age of ten yesterday. In the few minutes it took Amy to pick up Kallie, she'd seen a little girl about five push down a toddler, who hit his head on a chair, and another little boy bite a girl.

No. She wouldn't subject Kallie to that, again.

"I usually put Kallie to bed around eight. She's a bear if she stays up too late, but I'd hate to have to leave that early."

"I'll tend her." Ben's voice was so quiet, Amy wasn't sure she'd heard him correctly.

This was the last thing she expected to hear out of Ben's mouth. A quick glance at his parents told her they were equally surprised.

"I don't know, I... she..." Amy couldn't let a man tend her daughter. Could she? Since learning Ben's daughter had been kidnapped, she hadn't been concerned about his fascination with Kallie, but that didn't mean she trusted him to take care of her daughter.

She'd never trusted Lance to take care of Kallie, not that he wanted to. Celeste's husband, Grant, and Charlie had been the only men she'd trusted around her daughter.

Ben met Amy's gaze. She read the lingering raw emotion in the depths of his blue eyes along with something else. Hope?

"That's a wonderful idea," James said. "I'll be here, so I can help if Ben needs it."

Amy looked at James. He gave her a confident smile and a nod of encouragement. James wanted her to let Ben tend Kallie. Did he think it would help him heal?

Kallie loved James. He read her stories and took her for walks out in the yard all the time. And Kallie appeared content on Ben's lap. Surely, it would be okay to let Ben take care of Kallie as long as his father was there. Wouldn't it?

"Okay. Thank you, Ben." Amy pasted on a smile to mask her concern. "On one condition." When he looked up, she added, "You come over for dinner before."

"Deal." Ben smiled, and Amy's heart skipped a beat at the sight of his dimple.

CHAPTER 14

"*I* already bathed her, so you don't have to worry about that, but she might need a dry diaper before bed. I usually read her a couple stories before I put her down. She'll fall asleep on her own." Amy continued to rattle off more information than Ben would ever need to care for Kallie.

The meatloaf she'd fixed for dinner sat in her stomach like a brick now that it was time to leave her daughter. She'd worried all day about how Kallie would react to having Ben and James tend her. Add to that, the stress over talking to Robert and Jake about the auction, and Amy was a bundle of nerves.

Rumors were circulating that most of the bachelors had already agreed, and Amy had yet to ask Robert and Jake. She'd stood outside Robert's closed office door for a full minute this afternoon, but then she'd chickened out and retreated to her desk. Focusing instead on calling businesses to solicit donations for the gift baskets to be raffled off at the Festival.

It didn't help that Amy couldn't seem to get the image of a blue-eye baby in a pink snow suit out of her head. The familiarity of a blue Suburban with a grill guard perplexed her too. Her frustration grew with each day that passed, making her anxious.

Ben put both hands on Amy's shoulders, making her aware of his proximity. His spicy, earthy scent made her want to lean into him and inhale deeply.

"Relax, Amy. I remember how to change a diaper. I'll put her to bed on time. We'll be fine, don't worry."

He pulled his phone from his pocket and handed it to her. "Give me your number, and I'll give you mine." He held out his hand for her phone. "I will give you hourly updates, so you know everything is okay."

His fingers brushed hers when they swapped phones, and a tingling sensation worked its way up her arm.

"Okay." Amy took a deep breath. "Thank you for tending Kallie."

"Baa-baa." Ben held out a toy sheep to Kallie.

When Amy walked out the door, and Kallie got a concerned look on her face, Ben grabbed the bag he'd stashed in the front room when he arrived. He distracted her with the barn and animal set he'd purchased on impulse yesterday in Kennewick.

Kallie picked up the pig and held it out to Ben for the tenth time. She laughed every time he 'oinked'. Then he and his dad laughed every time she scrunched up her nose as she attempted to mimic the sound. Ben took a picture of one such facial expression and sent it to Amy.

Haha. I can see she's having fun, so I'll stop worrying about her. Thanks.

It relieved Ben to know Amy wasn't just concerned about him caring for Kallie; she was concerned whether Kallie would take to him. He'd seen Amy's reticence on Sunday when he offered to tend. If he could prove he was capable of taking good care of her daughter, maybe she wouldn't be so hesitant next time.

And he really wanted there to be a next time.

About an hour after Amy left, his dad's cell phone rang, and he excused himself to take the call. He returned less than a minute later. "Sorry, son, but I need to assist Dr. Spencer with an emergency appendectomy. Will you be okay by yourself, or should I ask your mom to come home?"

"We'll be fine, Dad."

His dad had carefully watched him for the past hour. What he expected to see, Ben didn't know, but he'd thoroughly enjoyed playing with Kallie.

Realizing it was Kallie's bedtime, he took her to Amy's room, trying in vain not to remember what happened the last time he was here and how much he enjoyed it. After a quick diaper change, Kallie rolled onto her tummy and slid off the bed before he could get her feet back into her pajamas. She grabbed a bottle of baby lotion from the nightstand and held it out to him.

"Some."

Amy probably put lotion on Kallie after her bath, but he couldn't deny those beautiful puppy-dog eyes.

"Okay, just a little." He sat Kallie on the bed beside him, squirted a small amount into her palm, and watched as she rubbed it on her tummy, then held out her hand again.

She barely smeared the next squirt on the other leg before raising her hand again. "More."

After multiple squirts, Kallie had enough lotion on her body for two children, not to mention the amount she'd rubbed on his arms.

Putting the lotion out of sight on the dresser, he helped her rub it all in. As he did so, the familiar baby scent tugged at his memories, and an intense longing swept over him. The routine, though foreign, was the most wonderful thing in the world.

He stumbled his way through *Five Little Piggies* with lots of *oinking* as he rubbed the lotion into her chubby feet. She squealed and jerked away.

"Ah, you're ticklish, huh?" Ben growled and tickled her feet again, then her tummy. She squealed in delight each time he touched her.

Kallie patted her tummy. "More."

He put her legs in her pajamas and zipped them up. Then he nuzzled her tummy and neck with his chin. She squealed and laughed until tears filled her eyes.

Tears filled Ben's eyes too, but they weren't from laughter.

He had been able to elicit giggles from his Cassey by nuzzling her neck, but nothing like the squeals that came from Kallie. Now that his princess was older, would she respond like this little angel?

He'd never get to find out.

Heaviness filled his heart as he read Kallie her bedtime stories. She grew sleepy in his arms, but he loathed the thought of putting her in bed. His arms and heart would feel so empty.

After laying her down, he took another picture to send to Amy.

"Night-night," he whispered, stroking her cheek one last time.

Kallie waved, giving him a sleepy smile, and his heart twisted.

He returned to the family room and turned on the television. He needed a movie with some action and a fast moving-plot to dispel the loss that consumed him.

An hour later, he turned the TV off after hearing Kallie cry. Amy hadn't said what to do if she woke up. Should he leave her? Give her a hug and lay her back down? Or rock her back to sleep?

He chose the latter. Not because Kallie needed it, but because he did. For a few minutes, he needed to hold this sweet little angel and pretend he hadn't failed his own daughter.

WHEN AMY RETURNED, the house was dark except for a lamp in the corner of the family room. She walked in to find Ben asleep in the recliner with Kallie sound asleep on his chest, one large, masculine hand on her back. She stood for a moment, taking in the scene. Another chunk of her frozen heart thawed at the domestic sight.

Ben's face looked so peaceful. This was the most pleasant expression she'd seen on his face since her arrival in Providence, except when he teased her.

She touched his arm. "Ben."

He blinked and instinctively put his other hand on Kallie's back. Amy whispered his name again, and he finally acknowledged her presence.

"You should have put Kallie in her bed," she whispered.

"I did, but she woke up crying about an hour ago."

"She would have gone back to sleep if you'd given her a hug and laid her back down."

"But that's no fun."

"You'll spoil her."

He grinned. "Maybe, but that's your problem. Not mine."

Amy propped her hand on her hip and scowled at him. "Do you want me to take her?"

"No, I'll take her back to bed." He lowered the legs of the recliner and held Kallie tight as he stood.

Remembering what happened the last time Ben carried Kallie to bed, Amy waited in the hall until he came out of the room.

"Where's your dad?"

Ben shrugged. "He got called into the hospital hours ago."

"I'm sorry you had to tend her by yourself."

"Why? Did you doubt I could handle it?"

"Not at all. I know you used to be a father."

Ben's head jerked back as though she'd slapped him.

Realizing how hurtful her words sounded, Amy clapped a hand over her mouth.

"I'm so sorry. I didn't mean for that to come out like that."

He glanced away, but Amy saw the muscle in his jaw clench in the dim light.

"Please forgive me." Tears filled her eyes, and her throat burned. The last thing she wanted was to hurt Ben. She grabbed his arm. "Ben…"

He looked at her. "You're right." The pain in his eyes and voice tore at her heart and her chest tightened.

"No, I should never have—"

"I used to be a father," he said, his voice raw with emotion. "But I'm not anymore, and I used to be a husband, but I'm not anymore."

Hot tears ran down Amy's cheeks. The anguish in his voice broke her heart.

"I don't know what I am anymore."

"Listen to me." She put both hands on his shoulders much as he'd done to her earlier that evening. She gave him a slight shake, waiting for him to look at her. "You're still a father. That hasn't changed because Cassey isn't here. You're also a son, a brother, a nephew, and a cousin, but most importantly you are a wonderful, kind, compassionate man, to whom I am very grateful." More tears spilled onto her cheeks. "Please, don't let my careless words hurt you. You know I tend to speak without thinking, and I'm so sorry. I can't bear for you to leave without forgiving me."

Ben cupped her face with both hands and wiped her tears with his thumbs. "It only hurts because it's true. Unfortunately, the pain of acceptance is almost as bad as the pain of the actual loss." He dropped his hand and turned to leave.

"Please, don't go." She grabbed his arm again.

He covered the hand on his arm and squeezed. "There's nothing to forgive, Amy. I'm not angry with you," he said, his voice flat. Then he turned and walked out the door.

Amy dropped onto the couch and buried her face in her hands. These emotions had been building ever since she saw the pictures of Melanie's lifeless brown eyes and that empty car seat base. And now, her careless words were another source of pain for Ben.

Will I ever learn to think before speaking?

Hope came home a few minutes later and found her crying. She sat beside Amy and put her arm around her. "What's wrong, dear?"

"Oh, Hope. I said something awful to Ben. I didn't mean to. It just slipped out."

"Tell me what happened."

Fresh tears filled Amy's eyes when she told Hope about seeing the file on Melanie's accident, and how it made her feel, despite the fact she didn't even know Melanie.

Hope's arm tightened around her, and she cried with Amy as she shared how difficult losing Melanie and Cassey had been, especially on Ben.

Amy told her about the careless words she'd said to Ben. "He said he wasn't angry at me, but how can he not be hurt by what I said?"

"Ben has always been that way. After the accident, I rarely saw him cry. He often had red eyes, so I know he cried in private, but he rarely did in front of others. He prefers to be alone with his grief, but I'm not sure he's dealing with the loss very well."

"I wish I could say or do something to help him." Maybe she could, if she could only remember where she'd seen the baby from the photograph on Ben's desk.

"We all do, dear." Hope hugged Amy again. "But you've done more than you realize."

Amy pulled back. "What do you mean?"

"Ben has smiled more since you and Kallie came to town than I've seen in almost a year. And he comes around more often than he used to."

"I keep worrying Kallie is a constant reminder of what he lost."

"In some ways, I'm sure she is, but I'm hoping she will be his own little form of therapy." When Amy's brow furrowed, Hope added, "Maybe she can help him accept his loss, and be the reason he decides to build a new life."

Could Hope be right? Ben did seem more comfortable with Kallie lately, and Kallie liked Ben. Could she pull him out of his grief?

Amy frowned. If for some reason she needed to leave Providence, both Kallie and Ben would be hurt.

"I still wish I could make things easier for him."

Hope hugged her again. "Sometimes the only thing you can do is pray."

BEN PARKED behind the repair shop and turned off the engine of his truck. He made no move to get out, letting the darkness envelop him. Just as it had his heart almost a year ago.

He'd enjoyed taking care of Kallie tonight. He had almost been able to pretend she was his daughter, and he was still part of a family. Allowing himself to think like that probably wasn't healthy, but Kallie's sweetness made it so easy.

Amy's words stung, but he knew she didn't mean them maliciously. Forgiveness was easy. Forgetting wasn't. He couldn't forget the night his life fell apart, and no matter how hard he tried, he couldn't pick up any of the pieces and put them back together.

He didn't know how long he sat in his truck, but the chime of a text notification startled him.

He read the text from Amy.

I know my words hurt you, and I'm truly sorry. Please tell me what I can do to make it up to you. Thank you for taking care of Kallie tonight. I appreciate it.

If only someone could take away his pain. He'd reached the point where he was ready to let them. But no one could take it away. He needed to be willing to let it go. He wasn't ready to move on by any means, but maybe Paige had a point. He needed to make an effort to live a little.

He'd involved his heart a little tonight. That hadn't turned out so well. Maybe, he needed to focus on things that didn't involve his heart.

He picked up his phone but didn't text Amy back. Instead, he typed a group text to Robert and Jake asking if they wanted to go four-wheeling and target practicing Friday night. He paused before hitting send.

It was after ten. Robert was undoubtedly asleep with his phone by his bed in case of an emergency. He shouldn't disturb him.

He'd send the message in the morning.

Maybe.

If I don't change my mind by then.

A HEADACHE GREETED Amy the next morning, a lingering effect of last night's tears. A lack of response to her text confirmed Ben was more upset than he let on.

When she spotted the toys Ben brought over, she wanted to be angry that he felt the need to buy toys for her daughter, but she couldn't bring herself to say anything. She'd already hurt him enough.

Focusing on her work, she mulled over the best way to get Robert and Jake to agree to the auction.

When Robert walked through the front door whistling an unrecognizable tune, Amy fought the urge to bolt to the restroom.

"Good morning, Amy. How are you?"

"Fine."

She tried to match his cheerfulness but apparently failed, because he sat on the corner of her desk and stared at her.

"What's the matter?"

"Nothing."

His eyes narrowed. "I don't believe you."

If she didn't respond, would he walk away? Probably not.

"I said something I regret to Ben last night. I didn't mean to, it just came out wrong."

"Something embarrassing?" A spark of amusement lit Robert's eyes.

"No, something hurtful. He said he wasn't mad at me, but I'm mad at me, and I don't know how to make it right."

"What did you say?"

Remembering her breakdown last night, she didn't dare tell him for fear of a repeat of last night's waterworks. She shook her head and bit her lip.

Gratefully, he took the hint and let it go.

He stood. "I wouldn't worry about it. Ben asked Jake and me if we wanted to go four-wheeling and shooting on Friday. He hasn't done that in over a year, so I don't think he's too upset."

Robert's words made her feel better, but relief swept over her at quitting time.

When she prepared for bed that night, she spotted Ben's truck parked in front of Debbie's house. *Again?* Why did he spend so many evenings with her? Did he seek comfort in Debbie's arms despite his grief?

Remembering Ben's reaction to their kiss last Thursday, she

doubted it. She touched her lips. They'd agreed to forget the kiss ever happened, but she couldn't. She'd replayed it in her mind a dozen times, and every time, she couldn't deny she'd responded and enjoyed the kiss. Worse, she longed for a repeat.

Then it hit her. Today was Thursday. Ben never came to mow, like he did the last two Thursdays. Swallowing the lump in her throat, she closed the blinds and undressed.

Temperatures are dropping. The grass isn't growing as fast. It doesn't need to be mowed as often now.

Maybe if she kept telling herself that, she'd eventually believe it and wouldn't feel so horrible.

BEN SQUEEZED ONE EYE SHUT, sized up the target, and pulled the trigger. Bullseye. *Finally.* Not dead center, but at least he'd hit the center ring with that shot.

Rusty. That's what he was. Not just at shooting either. Working his way through the gears on the four-wheeler had resulted in a choppy ride until he'd relaxed and allowed himself to enjoy doing something that used to be second nature to him. They'd ridden for nearly an hour across the ranch's varied landscape before heading to the shooting range.

A measure of peace had settled over him like a favorite, comfortable sweatshirt as they'd ridden over barren foothills—common in this region of southeastern Washington—to fertile pasturelands and on to greener alfalfa fields.

Both Robert and Jake offered encouragement, commenting on how glad they were he'd come. They watched him like hawks, though. He wasn't sure what they were looking for, but it made him feel like a child.

As Ben strapped his gun back onto his four-wheeler, Robert disrupted the peace he'd found tonight.

"Amy was pretty upset yesterday."

Ben's hands froze. He straightened and met Robert's eyes.

"Did she say why?"

"She felt bad about something she said to you. She said it came out all wrong."

"Did she tell you what she said?"

"No. Do you want to tell me?" Robert emptied the shells from his gun.

Ben turned his face toward the setting sun. Tonight's sunset, with golden rays arcing up from the horizon, wasn't as beautiful as the one he'd watched with Amy, right before he kissed her. Warmth settled in his stomach—as it did every time he thought about their kiss. She felt bad for her careless words, but he'd been the one out of line last week. She'd quickly forgiven his actions, but he couldn't forgive himself so easily.

Will it always be like this? Every time he attempted to start living again, something or someone reminded him of his situation. Amy's words had been like a slap in the face, but he knew she didn't mean them, and he wasn't upset with her. He was upset with himself. *Why do I allow these things to bother me?*

He scowled at Robert. "No."

If he told his two best friends what Amy said, they might think less of her. He didn't want that. His problems didn't need to be their problems.

"Fine. But are you mad at her?"

Ben let out a sigh and dropped onto the seat of his four-wheeler. "What she said hurt, because it was true. I know she didn't mean to say it, so I'm not mad at her. But when she started crying..." He shrugged his shoulders. "I tried to reassure her everything was okay, but I couldn't comfort her, so I left."

"You made her cry?" Robert and Jake said in unison.

"No." If he wasn't so miserable, he would've laughed at their protectiveness. "She cried because she felt bad about what she'd said." Raking his fingers through his hair, Ben let out a tight chuckle. "You guys have no idea how hard it was to come out this evening. I was having a good time, but you're ruining it."

"We're glad you texted, Ben." Jake slapped him on the shoulder. "I know it's been hard, but it's good to have you back."

"I wouldn't say I'm back, yet." He let out another sigh. "It's a start, I guess, but I've got a long way to go."

"I'm glad you're trying." Robert sat on his four-wheeler. "But maybe you should try to think of a way to make Amy feel better. She's really upset with herself."

Robert started his four-wheeler and took off, leading what turned out to be a rather dangerous race back to the ranch house.

Not only did Ben lose the race, he had no idea how to make Amy feel better.

CHAPTER 15

"Oh, my," Hope said as she walked into the kitchen early Saturday afternoon to find Amy putting the final touches on three triple-layer, triple-chocolate cakes. "Those look delicious. What's the occasion?"

Amy pointed at two of the cakes and grimaced. "Bribery." Then she pointed at the third cake. "And that one's an apology for Ben."

She'd finally come up with a plan to get Robert and Jake to agree to the bachelor auction. She was going to sweeten them up. She'd seen it work time and again at the restaurant. Bringing a belligerent, unhappy diner a sweet treat, often calmed the most stubborn customer.

She'd gotten a jump start on the cakes last night while James and Hope had been in Spokane for a cousin's birthday. Now, she added the final touches.

"I see. I take it you haven't talked to Robert or Jake?"

"Not yet."

"You come bearing gifts like that, they'll have a hard time saying no."

Amy prayed Hope was right as she rang Robert's doorbell an hour later. Gratefully, Hope had offered to watch Kallie while she did her sweet talking. She hoped the sweets would do most of the talking, and the men would easily agree, but she doubted it.

Robert's house was a modest rambler-style home in the same neighborhood as Charity's house. His flower beds were not over-flowing with colorful flowers, but his yard appeared well kept. In fact, a recent mowing lent a fresh-cut grass scent to the air.

He'd invited her to lunch again yesterday, but she'd been relieved when he'd gotten called away shortly before lunchtime. The subject of the bachelor auction would undoubtedly come up, and she hadn't decided how to convince him to participate.

Robert opened the door dressed in worn, well-fitted jeans and a snug, white t-shirt that showed off his muscled chest and biceps.

Amy's breath caught in her throat. This was the second time she'd seen him wearing casual clothes. Robert looked handsome in his sher-iff's uniform, but he sure wore his casual clothes well. It amazed Amy that some woman hadn't taken him off the market. Not only was he handsome and owned a nice house, he was the sheriff, for goodness sake.

"What do we have here?" Robert leaned against the door frame, arms folded, biceps bulging.

She pulled her eyes up to his face, her cheeks warm. "Um… I made you a cake." She thrust the plate into his hands.

Pull yourself together.

He took the cake and motioned her in. "What's the occasion?" Leading her to an L-shaped kitchen, he set the cake on a small table in the corner and studied her.

"It's bribery." She bit her bottom lip, waiting for him to blow up.

His eyes darkened. "I see. So, the rumors are true."

"It's for a good cause." She listed the things they hoped to buy with the proceeds from the festival before he could stop her.

As she talked, Robert set two plates, glasses, and forks, and milk on the table. He sat down, motioning for her to join him.

"It's for a good cause," he mimicked. "Says the woman who has never had to spend more than a few minutes with Debbie Wheeler."

With a growl, he added, "You know she'll win, don't you? *If* I agree to the auction, that is."

She bit her lip again and gave him an apologetic glance. "I guess you've heard it was my idea."

He nodded, his lips tight.

"Actually, it's your fault."

Robert's eyebrows shot up. "My fault? How is this my fault?"

"You told me Debbie always likes to make sure people know how much she donates. I found a way to capitalize on her donations?"

"I see, so Jake and I are your pawns. What about Ben? Will you ask him to participate too?"

Amy lowered her eyes. "No. I'd never ask that of him."

"Good. By the way, he's not mad at you."

"Did you talk to him last night?" Amy grimaced. "Did he tell you what I said?"

"No, and unless you've changed your mind about telling me, we should drop the subject." He paused for a second, giving Amy the chance to speak up. When she didn't, he said, "For the record, I don't appreciate being used like this." Robert cut the cake, revealing the layers of chocolate mousse in the center. "Did you bring insulin too?"

Amy gasped. "Are you diabetic?" Was that why he always got his dessert to go when he took her to lunch on Fridays?

"No, but I probably will be after eating this."

She breathed a sigh of relief. *He's teasing me.* Had his anger a moment ago been genuine, or was he teasing then too? She wasn't sure. He'd seemed mad, but it had dissipated quickly.

Robert put a wedge of cake on each plate, and Amy cringed at the size of the piece he put in front of her. She usually only ate a thin sliver when she made this incredibly rich cake.

Robert took a bite and closed his eyes. "Mmm… This is amazing! Did you make this yourself?"

"Yes." She nibbled on a bite, savoring the rich chocolate flavor.

"Are you bribing all the bachelors with cake?"

"No."

"Ah, so I'm special?"

"Yes, you're special."

Robert grinned, and she realized how that sounded.

She blushed as she rushed to explain. "I mean... you... I made a cake for... you and Jake... because... you two are... I mean, you're the only ones I'm supposed to ask."

Robert laughed at her. "So, if you'd been assigned to ask other bachelors, would you have made cakes for them too?"

Amy shook her head, not trusting herself to open her mouth.

"I see," Robert said, enjoying her discomfort. "So you made them because we're the best-looking bachelors in the county?"

"No. I mean yes... you are... but that's not..."

Amy buried her face in her hands. First Ben, now Robert. Would she ever learn to curb her tongue around these men? She'd waited on plenty of handsome men in the restaurant, and many of them had even flirted with her. She'd never become a bumbling idiot around any of them. Ben and Robert seemed to take great delight in her discomfort, which made it worse.

Robert sobered. "Right, it's bribery." Then he got a gleam in his eye. "So, what's in it for me?"

Amy's eyes widened. "Do you realize how many hours I spent making this cake?"

"Mmm..." He moaned as he took another bite. "Delicious. But come on. You're asking me to put myself out there where Widow Wheeler has full access to me. As good as your cake is, you've got to give me something more." Desire lit Robert's eyes.

Amy's stomach clenched. "What do you mean?"

She'd seen that look in men's eyes many times before—in Dennis' eyes the night she quit her job—but she wasn't sure if Robert was kidding or not. She remembered Ben's discomfort when she'd misunderstood his intentions the day they met. From everything she'd seen, Robert was every bit the gentleman Ben was.

"Well, if I'm going to risk getting stuck taking Debbie on a date." Robert's tone sounded calculated. "I think I should have a little more of a reward."

Amy felt the blood drain from her face, and her stomach churned.

"What do you have in mind?" She shrank back in her chair, folding her arms across her chest.

Robert must have recognized her unease because his smile faded, and concern filled his eyes.

"Relax," he said, his voice light. "I only thought if I'm willing to go out with the Widow, maybe you'd be willing to go out with me."

"On a date? I don't... I'm not..." Amy stopped talking and took a deep breath. "I just left a bad relationship, and I'm not interested in getting involved with anyone."

"I'm not asking for a relationship, Amy. I'm asking for a *date* because I'd like to get to know you better." When she continued to frown, he said, "I'll agree to the auction, if you'll go on a date with me."

"That's blackmail. And you're an officer of the law."

"Yes." He grinned, holding up another bite of cake. "And this is bribery. Don't forget *you're* employed by a law enforcement agency."

He was teasing again. She was more comfortable with this side of Robert, and she kind of liked it.

She gasped and put a hand on her chest. "Are you saying if I don't go out with you, I could lose my job?"

He ignored her question as he ate another bite of cake. "If I agree to the auction, will you agree to go out with me?"

"Okay. I guess it's for a good cause."

"You make it sound like it'll be unpleasant." He acted hurt. "Trust me, Jake and I are the ones who have to worry about an unpleasant date."

"We've set a rule that Debbie can only win once, so—"

"Woohoo!" Robert dropped his fork and pumped his fists in the air. "So, if I can find someone to give the widow a run for her money, I won't get stuck with her after all?"

Amy could practically see the wheels turning in Robert's mind and felt sorry for Jake. According to Faith, Jake rarely left the ranch. He wouldn't stand a chance against Robert.

"Will you bid on me?"

"Of course, but I can't possibly give Debbie a run for her money."

"Well, we need women to drive the price as high as possible." He pointed to her plate. "You're not eating your cake. Makes me think you're trying to poison me."

"You cut me too big of a piece." She took another small bite.

"Tough, eat it. By the way, Ben was right." When Amy shot him a questioning look, he said, "You're not only cute when you're angry, you're also cute when you're flustered."

Amy stood on Jake's front porch, cake in hand, trying to get up the nerve to ring the doorbell. The last time she was here, she made a fool of herself by falling off the fence.

Would Jake make this easier than Robert?

She pressed the doorbell, half hoping he wouldn't answer. But she wasn't that lucky. The door opened to reveal Jake in snug jeans and a t-shirt every bit as tight as the one Robert had worn. If his wet hair and bare feet didn't attest to the fact he'd just showered, the fresh, zesty scent surrounding him did.

Amy inhaled, appreciating the fragrance of his soap or deodorant. Maybe both. It couldn't be aftershave, because he had at least a day's worth of stubble on his face, adding to his rugged good looks.

Flustered by the wave of attraction that swept over her, she ground her teeth to keep from saying so out loud.

"I've been expecting you." Jake swung the door open wide and motioned her inside.

"You have?" Then it hit her. "Robert?" She should have known he'd call Jake before she could get here—to give her a hard time.

"Robert," he agreed as he led her to a spacious kitchen.

If the sheer size of the kitchen hadn't taken her breath away, the expansive countertops, state-of-the-art appliances, and the large oak table would have. She'd thought the Young's kitchen was her dream kitchen, but she could be happy cooking in this one for the rest of her life.

She placed the cake on the counter and clasped her hands together to hide her nervousness. "So, you know why I'm here."

"Let's see. How did Robert put it? Oh yeah, you're here to bribe me."

"Did he tell you why?" She bit her lip.

He grimaced. "Warned me, you mean?"

"Did he tell you it's for a good cause?"

"No. But he said you'd be more than happy to fill me in, while you have a piece of cake with me. Which, I hear, is delicious." He put plates, glasses, and milk on the table.

Amy cringed as he cut a large wedge. She took the knife from his hand before he could cut a second piece. She dished herself a thin sliver. Robert had insisted she eat the whole piece he'd given her, and she could feel the effects of the sugar buzzing in her ears.

"That's all you're eating? I'll get even fatter if I eat this all by myself."

"You're not fat. You're perfect." Amy clapped her hand over her mouth. She'd done it again. "I mean... you're... you look... great."

Shut up, already.

True, Jake was not as slender as Robert, but she could tell by the way his t-shirt hugged his torso, he was all muscle.

Jake laughed out loud. "I see what they mean."

Heat rushed to her cheeks. Did these men freely share information about her? Should she be angry or flattered? The kiss she'd shared with Ben flashed through her mind. What all had Ben told them?

One thing was certain, they all delighted in her discomfort.

Jake smiled, a teasing gleam lighting his eyes. "Does this mean you'll bid on me too?"

He was agreeing to the auction. Just like that?

"Um... yes, of course, but I'm no match for Wid— uh... Debbie."

"No one's a match for her—financially or otherwise."

They sat at the kitchen table and Jake sampled the cake. "It's as delicious as Robert said."

"What else did Robert tell you?" Amy licked her suddenly dry lips.

"Let's see... he said I need to hold out for more than cake." His lips curved into a broad smile. "So how does next Friday sound?"

She bit back a groan.

Why did she get the feeling that despite the brothers' apparent closeness, they were competitive?

"Um... I'm going out with Robert on Friday."

"That's right." Jake's eyes sparkled with repressed humor. "How about Saturday?"

~

"I'VE BEEN LOOKING FORWARD to this since yesterday," James said, Sunday evening when Amy set the third chocolate cake on the dining table.

"Me too," said Ben.

Amy froze in the process of putting a slice of cake on a plate for Ben. Had Hope told him about the cake? She'd been nervous to see Ben again after what happened Wednesday night, but he'd greeted her with a smile, complimented her cooking, and acted like nothing was wrong.

She placed a generous slice of cake in front of him.

"I only get one piece? Not a whole cake to myself?"

"Do you... want a whole cake... to yourself?" Amy asked, eyebrows raised.

Did he know she'd bribed his cousins with cake? No doubt he'd heard about the auction and understood, as Robert and Jake did, what was at stake where Debbie was concerned.

Ben shuddered. "Not at its intended price, no. Although, the bonus prize sounds tempting."

Warmth crept up Amy's neck. *Robert!* She should have known he would gloat about the hard time he'd given her and brag about blackmailing her into going out with him. Did Ben mean it, though? Did he want to go out with her? Or was he teasing her?

"Actually, for you it's an apology. But I figured you wouldn't mind sharing."

"Stop apologizing for that, Amy." His voice was tight and held a warning.

She dropped her eyes and nodded. Ben didn't seem to be holding a grudge, so she needed to let it go too.

"You're not having any cake, Amy?" Hope asked as Amy settled in her seat.

"Um… I'm kind of full." She'd eaten enough of this rich chocolate cake with Robert and Jake to last for months.

"I imagine she got her fill yesterday." Ben gave her a sly grin as he took a bite of cake. His eyes closed in appreciation.

Amy's cheeks burned. Ben's parents exchanged amused glances across the table.

"So, did Robert tell you everything about my visit?" Amy kept her voice casual, pretending James and Hope weren't there.

Ben's eyes twinkled. He smiled, and that shy dimple appeared, causing Amy's heart to stumble. "Enough to know he agrees with me. Now I know it's not just me."

The heat in Amy's cheeks caused her eyes to burn. She resisted the urge to hide her face behind her hands. "Let me guess," Amy said. "You talked to Jake too?"

His gaze held hers as he gave her a slow nod. "I agree. He's not fat. But perfect? Really?" Then the amusement in his eyes bubbled out in a chuckle.

Amy's pulse raced despite her humiliation. She loved Ben's laugh. Too bad it was because she'd made a fool of herself. Again. She folded her arms on the table and dropped her head onto them with a groan.

"Is something wrong, dear?"

She raised her head and glanced at Hope, then she turned to James. They were enjoying her discomfort as much as Ben. Or maybe they were enjoying Ben's amusement. Is this what he'd been like before tragedy struck his life?

She asked James, "Do they make a medicine that can prevent people from saying stupid stuff they'll regret?"

Ben and his parents chuckled. *I'm glad I can provide such comic relief.*

Ben put a hand to his chest. "Stupid, huh? I think I'm offended."

She'd told him on more than one occasion he was good looking, and now he pretended to take offense because she regretted saying it aloud. He was enjoying this too much. She glared at him across the table. Then her eyes shifted to the cake in the center and an idea struck her.

A horrible idea.

A very unladylike idea, but once the idea struck, she couldn't stop herself. She reached out and swiped a chunk of frosting off the cake with her middle finger. A shiver of anticipation rippled through her as she bent her finger, wrapped her thumb around it, and aimed at Ben's smug face across the table. Releasing her finger with force, she let the frosting fly.

It hit Ben square in his dimple.

His eyes widened, Hope gasped, and James chuckled. She wasn't sure who she surprised more—Ben, his parents, or herself.

She couldn't believe she'd had the audacity to do that, let alone in front of his parents. A tense moment of silence settled over the room as Ben stared at her. Then he started laughing—a rich, full-bodied sound that made Amy tingle all over.

James and Hope joined in the laughter, and so did Amy. Hearing Ben's laughter made her happy.

His eyes held hers, and she envisioned cleaning the frosting off for him. She licked her suddenly dry lips, willing the warmth in her abdomen not to travel to her cheeks. With his eyes never leaving hers, Ben wiped the frosting from his face and licked his finger. He smiled, but the wicked gleam in his eyes made her fear retaliation.

"Where did you learn that trick?" James asked.

Amy turned to James, grateful for the excuse to tear her gaze away from Ben's. "When things were slow at the bar, the other waitresses and I used to have contests flipping peanuts into shot glasses at the opposite end of the bar."

"I imagine you stayed pretty busy on Friday and Saturday nights though, didn't you?" Ben said, biting back another smile. "Speaking of which, are you busy this weekend?"

Amy reached for the cake again, but he laughed and pulled it away.

"Okay, I'm done. I'm sorry." He fought to control his laughter. "Except... do you need me to babysit?"

~

BEN SHOVED his hands into his pockets as he walked home from his parent's house. He laughed again at Amy's reaction to his teasing. The emotion made him feel lighter than he had in a long time.

Teasing her wasn't nice, but he hadn't been able to help himself. He enjoyed seeing her flustered and frustrated. She was so fun to tease because she reacted so strongly. He couldn't believe he'd flirted with her like that again, especially in front of his parents.

He found her refreshing. She made him want to shake off the pain and gloom of the past year. As soon as the thought crossed his mind, a tightness settled in his chest. His smile faded.

With more force than necessary, he kicked a small rock, sending it tumbling across the street. He shouldn't feel this way about another woman.

He'd loved Melanie deeply, and he would probably mourn her death for the rest of his life. As for his daughter, he'd tried to accept the fact he'd likely never see her again. Most days, he felt like he'd succeeded, but other days he longed to hold her in his arms.

But he was tired. His feet slowed to match his mood.

Tired of feeling hopeless. Tired of the bleakness and loneliness that had become his constant companions. He wanted to move on, but he felt so torn. Every time he thought about building a new life, a life without Melanie and Cassey, he felt like he was being unfaithful.

CHAPTER 16

The next few days flew by for Amy. Fortunately, she kept busy at work, because whenever it got slow, she thought about the photos she'd seen in Melanie's file and the picture on Ben's desk. She couldn't seem to stop thinking about where she'd seen that baby and a blue Suburban with a grill guard. She'd seen a vehicle like that, she was certain of it—just as sure as she was about the baby—but she couldn't remember where. On both accounts.

It drove her crazy. She wanted so badly to help Ben, to find his daughter, but she didn't know how.

To stay busy, she called the local businesses, including some in neighboring counties, for donations to the Fall Festival.

Wednesday afternoon, she received a text from Ben.

Do you want me to tend Kallie tonight?

Yes. Please. I promise I will keep my mouth shut.

And she did. After dinner she kissed Kallie and walked out without giving him a single instruction.

She enjoyed getting involved with the festival, making new friends while cutting fabric and assembling crafts. It felt good to be a part of the community. Providence was really beginning to feel like home.

When she returned, she sat stiffly on the couch, reminding herself not to say anything she would regret.

Before she could ask if everything went okay, James got a phone call and excused himself. Amy wanted to follow him. As much as she liked Ben, she didn't want to be alone with him. Now, if she asked how things went, he might take it wrong.

Ben watched her. "Are you okay?"

She nodded.

"You meant it when you said you'd keep your mouth shut, didn't you?"

"Trust me, it's better this way," she said with a tight smile.

He tilted his head and smiled. "Not as fun, though. For me, anyway."

"I don't trust myself to not say something I'll regret."

"You mean like, you find me attractive?" A twinkle lit his eyes.

Her lips curve up of their own accord. "Something like that."

"Guess what I caught my dad doing?" Ben said, changing the subject.

"What's that?"

"He was trying to get Kallie to call him Papa."

"I guess you've heard that she calls your mom and Faith Nana." Amy had mixed emotions when she first heard Hope trying to get Kallie to call her grandma. She was torn between feeling guilty that Kallie didn't know her own grandma and grateful that Hope wanted to be a grandmother to her daughter. Hope was a much better role model than Amy's own mom would be.

"Does it bother you that Kallie calls your mom Nana?" She cringed at the way that came out. So much for not saying something she'd regret. "I'm sorry, you don't have to answer that."

She hid her face in her hands.

Ben shifted from the armchair to sit beside her on the couch. His nearness made her insides flutter.

"Amy, don't." He pulled her hands away from her face. "Don't apologize for saying what you think." Then his lips curved up at the corners. "Especially if you think I'm good looking."

His teasing elicited another smile.

"Seriously, I can't dance around the fact my wife and daughter are gone, and I don't expect everyone else to either. No, it doesn't bother me that Kallie calls my mom Nana, or that my dad wants her to call him Papa. But I am sad that they'll never get to hear my daughter say it."

Amy's chest tightened in the way it usually did every time she thought about all Ben had lost. But she didn't think it was his loss that made her heart race and her breath hitch.

～

"Alright!" Robert cheered Friday morning, when Amy walked into work without her boot. "Change of plans for tonight."

She'd gotten the okay from James that morning to remove it as long as she took it easy.

"What do you mean? What are we doing tonight?" Robert had teased her all week about big plans for Friday night. Knowing Robert, he probably had something crazy planned.

"It's a secret," he said before walking away.

He had a meeting at lunchtime, and they had to skip their Friday lunch date, so she couldn't get any information out of him. Truthfully, she was relieved to not have two dates with him in one day. The man was way too attractive.

Leaving Kallie with Ben that evening, so she could go on a date with his cousin was awkward. Hope had offered, but James had reminded her they needed to attend the hospital board meeting, so Ben had volunteered again. Having no alternative, Amy accepted.

Now, sitting in the truck with Robert, his tangy, woodsy scent filling the cab, Amy reminded herself he was her boss, and they were just friends. "So where are we going?"

"Scooters. Out by the county line. It's the best dance hall in the state. Fridays are always swing dancing night, and they have line dancing on Saturdays."

Swing dancing? Amy's stomach knotted. She'd joked about her gracefulness, or lack thereof, when she'd broken her toe, but she honestly wasn't very coordinated. She'd broken a lot of dishes at the restaurant before she'd acquired the skill to bus and wait tables.

"Robert, listen, I'm not very good at dancing... or anything that requires any real agility."

"Relax. It'll be fun. Besides, I'm an excellent teacher."

They shared easy conversation while they ate pulled pork sandwiches and steak fries—the one good thing on the menu, according to Robert. Scooters was a fun environment, reminding Amy of an old-time saloon with wood floors, and a mixture of brass and wrought iron decor. Loud music, boot tapping, and laughter filled the establishment creating an air of excitement.

She enjoyed her time with Robert, but she couldn't seem to keep her mind off Ben. It didn't matter whether he was working in the garage across the street or miles away tending her daughter, Amy missed Ben. A part of her longed to stay home with him and Kallie, making cookies or watching a movie.

She relaxed over dinner, but her food churned in her stomach the moment Robert insisted they hit the dance floor.

"Sorry." Amy said the word so many times over the next hour she felt like a broken record.

Despite Robert's skills at leading, she repeatedly stepped on his toes as she struggled to follow the unfamiliar moves. Once she became familiar with the basic steps, and managed to relax, she enjoyed herself. Until Robert suggested they try some lifts.

"No way. I can't do that stuff." She'd admired the experienced dancers all night and was in awe every time one of the men lifted his partner overhead. "Besides, my toe is starting to hurt. I think I've overdone it." It sounded lame, but it was true. This stupid broken toe was so embarrassing.

Besides, she was more than ready for the evening to be over. The more time she spent with Robert, the more she liked being around him. And that was dangerous.

BEN MUTED the already quiet TV when he heard Robert's truck pull up in front of his parents' house. *Well, this is awkward.*

When he offered to babysit, he never thought he would still be here when Robert brought Amy home. His mom was supposed to take over, but she wasn't home yet.

Every muscle in Ben's body tensed a moment later, when Robert carried Amy through the front door. He was on his feet in an instant. "What did you do to her?"

"Nothing ice and rest won't cure. I tried to teach her to swing dance, but that—"

"That was a dumb idea, considering her toe has barely healed." The heat in his words surprised him.

A scowl marred Amy's pretty face. "You didn't need to carry me. I could have walked." She looked at Ben after Robert put her on the couch. "I'm fine."

Robert bent to take off Amy's shoe, and Ben darted to the kitchen for an ice pack. He returned in time to see Robert placing a pillow under Amy's foot. When his cousin reached out for the ice pack, Ben hesitated. He didn't want to relinquish it. He wanted to be the one to come to Amy's aid.

What is wrong with me? Ben tossed the ice pack at Robert with more force than necessary. It bounced off his wrist and fell to the floor.

Robert picked it up and shot him a *'What's with you?'* glare. After placing the ice pack on Amy's foot, he sat by her, in the spot Ben occupied a couple weeks ago—the night Amy told him about Lance's abuse.

Did Robert really need to sit so close?

Ben sat on the other couch and rubbed his hands on his thighs. "So, you went dancing, huh?"

Robert chuckled. "Amy kept insisting she wasn't very coordinated... but she was right."

Amy swung a throw pillow at Robert. He snatched it from her grasp a split second before it struck his face. She flinched when Robert acted like he might throw it back at her. Instead, he chuckled and tucked it behind him.

"I don't know. I hear she can flip peanuts into a shot glass." Ben gave Amy a sly grin. "I'd say that takes skill."

Amy smothered a chuckle and returned Ben's smile. "I'm especially good at it when the shot glass deserves it."

Ben relaxed as her attention shifted to him. Sharing the inside joke with her eased the tension in his gut.

Robert gaped at Amy. "How can you hit a shot glass with a peanut, but not be coordinated enough to dance?"

"It's an acquired skill."

"And when would you ever need such a skill?"

She glared at Ben. "It comes in handy when someone annoys me."

He smothered a laugh.

Robert's eyes bounced back and forth between Amy and Ben, his curiosity evident. Would Amy tell Robert what she'd done? Ben doubted it. She'd been embarrassed when she apologized to his parents for her lack of restraint. He'd almost felt bad for teasing her. Almost, but not really. He'd enjoyed it too much. That's probably why she hadn't apologized to him.

"If you can flip a peanut into a shot glass, you can learn to dance," Robert said. "I'll make you a deal. The day you master swing dancing, I'll let you flip peanuts into my mouth."

Amy's eyes narrowed as she studied Robert. Then she grinned and stuck out her hand. "Deal."

Robert hung onto Amy's hand when she tried to pull it back, a teasing gleam in his eyes.

Ben shot to his feet. "I'd better go."

Since when am I so eager to go home?

Anywhere was better than sitting here watching his cousin flirt with Amy.

Amy tugged her hand from Robert's. "Thank you, Ben. I really appreciate you watching Kallie."

Ben nodded and headed for the door.

As he started his truck, he finally admitted the reason he'd been so uncomfortable seeing Amy and Robert together. He was jealous.

Watching Robert tease Amy and hold her hand made him long to be in his cousin's place.

Was it simply having a woman, more specifically his wife, to cuddle with on the couch, that he envied, or did he envy Robert's relationship with Amy?

He wasn't sure at the moment.

He liked Amy as a person, admired her willingness to work hard, and her dedication to her daughter, but did his feelings for her go beyond admiration?

No. They couldn't. Because, if they did, that would mean he wasn't mourning Melanie like he should.

She hadn't even been gone a whole year. He shouldn't even look at another woman. Let alone be jealous of Robert.

He'd certainly grown fond of Kallie, though. He loved how she wrinkled her nose when she smiled and how she tried to say new words. He missed his Cassey terribly. But every time Kallie climbed on his lap and snuggled into his arms, he saw a glimpse of something worth looking forward to.

CHAPTER 17

*A*my berated herself for thinking Jake's deep voice sounded
sexy when he called the next morning. He only said a few
dozen words, stating the time he planned on picking her up, and
warned her to dress in comfortable, warm clothing, but it was enough
to cause Amy to dread her date that afternoon.

The text she received from Robert didn't help.

*Enjoy your date with Jake. You're gonna wish you were swing dancing
instead of what Jake has planned.*

Robert enjoyed teasing, so she never knew if she should take him
seriously. Ben also delighted in teasing her, but she could tell when he
was teasing. She'd spent less time around Jake, so she had an even
harder time reading him. Trying to put the whole thing out of her
mind, she focused on spending quality time with Kallie.

When Jake picked her up that afternoon, he drove back toward the
ranch. Did he plan on riding horses? The thought both thrilled and
terrified her. The horses were so big and powerful. It would be a good
way to keep distance between her and Jake, though.

As if he wasn't attractive enough, Jake's fresh, zesty, masculine
scent filled the truck's cab, making him that much more appealing.

After Ben left last night, Robert lingered for a while, and they continued to talk. At one point, he'd leaned toward her, and she thought he might kiss her, but he quickly pulled away at the sound of the garage door opening.

She was grateful for the interruption because she feared if Robert had kissed her, she would've responded the same way she did to Ben's kiss. The thought sickened her.

Jake pulled his truck up beside the sprawling ranch house and turned off the engine. He turned toward her. "I'm letting you choose today's activity. Horses or four-wheelers?"

A knot of tension coiled in her gut. "I've never ridden either. I'm sure you've heard by now, I'm not particularly graceful or agile, so I doubt I'll be good at either one."

He chuckled. "Yeah, I've heard conflicting stories about that. Ben says you're skilled with peanuts, and Robert says you have a long way to go when it comes to dancing."

Amy groaned. "Are you three always this aggravating?"

He winked at her. "Only when a pretty woman is involved."

Was he teasing, or were he and Robert actually competing over her? What about Ben? He hadn't shown interest in going out with her, but he enjoyed teasing her. And he'd kissed her. Did Ben tell his cousins about their kiss?

Trying to keep the color from flooding her face at the thought of that amazing kiss, she pretended to mull over her options.

Jake watched her expectantly. "Come on, relax and let yourself have a little fun."

Relax? Could he tell how tense she was from being in the truck with him?

"Well, dancing made my toe sore. So, we'd better go with whatever is least likely to make it hurt again."

"Sounds like a toss-up, so I say we go four-wheeling and shooting."

Shooting?

His enthusiasm did nothing to dispel Amy's anxiety.

Jake led her to the shed where he kept the four-wheelers. He gave her a helmet and a crash course on driving an ATV.

"Can't I ride with you?" she asked, not because she wanted to be that close to Jake, but because the powerful machine scared her to death. She didn't relish driving it by herself.

"There's not enough room. I need to strap guns, blanket, and a cooler to the back of both four-wheelers."

Jake patiently repeated everything she needed to know to drive the ATV. Then he climbed on behind her and talked her through the gears as she drove circles around the house and outbuildings. Her shoulders knotted, aware of Jake's rock-hard chest pressed against her back. The man smelled so good.

After a while, he told her to stop. He climbed off the four-wheeler but stood close. "Are you okay? You seem uncomfortable. If you don't want to ride, we can watch a movie… or something."

Amy chewed on her bottom lip.

What is wrong with me? Yes, Jake is a handsome man who happens to smell great. Get over it, already.

"Or, I can take you back home, if you really don't want to be here."

"I'm sorry." Amy grabbed his arm. "I do want to be here. It's just… new things like this make me nervous."

Jake covered her hand on his arm with his large calloused hand. "Relax and let yourself have fun."

She nodded. "Okay. Let's do this."

She waited while Jake loaded everything on the backs of the ATVs, securing it with bungee cords.

Amy followed Jake on her four-wheeler, willing herself to relax. Jake occasionally checked on her over his shoulder. After the third time, she smiled and gave him a thumbs up, then frowned when he picked up speed. When they arrived at the shooting range, disappointment filled her. She'd enjoyed driving the four-wheeler more than expected.

Jake built a fire in a preset fire ring with wood from a nearby pile. Then he again gave her another crash course—this time in gun safety and how to shoot.

He leaned the rifles against a large log. "No one goes beyond this point…" He pointed at the targets in the distance. "Unless the rifles are on the ground, against the log, safeties on."

Determining she was ready to shoot, Jake handed her a pair of earplugs and a rifle. He reached his strong arms around her to show her how to hold the gun and focus on the target.

Amy forgot to breathe.

Relax. He's just showing you how to shoot. Don't make a big deal out of this. Have fun.

His clean scent, now mingled with dust, exhaust, and smoke from the fire, didn't affect her so strongly this time. For that, she was grateful.

Amy's first few shots hit the dirt, nowhere in the vicinity of the target. Jake suggested she try shooting with her other arm, using the other eye to size up the target. Following his suggestion, she took aim and hit the edge of the paper target on her next shot. Excited, she shot again. And again. Each shot hit increasingly closer to the bull's eye.

After a while, Jake handed her a different gun—a shotgun. Again, her first two shots went wild, but she eventually closed in on the center of the target. She couldn't quite seem to hit it though.

After emptying the shotgun, she insisted Jake take a turn. "I've done all the shooting."

"Take one last shot. Then I'll shoot a few." He loaded a single bullet into the gun and handed it back to her.

Amy grabbed the gun in a tight grip and took careful aim. She wanted to show *The Men*—that's how she'd come to think of Ben and his cousins—she could hit the bull's eye, at least once. Probably because they took such delight in teasing her about her clumsiness.

She closed one eye, focused on the target, and squeezed the trigger.

A sharp pain ripped through her shoulder. The kickback of the gun propelled her backward so hard, she almost fell over. The deafening report of the shot echoed in her ears.

"Ouch!" Amy heard herself yell, despite the earplugs she wore. She stomped her foot and bit her tongue to keep from swearing.

Checking her arm to make sure it hadn't been ripped from her shoulder, she struggled to comprehend what had happened. Had she somehow shot herself?

No. That was impossible.

Jake's laughter penetrated her pain and confusion. He'd done something different to the gun that last time. She laid the shotgun against the log and hugged her arm to her side.

She scowled at him. "What did you put in the gun, Jake?"

He shrugged, but his laughter belied any innocence. Her eyes dropped to the phone he held in front of his chest.

"Did you video that?"

Jake laughed and nodded.

Amy walked over, doubling up her fist. "Make sure you video this." She punched him in the arm, which made him laugh harder. Again, she rubbed her shoulder where the butt of the rifle had hit with such force.

Jake's laughter died, and he slipped his phone into his pocket. His expression turned contrite. "Hey, I'm sorry."

"Your laughter says otherwise."

Jake smothered a final chuckle. "I do feel bad. I know how bad it hurts. Robert has sneaked that high recoil buckshot in my gun many times."

"Robert! This was his idea, wasn't it? That's why you videoed me." Any attraction she may have felt for her boss dissipated. The man was handsome, but he was the worst tease.

"Would you be less angry at me if I said, yes?" His face was hopeful.

"Maybe."

"He did suggest it," Jake said, then he scratched his neck. "But I decided to go along with it."

"Do you always do the stupid stuff your brother suggests?"

Jake cleared his throat. "Not always but most of the time."

"And have you ever regretted it?"

"Plenty of times."

"Then why do you do it?"

He shrugged, then defended Robert. "He knows how to have fun. Life can be stressful. Sometimes you need to let go and laugh."

Amy's childhood hadn't had much laughter. How many times had she wished she had a sister or a brother to get into trouble with?

She didn't like being the butt of these bachelors' jokes. Although, Ben's laughter—and that dimple—did something to her stomach.

She gave Jake the sweetest smile she could muster. "I don't suppose I could convince you to delete the video."

Jake shuffled his feet. "Um, I don't think so."

"Let me guess, you're more afraid of Robert than you are of me." Amy remembered Ben's words a couple weeks ago when he insisted on driving her to work.

"Definitely."

"Why? You're bigger and stronger than he is."

"Maybe, but he hits harder."

She pretended to pout. "Why do you three have to get your entertainment at my expense?" She obviously wasn't much of an actress, because Jake laughed.

"You should feel flattered. Guys tease the girls they like. If we didn't like you, we'd avoid you like we do Debbie."

"I guess that's a good thing."

"Besides, you're fun to tease because of your reaction. You're cute when you get angry or flustered."

Amy felt both angry and flustered, but she wasn't about to show it.

Folding her arms, she scowled at him again. "Well, if you get stuck having to take Widow Wheeler out, let her shoot one of those bullets. She won't want anything to do with you after that."

"I'm sorry, Amy. I really shouldn't have done that to you."

Feigning anger, she turned away from him and eyed the target. Had she hit the center with that last shot? Hopping over the log that supported the rifles, she ran out to examine her paper.

She'd done it. Her last shot had left a large hole in the right edge of the bull's eye.

"I did it!"

DESPITE TRYING to act angry with Jake, Amy enjoyed the rest of the afternoon. They roasted hot dogs to go with potato salad, fresh fruit, chips, and cookies. While they ate, Amy used Jake's remorse over the buckshot to her advantage. With much coaxing, she convinced Jake to tell her something Robert and Ben would rather have kept secret.

By the time they finished eating, Amy had learned that Robert made out with twin sisters in high school and got punched by their brother. All within a twenty-four-hour period. And Ben, in a freak accident, managed to break his ankle by running over it after popping a wheelie on a motorcycle.

It was dusk by the time Jake brought Amy home. She gripped the edge of her seat as he turned into the cul-de-sac, dreading the good-bye-on-the-doorstep moment. Would he kiss her? Could she keep herself from responding if he did? She jumped when he spoke.

"Poor guy." He nodded his head toward Ben's truck parked in front of Debbie's house.

Again? Grateful for the distraction, Amy reflected on how frequently Ben visited Debbie. What was going on between them?

Jake parked his truck and climbed out before she could ask what he meant by 'poor guy'.

Her stomach knotted at his proximity as he walked her to the door. She stumbled up the steps, and Jake grabbed her arm to steady her.

"Are you okay?"

Amy's eyes widened. He stood so close. Warmth seeped through her sleeve from his hand. His masculine scent, though weaker than before teased her nose. Her breath caught in her throat.

Amy nodded, unable to speak.

"Good." Releasing her arm, he shoved his hands into his pockets. "I'd better leave before you pass out or something."

"What?"

Jake chuckled. "You're jumpier than the colt I've been trying to break. I'm not sure whether you're afraid of me, or something I might do, but let me just say thanks for going out with me. I had a fun time. And I'm sorry again about the buckshot thing."

He gave her a small wave and turned toward the steps.

"Jake, wait."

He turned back. With him on the lower step, they stood eye to eye.
"I'm sorry. It's not you… It's me." Squeezing her eyes shut in frustration, she took a deep breath. She couldn't say the words racing through her mind.

Don't mind me, I'm just freaking out because I'm afraid you might kiss me, and I'll enjoy it.

She felt like an idiot. A slow smile spread across her face. Wouldn't *The Men* get a kick out of her inner turmoil over a kiss? She put a hand on Jake's shoulder.

"I'm sorry, I'm acting so… ridiculous. I really did have a great time. I'm obviously not very good at this kind of thing." She waved her hand in a broad circle.

"No kidding," Jake chuckled. "And I thought I didn't get out enough." Taking her hand from his shoulder, he held it in his. "Let's not ruin a nice date by making it more awkward than it needs to be." He bowed his head and pressed a quick kiss to the back of her hand then released it. "Bye, Amy. I'll see you around."

"Thank you, Jake." Amy remained on the porch until he'd driven away.

She placed her hand on her chest where her heart had skipped a beat. No man had ever kissed her hand before. Surprisingly, Jake's kiss affected her almost as much as Ben's, in an entirely different way, of course. Jake's gentleness and respect triggered in her a longing for something she'd never had before. She'd met few men in her life who were as kind and respectful as Jake, Robert, and Ben, even though they loved to tease. She wanted to spend more time with a man like that. Wanted that kind of a man to be a part of her life.

She shook her head at her foolish thoughts. She'd gone from responding to a kiss from a handsome man to thinking she could have the fairytale dream.

The problem was fairy tales didn't happen in real life. Not to poor little nobody's that were unlovable.

CHAPTER 18

"*I*t smells great in here." Ben walked into his parent's kitchen Sunday afternoon and greeted Amy.

Startled, she spun around on bare feet.

The air whooshed from his lungs. He didn't think he'd ever seen her look so beautiful. Her simple, floral dress, covered by a bright yellow apron, hugged her figure in all the right places. But it was her flushed cheeks, framed by the loose ringlets that had slipped free from her ponytail that took his breath away.

This was the reason he'd come over early. Because he couldn't get Amy off his mind. The jealousy he experienced Friday night crept into his mind. Then he remembered the way Jake kissed Amy's hand last night, and how she'd held it to her heart like she'd met her one true love.

He hadn't meant to be a Peeping Tom, but when he caught sight of Jake walking Amy to the door, he'd been unable to look away.

Taking a deep breath, he pushed the annoying thoughts away and took in the aroma of bread dough. He peeked in the oven to see garlic bread sticks. From scratch, no doubt, knowing Amy.

She shot a glance at the clock. "You're early."

Ben shrugged. "I thought you could use a little help."

She smiled at him. "I *could* use a helping hand. Your mom was helping me, but so was *Kallie*."

"Ah, I imagine she's not much help."

"No, she's not. Besides, I'm lame, so you can be my left arm." When Ben tilted his head, she asked, "You didn't see the video?"

He chuckled as he remembered her reaction to shooting the buckshot. She sure was cute when she was mad.

He inhaled sharply, frustrated with the direction his thoughts had gone, again. "Yeah, I saw the video. Jake felt bad and wasn't going to share it. But Robert begged—or maybe threatened—and Jake showed us. I have to say I'm impressed you held your tongue. I said every swear word in the book when Robert slipped one of those bullets in on me. And Jake gave him a bloody nose when he did it to him. We both eventually got even. We all load our own guns now. There's no trust there anymore. Did it give you a bruise?"

Amy pulled the capped sleeve of her dress up to expose the joint of her shoulder. A large blue bruise, the size of an egg, marred her creamy skin.

Fighting the urge to reach out and caress the bruised skin, Ben grimaced. "I've never seen it bruise that bad. You must have been holding the gun really tight."

"I was. I was determined to hit the bull's eye."

"I heard you did it with that last shot." He couldn't hide his admiration. "Nice aim. Peanuts, frosting, and guns. Remind me not to get on your bad side."

"You'd better believe it." She poked him in the stomach with a bunch of celery. "Wash this!"

Grateful for something to do that took his attention off Amy, Ben grabbed the celery and set to work. They worked side by side with casual conversation for some time, and then Amy chuckled, and Ben's pulse sped up at the sound of her laughter.

"What's so funny?"

Amy bit her bottom lip to calm herself. "Nothing."

Ben studied her face. "Come on, tell me, or I'll slime you with this." He held up a spatula full of cheesecake filling and took a step closer to her, leaving little space between them. He owed her for flipping frosting on his cheek. Maybe he could smear pie filling near her mouth, then offer to clean it off for her. With his mouth. Heat filled his body, and his breath hitched at the thought.

Whoa. Where did that come from? His eyes lingered on her mouth.

Licking her lips, she backed away. "It was nothing. I was just laughing at something Jake told me yesterday."

Jake's name hit him like a bucket of ice water and his gut clenched. There was that feeling again. Jealousy. Thick, slimy, and green. He turned back to the cheesecake and let the matter drop. He'd been jealous of his cousins plenty when they were teenagers. Jealous that Robert had a brother, that they could ride horses whenever they wanted, and how the hard work had helped their muscles develop faster than his, and the girls that had drawn.

He wasn't a teenager anymore. Why was he jealous of them now? And what had Jake told her that made her smile like that?

Ten minutes later, when Ben insisted the Alfredo sauce needed more garlic, Amy kept him at bay with a whisk and threatened to kick him out of the kitchen. Tempted to push the issue, he stepped closer, giving her a mischievous grin. Then, after a moment's consideration, he stepped away. As much as he enjoyed it, he had no right to flirt with Amy. He shouldn't be jealous of his cousins' attention toward her, since he had no intention of making a claim on her.

Searching for a distraction from the direction his thoughts repeatedly traveled, he said, "You said you've always enjoyed cooking, even when you were young. Did your mother teach you to cook?"

Amy scoffed. "My mother didn't teach me much of anything. Nothing useful, anyway."

At the bitter tone in Amy's voice, Ben studied her face. Her eyes had darkened with an emotion he couldn't peg. Anger? Or hatred maybe?

"I learned to cook out of necessity."

He read between the lines. "Meaning you were left alone a lot. That must have been hard."

Amy shrugged, but the action was stiff, stilted. "Better than the alternative."

"Which was?"

Amy stopped stirring, and Ben followed her gaze to the hand that gripped the whisk. Her knuckles were white, and her hand trembled.

He closed the distance between them, touching her shoulder. "Amy?"

"I— I don't talk about my childhood, with anyone." She gave the Alfredo sauce another stir then turned off the stove and pushed it off the burner.

He took her by the shoulders as she turned away from the stove. She was shutting down. Closing him out. How many times had she done this throughout her life as a defense mechanism?

"Please talk to me," he said.

Pain filled Amy's eyes. "Do you really want to know about my childhood, Ben?"

As his heart screamed, 'Yes, I want to know everything about you,' his mind said, 'No,' because he had a feeling he didn't want to hear the things she might say.

"I do. *If* you want to tell me."

Amy stepped away from him, leaned back against the counter, and folded her arms over her chest. Brow furrowed, she stared at him.

He sensed she steeled herself against unpleasant memories, as she contemplated what to share with him.

Finally, she spoke. "My earliest memories were of Bruce, my step-dad. He was everything I thought a dad should be. He was the only one who ever made me feel loved." Amy paused, as though fighting to keep her emotions in check. "But he and my mom fought all the time, and they got divorced when I was seven. My mom's next two marriages were brief and volatile." She raised her chin and looked him squarely in the eyes. "Sometimes when the fighting got really bad, I hid under my bed."

"Oh, Amy—" Ben took a step closer.

She held up a hand. "I don't need your sympathy. It won't change anything. I've accepted that my childhood was different from most kids, and that my mother never loved me."

"She may not have been a very good mother, but I'm sure she loved—"

"Love is more than words, Ben. Even if she'd said the words—which she never did—her actions spoke louder."

Ben's heart twisted for Amy. What must it have been like to grow up feeling unloved? And for her to still believe it, now that she was a mother and knew what it meant to love a child unconditionally.

Ben took another step toward her, bringing him within inches of her. "Was she abusive?"

Amy gave a scornful laugh. "If she'd abused me, at least I'd know she felt something toward me. She never struck me, but she was neglectful, indifferent, and apathetic. I tried so hard to be the perfect daughter, thinking I could make her love me or at least make her proud of me. But I was never anything more than a mistake and an inconvenience."

Ben searched for words to comfort Amy even though she didn't want to be comforted. Having grown up in a home with two parents who loved him, he couldn't comprehend how painful Amy's childhood must have been.

She spoke again before he found words. "Naturally, I assumed there was something wrong with me, as any child would. But I spent a lot of time at my friend, Celeste's, house and I saw how a mother loved her daughter *and* her daughter's friend. I told myself my mom was the one with the problem. That she wasn't capable of love, but she had no problem saying the words to the steady string of men she brought home and showered her attention on."

Amy's voice took on a hard tone as she mentioned the men, and Ben got a glimpse of the alternative to being alone. He wanted to keep her talking, but again, he feared the things she might say.

He took her hand. "Nothing was wrong with you, Amy. Your mother was selfish and self-absorbed."

"She was also greedy… and jealous." Her voice dropped on that last word.

Ben tightened his hold on her hand. "How so?"

She tugged her hand from his and hugged herself again. "I swear she brought home the sleaziest guys she could find. If they were ever nice to me, she got angry. She usually took it out on me in some way, by sending me to bed without dinner, or making me do extra chores." Amy did a poor job at repressing a shudder. "Most of them were heavy drinkers who often became crude and vulgar when they were drunk. I locked myself in my room most of the time, especially when my mom wasn't home. Some of the guys respected that better than others."

A sudden bitter taste filled Ben's mouth and his skin crawled. His hands balled into fists. *What horrible trauma had Amy suffered?*

She dropped her gaze as she continued, but her voice was hard as steel. "Things got really bad when I was seventeen. Fortunately, I was able to fight Rick off and get away. I spent the night at Celeste's house, and when I went home the next day, I found two suitcases sitting in the hallway. Rick told my mom I threw myself at him—that I'd come on to him for weeks. She said if I couldn't keep my hands off her boyfriend, then I could find someplace else to live."

A chill swept through Ben's body, and he had a hard time hiding his disgust when he spoke. "She didn't even give you a chance to explain what really happened?"

Amy raised tear-filled eyes to him, and his heart broke for her. He pulled her into his arms, half expecting her to resist.

She didn't.

Her voice sounded fragile when she spoke with her cheek pressed to his chest. "It wouldn't have mattered. She never cared about me. Certainly not as much as she cared about herself... and the men she brought home."

Ben tightened his arms around her and rested his chin on her hair. He held her for a long moment. He thought she might burst into tears, but she sniffed a few times, then controlled her emotion with a few deep breaths. The warmth of her breath seeped through his shirt when she spoke again, strengthening his desire to protect her.

"Two months before my eighteenth birthday, I rented my first apartment. And I haven't seen my mother since."

He pulled away enough to cup her face with both hands. He stared deep into her eyes, hoping she would truly hear the words he needed to say. "Amy, you have to understand you weren't the problem. Your mother was the one who was flawed. You... you're..." Ben searched for the right words to let Amy know what he thought of her.

You're perfect, beautiful, desirable.

The words were all true, but they hit too close to home. They conveyed the depth of his feelings. Feelings he shouldn't have right now. Not while he mourned Melanie.

"You're an amazing woman, Amy."

She gave him a sad smile before lowering her eyes and pulling his hands from her cheeks. "Thank you, Ben, but I'm sure you'll understand if I have a hard time believing you."

He wanted to pull her back into his arms and say, or do, whatever it took to convince Amy she was worth loving. But the timer on the oven buzzed, and his mother walked into the kitchen with Kallie.

AMY LOOKED up from her computer Monday morning when Robert pulled into the parking lot. Putting a scowl on her face, she pretended to be busy.

"Good morning, Amy," he said, sitting on the corner of her desk. "How was your weekend? After Friday night, of course, because I already know about that part."

"I'm not talking to you." She kept her eyes on her monitor.

"Why aren't you talking to me?"

"I'm mad at you."

"Why?"

She glared at him with raised eyebrows.

Understanding dawned on him, and he chuckled. "Oh. You're still mad about the buckshot thing?"

"Yes, I'm still mad about the buckshot thing."

"I have to say, you disappointed me. You kept your cool much better than I expected. Punching Jake was a nice touch. Too bad you're not strong enough to hurt anyone, especially with your great aim."

She scowled at him. "I can't tell if you're insulting me or complimenting me. But I'm mad at you. And I'll stay mad at you until the bruise goes away." She turned away again.

"Ben said it was bad." His voice turned contrite. "Listen, I'm sorry. I shouldn't have insisted Jake play that joke on you."

The image of Robert sporting a black eye after making out with twins filled her mind and her lips curved in a smile. She turned away again, to hide her amusement. She'd rather he thought she was still mad at him.

"Hmm… maybe I should take you out again to make it up to you."

Amy's stomach tightened. *No. I can't go out with you again. I need to stay away from men.*

Gratefully, he stood up from her desk and headed to his office without pushing the issue. He turned in his doorway. "Did you see Ben this weekend?"

"Yes, why?"

"How did he seem?"

"I don't know. About the same as usual, I guess. Why?" Amy wasn't about to tell him she was the one who was a wreck yesterday. A comforting warmth stole over as she remembered Ben's embrace. She knew him telling her she was an amazing woman was only meant to comfort her, but a part of her wanted—needed—to believe his words.

"This Saturday is the one-year anniversary of Melanie's death." Robert's expression was grim.

The familiar tightness she felt anytime she thought about Ben's loss gripped her chest. "That's right. He did seem quiet, I guess." She'd thought his somberness during dinner was due to the things she'd told him, but maybe it was more than that.

"He's going to need a lot of support these next few weeks. But will he accept any?" Robert turned and entered his office, deep in thought, leaving Amy to her own thoughts of Ben. Thoughts she shouldn't be entertaining.

Later that afternoon, Amy opened the door to Robert's office to let him know he had a visitor. The unmistakable image laying in the open folder on his desk caught her eye.

Robert had Melanie's file.

Ben wasn't the only one who would find the next couple weeks difficult.

Would Robert ever be able to forgive himself for not bringing Ben's daughter home?

"I APPRECIATE you watching Kallie again, Ben." Amy sat on the couch in the family room.

Ben lay stretched out on the floor with Kallie climbing over him, and James was on the phone in his office with the door open.

Amy had taken her time cleaning up after dinner, and still she lingered, hoping to get a feel for how Ben was doing. He'd been quiet during dinner, but that wasn't unusual.

"Thanks for letting me watch her. I know it's not easy to entrust her care to me and my dad, but I've really enjoyed it."

Had he sensed her reservations about letting him watch her daughter?

Kallie picked up her doll and climbed onto Amy's lap. Ben got up off the floor and sat at the other end of the couch.

Feeling awkward, she searched for something to say. She couldn't come right out and ask him how he was doing. She certainly didn't want to remind him it would soon be the anniversary of his wife's death.

"Mommy." Kallie demanded her attention. "Baby."

"Yes, that's your baby." Amy acknowledged the doll she held. Then, because she couldn't figure out how to broach the subject without causing Ben pain, she kissed Kallie's hair in preparation to leave.

"Daddy," Kallie said, holding her doll out to Ben. "Baby."

A soft gasp escaped Ben's lips and his eyes widened. She felt him tense despite the distance between them. Shock enveloped Amy as a twinge of pain settled in her chest.

"Did she call me Daddy?"

Amy nodded, holding her breath.

Ben had said he didn't mind Kallie calling his parents Nana and Papa. Did he feel the same way about Kallie calling him Daddy? Would it be a painful reminder he'd never hear his own daughter say it?

Ben looked away, blinking his eyes.

"I feel like I should apologize but... I don't know... should I?"

"No," he whispered, not meeting her eyes. Instead, he smiled at Kallie.

"I'm sure she just said it because she doesn't know what to call you. I can teach her to call you Ben."

"It's okay," he said, his voice louder now. "It's the most beautiful word I've heard her say, yet the most painful to hear."

"I'm sorry. This must be so hard for you."

He let out a heavy sigh. "Everything is hard, Amy. Every time I turn around, I find another reminder of what I've lost. Some days, I think it's getting easier, but other days..."

There didn't seem to be words to make this situation any less painful for him, so she remained silent.

Sensing Ben's sadness, Kallie slid off Amy's lap, scooted across the cushion between them, and climbed onto Ben's. He wrapped his arms around her small body, and she laid her head on his shoulder, patting his arm with her tiny hand.

Both Amy and Ben chuckled. Her little angel, compassionate soul that she was, didn't need words to comfort Ben. A piece of Amy wished she had the courage to comfort Ben in such a manner. She doubted it would have the same effect if she'd been the one to lay her head on his shoulder, but the thought was sure tempting.

"What kind of relationship did she have with Lance? I got the impression he wasn't very involved in Kallie's life."

"He was usually there during the daytime, but I'd hardly call him involved. Kallie loved to listen to him play his guitar and sing, but that was about the extent of their interaction."

"The question is..." he paused, as though unsure how to say what he wanted to ask. "How do you feel about her calling me... Daddy?"

Biting her bottom lip, Amy's gaze darted away as pain gripped her chest and clogged her throat. Memories flooded her mind of Bruce giving her piggyback rides, ice cream cones at the park, and teaching her to ride a bike, promising to never let anything hurt her. Then suddenly the man she'd called 'Daddy,' and trusted to keep her safe chose not to be a part of her life anymore, and Amy experienced the bitter sting of rejection.

The last thing she wanted was for Kallie to know that kind of pain. But how could she withhold something from Ben that could help him heal and deal with the extraordinary loss he'd experienced?

She had no right answer.

She sucked in a shaky breath. "Ben, I—"

"I'm sorry." He cut her off. "That was unfair of me to ask."

"No, it's not you..." She needed to say this the right way. She'd never forgive herself if she said something to hurt Ben again. Taking a deep breath, she said, "I couldn't think of a better, more deserving person, for my daughter to call Daddy, but I—" Emotion choked her throat, cutting off her words. She swallowed hard, struggling to keep the tears at bay. "I told you the other day how I felt about Bruce." When Ben nodded, Amy continued, "After my mom divorced him, he made it a point to spend time with me each week, but he eventually got involved with another woman who had two kids... and he didn't have time for me anymore." Again, she swallowed hard. "I don't want my daughter to feel that kind of rejection when you're ready to move on with your life."

Kallie climbed back to her lap and laid her head against Amy's chest. Wrapping her daughter in a hug, she choked back the sob that threatened to escape. What a perceptive little girl.

Closing the gap between them, Ben put his arm around Amy's shoulders. "I understand."

Amy caught her breath at his nearness, the warmth of his strength surrounding her. She fought the urge to lean into him. She couldn't give in to the attraction. Taking a deep breath, she looked up at him. "Please don't take what I said the wrong way, I'd honestly never forgive myself..."

"I'm not offended." He squeezed her shoulder. "I wouldn't dream of hurting Kallie. Thank you for letting me take care of her. She has helped fill a small part of the void in my life."

Amy bit back a groan. Ben needed Kallie in his life, and deep down she wanted him to be a part of Kallie's life too. She wasn't ready, however, to analyze in what capacity Ben could be a permanent part of her daughter's life.

"I'm sorry, Ben, I can't call you... that."

"What do I do if she calls me... that, again?"

Was it as hard for him to say the word as it was for her? No. It was harder because he would never hear his daughter say it.

"Answer her." The words escaped her tight throat as a whisper. "But... please don't refer to yourself as 'Daddy'."

At such a young age, Kallie wouldn't recognize the distinction of whether Ben called himself 'Daddy' or not. Would her daughter come to regret this decision like Amy regretted so many of her mother's? Would Amy end up regretting this decision? The thought of Ben finding another woman and starting another family hurt Amy, and not only for Kallie's sake.

"You don't need to do this, Amy."

"Maybe not, but she needs a good, daddy-figure-role-model in her life as much as you need her in yours."

"Thank you," he said, his voice thick with emotion as he hugged Amy close to his side and pressed his cheek to her hair.

She relaxed and leaned into him. Maybe she could give in just this once. But only for a minute.

CHAPTER 19

Saturday morning as Amy finished breakfast, she received a text from Paige.

Please don't leave Ben alone today.

Amy frowned as she reread the text. Paige, like everybody else, was worried about Ben.

Amy stopped by the repair shop yesterday to make a payment on her car repair, hoping to discern how Ben was doing. But he wasn't there. Scott informed her Ben hadn't been in since Wednesday. Had Kallie calling him 'Daddy', and their subsequent discussion, upset him? Or was the knowledge that his wife and daughter had been gone a whole year too much for him to bear?

Spotting his truck in the back-parking lot, she'd knocked multiple times on his apartment door but got no answer.

She responded to Paige's text: *What am I supposed to do?*

Just be there for him.

He hasn't come out of his apartment for days. I doubt he'd let me in.

Make him let you in. Get a key if you need to.

I don't think I can do that. You should ask Robert or Jake.

No, he'd tell them to take a hike, but he wouldn't say that to you.

I wouldn't be so sure.

I don't want him to be alone and I can't be there. Please, promise me you'll try.

Amy chewed on her bottom lip. She wasn't sure she could do this. Talking with Ben about his wife and daughter always made her uneasy. She never knew what to say, or her words always came out wrong. What could she possibly do or say to make today more bearable for him?

She'd never lost someone close to her, and she didn't know anyone who had except for Lucy, one of the waitresses at the restaurant. She'd sat with her during a slow time and listened to the waitress talk about her dad. Before they returned to work, Lucy hugged her and thanked her for listening, saying it helped to talk about her dad and remember the good things.

Surely, Ben's family had provided plenty of opportunities for him to talk over the past year. Had he taken any of them? If he hadn't talked to them, how could she expect him to talk to her?

Amy became so lost in her own thoughts she forgot Paige waited for a response.

Amy? Are you there?

I don't know if I can do what you're asking.

Please, I need you to do this. Tell him I put you up to it. That he needs to exercise his muscle.

???

He'll know what I mean.

Amy let out a long sigh.

Okay, I'll try, but I doubt he'll even talk to me.

Thank you! You can do it! Be yourself!

That's what worried her. She wasn't good at these things. Certain she would end up stammering and stumbling over herself, she figured she'd better swallow her pride now.

Amy went to find Hope. She showed her the texts from Paige, and Hope, deciding it was worth a try, offered to watch Kallie for the day. Amy thanked her, feeling like she should add that it would probably only be for a few minutes since she wasn't likely to get anywhere with Ben.

185

She headed to the shower, wracking her brain for what she would say. What was she willing to do if he refused to talk to her? A knot formed in her stomach as she dressed and made the short drive to the repair shop.

It took a full five minutes to summon the courage to climb out of her car and approach the garage. A quick glance inside confirmed what she already knew. Ben wasn't there. She forced herself to climb the stairs to his apartment, the knot in her stomach expanding. She gripped the key Hope had given her so hard it dug into her palm.

Sucking in a deep breath, she raised a shaking hand and knocked long and hard. Then she waited, unsure what to say. After knocking a second, and a third time, she decided she would not let Ben tell her to go away.

You've dealt with belligerent drunks, surely a grieving man won't be any worse.

With a shaky hand, Amy raised the key to the doorknob. Before she could insert it, the door opened a margin.

There stood Ben in a gray t-shirt and well-worn sweatpants. He looked terrible. At least three days of stubble covered his cheeks above his normal beard line, and his hair stood on end. His blood-shot eyes reflected the pain she had seen when they first met.

She took a deep breath and pushed the door open a little farther. Ben groaned, put his arm up against the door frame, and hid his eyes against his forearm.

"Do you have a hangover?" Amy asked, surprised. She didn't think he drank. That was one of the things she liked about him.

Wait. Did I just admit I like Ben?

No. She only admitted there were things she liked about him. Okay, a lot of things.

"I wish," growled Ben, "then I would've had the pleasure of getting drunk."

Amy shifted from one foot to the other, unsure what to say.

"What are you doing here, Amy?" His harsh tone sent a shiver down her spine. He'd never spoken to her like this before.

Amy took a deep breath, intent on not stammering, although she trembled inside. "I came to see if you were all right."

He lifted his head from his arm, squinting in the bright light and stared at her like she had two heads.

"Do you know what today is?"

Amy dropped her gaze. "Yes."

"Then why would I be all right?" The acid in his voice almost made Amy lose her nerve. She grabbed the railing to keep herself from bolting down the stairs.

"How would Melanie feel, Ben, if you didn't take flowers to her grave and honor her today?" She wasn't sure where the words came from. She certainly hadn't rehearsed them.

Ben glared at her as though she'd punched him and knocked the wind out of him. He turned and walked away, leaving the door ajar.

Amy slipped the key into her pocket and stepped into the apartment. She paused, letting her eyes adjust to the dim interior. The only light in the room, and fresh air, came through the open door. She wrinkled her nose as stale air, resembling a combination of a locker room and a garbage dump, hit her. Her eyes adjusted, and she spotted Ben sitting at a small, round table with his head lying on his folded arms.

Opting to leave the door ajar, Amy sat in the only other chair at the table.

"I can't possibly understand how difficult this day must be for you, as well as every day for the past year, but—"

He lifted his head and glared at her. "You're right. You have no idea how hard it is to lose everything in the blink of an eye."

Amy recoiled. His words stung, like a slap to the face. She'd never lost a loved one to death, but she knew what it felt like to be all alone. Gritting her teeth, she pretended his words didn't hurt. "Today is not about you, Ben." She paused, to let her words sink in. "It's about Melanie. Today is a day for honoring her."

"Tell me, Ms. Grief Counselor," he snapped as he folded his arms across his chest and glowered at her. "How exactly do I *celebrate* my wife's death and my daughter's kidnapping?"

Amy wrung her hands under the table. What *was* he supposed to do? She had no idea what to say? The way he glared at her made her want to high-tail it out of there. She couldn't blame him for wanting to hide away from the world. She wanted to strangle Paige.

"Well? You come here pounding incessantly on my door, drag me out of bed and tell me I should honor my dead wife, but you're not going to tell me how to do that?"

Amy flinched at the anger in his words. She thought of all the abuse her mother had suffered at the hands of various men throughout her life and wished she'd been strong enough to stand up to them. That she'd stood up for Amy.

She didn't want to be like her mom. She'd walked away from Lance. Surely, she could stand up to a grieving widower. Springing to her feet, she took a deep breath. "Listen, I don't want to be here anymore than you want me here. But I made a promise to your sister, and I intend to keep it. So, like it or not, I'm not going away."

"Paige put you up to this?" he asked, his tone losing some of its bite.

"She made me promise not to let you spend the day alone." Amy's brow furrowed. "She said you need to exercise your muscle?"

Ben looked away, his jaw clenching. Absently, he pressed a hand to his chest and rubbed. He was quiet for so long, and his face looked so grim, Amy was certain he would send her away.

"You're seriously not going to leave me alone?" When she shook her head, he added, "Even if I promise not to crawl back into bed?"

"Nope."

"Fine." He let out a resigned sigh. "If I'm stuck with you, what are you planning on doing to help me make it through the day?"

"Well, first you need to shower." Amy tried to act more confident than she felt. "I don't think it appropriate to honor Melanie in your current condition."

He glanced down at his clothes and grimaced. "Okay. Then what?"

"Today, you need to celebrate the life you had with Melanie. Do the things she would do if she were here and remember the good times you had with her. Eat her favorite foods. Go to her favorite places and think about her. And of course, you should take flowers to her grave."

"Did you study psychology or something?"

"No, I just saw too many men trying to drown their sorrows in alcohol. It didn't prove effective."

Ben let out a deep sigh and stood. "Fine, I'll shower. Make yourself... feel free to..." Ben looked around the room, taking in the dim, untidy hovel he called home. He finally waved a hand as though to dismiss it all, walked out of the room, and slammed the door behind him.

Amy flinched. *It's going to be a long day!*

BEN SPOTTED Amy as soon as he opened his bedroom door. She stood by the sink, washing his dishes. An open window let in fresh air, and garbage bag sat by the door, waiting to be taken out.

She hadn't heard him come out. So, he leaned against the door frame and took the opportunity to study her from behind. He liked the way her faded jeans hugged her hips. Warmth coursed through him as he remembered how perfectly she'd fit in his arms the night they kissed.

Stop it. You shouldn't be thinking about how attractive Amy is—let alone kissing her—while mourning Melanie and Cassey.

Pain gripped his chest. How did he mourn for his daughter? She was alive, somewhere. He knew it. How did he mourn a piece of him, who was gone but not dead?

Paige's words echoed in his mind. He'd tried to take her advice. It had been difficult, but he had yet to truly get his heart involved. That's what Paige wanted him to do today. He didn't want to get his heart involved. It hurt too much.

A clamp tightened around his chest. He'd avoided so many things for the past year because they reminded him of her. It was simply too painful.

Melanie deserved to be remembered. But wouldn't spending the day doing things Melanie loved make him miss her more? Could he handle the pain that would come when he opened his heart and remembered all the wonderful things he missed about Melanie?

Could he do Melanie's favorite things and remember her with another woman at his side. It felt wrong somehow. Thanks to Paige, Amy wasn't likely to leave him alone today, so he needed to figure out how to make it through the day without thinking about the fact that the woman by his side wasn't his wife.

Ben cleared his throat and walked into the room.

Amy jumped and turned, hands dripping. "You look much better." She smiled as she studied him for a moment, then her cheeks turned rosy and she quickly turned back to the sink. "Give me a minute. I'm almost done."

Why did she flush like that? Was there something wrong with the clothes he wore? He'd dressed for comfort, in jeans and a white t-shirt with a long-sleeved denim shirt layered over it. He had the sunglasses he knew he'd need in the breast pocket of his shirt. Not because it was sunny, but because at some point today he'd need his them to hide behind.

Ben walked to the window and shoved his hands in his pockets. He watched the cars passing. Life wasn't fair. Those people out there had no idea how quickly it could come to a crashing halt.

"Okay, I'm finished." Amy dried her hands on a dishtowel. "Have you decided what we're doing first?"

With a scowl, he put on his sunglasses, picked up his keys, and walked out the door.

CHAPTER 20

*A*my climbed into the truck, expecting Ben to start the engine, but he remained still, keys in hand.

"Is something wrong?"

"I think you should drive." He dropped the keys in her lap.

"Me? Why?"

"The amount of sleeping pills I've taken in the last forty-eight hours is not conducive to driving." He reached to open his door, but Amy grabbed his arm.

"How many pills *have* you taken, Ben?"

He sighed. "Not enough to harm myself. Only enough to keep me sleeping... where I don't think... or feel." He climbed out and walked around the truck.

Amy lifted the center console and slid across the seat. She'd never driven such a large vehicle. She considered suggesting they take her car, but one look at Ben told her he wasn't in the mood to argue.

"It's an automatic, so it's just like driving your car but bigger. You'll do fine."

His voice lacked the bitterness and disdain she'd heard since her arrival. Encouraged, she started the engine and adjusted the seat and mirrors before putting the truck in gear.

Ben instructed her to pull into the diner and wait in the truck. Through the window, she watched Charity wrap Ben in a lengthy hug before she handed over his order. He returned with two bags tied at the top. Climbing in, he swung the bags into the backseat.

Following Ben's instructions, Amy drove out of town. Her stomach sank when she realized they were headed to the Double Diamond. Was Ben doing what Melanie enjoyed, or was he trying to make Amy regret forcing him out of his apartment? Did he plan on riding horses?

Anxiety tightened her chest. She'd never ridden a horse before. Sure, it sounded fun, but she wasn't sure she wanted to rely on Ben, in his current mood, to teach her. With him in a sleeping pill-induced haze, she sure hoped he wasn't planning on riding ATVs or shooting guns.

When they arrived at the ranch, she pulled up near the stables as Ben instructed. The knot in her stomach grew when Ben reached over the seat for the bags he'd placed there and climbed out of the truck.

They walked to the side of the stable, even though the massive double-doors of the main entrance stood open. They found Jake saddling a horse tied to a hitching post. A second horse stood nearby, already saddled, with saddle bags attached. Ben went straight to the second horse and transferred the takeout containers to the saddle packs.

Trying to ignore the strong odor of horses and leather that made her stomach turn, Amy grabbed Jake's arm. "I can't do this." She tried to whisper so Ben wouldn't hear her, but her words came out a hiss.

Jake put his hands on her shoulders. "Relax. Honey is a gentle, patient horse, and Ben is experienced with horses. He won't let anything happen to you."

"But I haven't... I've never... ridden a horse before." Her whisper—bordering on hysterical—was certainly loud enough for Ben to hear.

Jake took her arm and led her into the tack room where the horse scent wasn't as strong, but the leather smell intensified. "Listen, Amy, Ben told me Paige asked you to be his grief counselor today, and I have to say I think it's a wonderful idea."

Amy tried to find comfort in Jake's words. "I'm not so sure. He's in the foulest mood."

"He deserves to be. The simple fact he is even doing this, and letting you come along, is like a cry for help. The first cry he's made in a whole year." He gave her a pointed look.

This was Ben's first cry for help in a whole year? How had the man contained his grief for so long? She didn't know how to help him face his pain. The prospect of trying overwhelmed her.

"I don't think… I'm the best person… maybe you should ride with him."

"No," Jake insisted. "It needs to be you. He's not likely to open up to me. He needs to talk about Melanie to someone who has never met her. Besides, we macho types find it difficult to share our feelings with each other."

"I'm not sure he'll even talk to me."

"Be patient. Give him time. Ben needs this." Jake squeezed her shoulder. "Besides, riding horses really was one of Melanie's favorite things to do."

Ben stepped into the tack room. "Jake, I think we need to borrow some boots, mine are in storage and Amy…" he glanced at Amy's slip-on shoes and let his words die off.

Before Amy knew it, she wore one of Riley's cowboy hats and a pair of her old boots. Jake demonstrated how to mount the horse, with one foot in the stirrup. She tried twice to pull herself up but failed to make it high enough to swing her leg over. On her third try, Jake's hands encircled her waist, lifted her up, and deposited her in the saddle. Ben waited with an air of impatience, while Jake adjusted her stirrups and instructed her on how to use the reins to guide her horse.

"Keep the reins loose," Jake said. Gesturing toward Ben's horse, he added, "She'll follow Apollo, no problem."

Ben nudged his horse in the flanks with his heels, and Amy's heart leaped to her throat when Honey moved after Apollo. Keeping a tight grip on the pommel, she sucked in a steadying breath. *I can do this.*

The sun shone on Honey's shiny coat, and Amy thought how

appropriate her name was. She pictured flowing honey as she watched the fluid movement of her horse's muscles.

It took a full five minutes to convince herself she wasn't going to fall off and release the saddle horn. Honey's smooth gait made her body sway in a gentle rocking motion, and the tension in her body relaxed. A smile crept across her lips. She couldn't believe she was actually riding a horse and enjoying it.

She tipped her head back and closed her eyes. What a beautiful fall day. She wore only a light jacket, and the sunshine felt wonderful after the stormy weather of the last couple days.

She studied Ben on the horse in front of her. He rode with confidence, creating a striking figure in the saddle, with his broad shoulders and narrow hips. His posture had been rigid, but now, he appeared relaxed.

As she studied his shoulders, Amy's mind strayed to the night he carried her into the house after she broke her toe, followed by the memory of being held in his arms when he kissed her a few days later.

She licked her suddenly dry lips. She promised Ben she'd forget about the kiss, and she'd tried, but every time she saw him, she wanted him to kiss her again. She was as disgusted with herself for wanting him to kiss her again as she was for the way she'd responded. But she couldn't seem to stop her thoughts from going that direction whenever he was near.

Ben reached his left hand out to his side, clicked his tongue, and snapped his fingers. Honey picked up her pace, startling Amy. Honey pulled up to the side of Apollo and adjusted her gait to match the other horse.

"As attractive as my and Apollo's backsides must be... it's easier to keep an eye on you when I don't have to keep checking over my shoulder."

Amy's cheeks flamed as though she'd been caught doing something she shouldn't. She assumed he was teasing, but it was difficult to read his mood today. He seemed more relaxed than earlier, but did she dare make a joke about his backside being the best part of the scenery? Embarrassed she'd even thought it, she flushed more.

"You look hot. Do you need a water bottle?"

Amy turned away, so he couldn't see her face. "I'm fine."

They rode in silence for some time over gently rolling hills of dry desert lands, dotted with green pastures and the occasional forested area, creating a beautiful vista. No matter which way she looked, the view amazed her. She felt so small and insignificant here on the wide-open range.

Ben began to talk about the ranch. He explained how the thousands of acres owned by the Double Diamond extended in different directions, almost as far as the eye could see. "A small portion of the ranch is used to breed and raise horses. The majority is used to raise thousands of heads cattle, most of which were sold and shipped across the U.S. every fall. They also grow all the feed for the animals."

From her first visit here, Amy could tell this was no small operation, but she hadn't realized how large it was. The overhead costs must be astronomical, but Jake seemed to be doing well.

Ben remained quiet, lost in his own thoughts, and Amy wondered if he thought about riding out here with Melanie. After a while, he began to talk about time spent on the ranch and in his uncle's garage in his youth.

"I envied my cousins. Robert and Jake had the whole ranch to roam, horses and four-wheelers to ride, guns to shoot. Steven, Matt, and Damon had the repair shop to hang out in. I never could understand why they weren't fascinated with cars like I was."

Although Ben seemed to have a good relationship with his family, it didn't sound like he'd spent much time at home. Was that why he hadn't shared his grief with them?

"Before I turned sixteen and could drive myself out here, I had to make the long ride on my bike. So, I spent most of my summers at the garage. My parents sometimes let me come stay for a week at a time, though. Usually during branding or round-up."

"Sounds like you had a great childhood."

Ben nodded. "I wish you could say the same."

They hadn't talked about the things she'd told him last Sunday, and

Amy really didn't want to talk about them now, but she had a feeling Ben wanted her to.

Isn't that what she'd dragged him out of his apartment to do? Talk about his loss. To deal with it. As much as Amy would like to think otherwise, she hadn't truly dealt with her issues. She'd accepted them, but she hadn't dealt with them.

Ben must have thought the same thing, because he said, "Amy, any time you want to talk about... your childhood... or Lance... or anything, I'm here."

Amy dropped her eyes to her hand, resting on the pommel with the reigns dangling. "What if I don't want to talk about any of it? Maybe I don't want to admit how badly I screwed up my life?"

A sharp 'tssst' sound from Ben brought her head up. The horses reacted as sharply, coming to a stop. Ben really was skilled with horses. She was about to say so until she saw the intensity in his eyes.

"Screwed up your life? With the kind of upbringing you had, I'd say you turned out pretty amazing."

This was the second time Ben had used that word to describe her. Maybe if she heard him say it often enough, she'd believe it. Or maybe she should share with Ben another bit of truth.

"You know, after I moved out on my own, I wanted to believe I was better than my mom. I told myself I didn't need her, or anyone else to make me feel good about myself. I tried to keep a positive attitude, recognizing as bad as my childhood was, it could have been worse. I avoided dating because I'd seen how dependent my mom was on the attention from the men in her life."

"You viewed her need for attention as weakness," Ben stated.

"Yes, and I swore I'd never let it happen to me." A weight settled in Amy's stomach at the reminder that she'd failed.

"But then you fell in love with Lance."

Amy nodded. "The worst part was, deep down, I knew what kind of man Lance was. I knew he'd end up hurting me." She gave a wry chuckle. "I thought it would just be emotionally, but I guess I should have expected the physical abuse too."

Ben reached out and lifted her chin until she looked at him. The warmth she saw in his eyes touched something deep inside her. "We all want someone to care about us, Amy, and we have an innate need to love others. It doesn't make us weak; it makes us human." He smirked. "They say love is blind, but the truth is, love is powerful. Countries have gone to war over love."

BEN'S WORDS rang in Amy's head long after he clicked his tongue and flicked the reins to set the horses in motion again. She couldn't argue with him. Love *was* powerful, but she wasn't sure she'd ever felt that kind of love. Yes, Lance had flattered and charmed her, but she wasn't sure she would have ever been willing to fight for him, let alone go to war for him. Only Kallie had ever evoked that kind of intense emotion.

Amy couldn't ignore the tingles Ben's fingers under her chin had set off, though. Attraction. That's all it was. Not love. It couldn't be. Amy wasn't going to fall in love again. *But doesn't attraction often lead to love?*

They rode a little longer until they came to an area where the land rose above them in a steep, rocky slope. Before they hit the steepest part of the incline, Ben turned his horse toward a small clearing at the base of the outcropping. He led them to a pool of water—a result of a waterfall twenty yards upstream.

The view took Amy's breath away. Peace blanketed her as she took in the crystal-clear water, lush golden grass, and clear blue sky, scattered with fluffy, white clouds. She was convinced a prettier place didn't exist. Even the air smelled refreshing and inviting.

Ben stopped his horse near a fir tree and swung himself down in one fluid motion. Honey stopped near Apollo, patiently waiting for Amy to dismount. Amy was as unsure about getting off as she had been about getting on. Ben made it look so easy and graceful, but he'd also made getting on appear easy, and Amy was anything but graceful.

Seeing her hesitation, Ben stood close and told her to support her weight in the left stirrup while swinging her right leg over the horse's back and down to the ground.

Following his instructions, she slowly swung herself down, smiling at her success. She gasped when the muscles in her legs spasmed, and her knees buckled. Her hands flew out, grabbing a hold of the closest supports—Honey's saddle and Ben's shoulder.

Ben grasped her waist to steady her. "Sorry, I forgot to warn you about that part. It takes a moment for the muscles in your legs to adjust." His warm breath tickled her cheek.

Amy's breath caught in her throat and her mouth went dry at his nearness and the feel of the firm muscle of his shoulder beneath her palm. He exuded warmth and security, and his spicy-citrus scent mingled with the smell of the horses made her stomach take flight. Her legs experienced a whole new weakness.

"Are you okay?"

She nodded, not trusting her voice.

His hands lingered at her waist for a moment before he released her and turned to unstrap the blanket from behind his saddle.

Amy sucked in a deep breath. *What's the matter with me?* She remained near the horses and studied him from a distance. Ben looked especially attractive today in his jeans and denim shirt, but the man was grieving his wife for goodness' sake.

Ben walked to the water's edge and shook out the blanket in the shade of the trees. He turned upstream toward the waterfall, and his movements slowed. Then his shoulders slumped, and the blanket fell to the ground.

Catching the change in his demeanor, Amy walked over to him. "Ben?"

"I don't think I can do this." His voice came out choked.

"Memories can be painful." Sharing her own difficult memories had been one of the hardest things she'd ever done. "I'm sure you have many wonderful memories of this place. Don't fight them!" Her words came out a fervent whisper.

A pained expression filled is face. Turning, he walked upstream toward the outcropping where the water spilled down from above.

Amy watched him drop onto a large flat-top boulder near the stream's edge. She ached to go to him. To hold him, comfort him, as he'd held and comforted her last Sunday. But Hope had said Ben liked to be alone with his grief.

Does he really need to be alone though, or does he need a friend?

She watched as he planted his elbows on his knees and dropped his head in his hands. His shoulders shook. The tightness she hadn't realized had seized her stomach eased, and at the same moment her heart twisted.

Amy squeezed her eyes shut. *Please let these tears provide the healing he needs.*

Fighting the desire to go to him, she turned away to let him grieve in peace. Hopefully, he would feel like talking to her later.

She picked up the blanket Ben had left in a heap, shook it out, and spread it on the ground.

CHAPTER 21

*B*en set the borrowed cowboy hat on the rock beside him and pressed a hand to his chest as the memories flooded over him. He wanted to fight them, because they always filled him with despair. Knowing Melanie would never again wrap her arms around his neck, and that he would never again hold his infant daughter left him so empty.

Don't fight the memories.

He wasn't sure it would do any good to allow himself to remember, but Melanie deserved to be remembered.

Could he handle the pain that would come with really remembering?

Tears stung his eyes as he pictured Melanie the first time he took her horseback riding. She was so giddy. He'd always thought her beautiful, but the first time they rode together, she'd captivated him. His eyes dropped to the ground in front of him where he'd knelt to propose to her. He'd hardly been able to contain his excitement when she said yes, just as he could no longer contain his emotions now.

As the tears flowed, the urge to fight the memories dissipated. He wanted—no needed—to remember. All of it. The big things and the little things, the good times, and the bad—though gratefully, they were few. He needed to remember the laughter, the joy, and the intimacy.

His throat ached as he sobbed. Once he allowed himself to weep, he couldn't stop. He didn't want to. Not until he'd wept for the shortness of Melanie's life, the lost opportunities, the children they didn't get to raise together. He would never get to teach his daughter to ride a bike, or a horse, or walk her down the aisle.

He sat on the boulder for some time after the tears finally subsided. He felt bad for keeping Amy waiting, but he couldn't face her yet. Glancing her direction, he saw her laying on her back on the blanket like she didn't have a care in the world.

He knew better.

She'd had a difficult childhood, but instead of being angry for the bad things that happened to her, she was grateful things hadn't turned out worse. He wanted to be more like Amy, although in his situation, things had turned out for the worse. He couldn't seem to find a silver lining.

How did she keep such a positive attitude?

Not without great effort.

Her happiness was a choice.

Could he make that choice? It wouldn't be easy, but for the first time in a year, he wanted to be happy again.

He rubbed his eyes and raked his fingers through his hair. Pulling out his cell phone, he checked his reception, knowing cell service around the ranch was spotty. Two bars. It was worth a try.

Finding Paige's name, he sent her a text. *Exercise sucks!*

Whether it sent or not, he had to admit he felt a little better. Remembering was painful, but that pain was better than the guilt he'd been carrying. Guilt over not wanting to remember because it meant acknowledging all he'd lost.

He sent a second text. *But it's good, I guess.*

He stood and stretched. He didn't want to face Amy, but he'd kept her waiting long enough. Besides, he was starving. Sighing, he put his sunglasses on and pulled his hat low. It wouldn't fool Amy, but maybe she'd get the message and leave him alone.

He walked toward where she lay on the blanket. She lay so still, as though sleeping. He slowed his steps and studied her. For the second time today, he admired her figure, then his eyes lingered on her face, fair skin, dainty nose, thick lashes, pink lips.

Tightness seized his chest. He should be remembering Melanie today, not noticing all the things that made Amy beautiful. He cleared his throat.

Amy shot up, a flush tinting her cheeks, making her all the more attractive.

She tucked her hair behind her ear. "It's so beautiful and peaceful here."

"It is." He lowered himself to the blanket. "Melanie loved this place."

Amy held out one of the to-go containers containing chicken salad on croissants and fresh fruit. He took it, grateful she didn't comment on his emotional state.

They ate in silence for a time, then Amy asked, "Will you tell me about her? Where did you two meet?"

Ben didn't want to talk about Melanie. Not with Amy or anyone. Was that why he struggled so much? Because he wasn't willing to talk about her. He'd begged Amy to share with him something difficult and painful, shouldn't he be willing to do the same?

He cleared his throat. "We worked in the same building. We didn't work the same schedule, but once she caught my eye, I made it a point to linger over my work so I could see her. After we got to know each other, we spent as much time together as our conflicting schedules allowed. We loved it when we could both break away for the weekend." His lips curved into a smile. "She was so cute the first time I took her riding. I brought her here, and she fell in love with this place. That was the day I realized I'd fallen in love with her."

The memory was a balm to his troubled soul.

Amy let out a lengthy sigh. "I was so scared to get on a horse, as I'm sure you heard this morning. But riding is fun. I can see why she enjoyed it. And I can see why she loved it here." Amy's gaze roamed from the waterfall to the nearby wildflowers.

Ben glanced over his shoulder at the large boulder he'd sat on.

"I proposed to her a couple months later on that rock over there."

"No wonder this is such a special place. Is this the first time you've been here since... the accident?"

His stomach clenched. He had been such a coward to avoid facing the memories of his wife in this place because of the pain they would bring. Wonderful, beautiful memories, and he had fought them for so long.

Not trusting himself to speak, he nodded.

Looking away, Amy opened her cheesecake container.

Thank you. Talking about Melanie was hard enough, he couldn't bear to see the sympathy in Amy's eyes.

"I've seen the pictures of her on the mantle at your parent's house. She was beautiful. I envy her long hair and perfect curls." She took a bite of cheesecake and closed her eyes in enjoyment.

Ben chuckled. "She spent hours trying to get those perfect curls. Sometimes she straightened it. She hated her hair. It wasn't as curly as yours, but she always thought it was a mess and complained about the frizz."

Amy patted her own thick, curly hair. "I feel the same way."

"Melanie used to have my cousin, Steven, order this special hair stuff for taming curls. I'll try to remember the name of it and we can see if he keeps it stocked at the store."

"What else did she like besides riding horses and your Aunt Charity's chicken salad and cheesecake? Which are delicious, by the way." She set her container aside.

"Melanie liked reading. She'd start a book and get so caught up in it, she'd stay up all night." He absently twisted his wedding band around his finger and smiled as he remembered more wonderful things about the woman he loved. "She liked bubble baths and being barefoot. I introduced her to swing dancing, and she loved that too."

He raised his eyes to find her watching him twist his ring.

He shrugged. "I probably shouldn't wear a ring while working as a mechanic. But I'm not ready to take it off."

"Safety aside, unless you're ready to move on with your life, I don't see any reason you shouldn't wear it."

Would he ever be ready to move on? Ben's eyes met and held Amy's. He'd had a hard time keeping his eyes off her today but finding a woman attractive didn't mean he was ready to move on.

Color flooded Amy's cheeks, and her gaze darted away.

This was the third time she'd blushed today. *Is she fighting the same attraction I am?*

"Will you tell me about her family?"

Change the subject. Smooth move.

"Her father left when she was young, so she and her younger sister were raised by a single mom. She dropped out of college to take care of her mom and younger sister when her mom was diagnosed with pancreatic cancer. After her mom passed away, she worked two jobs to help take care of her sister and pay the medical bills."

"That must have been hard. She sounds like an amazing woman."

"She was. That's part of what I loved about her. She was selfless and compassionate." He studied Amy. "You remind me of her."

"Is that good or bad?" she asked, biting her bottom lip.

Ben took his time answering. The fact he'd even noticed their similarities wasn't good. It meant he thought too much about Amy and not enough about Melanie. It also meant he was being disloyal to Melanie's memory. "I don't know." He shrugged. "You have a lot in common."

They lapsed into a comfortable silence.

Though they had similar upbringings, Melanie hadn't faced the kind of challenges Amy had. Amy's resilience and positive attitude were every bit as impressive as Melanie's. He admired Amy's determination to make a better life for herself and her daughter.

And he was doing it again. Thinking about Amy, when he should be thinking about Melanie. He *had* thought about Melanie, though. It had been both painful and wonderful. Maybe if he allowed himself to remember Melanie and Cassey more, he wouldn't have nightmares so often.

"I dream about her... about them." He hadn't meant to say the words aloud.

Amy's head tilted, and her brow furrowed.

Unable to take the words back, he forged on. "That's why I took the sleeping pills so frequently this week because I didn't want to dream about them." He shared his reoccurring dreams of following his wife and daughter through bizarre mazes, where they always remained out of reach, then disappeared into a black abyss.

Amy placed a comforting hand on his arm. "That must be terrible to experience over and over."

"It is. But I can often hear Melanie's voice in those dreams... and Cassey's laughter..." He paused to control his emotions. "I think that's why I've tried to block out the memories and why I avoid talking about them. Hoping it would lessen the pain of losing them again and again."

"Has it?"

He let out a heavy sigh. "No. I don't have the dreams as often as I used to, but when I do..."

"Do you have pictures of them on your phone?" Amy asked after a few moments. "Would you share them with me?"

Ben pulled out his phone and swiped through his pictures, showing them to Amy occasionally.

"This is a picture of her, first thing in the morning." He angled the phone toward her. "She hated it when I took pictures of her without her hair and make-up done."

Ben couldn't hold back his smile. This was his favorite picture of Melanie. She'd taken a pregnancy test that turned out to be positive. She was so happy and beautiful in that moment.

He blinked back the tears that filled his eyes.

"She's pretty without it, but as a woman whose hair needs taming in the morning, I completely understand."

If Amy noticed he'd choked up again, she didn't show it. Or maybe she chose to ignore it. Either way, he was grateful.

They looked at several more pictures of Melanie and Cassey. Ben was even in a few of them. He swiped sideways until the picture of

Cassey in a puffy, pink snowsuit filled his screen. He'd framed this one and kept it on his desk at the garage. It helped him feel like he was close to her even though she was gone.

"You've seen this one. Taken that day." He was about to exit his photo gallery, when Amy took the phone from his hand.

Her brow furrowed as she studied the picture.

Expecting her to give the phone right back, he held out his hand, then dropped it when she didn't. Why was she so fascinated with this picture? It wasn't the one that had been plastered everywhere for months after Cassey's disappearance, but she seemed interested in it.

Confused but not wanting to appear rude by demanding his phone back, he busied himself cleaning up their lunch.

AMY'S CHEST tightened as goosebumps covered her arms. Her reaction to seeing this picture again was even stronger than last time. She'd seen this baby somewhere. She was sure of it.

This picture had occupied her thought so many times over the past month, but she simply couldn't remember where she'd seen Ben's daughter. She'd done numerous Internet searches on Cassey's disappearance, reread all the articles, studied her picture. And every time, she came up blank.

She used to believe she'd been led to Providence for a reason, but now she wondered if it was all a fluke. If she was supposed to somehow find Cassie, then why couldn't she remember where she'd seen this baby and the blue Suburban?

She grabbed Ben's phone and studied the image, hoping to jog some long-forgotten memory.

Nothing came. She bit back a growl of frustration.

Ben started to clean up the mess from their lunch, but Amy couldn't take her eyes off the image of Cassey. She tapped the photo and texted it to herself. Hopefully, Ben wouldn't notice and wonder why she'd done it. He'd probably think her interest in his daughter was as creepy as she'd thought his fascination with Kallie was the first day they met.

She handed his phone back and helped him fold the blanket.

"Let me guess... you had déjà vu again?" He chuckled. "Oh wait, would this be déjà vu of your déjà vu?"

Amy forced a laugh. "Is that possible? She's just so cute. She has the prettiest blue eyes."

Ben's movements stilled, and he stared at her.

Her face grew warm under his scrutiny. She couldn't see his eyes behind his sunglasses, but everyone knew Cassey had her daddy's eyes. So, Amy had basically said that Ben had the prettiest eyes.

It was true, so she wouldn't try to deny it. She'd end up digging herself a bigger hole. She carried the blanket over to the horses, pretending she hadn't said anything. Thankfully, Ben followed and within minutes, everything was packed up.

Before they mounted their horses again, Amy grabbed Ben's hand. "I know this hasn't been easy but thank you for sharing with me today. I'm so sorry for everything you've lost."

"Thank you, Amy." He removed his sunglasses, and his electric blue eyes bore into hers. He squeezed her hand. "Thank you for being stubborn, for making me face the memories. It hurts. A lot. But it's been good."

"I won't pretend I understand your pain because I don't. I've never suffered a loss like you have, but whenever I've struggled with something difficult, I take life one day at a time, then try all over again the next day."

"I've been taking life one day at a time for a year now, but I haven't been trying to make it any better. Consequently, I don't think it's improved." The corners of his mouth turned up. "How did you and Paige get so smart?"

Amy gave him a wry smile and turned to her horse.

Ben stood by as she climbed on Honey. It took two tries, and a nudge from Ben against her hip to get her into the saddle.

Before they returned to the ranch, they skirted around the rocky out-cropping, riding the horses uphill. When they arrived at the top,

Amy caught her breath. The view was incredible. Gently rolling hills blanketed in grass starting to turn gold were broken by stands of trees with leaves in various shades of yellow, orange, and red. A wide stream snaked across the landscape like a silver serpent. The sky, still a vibrant blue, held more fluffy clouds than before.

Amy sucked in a deep breath of fresh air. "Beautiful. This is my new favorite place in the whole world."

THEY TALKED as they rode back to the ranch, and Amy shared tidbits of her past as well as her dreams of someday going to culinary school and owning her own restaurant. She talked about her early days at Charlie's. "And then the entire bin of dirty dishes slipped from my hands, right there in the middle of the restaurant. There were broken dishes and food all over the floor. I was so embarrassed. Charlie made me clean it up all by myself."

Ben laughed. "So, you've always lacked coordination, huh?"

The most genuine smile she'd seen since her arrival in Providence lingered on his face, and she caught her breath at the sight of his dimple. Again, she chided herself for being attracted to the man while he grieved for his wife and daughter.

Reminded of the photo on Ben's phone, Amy again tried to remember where she'd seen that baby. If she could remember the baby, why couldn't she remember where? She was almost certain she'd seen Cassie after she was kidnapped.

But how? Where?

"How about it?"

"How about what?" Amy said, pulling herself from her thoughts.

"Shall we pick up the pace? Let the horses run a little?"

Amy shivered as she felt the color drain from her face. "No. I don't want to fall off." She was enjoying herself. *Why ruin a good thing?*

"You'll be fine. We'll start off with a trot."

"Ben, you know I'm not that coordinated."

"Relax and feel the motion of the horse and let your body move with it. Hold onto the saddle horn if you need to."

Before she could protest again, Ben nudged Apollo's flanks, and he quickened his pace to a trot. Honey followed suit to keep pace with Apollo.

Wide-eyed, Amy grasped the pommel in a death grip as she bounced in the saddle.

"Relax into it."

Jaw clenched, she studied Ben. His body came upward in a single fluid motion with the horse and back down again. Taking a deep breath and loosening her hold on the pommel, she attempted to relax and focus on the motion of her horse.

After several more strides she felt like she bounced less, but she was certain she didn't look nearly as graceful as Ben. As she relaxed into Honey's rhythm, a lightness settled over her. *Exhilarating.*

"Let's take it to a gallop."

"Ben, no. I—"

She'd finally relaxed enough to let go of the saddle horn, and Ben instructed her to hang on and lean forward.

"If you want to stop, pull on the reins, and Honey will slow down or stop, depending on how hard you pull."

He nudged Apollo's flanks again, and the horses took flight. At least that's what it felt to Amy. She hung on, wanted to pull back on the reins, but not wanting to be a quitter. Following Ben's instructions, she leaned forward, but couldn't seem to relax.

Certain she was going to fall, she tugged on Honey's reins. The horse slowed, no longer trying to match Apollo's pace but still galloping. Feeling more comfortable with the slower pace, Amy tried to relax and enjoy the ride. She could see why Melanie loved riding—the wind on her face was intoxicating.

The ranch house was in sight when Riley's hat slipped back on Amy's head. She couldn't bring herself to let go of the saddle horn to adjust it, and within seconds, it flew off. She called out to Ben, but he was too far away. If she stopped to pick it up, she wasn't sure she'd be able to get back on her horse by herself.

Ben stayed mounted after reaching the stables, waiting for her to get there. Honey came to a stop at the fence beside Apollo.

"Where's your hat?"

"It blew off, back about a hundred yards."

"I'll get it." Ben turned Apollo and took off at a thundering pace to retrieve her hat. Her eyes followed him. He never once held onto the saddle horn like he'd instructed her to do. Jake was right. Ben was skilled with horses.

Honey waited patiently for Amy to get off, but she didn't dare attempt it by herself. Thankfully, Jake walked out of the stables and came to help her down.

Amy put her weight in one stirrup and swung her other leg over the back of the saddle, dropping to the ground like Ben taught her. She would've done fine except for the pins and needles in her feet and the weakening of her leg muscles.

"Ouch."

Jake's hands encircled her waist. "It takes some getting used to." His chuckle near her ear made her mouth go dry.

She tensed, expecting her heart to race and her breath to catch at his nearness like it had at Ben's. When it didn't happen, she relaxed. He smelled more like horses today than his tantalizing soap. *Thank goodness.*

Why had she reacted so differently to Ben's touch?

BEN ARRIVED BACK with the hat just as Jake released Amy's waist. Jake remained close to Amy even though she looked fine. He understood why Jake would take an interest in her, what he didn't understand was why it bothered him.

"Did you two have a nice ride?" Jake gave Ben a probing look.

Ben met his gaze. "We did."

"Yes!" Amy said.

"Good." Jake took Honey's reins and led her to the hitching post outside the tack room.

Ben followed with Apollo. As he helped unsaddle and brush down the horses, a sense of rightness, of belonging surrounded him. When Melanie died and Cassey disappeared, he'd lost more than a wife and daughter. He'd lost a piece of himself, of his very identity because he'd stopped doing the things that had been a part of his life even before Melanie.

Why?

Because you shouldn't enjoy life. Not without them.

He'd enjoyed himself today, though. His gaze drifted to Amy who sat on a bench removing her boots. Was it wrong to have some of his grief lifted by sharing it with someone? Would he ever be free of that burden?

No, because that would mean he'd forgotten Melanie, forgotten his daughter. He couldn't allow that to happen.

He rubbed the horse brush down Apollo's flank. Was there any way to remember them *and* be happy?

His phone chimed when he sat on the wooden bench to remove his boots. He pulled it out and read the message from Paige.

Sorry I'm not there with you on this difficult day. Be nice to Amy, she's only the messenger. I know it hurts but keep putting one foot in front of the other.

Ben slipped his phone back into his pocket and lifted a foot to remove the boot, but Jake stopped him.

"Why don't you hang onto them for tonight?" When Ben gave him a questioning look, he added, "We should go to Scooters this evening."

Ben's foot dropped to the floor as the air whooshed from his lungs. Jake may as well have punched him. Melanie had loved swing dancing at Scooters. But like everything else, he'd avoided that place for the past year.

Could he face more wonderful, but difficult memories today?

He stood and stepped outside the tack room, as if doing so could help him catch his breath.

Jake stood behind him.

"Do you remember what my dad used to tell us when we got bucked off a horse?"

"Doesn't matter how far you ride. What matters is that you get back on." Ben heard Uncle Blake's voice as he said the words.

"Maybe it's time to get back on, Ben. I think Melanie would be pleased with your efforts today."

Ben rolled his shoulders as the weight of indecision rested on them. As painful as it had been, he'd enjoyed the afternoon. It had been wonderful remembering all the incredible moments he'd shared with Melanie. Knowing he'd never share one more single moment with her was painful, but it had felt good talking about Melanie to Amy. He hadn't done much of that since she died.

He couldn't ignore the guilt that ate at him for enjoying himself without Melanie by his side. If he went to Scooters, knowing how much she loved to dance, would he be able to handle that much more pain.

Worse, could he handle the guilt if he ended up enjoying himself?

He thought of Paige's text: *Keep putting one foot in front of the other.* Surely, she didn't mean by dancing.

Actually, Paige would be thrilled to know he considered going dancing.

"It's line night, so there's no pressure," Jake said. "Robert and I could come along and entertain Amy, and you can join in if you feel like it."

Ben groaned. "First Paige, then Amy, and now you. Why are you all so pushy?"

Jake clapped him on the shoulder. "Because we love you, man."

CHAPTER 22

hen they left the ranch, Ben assured Amy he was fine to drive. He remained quiet as he drove, his earlier joviality gone. She assumed they'd go to Scooters later, since Ben still wore the borrowed boots. He'd grabbed his tennis shoes and the boots Amy had already taken off, before climbing into his truck.

Would line dancing be any easier than swing dancing?

Ben's whole demeanor had changed as soon as Jake suggested going to Scooters. Because Melanie had loved to dance, Scooters would likely be full of more memories Ben hadn't faced in a year. Would going there, on top of riding, be too much for him to face in one day?

Jake's response when Ben asked why they were all so pushy filled her head. Of course, Paige and Jake loved Ben, but what did she feel for him? She thought of him often, but she didn't think of him as a brother or a cousin. She was too attracted to him for her feelings toward him to be platonic.

Lately, her body had reacted strangely whenever he was near. She felt things she'd never felt, not even with Lance. Things she didn't want to feel. She couldn't seem to get the kiss they'd shared out of her head and didn't like what that said about her.

No, she wouldn't say she loved Ben. But she had to admit, she cared a great deal about him. Enough that she'd do almost anything for him, including pushing him to confront painful memories, to help him heal. She was even willing to make a fool of herself on the dance floor if it would help him.

Ben pulled his truck to a stop at the grocery store. "I assume my mom has Kallie?" At Amy's nod, he said, "You should let her know you won't be home until late."

Then he was gone.

After a quick call informing Hope they'd be going to Scooters tonight, during which Hope squealed in her ear and thanked her profusely, Amy caught up to Ben. He stood in front of the store's small display of fresh flowers, looking lost. She hung back, not wanting to intrude on his privacy, but wanting to give moral support.

"What was her favorite flower?" She stepped closer when he didn't make a move to choose anything.

"Roses." His voice was quiet. "She loved red roses and lilies."

"This is not a good time of year for lilies, but maybe you can get her those roses, and we could get some daisies or carnations to go with them."

Ben thought for a moment more, then gathered arrangements of red roses, white daisies, and pink carnations. Instead of heading for the registers to check out, he grabbed a shopping cart, laid the flowers in it, and headed to the opposite side of the store.

Wishing she could read his mind, Amy followed at a distance.

Knight's Grocery store was the one real store in Providence. Besides groceries, it contained a pharmacy, where Ben's cousin, Matt, was the Pharmacist. It also had small sections of toys, hardware, housewares, and clothing.

Amy followed Ben as he pushed his cart up and down aisles of soaps, lotions, and hair products, only to double back to a previous aisle. Finally, he stopped and searched the shelves. He reached up to the top shelf and pulled down a white bottle with a red logo and black lettering. He handed it to Amy.

"That's the stuff Melanie always used for the frizz."

Amy took the bottle and studied it. She'd never seen this brand before. The name looked French. She glanced at the shelf where Ben had gotten the bottle and sucked in a sharp breath. No wonder she'd never noticed it before. *Talk about expensive.* But as she'd come to learn while staying with the Youngs, expensive products were usually worth it.

"Thanks, I'll try it."

Reaching the end of the aisle, Amy turned to find Ben had stopped. He held a bottle of perfume in his hand. She watched as he took off the lid and raised it to his nose. He closed his eyes, and Amy's heart broke.

It must be Melanie's perfume.

She left him and found the clothing department. Finding what she wanted, she snatched a package off the hook and returned to where Ben stood, still holding the perfume. His face reddened when he saw her approaching, and he put the bottle back on the shelf.

Amy opened the package of men's handkerchiefs and took one out. Grabbing the perfume, she sprayed the handkerchief twice. After replacing the bottle on the shelf, she folded the handkerchief and tucked it back in the package between the other two. She tossed the package in the shopping cart and walked away.

He might not appreciate what she'd done, but she wouldn't stick around and let him argue. Ben needed to remember everything about Melanie, again and again. He needed to enjoy those memories, and he couldn't do that in the middle of the grocery store.

At the checkout, when Amy tried to pay for the hair product, Ben insisted on buying it.

The cashier picked up the package of handkerchiefs. "This one is open. Would you like to get a different one?"

Amy grabbed the package. "No, this one is fine."

Ben bit back a smile.

On their way out, they crossed paths with Ben's cousin, Steven. He shook Ben's hand and gave him a quick one-arm hug, slapping him on the back. "I've been thinking about you, man."

Ben mumbled something, and Steven released him.

Before Steven walked away, he brushed Amy's arm behind Ben's back. She glanced over her shoulder to see him giving her a thumbs up. The family grapevine must be working overtime.

When they arrived at the cemetery, Amy climbed out of the truck and stared at the sky. Clouds had continued to move in until the whole sky was overcast. The temperature hadn't dropped though, nor did it look like it would storm. She hoped the weather held.

Amy helped Ben carry the three packages of flowers to Melanie's headstone, where she spotted a vase attached to the monument.

"Do you mind if I arrange some flowers in the vase?"

Ben shrugged, and Amy set to work. She arranged flowers from each of the packages together in the vase, doing her best to make them presentable despite not having anything to trim the stems with. Putting the remaining flowers together in a semblance of an arrangement, she wrapped plastic around them, and laid them on the ground next to the granite.

Gathering the remaining wrappers, she stood beside Ben. She studied the small oval frame embedded in the headstone with a picture of Melanie, and her chest grew tight. She was a beautiful woman, who'd died so young.

She turned to Ben. "If you'd known how things would turn out, would you have still married her?"

Anger flashed in Ben's eyes, just like she'd expected.

She grabbed his arm. "Cherish the life you had with her, Ben. Instead of regretting the life you didn't get to have." She paused to let her words sink in. "Take all the time you need." She squeezed his arm and walked away.

She wandered aimlessly, looking at various headstones. Looking, but not really seeing. Her thoughts were on the man who stood alone at his wife's grave. Ben had endured so much. His life had been perfect with a beautiful wife and baby girl with the possibility of more children. Then suddenly everything was gone.

Her sorrow for Ben turned to anger. How could someone have been so selfish and callous to not seek medical help for Melanie?

Instead, they walked away with her child? Ben's whole world was gone in a single, selfish act.

She pulled her phone out and studied the picture she'd sent from Ben's phone. If she could figure out where she'd seen this baby, maybe she'd have a clue to where Ben's daughter was.

She let out a frustrated growl. It was futile. She simply couldn't remember.

Glancing in his direction occasionally, Amy wandered back to the truck to wait for Ben.

~

BEN DROPPED to his knees in front of Melanie's headstone. He closed his eyes and inhaled the fragrant scent of the flowers Amy had arranged.

He was glad he came.

Despite his desire to sleep through this difficult day, it had never been his intention to let the day pass without bringing flowers. He brought flowers often, but today's visit felt different.

In the past. his heart had always been filled with bitterness and anger. Anger at the person who caused the accident. Anger at Melanie for leaving him alone. Anger at law enforcement, who had come up empty-handed in the search for his daughter. And anger at God for allowing it all to happen.

He thought about Amy's words. If he'd known Melanie would be taken from him so soon, he would have still married her. He'd loved her deeply.

He'd been unprepared for the powerful memories and emotions that had swept over him with the scent of her perfume. It had carried him back to the janitor's closet of the building they'd both worked in. He'd kissed her for the first time in that closet, her perfume blocking the odor of the cleaning products. He remembered how she smelled when she greeted him at the end of the day by wrapping her arms around his neck and kissing him.

"I'm so sorry." A sob tore from his throat and he squeezed his eyes shut. "Please forgive me for my stubbornness. For my reluctance to remember and cherish everything we had." His throat grew so tight, it choked off his words. He begged Melanie's forgiveness in silence. *Forgive me for not being able to find Cassey and care for her. Forgive me for enjoying riding horses without you and enjoying the time I spent talking to Amy.*

A sensation of warmth flooded Ben even though he hadn't felt cold. He opened his eyes.

The sun had broken through the gathering clouds, shining directly on him. He glanced around, realizing it shone only on him. Six feet away, the headstones and grass remained in shadows. He searched for Amy. He spotted her sitting on a bench near the truck with her back to him. She too, had a ray of sun shining directly on her, causing her platinum hair to shine like a halo, much like it had the first time he saw her.

He discounted it as an odd coincidence until a peaceful feeling surrounded him—a warmth that radiated from within—so powerful he had to question where it came from. He'd never felt like this before when visiting Melanie's grave. Peace was something he hadn't felt in forever.

All the anger and bitterness he'd harbored for the past year dissipated. He couldn't understand what had changed, but the fear and pain he'd lived with the past year seemed to lose their grip on him. Even the guilt he'd experienced today felt insignificant compared to the warmth and love that encompassed him.

Melanie's love for him. That's what it was.

He sensed her presence, and that she wanted him to accept the things that had happened and find a way to move on. Ben closed his eyes again, trying to absorb everything he felt.

"I love you." Could she feel his love the way he felt hers?

He remained still long after the clouds again blocked the sun, and the warmth faded. Fortunately, the peace remained. He wanted to remember this moment forever.

During the drive to Scooters, Amy studied Ben out of the corner of her eye. He'd been quiet since they left the cemetery.

There was something different about him. His eyes, that had always been so full of pain, shone with a light she'd never seen there before. The haunted look she'd grown accustomed to was gone, and he looked at peace.

Was this really the same man who had snapped at her this morning?

When they pulled into the parking lot of Scooters, Ben turned off the engine but made no move to get out of the truck.

"Are you okay?" Amy asked. "You've been quiet since we left the ranch."

Ben opened his mouth, then closed it again. He cleared his throat before speaking. "Thank you... for making me go to the cemetery. I needed that."

"Something happened to you there, didn't it? Do you want to talk about it?"

"Not right now. Maybe someday." He removed the keys from the ignition and reached for the door. Amy stopped him with a hand on his arm.

"Are you sure this won't be too much for you?" She tilted her head toward Scooters. "You've faced a lot today, but I don't want you to... I want it to end on a positive note for you."

"I'll let you know if I need to leave." He opened his door, then smiled at her over his shoulder. "You're not getting out of line dancing that easily."

When they entered Scooters, they spotted Robert and Jake sitting at a corner table. They stood as Ben and Amy approached.

"Hey, Amy," Robert said. "How was your ride today?"

"I had a blast, and I didn't fall off once." Her smile turned to a wince as she sat on the hard, wooden chair. "But I think I'm saddle sore."

Everyone chuckled, including Ben. She loved his smile. He seemed to be in a good mood, so she decided to risk some teasing. She gave Ben a quick wink. "It serves me right, I suppose, for being so pushy."

"That's right." Ben returned her smile. "If it makes you feel any better, I'm sore too."

"It does."

Amy caught the glance Robert and Jake exchanged across the table, and she knew Ben saw it too. She couldn't believe she'd winked at him in front of his cousins, but when he returned her smile, she decided it was worth any teasing she might get. By the look on their faces, they were glad to see Ben smiling too.

"Have you ordered?" Ben asked.

"Yes," Robert said.

Their food soon arrived, and Amy ate with gusto. She couldn't believe how hungry riding horses made her. She enjoyed the food and the company so much, Jake surprised her when he insisted she go to the dance floor with him.

Amy shifted in her seat. "I shouldn't. I'm not very graceful, ask Robert."

"Don't worry, there aren't any fences to fall from," Ben said.

Amy shot him a quick glare before Robert grabbed her arm. "Come on, Amy. Practice makes perfect."

With a brother holding onto either arm, she couldn't very well back out.

Self-consciously, Amy stumbled through the steps. She took turns stepping on Robert's toes then Jake's as she repeatedly turned the wrong way. They stepped on her toes a couple times also, because she was always a step behind.

Just when she grew comfortable with the steps, the song ended. She made no attempt to hide her frustration when the next song used a completely different series of steps.

BEN WATCHED AMY, Robert, and Jake from his seat at the table. He laughed at Amy's frustration over the dance steps. She wasn't particularly graceful, but she was a good sport. She didn't like being the center of attention or doing something new, but she did it anyway.

For me.

Just like she'd climbed onto Honey's back to ride with him even though she'd been terrified. She was here because he needed to be here.

He recalled the first time he brought Melanie to Scooters. The different dance steps had frustrated her too, but she was naturally graceful and had quickly picked up the moves. She'd loved swing dancing, often insisting he dance with her in the kitchen while they fixed dinner.

Every time he'd held her in his arms, he'd forgotten the rest of the world existed. Dinner had burned on multiple occasions when their dancing in the kitchen had led to other things.

Determined not to fight the memories, Ben shifted his chair back and leaned his head against the wall. He closed his eyes and let the music carry him away. For the third time today, he cherished the memories. Melanie's smile and excitement for new things brought a smile to his face. The feel of her in his arms, the sound of her voice when she whispered seductively in his ear, then laughed, letting him know she was teasing. Remembering the intimate moments brought a flush to his cheeks.

Life had been wonderful with Melanie. Almost perfect.

But that life was over. He didn't want it to be, but he needed to accept it, because no amount of wishing, or praying, would change the fact that his wife and daughter were gone.

He pondered on his experience at the cemetery. Peace still enveloped him. He missed Melanie and Cassey terribly. He would continue to mourn them for a long time but, for the first time in a year, he felt like maybe he could actually go on living without them.

Opening his eyes, he contemplated joining the others on the dance floor. Jake stood behind Amy with his hands on her hips, guiding her through the steps, his head bent close to her ear. Was he telling her the dance moves or whispering something else entirely? Irritation flared as he thought about Robert's and Amy's Friday lunch dates.

Why was he jealous? He was mourning his wife. He shouldn't be interested in another woman yet. So why was he always thinking about Amy? And why did he want so badly to take her in his arms and kiss her again?

Did the sun shining on her at the cemetery mean something? Or was it only a coincidence?

Stop trying to over analyze this. You're making mountains out of molehills.

Standing, he shook off his somber mood and headed toward the dance floor. Maybe his rusty dance moves would make Amy feel better.

～

BEN PARKED behind the repair shop and walked Amy to her car. He was both relieved and disappointed to have this day come to an end.

"Thanks for letting me spend the day with you," Amy said.

"No, thank *you*. It's been a rough day, but you helped me through it." He swept Amy into a hug. When she tensed, he told himself to let her go, but she relaxed into him before he could.

She wrapped her arms around his waist and Ben relished her touch. Holding her felt right, somehow. He waited for the guilt to hit. When it didn't, he tightened his embrace. He wanted to enjoy this one moment with her.

Despite the activities of this Fall day, she smelled like spring. Like sunshine and flowers. Happiness and anticipation. She felt as good as she smelled. If he kissed her again, would it be as amazing as last time?

Yes. He was sure of it, but tonight was not the right time to find out. Reluctantly, he released her.

Amy looked as disappointed as he felt, but she quickly hid it by pulling the package of handkerchiefs from the grocery bag she carried. She pressed them to his chest. "Don't fight the memories, Ben. They're part of you, but don't let them keep you from living your life."

She slipped into her car, and Ben watched her drive away before climbing the stairs to his apartment.

Had he only been gone twelve hours?

Everything he'd experienced today had made the day seem to last an eternity. Without turning on a light, he went straight to the bedroom and sat on the edge of the bed. He pulled off the borrowed boots and opened the package of handkerchiefs, this time, prepared for the familiar scent. He laid back on the bed, inhaling deeply, a smile on his face.

CHAPTER 23

"Is everything okay?" Amy asked when she saw Charity laying on the couch the next Monday.

Charity was never home when Amy dropped off and picked up Kallie. She was always at the diner, so it surprised Amy to see her here today.

"I'm fine."

"No, she's not," Faith said. "She had a dizzy spell and almost passed out. The cook called me, and I made Robert bring her home."

"You're so bossy," Charity grumbled, trying to sit up.

"I am not. Now, stay down." Faith pushed against Charity's shoulder, preventing her from sitting up, and wrapped a blood pressure cuff around her arm.

"You took my blood pressure for the hundredth time two minutes ago."

"Well, it's still a little high."

"It wouldn't be high if you'd let me go check on the diner."

"The diner is fine. Susan is the evening, head waitress for a reason. She's perfectly capable of taking care of everything. You're working too hard."

Amy bit back a smile. *Is this what it's like to fight with a sister?* As annoyed as Charity acted, it must be nice to have someone care about you like Faith did.

Amy sat in the chair opposite Charity. "Do you need help at the diner?" She'd been in Providence for six weeks already and she was uncertain what would happen with her job. Robert hadn't said anything about Janice's maternity leave ending soon, but Amy knew she should search for another job, just in case. She had no desire to leave this beautiful small town.

"Yes!" Faith said.

"I suppose I could always use more help." Charity nodded. "Especially in the afternoons. That's when I do most of the baking. I have a couple waitresses for the mornings, and a head waitress for the evenings along with a couple teenage girls. And I have plenty of teenage girls for the weekends, but I probably ought to hire someone else to help in the afternoons."

Faith eyed Amy, a spark in her eyes. "Didn't you used to wait tables, Amy?"

"I did, and I may be looking for a job soon. I'm not sure when Janice will return from her maternity leave."

"Oh, this is perfect." Faith clapped her hands.

Yes, almost too perfect. Amy stared at Faith. If she didn't know better, she'd have accused her of orchestrating Charity's dizzy spell. Had Robert told Faith Amy would need to find another job soon?

"Would you like to come work at the diner, Amy?" Charity asked. "It would be a combination of waiting tables and baking."

The idea of being in the kitchen of a restaurant again appealed to Amy. It would be a step in the right direction to getting her life back on track. Maybe, Charity would be willing to share her recipes and secrets with Amy.

"I'd love to, but I'm not sure yet what will happen at the Sheriff's Office. I'll talk to Robert and let you know how soon I can start."

"SOMEONE IS HERE to see you, dear." Hope's brow furrowed as she leaned against Amy's bedroom door.

Amy sat on her bed memorizing the menu from the diner. She'd talked to Robert earlier this week, and he followed up with Janice, who only wanted to work half days until her baby slept through the night better. Starting Monday, Amy would work mornings at the Sheriff's Office and afternoons at the diner. She looked forward to the hustle and bustle of waitressing—somewhere other than a bar—and the opportunity to get to know more people. The Sheriff's Office was not a place where people came to socialize.

"Who is it?"

Hope grimaced. "Lance."

Amy frowned. "How did he find me?" And what did he want?

Money. But was that all?

"Should I call Robert?"

"No, I'll be fine. But keep Kallie out of sight, please." Amy grabbed a jacket and went to the front porch where Hope had left Lance waiting. Out in the cold where he belonged. She bit back a smile.

The air smelled like rain, though none had fallen, and a chill—that hadn't been there a week ago—filled the air.

Stepping outside, she pulled the front door closed behind her.

"What do you want, Lance?" She hoped her voice sounded steadier than she felt.

Lance's tousled golden hair was longer than he'd ever worn before, and he sported a three-day stubble. The style suited him. He never tried to be attractive, he didn't need to. His brown eyes, rimmed by thick lashes, a prominent jaw, strong cheekbones, and full lips, drew women like a magnet. Though not muscle-bound, Amy had always thought he had a nice physique. No wonder he never had a shortage of women hanging on him.

Shaking herself for getting caught up in his good looks, she pictured the last woman she'd seen hanging on Lance, in her own bed. She couldn't help but compare him to *The Men*, and suddenly he wasn't as good looking as she'd once thought. Attractiveness was so much more than looks.

"It's so good to see you." Lance stepped close as though to hug her, but Amy put a hand on his chest, stopping his advance. "Baby, I want you to come home."

Amy shuddered. The endearment always sounded so condescending. "How did you find me?"

Lance glanced down at his feet. "I talked Celeste into telling me where you were."

Amy had talked to her best friend two nights ago. Celeste had said Lance had been asking about her, but she didn't say she'd told him where Amy was staying.

"As much as I miss you, it's a good thing you left when you did," Celeste said. "Lance's band is struggling, and he's drinking all the time now."

"I'm glad I left when I did too, C. I like it here and things are going so good for me right now. I'm almost afraid it won't last." In a moment of weakness, Amy had told Celeste about her attraction to Ben, and her fear that she was turning out like her mom, especially since she wasn't sure Ben would ever be able to move on.

Celeste's words came back to her now: "You are a strong, capable woman, Amy. You don't need a man to complete you. I'm not saying you shouldn't keep your heart open, but don't make your happiness dependent on a man."

Amy studied Lance and agreed whole heartedly with Celeste. She didn't need a man to complete her. Especially not the man standing in front of her. And she didn't need a man in her life to be a good mother.

But what if I want a man? A man like Ben?

Pulling her thoughts back to Lance, Amy crossed her arms over her chest. "You should have saved yourself the trip. I told you I wasn't coming back the last time you called."

"I missed you, Baby."

"I doubt that. You miss having someone to pay the rent."

Lance shrugged. "I admit times are tough. We lost our drummer to a bigger band, and we've had a hard time finding a replacement, and

227

keeping the gigs lined up. Dennis is trying out a new band tonight." His brown eyes sought hers.

Amy glared at him.

Realizing he wouldn't get any sympathy from her, he changed tactics. "I miss you and Kallie."

"No, I'm sure what you miss is someone to support you."

He shoved his hands into his pockets, shifting his weight. His short-sleeved t-shirt revealed something on his right bicep that hadn't been there a few weeks ago.

"I see you got a new tattoo. How much did that one cost?"

Ignoring her question, he grabbed her shoulders. "I'm sorry for the way I treated you, Amy. I'm sorry for sleeping around with all those girls. I swear I'm done with other women."

Amy shook her head. She'd heard so many of his empty promises. He always said what he thought she wanted to hear. But he never meant the words.

He shook her to emphasize his next words. "I've changed! I'm a different person now, I promise. I need you back in my life. I haven't been able to write a single piece of music since you left."

A twinge of sympathy pulled at Amy's heart. Oh, how she wished the words were true. Not because she had any interest in going back to Lance, but because she needed to believe he really had loved her at some point.

She looked over Lance's shoulder in surprise as two trucks entered the cul-de-sac. Robert's sheriff's vehicle followed by Ben's Dodge. Hope must have thought she needed back up.

Seeing them boosted her confidence. She could deal with this. If she didn't take care of the situation herself, Lance might drive away with a broken nose and missing a few teeth. His career was struggling enough, he didn't need that kind of setback.

Raising her elbows, she shook his hands off her shoulders.

"I'm glad you've changed, Lance. I really am. Unfortunately, nothing you say or do will change the things you've done. I've changed too, and I'm done making bad choices. I'm not coming back.

Ever. I'm making a new life for myself and Kallie here, and you're not going to be a part of it."

"Is there a problem here?" Robert asked, approaching Lance from behind.

Lance spun around. The surprise, followed by a flash of fear that crossed his face as he spotted the two men, suggested he hadn't paid attention to their arrival. Robert and Ben both stood a few inches taller than Lance and their athletic builds, no doubt intimidated him, not to mention Robert's uniform.

"Thanks, gentlemen," Amy said, smiling at them, "but he's leaving." She folded her arms and glared at Lance, daring him to argue.

"Amy, wait," Lance said in a pleading voice. "I want to see Kallie."

Amy's stomach dropped. No way would she let Lance have Kallie. "Why now? You wanted nothing to do with her before."

"She's my daughter. I have a right to see her."

"Lance, I don't think that's a good idea. She—"

Ben stepped between her and Lance and pulled his wallet from his back pocket. "It's time for you to leave." His voice was firm, authoritative. "If you want to contact Ms. Lawson again, I suggest you call her lawyer."

Robert's gasp startled her. She stepped sideways and glanced at him. He stared at Ben, his mouth curved into a broad grin. She didn't understand what just happened, but when Ben stepped aside, she saw Lance walking to his car holding a business card in his hand.

Good.

Lance paused after opening his car door and turned to give her one last look like he'd done every Friday and Saturday night after his band finished their gig at Charlie's. The sight of Lance standing there triggered a memory with such clarity, she couldn't believe she hadn't recalled it before.

The air whooshed from her lungs as she remembered an older-model blue Suburban belonging to Lance's greasy-haired drummer always parked next to Lance's car in the back-parking lot at Charlie's.

Amy sucked in a sharp breath. Could it be the Suburban Robert searched for?

No. It's just a coincidence.

She searched her memory—did the drummer's Suburban have a grill guard?

Yes! It looked like the pictures she'd seen online.

Another memory flooded her mind of accompanying Lance last October when he went to fire his drummer for missing gigs.

Walking down the lane with Lance, Amy spotted the drummer's wife in the backyard pushing a baby in a swing. When she walked over to her, the woman lifted the baby from the swing and held her close. A blue-eyed baby dressed in a pink snow suit, with a tuft of blond hair sticking out from under the hood.

Amy's heart thundered in her chest, and a tingling spread throughout her body. *Was that Cassey?*

"Lance, wait!" She ran down the steps to his car.

He stopped in the process of getting into his car, his face full of hope.

"What was the name of your drummer last year?"

Lance's face fell, and his brow furrowed. "What?"

Amy grabbed the front of his t-shirt in both fists. "I need you to tell me the name of the drummer you had to fire a year ago." Her mind reeled as she pieced the memories together.

"Why? What does he have to do with anything?"

"You said things have been hard since you lost your drummer, and it reminded me that you had to fire your drummer last year when he became so unreliable. I need to know his name."

"We always called him *Sticks*, you know that."

She yanked on his shirt. "I need his real name."

"Um… Eddie, I think."

"Eddie what?"

"Eddie… Green."

"Eddie Green. That's it!" Amy's breath came in short rapid bursts. "Now, where did he live?"

"I don't remember." Lance shrugged. "Why do you care?"

"Please, Lance. I need you to remember. This is important. You took me with you last year when you went to fire him." Hoping to spark his memory, she said, "He and his wife lived down some country road, in a heavily forested area."

"That's right, they lived outside Glenwood," he said with enthusiasm. "I remember having a hard time finding his place. I missed the lane once because of all the trees. Seriously though, what does Sticks have to do with anything?"

"I need to know where to find him," she said, incredulous over the sudden rush of memories.

"Are you trying to tell me Eddie is actually Kallie's father? If that's the case, I would think you'd be able to remember his name." The accusation in Lance's voice stung.

Amy gasped. "How dare you even think that?" Just because Lance had no problem sleeping around, didn't mean she ever did.

She slapped him hard across the face. Spinning on her heel, she marched past Robert and Ben standing like sentinels at the edge of the porch.

"Are you okay?"

Ignoring their simultaneous question, she went straight to the kitchen and got a glass of water. Her hand trembled so badly she set the glass down after a couple swallows. A tornado of emotions tumbled around inside her: anger and excitement, disgust and hope.

She splashed cold water on her heated cheeks. Grabbing a handful of paper towels, she blotted her face dry. Her bodyguards came into the house, and she sensed their presence at the entrance to the kitchen. She kept her back to them.

I can't face anyone right now. She needed more time to process everything.

She stared out the window at Hope's barren flowerbeds, her heart feeling equally as empty and confused. A leaf broke free from the maple tree closest to the house and drifted to the ground, claiming its spot among the leaves already littering the lawn. Like a puzzle piece fitting into place.

The memories she'd recalled, and the information about Eddie filled her mind like pieces of a puzzle. She closed her eyes and pictured Eddie's blue Suburban. He'd told Lance it had broken down. That's why he'd missed so many gigs.

He'd lied.

Hadn't he?

Picturing Eddie's wife, with a baby in her arms, she rearranged the puzzle pieces in her head. Another memory pushed to the surface.

Amy held a two-month-old Kallie in her arms at a corner table at Charlie's, visiting with the drummer's wife while listening to the band play. The quiet, plain woman, whose name she couldn't recall, grew emotional as she expressed her disappointment that she and Eddie hadn't been able to have children.

Amy replayed the scene when she accompanied Lance to fire Eddie. When Amy waylaid Eddie's wife from taking the baby in the house, the woman said they were fostering the baby, hoping to adopt. Amy had been so happy for her.

Holy cow! Amy's pulse raced again, and her chest heaved. *Eddie and his wife kidnapped Ben's daughter.* Could she find Cassey and bring her back to her father? Warmth filled her body as understanding filled her mind. *That's why my car broke down in Providence. I'm supposed to bring Cassey home.*

Hope surged through her. She'd need to figure out exactly where Eddie lived. Given time, maybe she could piece it together, but right now Ben and Robert were concerned about her.

Pasting on a smile, she turned to face the two handsome men who filled the wide entrance to the kitchen. They probably didn't dare come any closer for fear of her slapping them too.

"I'm fine." Her voice sounded steadier than she felt. She rubbed her right palm against her thigh. "Except, my hand stings a little."

Robert and Ben both breathed a sigh of relief and stepped into the kitchen.

"Heck of a right hook you have there," Robert said, grinning.

Ben didn't say anything. He simply studied her face.

She avoided eye contact with him. When he looked at her like, that she felt like he could see right into her soul. She couldn't have him seeing the hope and uncertainty she felt concerning his daughter. Not yet.

"Do you want to tell us what that was all about?" Ben's voice was quiet.

She shrugged. "He said something that made me mad, that's all."

"Remind me not to make you mad," Robert said with a laugh. "And Hope thought you might need backup."

Ben's lips slowly turned up. "I bet that felt good."

Amy grinned. "Yeah, it did." Then she changed the subject. "What was that whole 'call my lawyer' thing about?"

Robert turned to Ben. "That's right, Bro. Are you serious?"

Ben took a deep breath and slowly let it out. "I think it's time." A smile spread across his face.

Robert wrapped Ben in a bear hug and slapped his back.

Did I miss something? Something significant.

Hope came into the kitchen with Kallie on her hip. "Is everything okay?"

"Aunt Hope, you should have seen the way Amy slapped Lance, and Ben told Lance if he ever wanted to contact Amy again, he should call her lawyer," Robert's voice was full of pride.

Hope gasped, then she set Kallie down and hugged Ben.

Amy's brow wrinkled. "Would someone like to tell me what's going on?"

Beaming with pride, Hope turned to Amy with her arm around Ben's waist. "I'd like you to meet my son, Benjamin James Young, the attorney."

"Attorney? I don't understand. I thought he was a mechanic?"

Ben smiled at his mother. "I'll explain." He motioned for Amy to follow him to the family room.

"You do that, son. Kallie and I will make some lunch."

"Not for me. I need to get going." Robert kissed his aunt's cheek and left.

Amy sat on the couch in the family room. Ben sat on the same couch, turning his body sideways to face her, so she did the same.

He took a deep breath. "I got a law degree at UCLA, and after two years working at a large firm in Los Angeles, I'd had enough of the city and was ready to move home. Melanie and I were ready to start a family, and we both agreed we didn't want to raise our children in the city. So we moved back to Providence, and I went into partnership with Uncle Brent, my dad's brother, at his law office." He paused to let his words sink in.

"Why are you working as a mechanic then?"

"When Melanie died last year and Cassey went missing, I nearly went insane. I exhausted all my resources, professionally and finan-cially, including Melanie's life insurance, trying to find my daughter. As each day passed without a single credible clue, my hopes of finding her alive sank lower and lower. About six weeks after the accident, Robert made me realize that *if* Cassey was alive, she could be anywhere in the world." Ben paused, taking several deep breaths to control the emotion that had deepened his voice. "The chances of finding her were so low, I couldn't eat or sleep, much less focus on cases. I couldn't do it anymore. Any of it. I couldn't stand the pity I saw in people's faces every time they looked at me, so I rarely left my house. But that didn't stop all the wonderful, annoying do-gooders in this town from bringing casseroles and cookies to my door all the time."

He said it with a smile, but Amy knew it must have been difficult to have to pretend he was fine when he was anything but.

"So, I left. I had to get away from this wonderful, claustrophobic town I love. I couldn't stand the silence in my house anymore, where every room was full of memories of them." His voice grew husky again, and he paused for a moment. "But I couldn't bear to be too far away in case we got news about Cassey. I went to my mother's family cabin out by the lake where I'd spent some of the greatest times of my childhood. I became a recluse. If my family hadn't checked in on me from time to time, bringing me food so I didn't starve, I would have gone months without seeing another human being. It was a dark, difficult time."

Amy longed to say something to comfort him, but words seemed inadequate.

"Robert and Jake were my lifesavers. They visited me as often as they dared, without driving me farther away. They were content to spend hours fishing with me in silence, or sitting, staring out the window. Paige came as often as she could too. She'd arrive, give me a hug, then go into cleaning mode. When she was done, she would sit and share her life with me." He smiled as he remembered this. "Their presence reminded me I had people who cared about me. That's what kept me from doing something stupid to myself that would have caused my family even more grief."

"I can't imagine how hard that must have been for you." She reached out and covered his hand with hers. He put his other hand over hers, trapping it there.

A strange fluttering hovered between her stomach and her chest at the gentle pressure of his warm, strong hand. She'd reached out to him as a gesture of comfort, but his touch was anything but comforting.

"One day, after I'd been holed up at the cabin for about five months, Robert came with news that my Uncle Richard had died suddenly of a heart attack. I was shocked. He was only sixty-three. I'd practically grown up in his garage. He taught me everything I know about cars." Ben sucked in a deep breath. "That's when I realized, despite my additional grief over my uncle's death, there were people who needed me. Aunt Charity needed help running the gas station and the repair shop. I'd finally found something to live for, if you can call it that. My family would argue I've not really been living, rather simply going through the motions, but taking care of the garage has given me a reason to get out of bed every morning. Which is something I hadn't had since... the accident."

"I'm sure she's been very grateful, as well as everyone else in this town." Amy squeezed his hand. "I'm grateful you were in the garage the day I broke down."

"I am too." His eyes lingered on her face, and her heart stumbled. "Despite joining the land of the living again, I couldn't bring myself to look people in the eye. All I saw was pity, so I interacted with people as little as possible, and spent my time working on cars. I think your face was the first one I actually saw for almost a year." He reached up and stroked her cheek with his thumb, setting her skin afire. "I could look you in the eye because you didn't know what I'd been through. And when I saw you were going through something difficult too, I had to help you."

Warmth filled her chest. "Do you realize the lifesaver you were to me that day?" she asked, struggling to keep her emotions in check. "You rescued me and Kallie."

He shrugged. "I don't know about that. But when I heard Lance try to threaten you with Kallie, I decided I needed to start living again, and that means returning to the law practice." He gave her hand a squeeze before releasing it.

Amy missed the contact immediately.

"Smells like Mom has lunch ready. If I'm going to eat here, I need to hurry. I've got a lot of work to do. Besides, I need to make Aunt Charity realize Scott is capable of running the garage and see if Uncle Brent is willing to take me back."

Amy's mind raced while they ate grilled cheese sandwiches and fruit. She couldn't seem to clear it of the revelations she'd had before Lance left. The year-old memories that had surfaced left her reeling. Then Ben's announcement had taken her by surprise. She needed time to process everything.

"You're quiet, Amy. Is everything okay?" Hope asked.

Amy jumped, startled out of her revelry. She shrugged. "I'm fine. I just have a lot on my mind right now."

Aware of Ben's eyes on her again, she studied her food. He probably thought her conversation with Lance occupied her thoughts, but he couldn't be further from the truth. Amy couldn't get her mind off Ben and possibly reuniting him with his daughter.

Could she do it?

Yes. She was going to find Eddie and bring Cassey home to her father. But she needed time to sort things out and do some investigating.

Problem was, she had no idea how to do investigative work.

CHAPTER 24

*B*en paused on the wide church steps and sucked in a deep breath. The ivory sandstone structure, though modest felt imposing. He looked up at the stained-glass window above the door, knowing it cast interesting geometric prisms on the back of the heads of the gray-haired widows who always occupied the front pew.

Ben wiped his damp palms down his slacks. He hadn't thought this through very well. He'd purposefully arrived late to avoid having to talk to anyone before the service, but now all eyes would be on him as he entered.

The strains of a familiar hymn crept through the door, and peace settled over him. He closed his eyes for a long moment. *I can do this!* This was where he needed to be. He recognized that now. He just wished it hadn't taken him so long to realize it.

Opening the door, he strode in, hoping he looked more confident than he felt. He kept his eyes straight ahead as every head turned and whispers filled the church. There were his parents in the fourth pew, like always. Thank goodness some things never changed. Beside his mom sat the curly-haired, blue-eyed blonds that always seemed to brighten his day.

He slid onto the bench beside Amy. Her wide-eyed stare, followed by a dazzling smile, was exactly the reaction he'd hoped for when he shaved his beard and cut his hair yesterday. He returned her smile and faced forward. The scent of sunshine and flowers reached him and his attraction for Amy skyrocketed.

He held out his hands to Kallie. Maybe if he held her, he'd be able to keep himself from lacing his fingers with Amy's—like he'd wanted to do ever since she'd clasped his hand yesterday. Kallie shied away and scooted to his mom's lap.

Shoot. He hadn't stop to think that Kallie might not recognize him without the beard. Amy gave him an apologetic smile and clasped her hands in her lap.

He forced his gaze to the pulpit, instead of letting it linger on her long, slender fingers. Twisting his wedding band, he fought the urge to draw her hand into his. *This will be the longest sermon of my life.*

When he arrived at his parent's house for dinner later that evening, Kallie ran away from him.

Amy picked her up and stepped close to Ben. So near he caught the scent of her perfume again.

"It's Ben." She took Kallie's hand and stroked his cheek. "See."

An electric shock heated Ben's smooth skin under Amy's fingers, sending warmth through his veins. His eyes jumped to hers.

She gasped and let go of Kallie's hand.

Had she felt the same electricity he had? Ben tried to search her face, but she looked away.

Kallie's hand rested on his cheek. "Daddy?"

Pulling his eyes away from Amy, Ben reached up to take Kallie. "Come here, Angel."

Amy pushed Kallie into his arms and stepped away.

He tamped down the disappointment that filled him.

"It was nice to see you… at church… today." Amy's cheeks flushed as she stammered out the words.

He loved it when she got flustered. She was so cute. And he loved the way her cheeks colored when she blushed.

"You were right. I need to stop blaming God for everything." He blew out a quick breath. "I sure had a hard time walking through those doors though, after such a long absence."

She gave him an understanding smile. "Are you glad you went?"

"Of course, I got to sit by the prettiest woman in the congregation."

Amy's cheeks flushed again, and she mumbled something about needing to check on dinner before heading to the kitchen.

Idiot. You're going to scare her away.

She turned in the doorway and gave him a dazzling smile. "By the way, you look... nice." Then she was gone, leaving him elated.

Following dinner, Ben found himself with Kallie and Amy in the family room while his parents did the dishes. Ever since Amy started cooking, they'd insisted on doing the dishes. He'd been banking on their predictability tonight. He needed Amy to himself for a little while. It had been all he could do to not stare at her all through dinner.

Amy sat on the floor and leaned back against the couch, her legs outstretched. Ben joined her, sitting close enough to touch her, but not so close to make her uncomfortable, he hoped. Kallie took turns climbing over his legs, then Amy's.

After a few minutes, he bent his knees and turned his body to face Amy. He propped his elbow on the couch and leaned his head against his hand. He studied her. Something was wrong with Amy. Ever since Lance's visit, there had been a tension in her. She looked like she was about to either break down or bolt.

He supported Kallie as she climbed over his knees again, then turned back at Amy. "Are you okay?"

"Of course. Why wouldn't I be?" She didn't meet his eyes as she helped Kallie over her legs.

"You seem... distracted." Did it have something to do with Lance? Or was it the attraction sparking between them? He hoped it was the latter.

"I'm fine. I have..."

"A lot on your mind?" he asked. "Still? Is it something I can help with?"

"No." He suspected the word came out faster and louder than Amy intended. "I just need time to sort some things out."

Did she regret sending Lance away? Or maybe it had to do with Lance's accusation about some other guy being Kallie's father. No. Amy's anger toward Lance told Ben she'd never been unfaithful to the jerk.

A glimmer of hope surged in him. Was Amy trying to sort out how she felt about him?

"Well, while you're sorting things out, will you go out with me?" Ben held his breath.

Amy's head jerked up. "What?"

"On a date. You know, where two people spend time together to get to know each other better? It usually starts with dinner, then maybe—"

"Why?"

Ben chuckled. "Well, I find you attractive, and I enjoy spending time with you. Don't get me wrong, I love this little monkey..." He caught Kallie as she toppled over his knees and nuzzled her neck with his chin until she squealed and struggled to escape. Ben released her, and she raced to the kitchen seeking Nana's protection.

Good. He had Amy's undivided attention. He turned back to her. "But I want to have you to myself for a change."

Amy sucked in a sharp breath, then her brow wrinkled. "What about Wid—" She blushed. "uh... Debbie?"

Ben scowled. "What about Debbie?" The woman had become a nightmare, constantly calling about the most ridiculous things. He'd taken to walking to his parent's house—entering and leaving by the back door—so she wouldn't know he was here.

"I've seen you going over to her house a few times." Did he detect a hint of jealousy in Amy's words?

"A few times?" Ben ground his teeth together. "If I'd known what a nuisance that woman was, I never would have rented her my house."

Amy's jaw dropped. "*Your* house?"

"My parents gave us the land as a wedding present, hoping we'd someday come home. When Melanie and I moved back to Providence,

240

we built a big house hoping to fill it with a large family, but…" Ben shrugged, fighting the grief that sneaked up on him.

He cleared his throat. "So, will you go out with me?"

Amy hugged her knees to her chest. "Ben, you don't really even know me."

"Hence the reason to go on a date." When Amy rolled her eyes at him, he said, "Fine. I know you're a wonderful mother, a hard worker, and a great cook." Grinning, he added, "You're stubborn and independent. You have great aim, a powerful right hook, and aren't very graceful."

Amy's breath came out in a huff, and she slapped his arm. "What I mean is, two months ago I was a waitress, living with a musician."

Dread tightened Ben's chest. "Are you still in love with him?" He dropped his gaze, fearing her answer.

"No," she said without hesitation. "Honestly, I'm not sure I ever was. I think I was in love with the idea of having someone love me."

Ben's relief was short-lived. Why didn't Amy want to go out with him then? "So… you think because you were a waitress, I shouldn't want to go out with you?" He couldn't hide the confusion he felt from his expression.

Amy shifted to face him. "You were raised differently than I was. You were raised with two parents in your home who cared about you. They made religion an important part of your life. You're educated. You're a lawyer, for goodness sake."

"You say that like being a lawyer is a bad thing." Ben debated whether to take offense.

"No. We're just… different."

He tried to follow her logic. "If I continued working as a mechanic, would you go out with me?"

Amy dropped her eyes and fiddled with the hem of her blouse.

Why was she so reluctant? Was the attraction between them all one-sided? His voice was tinged with anger when he spoke again. "So, it's okay for a waitress to go out with the well-to-do sheriff or a wealthy rancher, but not a lawyer?"

Her eyes jumped up to meet his. "I only went out with them so they would agree to the auction, you know that."

Ben bit his tongue to keep from volunteering for the auction so Amy would agree to go out with him. The last thing he needed was Debbie winning.

"But you go to lunch every Friday with Robert."

"That's not…"

"Not what? A date? I can assure you Robert considers it a date."

Amy's eyes widened.

Hope surged in Ben's chest, and his eyes narrowed on Amy. "I hope your surprise means you don't consider Robert and yourself a couple."

"What? No. We're just friends." A blush belied Amy's words.

The same kind of blush he saw on her face multiple times last Saturday. Amy was attracted to Robert. Ben's stomach tightened.

"Listen, Ben, I've made some bad choices and haven't lived the kind of life most people of your social standing would approve of."

What was she saying? He stared into Amy's eyes, trying to understand the real source of her reluctance.

"Have you ever been a prostitute or a stripper?"

Amy gasped. "No!"

Ben couldn't hide the relief he felt at her response. "Then there's nothing you could say to make me change my mind about wanting to go out with you. Have I ever done or said anything to make you feel you aren't good enough because you were raised differently or grew up poor?"

"No, you and your parents have been very accepting of me, despite my background."

"Does social status matter that much to you? Have you always been this insecure about your upbringing and lack of wealth?"

She shrugged. "I don't know. I've always been aware there were people much better off than me. But instead of letting it get me down, I've usually tried to make the best of my circumstances. I've always worked hard to improve my situation, but after my experience with Lance… The more popular his band became, the less he wanted to do with me. Sometimes, I feel like I can't rise above my upbringing."

"Well, Lance is a ja—" He cleared his throat and glanced over his shoulder toward the kitchen. "A jerk. I can think of a more appropriate word, but like you said, my parents raised me with religion and would wash my mouth out with soap if they heard me use it."

Amy laughed. "You're right, Lance *is* a jerk!"

"Glad we agree on that." Raking his fingers through his hair, he took a deep breath. "I didn't think this was going to be so hard. If you don't want to go out with me, you can say so."

A LUMP FORMED in Amy's throat as she considered how difficult it must be for Ben to open up like this and put himself out there again.

"I do want to go out with you."

It scared her how badly she wanted to go out with Ben, and that was the problem. She couldn't fall for the first man to come along. And she was definitely falling. The more time she spent with him, the deeper she fell.

Ben may find her attractive, but when he really got to know her, he'd find she wasn't lovable. Like Lance did. And like her mother.

When she left Lance, she vowed never to get mixed up with a man again. Especially not a man who couldn't fully commit to her. She couldn't endure the heartache of betrayal again, and she had to protect her daughter. She couldn't control the men she dated. She could hardly control herself. That's why she needed to avoid dating altogether.

She dropped her eyes. "But I can't."

Ben leaned closer, lifting her chin, his fingers warm against her skin. "Can't or won't?"

His deep blue eyes robbed Amy's lungs of air. Her heart stuttered then raced, as his breath caressed her cheek. She sucked in a sharp breath, and closed her eyes against his probing gaze, hoping he couldn't see the affect his nearness had on her.

"I see." Her eyes flew open again at his quiet words. Understanding dawned in his. "This isn't about Lance, not really. Nor does it have anything to do with your upbringing."

Pulling away from Ben's fingers, Amy blinked back the sudden hot tears that flooded her eyes. "It has everything to do with my upbringing. I'm a product of my environment. I'm my mother's daughter."

Ben's brow furrowed. "Amy, you are not your mother."

"No, I'm worse than my mother." She buried her face in her hands.

"How so?"

No way would she tell him how strongly she was affected by his kiss, a mere two weeks after leaving Lance. How she longed for him to take her in his arms and kiss her again.

"When you left Lance, why did you run?"

Amy dropped her hands and frowned at him.

"Why didn't you stay with a friend until you found another job and got on your feet again?"

"I couldn't..."

"Couldn't what?"

Amy bit her lip to keep the thoughts racing through her head from escaping out her mouth. *I couldn't risk making the same mistake and getting rejected again. So, I left, only to find myself falling for the first single man I meet, as well as the second, and the third.* Technically, Rudy was the third, and he was cute, but he was young. Stifling a groan, she started to get to her feet. She had to put some distance between her and Ben.

But he caught her hand. "Amy, please don't run from this. From me."

Sitting back, she watched James carry Kallie from the kitchen to his office, with Hope hot on his heels. The click of the closing door made her long for Kallie's distraction. Had Ben planned this with his parents?

She let out a deep sigh. "I'd already given Lance so many chances. I was afraid if I stayed, I'd give in again, only to have him take advantage of me and cheat on me all over again."

"It was more than that though, wasn't it? You couldn't stay in Portland and continue working at a bar because you were afraid you'd turn out like your mother, weren't you? Make the same mistake, again and again. If not with Lance, then with someone else."

Lowering her eyes, she gave a slight nod. She couldn't believe how perceptive Ben was. Would he guess her deepest fear?

I'm not lovable.

"You said it yourself, you're a product of your environment. You're in a different environment now, Amy. You won't make the same mistakes here that you did in Portland."

A new environment can't suddenly make me lovable.

Amy bit back the words, instead she said, "A new environment doesn't change who... or what I am."

"And what are you, Amy?" Ben laughed, his eyes lighting with amusement. "That's what this is about? You don't want to go out with me because you're attracted to me?"

The conclusion he'd jumped to surprised Amy, and she wanted to deny it, but she couldn't. "I... um... how...?"

"You think something is wrong with you because you're a red-blooded female who responds to a man's kiss?"

Amy's eyes widened, and heat filled her cheeks as she remembered exactly how she'd reacted to his kiss a few weeks ago.

"Yes, I noticed you responded when I kissed you." Pride laced Ben's words. He reached out and played with a lock of her hair, shooting tingles across her scalp.

"I... um, yeah, but it's not... just...." The heat in her face made her eyes burn.

"Let me guess, you're disappointed in yourself because you find Robert attractive too."

Wishing the floor would open up and swallow her, Amy groaned and leaned her head against her knees. Her silence, an admission of guilt.

"Did Robert kiss you?" Ben's question was quiet.

Her head flew up. "No, but..." She bit her lip to keep from admitting she'd kind of wanted him to.

"But if he had, you're afraid you would have kissed him back." When Amy lowered her eyes, he went on, "So what? That's what you're supposed to do when someone kisses you. It doesn't make you some sort of… slut."

"You don't understand. I can't… do this. I can't trust… myself around… men."

"All men? Or just me and Robert?"

Amy looked anywhere and everywhere except for at Ben. "I don't know. I mean, the smell of Jake's—" She cut herself off as she realized what she was about to say.

Ben chuckled. "But Jake didn't kiss you either."

Amy cringed. "Did he tell you I was a basket case when he brought me home?"

"Is that why he kissed your hand and left so quickly?" Amusement danced in his eyes.

Amy's eyes narrowed on Ben. Somehow, Jake didn't strike her as the type to tell his cousin, no matter how close they were, that he kissed a girl's hand at the end of a date.

Ben blushed this time. He scratched his neck. "I… uh… may have been working on Debbie's blinds… when he brought you home."

How had the conversation turned to Amy *not* kissing Ben's cousins? The absurdity of their conversation hit her. Remembering how flustered she'd been and picturing a jealous Ben peeking through Debbie's blinds to see if Jake would kiss her suddenly struck her as funny.

She burst out laughing. "I was so afraid Jake might kiss me and I'd respond to him like I had you, that I totally freaked out. He probably thought me the most socially awkward person ever."

Ben's laughter joined hers. She loved his laugh.

After a few moments, he sobered. "But you felt something when he kissed your hand, didn't you?"

Amy met his eyes. "Do you ever miss anything?"

Something darkened in Ben's gaze. "Not when it's important to me."

Amy's heart somersaulted. *Am I important to you?*

Ben took her hand, causing her heart to stall altogether. "Were you ever unfaithful to Lance while you were with him?"

"Never."

"You slapped him because he doubted your fidelity."

"You heard that?" The color drained from her face. Had he also heard her question Lance about Eddie? Of course, she hadn't told Lance why she needed to find the drummer.

"You were angry when he questioned your morals. So why do you question yourself?"

Ben was right. Lance was the only man she'd ever been with, and she'd been with him a little over three years. In all that time, she'd never looked at another man. So why was she so drawn to Ben *and* his cousins?

Was it because of the kind of men they were? The quality of men in her current environment were much better than any man she'd ever met before. But that didn't change who she was inside. Whether Ben was the first man to come along or the tenth, she'd probably still have fallen for him. His sapphire eyes and dimple did funny things to her insides.

Ben stroked the back of her hand. "Amy, you are not your mother. And I am not Lance."

Warmth spread through Amy as Ben's thumb drew lazy circles on the back of her hand. No, he was nothing like Lance. Lance had never made her feel this excited and confused. Which meant it would hurt that much worse when Ben realized he couldn't find anything to love about her.

Knowing she was probably making the biggest mistake of her life, she relented. "Okay, I'll go out with you." She tugged her hand away. "But I need you to stop doing that."

Ben chuckled and straightened his legs, leaning his back against the couch again. Picking up one of Kallie's toys, he played with it absently.

"Did I ever tell you what job Melanie was working when I met her?" When Amy shook her head, he said, "She was a night janitor at the law offices where I worked." He winked at her. "If I can handle being seen in public with a janitor, I think I can handle going out with a waitress or a dispatcher or whatever you want to call yourself."

But could he really, truly love her?

CHAPTER 25

*M*onday morning, Amy sat at her desk wondering where to start.

She was almost certain, if she could find Eddie, she'd find Ben's daughter. She'd studied the picture on her phone last night and was convinced Cassey was the baby she'd seen Eddie's wife holding. But where did she find Eddie?

Chewing her bottom lip, she did a general Internet search on Edward Green. The whole first page of results were of an English shoemaker, creator of the *Gentleman's Footwear*. She scrolled through other results finding nothing of interest.

Returning to the search bar, she typed in Eddie Green and hit enter. Leaning forward, she studied the results. A Great Depression era bank robber, an African American actor who died in 1950, and a football player for Brigham Young University, wherever that was.

Something tightened around Amy's midsection and a restlessness filled her as she studied the remaining results. None of them looked like the Eddie Green she knew. Searches of social network sites yielded nothing, which didn't surprise Amy. Of course, if Eddie had kidnapped Cassey he would keep a low profile.

How am I supposed to find Cassey if I can't figure out where Eddie lives?

If only she could remember Eddie's wife's name.

Frustrated, she went to the records room and got Melanie's file. She thought she was prepared this time for the photos it contained, but they still hit her harder than she expected.

She took a deep breath and searched for the information about the vehicle that hit Melanie. There it was. Atlantic blue metallic 1996 Chevrolet Suburban. What shade of blue was Eddie's Suburban? It had always appeared almost black under the streetlights. For the third time since hearing about the accident, Amy searched for '96 Suburbans and grill guards.

After seeing both on her computer screen, she was certain that's what Eddie's Suburban had looked like.

How do I find Eddie, though?

Amy's eyes darted to the clock when she spotted Janice's car pulling in the front parking lot. *Is it almost noon already?* She shoved Melanie's file into the top desk drawer under other miscellaneous papers.

Hopefully, she'd find more information tomorrow.

AMY LEANED against the corner of Rudy's desk. "How would I go about finding out where an old friend lives now?"

"I have access to an awesome database that has all the information you could ever want on a person." Then he grimaced. "But I could get fired if I used it for personal reasons."

Amy's face fell. "That's what I was afraid of."

"You can get most of the same information yourself online. Here, I'll show you." Rudy turned to his computer. "What's the name?"

She thought about giving the name of a high school friend, but she might only have one chance at this.

It would be easier to tell Robert or Rudy her suspicions and let them help find the information she needed. But as certain as she was, she didn't want to get anyone's hopes up, in case she was wrong. Or in the event they found Eddie Green, but he no longer had Ben's daughter.

Melanie's death and Cassey's disappearance had rocked this community. She didn't want to open any wounds or give anyone hope until she had a worthwhile lead.

"Eddie Green."

Rudy's eyebrows raised. "An old boyfriend? Do I need to warn the sheriff?"

"No!" Amy said, louder than she intended. She lowered her voice. "He's just a friend. I'm curious where he's at and what he's been up to. That's all."

I'm really curious about what he's been up to.

Why would Rudy think he needed to warn Robert? Did he assume there was something between her and Robert? She'd only gone out on one date with him, but Ben did say Robert viewed their lunches as dates. Technically, Robert was on duty when he took her out to lunch, so it couldn't be considered dating, could it?

That would stop now that she worked afternoons at the diner. Either way, she didn't want Robert to know anything about Eddie, yet. Not until she found out whether he had Cassey.

Rudy scrolled through the Eddies who were basketball and rugby players and clicked on a link that opened a list of additional Eddie Greens. "Let's see. There are several Eddie Greens here," Rudy said. "Do you know his parents' name, or siblings, maybe a spouse?"

"Um… I don't remember."

"Look at the names of relatives associated with these Eddies and see if any of them ring a bell."

Amy leaned close to Rudy's shoulder and studied the names. She scanned through most of the list before she saw a familiar name.

Clara. That was Eddie's wife's name.

She pointed at the monitor. "This one."

"Are you sure?" When she nodded, he clicked on the name. "At this point, you can do some cyber-stalking to see if you can find him on any of the social media sites." He clicked on something and more sights popped up. "Or you can go to these people-search sites that provide more specific information for a fee. You have to decide how badly you want to find him. I'd recommend this one." He clicked again. "It's a little pricier than the others, but it's more reliable than most of the sites, and it allows you to do as many searches as you want in a month for a single fee."

"Thanks, I'll check these out on my computer and see what I can find."

"Now you're being secretive. Are you sure I don't need to tell the Sheriff?"

"Why would Robert care that I'm looking up an old friend?" Amy asked. "There's nothing between us."

"Seriously? He took you dancing a while back and you have lunch together every Friday."

How did Rudy know she'd gone dancing with Robert?

Right, this was a small town and people liked to gossip. Was that why Robert took her to lunch on Fridays? To establish a relationship between them, knowing word would get back to a certain widow?

Had it worked? Debbie hadn't called the Sheriff's Office for a couple weeks now.

Was Robert interested in more? After the buckshot thing, He'd joked about asking her out a gain, but he hadn't—other than their Friday lunches—and Amy was glad. He was a nice man, but she wasn't ready to jump into another relationship yet.

She kept telling herself that, but she couldn't wait for her date with Ben this Friday.

Ignoring Rudy, she returned to her desk and paid the fee to the website the deputy had suggested. If she found Ben's daughter, it would be worth every penny. She hated using her debit card, but since she no longer had a credit card, she didn't have a choice.

Adrenaline rushed through Amy twenty minutes later as she wrote down Eddie's last known address. With an address in hand, she couldn't wait to find him.

And Cassey.

AMY PULLED her car to a stop where State Road 22 met Highway 15. This was where it happened. This was where Melanie died.

The state road ended in a "T" at the two-lane highway. She could easily see how a distracted or speeding driver could easily miss the turn.

Putting her car in gear, she turned down the country road toward Eddie's last known address. She'd left early this afternoon after telling Charity she had some personal things to take care of. She felt bad taking time off already, but she needed to track down Eddie.

A few minutes later, Amy pulled her car up to a small white clapboard-sided house. It looked old with a tiny unkempt yard. A small detached garage, missing a door, stood beside the house. An old, pale blue Oldsmobile filled the small structure.

Disappointment tugged at her when she didn't spot a blue Suburban anywhere on the property. *Of course, that would be too easy.* Besides, she doubted Eddie actually lived here. She knew he lived some distance outside of Portland and had a lengthy drive to come play with the band. That was why he was often late or a no-show, especially if he had car problems, which he often did.

This place was only forty minutes from Providence. If Eddie lived here, he'd have at least a three-hour drive to Portland. When she'd gone with Lance last year to talk to Eddie, she remembered it being a long drive, but not this far from Portland. Besides, this house looked nothing like she remembered from last year.

Amy approached the front door and knocked. No one answered, so she knocked again, longer, and louder. She was about to walk away when the door finally opened. A young woman squinted at the bright sunlight. Judging by the dark shadows around her eyes and her tousled, mousy-brown hair, Amy had woken her.

She was too desperate for answers to feel bad. "I'm sorry to bother you, but I'm trying to find Eddie Green."

The girl stifled a yawn. "Um… he hasn't lived here for years."

"Are you related to him?"

"He's my cousin."

"Do you know where I can find him?"

"Who are you, and why are you looking for him?" The girl asked, now more awake.

"He's an old friend," Amy said. "He used to be the drummer in my boyfriend's band, the Lance—"

"The Lance Hayes band." The girl cut in. "I remember that. They used to call him Sticks. He was really mad when Lance fired him."

"I'm sure he was. I know Lance felt bad about having to let him go." Amy hoped to get the girl talking. "When was the last time you saw Eddie?"

"It's been forever." She brushed the hair out of her eyes. "He came to pick up some stuff shortly after my grandma's funeral last October. That was right around the time he got fired from the band. I bet if he'd just told Lance what he was dealing with, Lance would've understood and wouldn't have fired him."

"You're probably right," Amy said, although she doubted it. Lance had only ever been loyal to himself. "So, your grandmother was Eddie's grandmother too?" She asked, trying to get as much information as she could.

"No, my grandma was his aunt, but she was like a mother to him. His own mom walked out when he was young. He lived with my grandma as a teenager, after his dad went to prison. She got sick last year and died. Eddie took it hard. And to lose his job about the same time, it wasn't fair, you know."

"It wasn't." Amy nodded. "Do you know where Eddie lives now?"

"Not really. I think he's living in his dad's old house."

The house I visited with Lance?

"Do you know the address of his dad's house?" Amy held her breath. When the girl didn't say anything, she said, "You see, my boyfriend lost his drummer again." It was true. Although, she doubted Lance would ever hire Eddie back. He'd been too flaky.

"I don't know… I barely remember going there once or twice when I was young, but I do remember it was on the other side of Kennewick. Way out in the middle of nowhere, in the forest or something. I remember a lot of trees."

Amy's heart rate kicked up. *A lot of trees.* That's what she remembered too. Further questions to the woman, didn't provide any more information concerning the location of Eddie's dad's house. But she did get his father's name, Larry Green, and his aunt's name, Gladys Pike. She wanted to check obituaries to see exactly when she died in comparison to the accident that killed Melanie.

As Amy left, she paused again where the state road met the highway. Had Eddie been visiting his sick aunt last year on that rainy night?

She hurried home, anxious to see what she could find out about a property owned by Larry Green.

CHAPTER 26

*A*my parked her car as far off the road as possible, hoping it wouldn't be spotted. If she'd found the right place, Eddie's dad's house, and hopefully Ben's daughter, would be at the end of the lane.

With no address posted, not even a mailbox, she had to assume this lane—the only one for miles—was Deer Creek Road, which meant the surrounding property belonged to Larry Green. A sagging gate with a 'No Trespassing' blocked the narrow opening in the trees.

Climbing from the car, she approached the gate and crouched, slipping first one leg through the rails then the rest of her body. Once through, she hurried to the cover of the trees, wishing there were more leaves to hide her and her fuchsia jacket. Fall had taken its toll on the aspen and cottonwood trees. Thank goodness for the evergreens.

Her feet crunched on the dry leaves, and Amy froze. Any other time, she would've appreciated the beautiful colors of the Autumn leaves, but today, she shivered despite the mild temperature. Breathing in the crisp fall air, she let it out slowly, and attempted to calm her nerves. Zipping her jacket a little higher, she shoved her hands in her pockets and walked down the lane.

Her stomach hardened. *I should never have come alone. I'll take a quick look around. If I find anything concrete, I'll leave and call Robert.*

But she couldn't get his or anyone else's hopes up until she knew if Eddie lived on the property she'd found registered in Larry Green's name. She'd also discovered Gladys Pike had died the day after the accident that killed Melanie Young. After she discovered this information yesterday, she asked Rudy to cover the last two hours of her shift at the Sheriff's Office and arranged for one of the morning waitresses to cover for her at the diner so Charity wouldn't overdo it.

Amy needed to investigate.

With every step, she prayed she'd find the blue Suburban and Cassey. Of course, if she found Cassey she'd find Eddie, and she had no desire to confront him.

This is a stupid idea. Amy thought she'd stopped making stupid decisions. *Apparently not.* She was too close to turn back now.

Fifty yards down the lane, she rounded a curve in the dirt road and spotted a large, old, wooden barn, long since devoid of any paint. Its tin roof, brown from rust, curled up at one corner, the casualty of severe windstorms. The entire structure leaned precariously to one side.

An empty round corral with several missing poles guarded giant tumbleweeds behind the barn. Not an animal in sight.

Twenty yards to the south of the barn sat a small farmhouse, in desperate need of paint and new shingles. Its screen door hung crookedly on its hinges.

Her trip here last year flashed in her mind. When she and Lance walked down this lane, they'd found Eddie working on the engine of a green van. Lance had gone straight to Eddie, but Amy had spotted Clara in the backyard.

Amy's gaze shifted to the old, rusted, swing set that looked like it had been there for decades. The only swing, a new, blue, plastic baby swing, swayed in the breeze. Had it really been Ben's daughter she'd seen a year ago?

She studied the house and yard for signs of life. An old gray Buick missing both front tires sat on cinder blocks on the far side of the house, surrounded by tumbleweeds. The raised hood created an ominous, gaping mouth with a single headlight hanging from its casing.

The place appeared deserted.

Catching a faint scent of wood smoke, Amy's gaze jumped to the chimney of the house. She couldn't see any smoke rising, but the fact she could smell smoke told her someone lived here. Was Eddie trying to live off the grid? Power lines running to the house suggested he wasn't completely successful. But according to county records, the land was still in his father's name, making Eddie a difficult man to find.

Will I find him?

Her eyes returned to the barn. If Eddie's Suburban was here, that's where it'd be. She spotted a man-door to the right of the large double doors. Hopefully, it wasn't locked.

She rubbed suddenly damp palms against her jeans. *Get in, take a quick look, and get out.*

After a final glance around, she darted to the door and slipped into the old barn. Closing the door behind her, she let out the breath she'd been holding and waited for her eyes to adjust to the dim interior. The small window on the far wall, covered in dirt and cobwebs, let in little light.

She wrinkled her nose as the dank, musty air mingled with mildew and oil hit her. Pressing her back to the door, she shuddered at the scurry of rodents in the dark recesses of the barn. She hated mice and rats.

Forcing herself to take a deep breath, she stepped away from the door. *You can do this.*

Now that her eyes had adjusted, she focused her gaze on the massive tarp-covered object in the center of the barn. Her heart leapt to her throat. Could this be the evidence she wanted?

Excitement out-weighed caution, and she lifted the tarp, pushing it back to reveal an older-model blue Suburban with a grille guard. Amy's heart pounded so hard, that if Lance was here, he would hire her to be his new drummer.

This is it! This is the Suburban Robert has searched for.
She was sure of it.

One edge of the grille guard pressed into the radiator, and the corner of the hood was crumpled. But the real damage was to the headlight and its casing. She knelt and peered at the bumper—originally silver, now a dull gray. One end pushed back into the dented frame of the vehicle. Deep scrapes, like an unattended, bloody wound, left an angry scar complete with flecks of red paint.

Amy's breath came faster as her pulse picked up again. She studied the dents and scrapes and found more red paint around the crumpled headlight. Excited, she pulled out her cell phone. Because of the dimness inside the barn, she used her flash, hoping it wouldn't distort the colors. She snapped several pictures including one of the front tire. Her untrained eye saw a tread that might match the tracks left in the mud near Melanie's car.

I did it! Now what?

She couldn't wait to share the news with someone. Swiping through the photos she'd taken, she selected the best one to send to Robert, hoping two bars of reception would be enough to send the message. She deliberated over the words to include in the text. Finally, she typed in the words: *I think I found the Suburban that killed Melanie Young.* On impulse, she added Ben's name, creating a group text. She wanted to tell Ben she'd found his daughter, but she hadn't.

Not yet, anyway. But she was confident this lead would help them find Cassey soon.

She hit send.

As soon as she did, she regretted adding Ben to the message. Would her words be too direct for him? Too painful? She wanted to give him some hope. But was she premature in doing so?

Wishing she could undo what she'd just done, she stepped to the door. She needed to leave and call Robert. She grasped the knob then froze at the sound of a child's laughter. Turning, she walked to the window and peered through the dirty pane.

A woman with brown hair pushed a toddler-sized child in the

plastic baby swing. The child wore a red coat with the hood snug over its head.

Is it Cassey? Amy couldn't see the child's hair or eyes from this distance.

The toddler squealed again as the woman—Clara—snatched at her toes.

A fist squeezed Amy's heart. Ben should be the one pushing his daughter, making her laugh. She ached to march out there and confront the woman, to take the child back to her father, but that could be disastrous.

She'd already pushed the limit on stupid risks today. *This was dangerous,* she needed to remember that. She'd already been careless in including Ben in her text, she couldn't afford any more mistakes.

Turning off the flash, she raised her phone to the window, and took a picture. It'd be poor quality at this distance and through the dirty window, but at least she had proof of a child here the same age as Cassey. Now, she needed to leave and call the police.

She'd gripped the door knob a second time, when her cell phone rang. Startled, she jerked it from her pocket and answered it, hoping Clara hadn't heard it over the child's laughter.

"Hello," she whispered.

"Amy!" Ben's voice filled her ear. He definitely wasn't whispering. "Where on earth are you?"

"Ben, I'm pretty sure I found the suburban that caused your wife's accident." She struggled to keep her voice down amid her excitement.

"What? How?"

Amy didn't have time to answer his questions fully, but she owed him an explanation. Trying to speak in hushed tones, she walked back toward the window as she talked. "I saw the police report of your wife's death and Cassey's disappearance, and I couldn't stop thinking about it. For some reason, the details seemed familiar. When Lance came last week, I remembered some things, and I started putting the pieces together. So, I found Lance's old drummer's house. It's hard to find, because it's hidden in the trees out on Deer Creek Road. My hunch paid off, and I found the SUV."

She bit her tongue to keep from telling him she'd found his daughter too. *What if the child in the swing isn't Cassey?*

"Amy, I can hardly hear you, and you're not making sense."

A vehicle suddenly drove past the barn spraying gravel as it skidded to a stop. She peered toward the front of the house. A man jumped out of a green van. "Clara!"

Amy's stomach dropped. *Eddie.* He'd seen her car and knew someone was here.

Would he search for her?

Yes.

Did she dare make a run for it?

No. He'd catch her before she could get to her car.

"Amy?"

She jumped. She'd forgotten she was on the phone with Ben.

"Ben, someone's coming. I have to go," she whispered, hopefully loud enough for him to hear. "Don't call me back, he might hear my phone. Call Robert!" She ended the call, muted the volume, and stuffed her phone down her bra. Hopefully, if it vibrated, Eddie wouldn't hear it.

Heart racing, she pulled the tarp down over the front end of the Suburban and searched for somewhere to hide. A loft at the back of the barn looked promising, but Amy dismissed it as a possible hiding spot after one glance at the broken rungs on the ladder. Rusty oil drums filled one corner of the barn, and a short stack of old straw bales occupied the other. She approached the straw, intent on hiding behind it, but a scurry of rodents caused her to back away as quickly as she'd approached.

Panic rose in her throat as she realized her lack of options. Seeing no other place to hide, she dropped to the floor and rolled under the Suburban. The motion stirred up dust, and she inhaled the filthy air. Coughing, she squeezed her eyes closed at the sight of mice droppings scattered across the dirt floor.

When Eddie came to check the barn, and she knew he'd come to make sure his secret was safe, hopefully, he wouldn't find her. Then later, she could sneak out or at least call 911.

Wishful thinking? Yes, but it was the only positive thought she could conjure at the moment.

She jumped at the sound of the door to the house slamming. *He's coming.*

Blood pounded in her ears, and spots filled her vision. It's a good thing she was lying down because she thought she might pass out. She was in trouble here. With no one to help her.

Oh, why did I come alone?

Her desire to find Ben's daughter had driven her to make stupid decisions. Decisions that might cost her life and rob Kallie of a mother.

Amy bit back a scream when the door she'd used to enter the barn swung open.

"DON'T CALL ME BACK, he might hear my phone. Call Robert!"

"Amy?" Ben shouted.

The line was dead.

A vice closed around Ben's heart. Amy was in danger. His thumb hovered over Amy's name on his call list. Instead, he scrolled down a few calls and tapped Robert's number.

Not bothering to tell his secretary where he was going, he walked out of his office. He was on the street, headed toward the Sheriff's Office two blocks down by the time Robert answered.

"Did you get Amy's text?" Ben asked.

"I've been in a meeting with the Mayor. I was looking at it when you called."

Ben spun around and headed the other way, taking long strides. The city offices were around the corner from his office.

"What's going on? Where is she?"

"That's what I want to know," Ben demanded. Spotting Robert standing on the sidewalk, Ben walked up behind him and spun him around with a firm grip on his shoulder.

Both men dropped their phones into their pockets. Then Ben

grabbed the front of Robert's uniform in both fists, taking him by surprise. "What have you put her up to? Do you realize the danger you've put her in?"

Robert grasped Ben's wrists in a defensive hold. "Chill, Bro." He ground out through gritted teeth. "I have no idea what you're talking about. Amy was at the office when I left this morning."

Ben released a pent-up breath and the front of Robert's shirt at the same time. "She's in danger." Robert's eyes widened, and Ben spoke talking over his shoulder, as he walked toward Robert's Tahoe. "I called her after I received her text. She spoke really fast and quiet, like she was afraid someone might hear. She said something about Lance and his drummer and something about Deer Creek. Then she said someone was coming, and she didn't want me to call her back for fear he would hear her phone. She sounded terrified, Robert."

They drove the two blocks back to the sheriff's office and raced in, hoping to find Amy at her desk. Instead, Janice greeted them.

"Where's Amy?" Both men said in unison.

"I don't know. Rudy was covering when I came in."

Hearing his name, Rudy walked out of the large office he shared with the other deputies.

"Where's Amy?" Robert demanded again.

Rudy's eyebrows rose as though surprised by Robert's gruff tone. He shrugged. "She said she had some personal things to take care of this morning and asked if I could cover for her for a couple hours. I assumed she'd cleared it with you. She's probably at the diner by now."

Robert pulled out his cell phone.

He snapped it closed again after a quick call to Aunt Charity. "She asked for the afternoon off." Scowling, Robert turned to Ben. "Tell me, again, everything she said on the phone."

Ben paced as he repeated every detail from his brief conversation with Amy. His chest grew tighter with each step.

"Rudy, search for a Deer Creek. Let's see if we can get an idea of where she might be," Robert said, pinching his bottom lip. He joined Ben in his pacing. "What does Lance and his drummer have to do with anything?"

Janice stood and stepped back to let Rudy have access to her computer.

Ben stepped in front of Robert, nearly colliding with him. "Did you ask her to investigate Melanie's death and Cassey's kidnapping?"

"No," Robert said. "She asked about Melanie's accident once, shortly after she first came to Providence, but that was it."

"Um... I may know something about that." Rudy tugged at his collar. "She asked a lot of questions about... the accident, when she first started working here, so I got the file out and showed her the evidence we gathered and explained the findings from the State Crime Lab." Robert glared at him as he continued. "I put the file back, myself, that same day, but I found it in her drawer earlier this week when I was searching for some paper clips." He pulled open a drawer and rifled around. "It's gone now."

"I'll go check the records room," Janice said.

Robert and Ben paced the small reception area again, waiting for Janice to return.

"Here it is."

Robert took the file and flipped through its many pages while Rudy focused on the computer. He closed the file and slapped it down on the desk. "Nothing's missing."

Ben was torn between wanting to see the file and knowing he couldn't handle the pictures he'd find in there.

"The nearest Deer Creek I can find is in Klickitat County. Deer Creek Road is on the outskirts of Glenwood. It looks pretty remote."

Ben glanced at Robert. "Didn't Lance and Amy discuss something about Glenwood last Saturday?"

"That's about two hours away. What time did Amy leave?"

Rudy checked the clock. "About two and a half hours ago."

Robert pointed at Rudy as he backed toward the door. "Send me a link with that map and the number for the Klickitat County Sheriff. We'll see if they can track Amy's cell phone and find out exactly where she is. And get a hold of Lance Hayes. Find out any information you can about his drummer, let's find out what he's got to do with this."

Ben followed Robert out the door.

Robert paused when they reached his Tahoe. "Are you sure you want to come? I have no idea what we may find. I don't want you to get your hopes up. Nor do I want to cause you any more pain."

"I'm coming," Ben said, without hesitation. He climbed in and slammed the door.

CHAPTER 27

*T*he hair on Amy's neck rose as well-worn work boots entered the barn. They scraped the ground, stirring up small swirls of dust, as they circled the Suburban. Were these the boots that left the prints in the mud at the scene of the accident?

Her heartbeat, along with each breath, thundered in her ears. Could he hear her breathing?

The boots paused near the window, then turned toward the Suburban again, and Amy held her breath.

Dark images of being a child, hiding under her bed to avoid her abusive stepdads crowded her mind. Her childhood fears intensified as she acknowledged the danger she was in. Fighting the panic, she focused on taking slow, even breaths.

"I know you're in here." A deep voice pierced the silence and Amy flinched.

Was that the drummer? For the life of her, she couldn't remember what Stick's voice sounded like. Not that she'd ever heard the drummer talk much. This voice sounded cold, menacing. "You may as well come out because I'm not leaving this barn until I find you."

Amy lay frozen in fear. She watched as he again circled the Suburban, coming to a stop where she'd rolled under. A jolt of fear arced through her as he dropped to one knee and lay a hunting rifle on the ground.

A gun? *I'm in so much trouble.*

The tarp lifted and strong hands grabbed her ankles.

She screamed as he yanked her out from under the vehicle.

He released her legs and grabbed the gun again, pointing it at her as he stood. "Who are you? And what are you doing in my barn?"

Amy had been in some terrifying situations when she was young, but she'd never felt the kind of fear that surged through her now, staring at the barrel of the rifle aimed at her. Every muscle in her body tensed as she contemplated making a run for the door.

No. I'll never make it.

Eddie would shoot her in the back.

Afraid to make any sudden movements, she held her hands out in surrender as she slowly sat up and leaned her back against the Suburban.

Eddie hadn't changed much. Long, greasy hair still hung to his shoulders and thin, straggly facial hair did nothing to improve his appearance. The nickname Sticks was not only because he was a drummer but also because of his tall, slender build. He looked like he'd lost weight in the past year. Was it the stress of keeping his secret? His sunken cheeks made him look terrifying.

Or maybe it was the gun that terrified her. Amy repressed a shudder.

He'd never believe she'd wandered in here by accident, so she decided to tell the truth in the least threatening way possible. Clasping her trembling hands together in her lap, and keeping her voice as calm as possible, she smiled with feigned bravado. "Hello, Sticks."

Eddie's eyebrows shot up. "Aren't you Lance's girlfriend, the waitress?"

"Ex-girlfriend."

"What are you doing here?" Lance's girlfriend or not, he considered her a threat.

267

"You can put the gun down. I'm no threat to you." Amy said, trying to sound nonchalant, hoping to hide the quivering she felt inside.

"You're trespassing on private property." His face was hard.

"What are you worried about? Are you hiding something?" Could she get him to talk, without divulging she knew exactly what he was hiding?

"I'm asking the questions here," he said, leveling the gun at her head. "And you still haven't answered my first one. What are you doing here?"

Ignoring his question, she cleared her throat. "I left Lance, you know." She wasn't sure why she said that, other than to ease the tension in the barn and buy herself some time. Eddie's only response was a grunt. "He started cheating on me when his band went on tour last year."

"Started?" Eddie's smirk held no sympathy.

Amy reeled.

"What's that supposed to mean?" Though she feared Eddie, at the moment, she didn't care what kind of threat he posed, she needed answers.

He sneered, making no attempt to hide his disdain for Lance. "To say Lance started cheating on you would imply he'd been faithful for a time."

Eddie may as well have struck her—the words stung that bad. But deep down she knew they were true. *Why had I ever thought Lance loved me?*

"Was he ever faithful to any woman?" She asked, her voice barely above a whisper. She needed to know if it was her or if Lance was incapable of loving *anyone*.

Eddie gave a short shake of his head. "Nor were you the first girl he ever got pregnant."

Amy squeezed her eyes shut to hold in the sudden tears that flooded them. *Lance fathered other children?* Amy had already admitted to herself, and Ben, that she didn't love Lance, so why did this news hurt so much?

"He only moved in with you because you had a steady job and a decent apartment."

Bile rose in her throat. Lance had used her. He'd always used her, and she had let him. *How could I have been so stupid?*

She'd had so many examples in her mom's string of boyfriends. She should've seen Lance was not the kind of man she wanted to get mixed up with. But no, she'd let herself be swept away by his charm.

Was I so desperate to be loved that I overlooked the kind of person he really was?

She didn't have time to mull over and answer her own question, because Eddie took a step closer and lifted the gun a little higher. "Enough about Lance. Now, tell me what you're doing here."

Just as well. She wouldn't have liked her own answer.

Amy let out a nervous chuckle and pushed the hair back from her face with a shaky hand. "The night I left Lance, my car broke down in a nice little town called Providence." She watched him carefully to gauge his reaction.

His eyes narrowed.

She continued, choosing her words with care. "I met a nice man there, a widower, by the name of Ben Young."

The muscle in Eddie's jaw tensed.

She waited a moment, biting her bottom lip to see if he would say anything, but he remained silent, holding the gun steady. "I also started working at the Sheriff's Office."

Panic flashed in his eyes.

Oops. Shouldn't have mentioned the Sheriff's Office. She would be signing her death warrant if she pressed for a confession, but she couldn't seem to stop herself.

She took a slow deliberate breath. "The more I got to know Ben and saw how deep his grief was, the more interested I became in learning about the circumstances of his wife's death, and his daughter's disappearance. When I read the police report, certain details stuck with me, and I couldn't get them out of my mind. Then last week, Lance came to see me, and I remembered some things. I knew someone who drove a blue Suburban. *You.* And you mysteriously stopped driving it about a year ago."

Eddie's shoulders hunched, and he shifted from one foot to the other.

"I also remembered coming here with Lance a few weeks later and seeing your wife with a baby girl. She said you were fostering to adopt, and I didn't question it, because I was happy for her. Despite the pictures everywhere, of the missing Cassey Young, I didn't put two and two together. Of course, I had my own problems at that time. You see, when you started missing gigs, Lance started drinking more. You knew Lance well enough to know he got angry when he drank heavily and guess who he took his anger out on."

"Lance's drinking problem was not my fault," Eddie said through gritted teeth.

"You're right." Swallowing hard, she said. "But the hell Ben Young has endured this past year is." The words were bold, but she knew she was right. It was dangerous, but if she was going to get the truth out of him, she couldn't be meek about this. "What happened, Sticks? Why did you do it?"

A pained expression crossed his face, surprising her. "It was an accident. I never meant to hurt anyone. It had been raining, and the road was wet. I swear I tried to stop."

"Why didn't you call 911?"

"My cell phone had died," he said. "Besides, I was afraid... if I called, they'd find out I hit her... and I couldn't have anyone know it was my fault."

"Why were you afraid?" Amy's brow wrinkled. "If it was an accident..."

"It *was* an accident!" His eyes flashed. "But I couldn't let the police find out I'd hit her."

"You said it yourself, it had been raining," Amy prodded. "You might have been fined, but leaving the scene of the accident, that's a hit and run."

Eddie glared at her.

She softened her voice. "I'm trying to understand why you did it, Eddie." Would using his real name help her situation?

"I'd been visiting my dying aunt, and I had a few beers before heading home. If I'd been caught drinking and driving one more time, I would have lost my license, maybe even done some jail time."

Eddie's confession both excited and terrified her. Determined to hide her fear, she tried to keep him talking. "So, in addition to drinking and driving, and hit and run, you decided to add kidnapping because you'd already screwed up? Is that why you took the baby?" She shouldn't accuse him like this, but she needed to hear the whole story.

"No!" He raked his left hand through his hair while holding the rifle with his right. "I never wanted to hurt anyone. But when the woman asked me to check on her baby, something hit me, and I thought if I took the baby, it would solve my problems."

"How was kidnapping going to solve your problems?"

"Clara was going to leave me," he said, the pain evident in his voice. "She wanted children so badly, and I hadn't been able to give her any. We'd talked about adopting, but we couldn't afford it. I couldn't lose her, so I took the baby because that's the one thing Clara wanted."

"Did it actually solve your problems?" Amy couldn't understand his twisted reasoning.

"Sort of." He paced a tight line in front of her. "At first, she was angry with me and insisted I take the baby to the police and turn myself in. But it was late and storming, so I promised I would do it in the morning. But by the next morning, she'd grown attached to the baby. I told her if I turned myself in, I'd go to jail and she'd lose me *and* the baby. I convinced her that we could be a family."

"I bet that secret has been a difficult one to keep, with pictures of Cassey Young plastered everywhere."

"We never dared take the baby anywhere. One of us always stayed here with her, usually Clara. She's a homebody, anyway."

"Do you work?" How had they been able to take care of Cassey?

He shrugged. "After Lance fired me from the band, it took me a while to find work. I wasn't sure we could afford to keep the baby, but I finally found factory work, and we've been getting by."

Amy had the confession she wanted. But would she live to testify against Eddie? Her stomach clenched at the thought of not making it out of this barn. Eddie obviously regretted what he'd done. But could she convince him to do the right thing and turn himself and Clara in? Did she even dare suggest it?

Planting his feet in front of her, he ceased his pacing. "Why did you have to come snooping around?" The anger in his eyes matched his gruff voice as he once again pointed the gun at her.

"I had to find some answers," she said more calmly than she felt. "Ben has suffered more than any man should have to endure."

"You should have kept your nose out of it. Now, I've got to decide what to do with you."

Amy's heart sank, and a weight settled in her stomach. "What *are* you going to do with me?"

He scratched the back of his neck. "I don't know."

"Look, Eddie, the car accident was just that, an accident. I know you didn't mean to kill Melanie Young, and I can tell you've had a hard time living with that this past year. And I don't think you want to hurt me. You're not that kind of person."

At least she hoped he wasn't.

"I'm not a murderer!"

Amy flinched at his words. Was he trying to convince her, or himself? How many times had he said those words in the past year?

He stepped closer, pressing the gun at her temple. "This is all your fault."

She squeezed her eyes shut and bit her lip to hold in the scream that clawed at her throat. *This is it.* She wrapped her trembling arms around herself, certain her racing heart would explode before the gun did.

Would it be as fast and painless as the movies portrayed? Would Ben ever forgive her for letting them get away with his daughter? Or Kallie for leaving her?

Swearing, Eddie spun around and walked to the corner of the barn.

The breath, Amy didn't realize she'd been holding, rushed out in a sob. Clapping a hand over her mouth, she blinked away the rush of tears.

He kept a close eye on her as he searched the dark recesses of the barn. Returning with a long rope, he knelt and set the gun down behind him. "Turn around."

With sharp, rough movements, he tied her hands behind her back. Then grabbing her shoulders, he dragged her to the support beam of the barn. After he tied her with her back to the beam, he stood, breathing heavily.

Amy wasn't sure whether to be relieved he hadn't shot her, or terrified of being left out here to die a slow death of thirst, starvation, and freezing temperatures.

"Eddie, please don't do this!"

"I can't have you going to the police."

"The police have already been contacted." Amy bit back the desperation that choked her.

Hopefully, Ben had called Robert, but he'd hardly been able to hear her. Would they even be able to figure out where she was?

Eddie's face paled.

"You've got a cell phone?" Swearing again, he knelt and checked her jacket pockets, then her jeans.

Nausea filled her from his proximity and body odor. He hesitated a moment before checking her bra for her cell phone. His hands on her body brought back all the fear and revulsion she'd lived with as a teenager. She was completely at this man's mercy. If he wanted to do something unthinkable to her, she was powerless to stop him.

He pulled the cell phone from inside her shirt and grabbed the rifle before standing.

"I told Clara to pack some bags. We'll be long gone before the police find this place." He spun and exited the barn.

Amy let out a long sigh. Her relief was short-lived, however. The temperature would likely drop below freezing tonight. She wouldn't survive out here. She pulled at the rope around her wrists, but quickly realized it was futile. Eddie had tied the rope tight, with the knot on the other side of the beam. No matter how she tried, she couldn't reach the knot. Her struggles only succeeded in tightening the rope, causing her fingers to tingle. Her gaze darted around, searching for something to cut the rope.

Nothing.

Pressure built behind her eyes as hopelessness swept over her.

Hope's words filled her mind. *Sometimes, the only thing you can do is pray.* Feeling the slightest glimmer of hope, Amy put her small, newfound faith to the test. "Please God, don't let them get away with Cassey. And please, take care of my sweet Kallie."

Would the police, or anyone, ever find her? If Ben and Robert couldn't figure out where she was, would help ever come?

The door to the house banged closed, followed by muffled voices. Then the van doors slammed with an air of victory and the engine roared to life.

A vice tightened around Amy's chest. She'd found Ben's daughter, but the kidnappers were getting away, taking Cassey with them. She leaned her head back against the beam and allowed hot tears to spill onto her cheeks. What would happen to Kallie if she died in this barn?

When she didn't come home, would Kallie be given to her mother to raise, since Lance wouldn't want her? She refused to think about the things she'd learned about him today. And her mom was the last person Amy wanted raising her daughter.

Without a doubt, she knew she wanted Ben to raise Kallie, especially since she'd failed to bring Cassey home. He and Kallie had formed a special bond over the last six weeks, but he would never be allowed to have Kallie.

She was supposed to go out with him tonight. She'd anticipated their date all week. More tears flowed down her cheeks. *I'll never see him again.* A sharp pain filled her chest, making it difficult to breathe.

Ben may have been the first man to come along after she left Lance, but he was the right man. She knew that now, and she was never going to get the chance to tell him.

The screaming sound of sirens pierced the silence in the barn. Amy gasped, her tears turning to tears of Joy. *"Thank you, Lord!"*

BEN CAUGHT the glance Robert tossed his direction. Though Robert kept a close eye on the road—he was driving too fast to be distracted. Ben could see the worry etched in his cousin's face.

Was he worried about Amy, like Ben was? Or was Robert worried about him?

His behavior since getting in the Tahoe had been erratic, but he couldn't help it. His chest had grown tight, and no matter how hard he tried, he couldn't seem to catch his breath. He'd loosened his tie and unbuttoned his top button, but it hadn't helped. Opening his window for the second time, he leaned his head out and sucked in deep gulps of air. But the wind resistance was too strong and only made it harder to breathe, so he closed the window again.

Bouncing his knee, Ben raked his fingers through his hair. He closed his eyes and recalled the way his insides had churned when Amy went after Lance last Saturday. He replayed her conversation with her ex-boyfriend in his head, focusing on the tension and excitement in Amy's voice. A bitter taste filled his mouth as he recalled Lance's questioning of Amy's fidelity.

I should have punched the jerk when I had the chance.

Robert reached over and squeezed his shoulder. "You okay, Bro?"

He stared at his balled fists. "I don't know, man." It came out a groan. "I can't do this again."

"I know this is hard for you, but it's important you don't get your hopes up about finding Cassey. Even if Amy found the Suburban that hit Melanie, it doesn't mean Cassey is there. It might give us a lead on her whereabouts," his voice dropped to little more than a whisper, "but I think it's best to prepare yourself for the worst."

"I know," Ben said. "It's not Cassey I'm worried about right now."

Robert's eyebrows shot up. "You're worried about Amy?"

How could Robert not be worried about Amy? They worked

together every day, had lunch on Fridays, and they'd gone out on a date. Robert wasn't the kind to talk about his relationships, but Ben knew he liked Amy. The familiar and uncomfortable feeling of jealousy rose in him.

Tonight. This was supposed to have been his night with Amy. He planned to let her know how much he liked her. To tell her how beautiful, intriguing, and special she was.

"I'm worried about Amy too. But she's a smart, strong woman. I'm sure she'll be fine. The local law enforcement officers are on their way to her."

"What if they're too late?" Ben again struggled to catch his breath. "If she found the person who kidnapped Cassey, they'll do anything to protect their secret. I don't think I could bear it if something happened to her." He raked his fingers through his hair.

Robert's eyes were on him again. So long, Ben feared he might run off the road. "Have you fallen in love with Amy?"

If Robert had asked him that yesterday, he would have denied it. He wanted to deny it now, but he couldn't. Yes, he found Amy attractive, but was he in love with her?

Knowing Amy was in danger tied his stomach in knots, and the thought of never seeing her again pierced his heart. Rubbing a hand against his chest, he let out a deep sigh. "I don't know. I wouldn't say I've *fallen* in love with her. I mean, I haven't felt my heart race or had my stomach drop when I'm around her like it did when I fell for Melanie. But I think about Amy all the time, and I can't wait to spend time with her. I'm always searching for excuses to go to my parent's house, so I can see her. Being with her feels... right. She makes me laugh, and I find myself flirting with her just to see her smile."

Robert slapped Ben on the knee. "Sounds like love to me."

"I can't tell her, though. I mean... assuming we find her..." Ben swallowed the fear choking him.

Robert squeezed his shoulder again. "Of course, we're going to find her, and she's going to be fine."

Ben wished he had Robert's confidence.

"Who falls in love after only knowing someone a few weeks?" Ben scoffed at himself.

Robert laughed. "Plenty of people. You two have a lot in common and you've been through a lot together. You've developed a closeness that normally takes couples months to build."

"We have been through a lot," Ben said, remembering the things she'd shared with him. Things she'd never shared with anyone else. And how she'd bravely forced him to confront his memories despite his anger and bitterness. "But it's only been a year since Melanie…"

Robert gripped the wheel with both hands. "Listen to me, Ben. You loved Melanie deeply. No one doubts that, and you've mourned hard for her. But don't let an opportunity to love someone like Amy pass you by. Melanie wouldn't want that."

Ben looked at his cousin and best friend. "I know you like her. I never meant for this to happen. Believe me."

Robert's eyes stayed glued to the road this time as he raised a hand. "I do like Amy. She's a great person. But I will not stand in your way, man. You deserve happiness more than anyone I know. And if you feel that strongly about Amy, consider me out of the picture."

Ben relaxed a little. Did Robert mean it? Were his feelings for Amy not as strong as Ben thought? Or was he just trying to make Ben feel better?

"I'm not sure when or how it happened." Ben rubbed his chest, remembering the pang he'd felt there the first time he saw Amy. "I think I kind of grew to love her. After I lost Melanie, I didn't think I could ever love another woman that much again, but I do. And the thought of losing her…" emotion deepened his voice, "before I've even had a chance to tell her how I feel… is making me nauseous and light-headed, and my ears are ringing. I don't think I can do this again." He groaned as he propped his elbows on his knees and dropped his head in his hands.

Robert squeezed his shoulder.

~

"OH, THANK GOODNESS." Amy cried when the barn door finally opened to a slew of police officers.

It felt like an eternity since she'd heard the sirens.

"Did you catch them? The Greens?"

Please say they didn't get away.

"They are being detained," said the officer who untied her. "I take it you're Amy Lawson?"

"Yes." Ben and Robert had come through for her. She could totally kiss them right now. Well, Ben anyway. She may find Robert attractive, but her heart belonged to Ben.

Amy spent the next forty minutes being questioned by multiple police officers. After telling the Klickitat County Sheriff everything Eddie confessed to her, she was told that was all for now, but she couldn't leave.

As she stood in the shadows of the front porch, avoiding the paramedics, an officer approached her with a crying toddler and asked if she could help comfort the little girl.

Cassey. Amy's lungs seized.

Amy took the beautiful, blond-haired, blue-eyed toddler in her arms. Her heart pounded so hard, she thought it might burst. *This is Ben's daughter.*

She bounced the child and made soft soothing sounds as she walked away from the crowd of officers. If Eddie and Clara had never taken Cassey anywhere, this crowd of people—not to mention the strobing lights—could easily overwhelm her.

She studied the toddler's face. Not only were her deep, blue eyes the same color as her father's, she had the same shape around the eyes as Ben, and her curly, blond hair was the same color as Melanie's. Amy hugged the baby close.

I did it! She'd found Ben's daughter and she couldn't wait to show him his beautiful little girl.

Not long after Amy got Cassey settled, a female officer approached her saying Clara Green wanted to speak to her. The officer took Cassey from her and motioned for her to follow another officer, who led her to the kitchen where the Sheriff questioned Clara.

Amy was grateful Eddie wasn't in the room. She never wanted to face him again.

She spent the next ten minutes listening to a tearful Clara tell her about Cassey's routine, including her favorite toys, blanket, foods, and lullabies.

"The bags I packed... should have everything Cassey needs."

Amy was glad to hear they still called her Cassey. It would make one thing easier for this poor little girl, who would struggle enough having the only two people she'd known for the past year disappear from her life.

When Amy left Clara, she went in search of Cassey and was told she was with the paramedics. She'd started to make her way to the ambulance when a familiar voice called her name. Her heart surged in her chest. She turned to see Ben running toward her.

He pulled her into his arms. His crushing embrace felt so good. So right. Warmth radiated through Amy and she found it difficult to breathe. She didn't know if it was because he hugged her or because he did it so tightly, but she never wanted him to let go.

"I'm so glad you're okay," he whispered against her hair.

His breath raised goosebumps on her scalp. "I don't think I would have been if you hadn't sent help. Thank you for rescuing me, again."

She thought briefly about giving him that "thank you" kiss but she didn't want an audience.

When Ben finally released her, Robert stepped in and gave her a quick hug. "I want to see you in my office first thing Monday morning. We need to have a serious talk about your job responsibilities."

She gave him a sheepish smile. Turning back to Ben, she took his hand. "Come with me."

She led him to the ambulance where the female officer stood with Cassey in her arms.

"Ben, I'd like you to meet—"

He gasped. "Casandra."

The officer turned toward Ben and waited as he approached.

He reached out and gently stroked Cassey's cheek. "My princess—"

His voice broke as he took Cassey in his arms and held her tight. Tears ran down his cheeks.

The toddler fussed and pushed back. When he held her away from him, she studied his face.

Would she recognize her father? It's a good thing he'd shaved and cut his hair. He would have frightened her with the full beard he had a few weeks ago.

The joy on Ben's face blurred as tears filled Amy's eyes.

CHAPTER 28

*B*en stood over the borrowed playpen, listening to his daughter's steady breathing. *I can't believe she was only two-and-a-half hours away this whole time.*

Tears filled his eyes. He could see glimpses of Melanie in Cassey's high cheekbones, button nose, and full mouth. *She's so beautiful.*

It was a small consolation, but with all the horrible things he'd imagined his daughter going through this past year, he was glad to know she was well cared for and loved.

Accepting he would never see Cassey again had been the most difficult thing he'd ever done, even more difficult than burying his wife. But Amy and Kallie had brought the sunshine back into his life.

He'd grown to love Kallie, his little angel. His chest tightened as he recalled the first time she'd called him Daddy. It had been a beautiful moment. He couldn't wait to hear Cassey call him Daddy. He hoped the adjustment wouldn't be too hard for her.

Cassey had clung to Amy most of the evening, and Amy had insisted on putting her to bed. Fortunately, Kallie had been content to let Ben put her down. He hoped Kallie's closeness to him would help Cassey learn to accept him.

His thoughts turned to Amy. He'd almost lost her today. The

thought tightened his chest all over again. He couldn't believe he'd come to care for her and Kallie so strongly in the few short weeks they'd been here.

Thanks to Amy, he could find joy in a life with his daughter. He wanted to build a new life with more than just Cassey, though. He wanted Amy and Kallie to be a part of it. That's part of the reason he'd decided to stay at his parents' house. It provided a much better environment for Cassey than the small apartment above the garage, and here, he had Amy and his parents' help.

When his parents had hugged and thanked Amy before going to bed, he'd followed suit, needing to assure himself she was really okay. It had felt so good to hold her in his arms. He'd almost told her he loved her, but he'd chickened out. These feelings were still so new and overwhelming. Besides, he didn't want her to think he only said it out of gratitude for bringing Cassey home. Instead, he'd settled for pressing his lips to her forehead for a long moment.

Would he have scared her away if he'd told her how he felt?

Maybe. Maybe not.

She'd agreed to help care for Cassey. Hopefully, in time, she would come to care for him the way he cared for her.

AMY THRASHED IN HER BED, trying to free herself from the support beam of the old barn. It was pitch black, except for the one bright headlight of the Suburban blinding her. The engine of the SUV revved and panic surged in her throat, choking her. She pulled against her restraints, but they were too tight.

The engine revved again, louder, and the light grew bigger. Closer.

Soon, the Suburban would crush her against the beam. *I'm going to die in this barn.* Again, she struggled to free her hands, but a pressure on her shoulder pinned her against the beam.

A scream ripped from her throat. "Help!"

"Amy," Ben shook her shoulder. "Amy."

She awoke, sitting straight up in bed. "Ben?" She wiped sweat from her brow, her hands no longer tied. Fighting confusion, she focused on Ben's words.

"I'm sorry to wake you, but Cassey's crying, and I can't get her to settle back down."

Cassey's desperate cries—cries, Amy had confused as the revving of the Suburban's engine—grew louder by the second. She climbed out of bed and hurried from her room and closed the door, so Kallie wouldn't wake. Good thing she had a habit of sleeping in a t-shirt and sweatpants.

Hurrying into Ben's room, she picked up Cassey. "Shh..." Amy swayed and hummed Cassey's favorite lullaby.

A twinge pulled at Amy's back by the time she finally laid Cassey back in the playpen Faith had brought over. *Poor baby had been so upset.* When she left Ben's room, she found him sitting on the floor, back against the wall, his shoulders slumped.

She sat near him.

A tear glistened on his cheek in the dim light.

"Are you okay?" She put her hand on his shoulder, belatedly becoming aware he was shirtless. Her first instinct was to jerk her hand away, but she wanted to comfort him. If she abruptly pulled away, it might make things worse.

"That song... Melanie used to sing it to Cassey every night before putting her to bed."

"Clara said it was her favorite lullaby. It was the one thing that soothed her when they... first got her."

Ben was quiet for a moment. "I wish I'd tucked her in bed more often as a baby. I should have been the one to sing to her."

"It will come." Amy squeezed his shoulder, then dropped her hand. "She needs time to adjust. I think the reason she feels more comfortable with me is because Clara was the only one to care for her."

"I'm sure you're right," he said, "It's going to take some time. Thank you for being here."

Amy stood, intent on returning to her bed, but Ben rose also, blocking her way. He took her hand.

JILL BURRELL

"What about you? Are you okay?" Ben ran a gentle finger over the rope burn around her wrist.

She resisted the urge to pull her hand away. The burn wasn't very painful. Unfortunately, she couldn't say the same for the lingering weight of fear that tightened her chest. She rubbed her forehead with a shaky hand. "I dreamed I was tied up again, and the Suburban was about to crush me." At least she hadn't been staring down the barrel of a gun in her dream. A shiver snaked its way up her spine at the thought.

"Oh, Amy." Ben pulled her into his arms, pressing her cheek against his warm, hard chest.

Ben's strength reminded her she didn't need to deal with this trauma alone like she'd done with so many things in her life. The emotions she'd held back all evening broke free, and tears leaked from her closed eyelids as the fear she'd experienced in the barn washed over her again.

Ben pulled back and held her face in both hands. "Hey, what's the matter?"

"I was so scared." The words poured out.

As they drove home, Amy had glossed over what happened in the barn because she didn't want Ben to worry about her. But now, with his hands cradling her face, she wanted to share her burdens with the man she loved.

"Come here." Ben took her hand and led her to the family room. He switched on a lamp and pulled her down on the sofa beside him. "Talk to me. Tell me everything that happened."

With his arm around her shoulders, she told Ben about her desperate search for a hiding place, afraid of what would happen when Eddie found her. Tears stung her eyes as she recounted the horror of staring down the barrel of the gun, certain Eddie would pull the trigger. Despair filled her again, tightening her chest, as she recounted being left tied to the support beam in the barn, utterly helpless, knowing she would never see her daughter again.

"I'm so sorry you went through that, Amy, but I'm eternally grateful." Ben's arm tightened around her, and he pressed his lips to her temple.

She could get used to all this hugging. She put her hand on his chest and looked up at him. "Please don't misunderstand me. If I had to do it again, knowing what would happen... and how scared I'd be... I would. I'd do it again, Ben. In a heartbeat." She paused, debating whether to tell him the rest. "It's just that... hiding under that Suburban the way I hid under my bed as a child... and Eddie touching me, searching for my cell phone, triggered something, and I can't let go of the fear."

Ben placed a comforting hand over hers that had begun to tremble. "You're safe now. I won't let anyone hurt you, ever again." His words soother her as much as the warmth and strength of his strong hand. She sucked in a deep breath, relishing his masculine scent. Hints of his woodsy soap remained on his skin, and his natural male scent threatened to overwhelm her.

I'm safe. In Ben's arms. But my heart isn't. If Ben ever rejected her, she wasn't sure she'd ever recover from that heartache.

Her shaking subsided, but the fear was replaced by new insecurities as she remembered the things she learned about Lance and herself in that barn. She lowered her gaze and sniffed. "Eddie told me something about Lance that... hurt. Worse than his... cheating."

Ben pulled away enough to look into her eyes. "Before you say anything, let me remind you we've already established that Lance is a jerk."

She frowned. "No, he's that other word you would have gotten your mouth washed out for saying." She gnawed on her bottom lip for a moment before continuing. "Turns out, not only was he never faithful to me, he never loved me. He used me because I had a steady job and an apartment."

"Eddie kidnapped my daughter and let my wife die. You can't believe anything he said." The vehemence of Ben's words and the muscle clenching in his jaw testified of his hatred for Eddie.

Amy's voice dropped to a whisper. "No. It's true. Lance used me, and I let him."

285

Ben held her gaze. "Why?"

"Because I was so desperate to be loved." Amy stared at her hands. "I have to believe Lance isn't capable of loving anyone but himself, because the alternative hurts too much."

"Which is?"

"I'm not lovable." Uttering the words aloud hurt as bad as her mother's rejection of her nine years ago.

Ben sucked in a sharp breath. "You are lovable, Amy. You're beautiful, courageous, and kind. I... I love you."

Amy's gaze jumped back to his as her heart stalled. *Did he mean it?* Or had he only said the words to make her feel better? He raised his left hand to stroke her cheek with his knuckles, and she caught sight of his wedding band.

He doesn't mean it. If he truly loved me, he wouldn't need that link to Melanie. And I could never ask him to give that up.

Amy pulled away as Ben leaned in to kiss her. It was the hardest thing she'd ever done, because she desperately wanted his kiss. But she couldn't become involved with another man who wasn't fully committed to her. And Kallie.

And she couldn't expect a man to love her as long as she believed herself unlovable.

"You're saying that out of gratitude." She started to stand, but Ben grabbed her hand.

"No, I'm not. I mean, yes, I am grateful, but I'm also in love with you." When Amy shook her head, he said, "Listen. When I thought I might lose you today, it nearly drove me insane. I can't live without you, Amy. I can't lose the woman I love, again."

Warmth flooded Amy, and her heart hammered in her chest. He certainly sounded like he meant the words, but she couldn't let herself fall so easily. Yes, she loved Ben, but until she was certain he was ready to move on, she couldn't accept his love. She needed to guard her heart.

Taking a deep breath to steady her racing heart, and summoning all her willpower, she stood. "I'm sorry, Ben. I don't think I'm ready for another relationship, yet, and I'm not sure you are either. You need to focus on Cassey, right now." She hurried to her room before she did something stupid like throw herself into Ben's arms.

"Amy..." He followed her down the hall.

Turning back, she saw a stunned look on his face. *Poor man.* He'd told her he loved her, and she'd rejected him.

She opened her bedroom door. "If you need to comfort Cassey again you should... wear a shirt." She motioned to his muscled chest. "She's probably not used to being snuggled against... that." She quickly stepped inside her room, hoping he didn't see the color that burned her cheeks.

Judging by the smile that replaced his stunned expression, he'd seen.

CHAPTER 29

*B*en's heart skipped a beat when he spotted Amy weaving her way through the crowded high school gym toward their table. He stood and pulled out the chair next to him, hoping she'd sit beside him, instead of across the table in the only other available seat.

The Fall Festival was in full swing, and this was the first he'd seen of Amy, except when she'd served him spaghetti, earlier. He'd managed to hold her gaze for a full three seconds before being jostled along in line.

His feelings for her had intensified over the past two weeks since Cassey came home. He'd wanted many times to tell her again how much he loved her, but he wasn't sure how to prove to Amy he felt more than gratitude. He ached to pull her into his arms and kiss her again, like he had weeks ago.

Sharing parenting responsibilities with Amy made him long to be a real family with her, Kallie and Cassey. There seemed to be a solid bond between him and Amy, but she held back, and he couldn't figure out why. He was certain she was attracted to him, but he suspected she avoided being alone with him. Which wasn't difficult, considering their two daughters and his parents all lived in the same house.

Amy gave Ben a smile before sitting in the chair he held out. "Thank you."

Paige, who had come home for Providence's first ever bachelor auction, started talking before Ben could even greet Amy. "Riley and I took the girls to the cafeteria for the kids' games, but it was so crowded and noisy, I think it overwhelmed Cassey." Paige patted her niece's head. "They're too young to understand most of the games, anyway."

Each girl sucked a lollipop, sported a butterfly on her cheek, and had a balloon tied to her wrist.

Ben watched Cassey, who seemed to be handling the large crowd in the gym surprisingly well, considering they'd only taken the girls out in public a few times. She'd come a long way. She now spoke one and two-word sentences—mostly mimicking Kallie.

He recalled with satisfaction the first time Cassey called Amy *Mommy* five days ago. Ben couldn't wait to make Amy Cassey's mom. And he'd bawled like a baby last night when his daughter called him *Daddy* for the first time.

But Amy had been talking about moving out. She'd even asked Charity if the apartment above the garage was available to rent. Ben hated to think how Cassey might react to Amy leaving. She let him put her down for her naps now, but she always wanted Amy to put her to bed at night. He didn't mind—he enjoyed the few minutes of one-on-one with Kallie. He loved that little girl like she was his own.

No, he couldn't let Amy move out and take Kallie with her.

Ben itched to take Amy away from this noisy, crowded gym to a quiet classroom where he could convince her not to leave. Convince her to take a chance on him. But the specialty baked-goods auction would start soon, and he had every intention of winning Amy's chocolate cake. It was the best way he could think of to publicly stake some sort of claim on her. Never mind that desserts from the bake sale tables already littered the center of their table.

The auctioneer stood at the pulpit just as Amy finished eating. "Thank you all for coming out and supporting our community tonight. We'll be starting the baked goods auction soon, followed by

something I know all the single ladies have been anxiously waiting for
—Providence's first ever Bachelor Auction! Be sure to get your
auction paddles at the table in the front right corner."

As half the gym migrated to the auction table, Ben was glad he'd
gotten his paddle before sitting down to eat.

"Oh, Amy, I picked up your paddle for you." Paige slid an auction
paddle across the table.

Ben doubted Amy planned on bidding on the specialty baked
goods, so that meant she planned on bidding on the bachelors. Oh,
how he wished he could blame the sudden tightening in his chest on
indigestion.

Ten minutes later, the auctioneer again took the stand. He wasted
no time in starting the bidding on the first specialty baked good.

Ben's leg bounced as he waited for a tray of Aunt Charity's Big Ol'
Cinnamon Rolls, and Annie Tucker's famous pecan pie, as well as a
dozen other equally delicious desserts to be auctioned. Most items
sold for fifty to a hundred dollars. This was why he loved this small
town—they were very generous.

"And our final item up for bid tonight is a triple-layer, triple
chocolate cake made by Amy Lawson."

Finally. Ben picked up his paddle, and so did Robert and Jake. A
few others joined in for a while, but as the bidding approached two
hundred dollars most of them backed out.

A low murmur rippled throughout the gym, and Amy's cheeks
grew rosy as her name was linked first with Robert's name then with
his. A dull ache settled in Ben's jaw from clenching it.

Debbie raised her voice in disgust from two tables away. "It's only
a cake. What's the big deal?"

It was a big deal to Ben.

Amy squirmed in her seat as Ben fought Robert and Jake for her
cake. The bidding soon passed three hundred dollars, but Ben was not
about to back down to Robert.

"Let's combine forces, so we can keep Ben from winning," Robert
told Jake, loud enough for most of the gym to hear. Jake nodded and
laid down his paddle.

Robert and Ben continued bidding.

Amy leaned toward him. "Stop bidding. I'll make you your own cake."

Ben inhaled her floral scent and grinned. "But it's for a good cause, and I'm having fun."

"Stop, please. You're embarrassing me." She put her hand on his arm and warmth seeped into him.

"That means letting Robert win. He's insufferable when he wins."

"Ben, please."

He gazed into her imploring, sky-blue eyes. He would do anything for this woman, even let Robert win. "Fine, but you owe me a cake." He laid his paddle down and propped his elbows on the table. Out of habit, he fiddled with the wedding band on his finger.

"Four hundred. Going once. Four hundred going twice. Sold to Robert and Jake Winters for four hundred dollars!"

Robert and Jake gave each other a high-five, then Robert winked at Amy, and snubbed his nose at Ben.

"See what I mean?" Ben said.

Amy rolled her eyes.

Robert had outbid him on purpose. Was he trying to see how far Ben was willing to go to make a statement?

He'd planned on paying as much as was necessary to win Amy's cake, but was he willing to do more than that?

Realizing he still twisted his wedding band, he remembered Amy's words on the anniversary of Melanie's death; *'Unless you're ready to move on with your life, I don't see any reason you shouldn't wear it'.*

He'd always love and miss Melanie, but he loved Amy too. If he couldn't convince her he was ready to move on, he'd lose her. Amy's words about her mom rang in his head. *Actions speak louder than words.*

Amy needed actions.

Would removing his ring be enough?

Or did he need to do more?

A KNOT FORMED in Amy's stomach as the twelve bachelors paraded onto the stage. This whole thing had been her idea, and if it flopped, she'd feel horrible.

Many of the younger bachelors blushed at the catcalls and cheers from the eager female bidders.

"The bidding for each bachelor will start at one hundred dollars and increase by ten-dollar increments. You woman can bid on multiple bachelors, but you can only win once." The auctioneer's voice droned on as he explained the rules for the dates, then he asked the youngest bachelor to step forward, and the bidding began.

Amy laughed as the auctioneer's volume and speed picked up from what it had been during the baked-goods auction, causing excitement among the women. She listened closely as the bids were called, attempting to keep track of the dollar amount. The women appeared to be having a good time, and the bachelors on stage nudged one another.

Paige and Riley bid against each other for one of their high school friends but were ultimately outbid by someone else. Most of the bachelors sold for two hundred to five hundred dollars. It surprised Amy that women would spend so much money for a date. The bachelors' good-natured boasting and ribbing about how much they sold for kept the crowd entertained.

Robert and Jake were the last two bachelors to be auctioned, and though Jake was younger, Robert stepped forward first.

Debbie suddenly became vocal. "Two hundred dollars."

Judging by the number of women bidding on Robert, he'd been busy. Amy raised her paddle several times because she'd promised Robert she would bid on him, but she couldn't ignore Ben's eyes on her and the tension radiating off him.

Why did that muscle in his jaw keep clenching?

"He made me promise to bid on him," she said.

Ben nodded, but it didn't make it any less awkward each time she raised her paddle. As the bidding passed four hundred dollars, Amy quit. She'd only brought five hundred with her. It was money she'd been saving for a deposit on an apartment. She didn't anticipate actually spending any money tonight.

"Can we join forces?" a woman from the center called out. "Like Robert and Jake did on the cake?"

The auctioneer hesitated. Unlike the cake that was easy to share, this would mean the bachelor would have to take multiple women out.

Robert cupped his hands to his mouth. "Yes."

The bidding resumed and at fifteen hundred dollars, Widow Wheeler tossed her paddle on the table in disgust. "Fine, you can have him."

Robert turned to Jake and flexed his arms in a sign of triumph. The audience erupted in laughter, and Robert walked off the stage, beaming.

Jake tugged at his collar as he stepped forward on the stage. Debbie was the first to bid on him.

Amy bid a few times, her spaghetti roiling in her stomach as Ben continued to watch her. When the bidding approached a thousand dollars, a woman again asked if they could bid as a group. Jake readily agreed. When the bidding reached fifteen hundred, Debbie made it clear she was not going to lose out on Jake too.

"Three thousand dollars!" Debbie shouted, on her feet now.

A collective gasp rose from the crowd, followed by a hush. The auctioneer raised his hand high in the air. "Three thousand dollars! Going once. Going twice. Sold!" He slapped his hand down on the podium. "Three thousand dollars for Jake Winters!"

The crowd cheered as Jake left the stage. A flush crept up his neck to the tips of his ears, and he scratched the back of his neck. Robert loved this kind of thing, but the attention clearly made Jake uncomfortable. Not to mention the fact he had to take Widow Wheeler out on a date.

A twinge of guilt tugged at Amy. This was all her fault.

As the cheering died down, a warm breath tickled Amy's ear, sending a flutter through her body. "Don't let me down."

She turned to see Ben stand and walk toward the makeshift stage.

A hush fell over the gym as Ben climbed the steps. He talked to the auctioneer in hushed tones. Then the auctioneer stepped back to the microphone.

"Folks, we have one more bachelor who has decided to help raise some money tonight. Please welcome Ben Young to the stage."

Applause filled the gym.

"That's not fair. I want to bid again." Debbie waved her paddle in the air.

Ben stood, his feet shoulder-width apart, hands clasped in front of him, his eyes never leaving Amy.

Self-consciously, she dropped her gaze to the table. There in front of her, where her plate used to be, sat a gold wedding band. Her gaze flew to Ben.

Sure enough, the ring finger of his left hand showed a faint white line.

Heart pounding, she picked up the ring. *He's ready to move on.*

Amy had done a lot of soul searching the past two weeks, and a few nights ago—after Cassey called her *Mommy*—she'd come to the realization that no matter how hard she tried, she'd never be perfect. Yes, she made mistakes, but she was a good mom, doing the best she could for her daughter.

The last few weeks working at the diner had reminded her she was an awesome waitress. She was also shaping up to be a great pastry chef, thanks to Charity's tutelage. Her mother may have never loved her, and Lance wasn't capable of loving anyone but himself, but that didn't mean Amy wasn't lovable. She'd just needed to learn to love herself first.

That meant taking care of her own needs.

And she needed Ben to know how much she loved him.

Amy's pulse quickened and heat filled her cheeks under Ben's unwavering gaze, but she didn't care. She raised her paddle again and again.

So did several of the women who had lost out on the other bachelors.

As the bidding passed three hundred dollars, Amy's palms grew damp. *Will Ben be disappointed if I don't win the date with him?*

She wanted to win. She wanted to go out with Ben. More importantly, she wanted him to know how badly she wanted to go out with him. She'd pay every penny she had to let everyone know.

She leaned over to Hope. "I only brought five hundred dollars with me. If I bid higher, can I pay it later?"

"Yes, yes. I'll even lend you the money if I need to. Whatever you do, don't let anyone outbid you."

A silly grin split Amy's face. She was glad Hope was on her side.

Amy's stomach tightened as the bidding passed four hundred dollars. This would wipe out her meager savings. She wouldn't be able to afford her own apartment for some time now.

She raised her paddle again. *I don't want to move out, anyway.*

Out of the corner of her eye, she saw Robert turn to the woman who had become her main competitor and wave his hand under his chin as though to telling her to stop. Then a loud whisper meant for the same lady came from another table. "Let Amy win!"

Amy bit back a smile. It was nice to know people rooted for her. The other woman dropped her paddle on the table with a sigh.

"Four hundred-fifty," shouted the auctioneer. "Going once. Going twice. Sold! To Amy Lawson, our local heroine. Congratulations!"

Amy's face flamed. She hadn't gotten used to all the attention she'd received from the locals. Their praise felt ill-placed. Although she appreciated the generous tips she earned at the diner. How long would it take for the unsolicited fame to die down?

Ben left the stage and returned to his seat next to Amy. He gave her a devilish smile, his dimple making her stomach take flight.

"I've already told you I'd go out with you. You didn't need to make a public scene."

"Yes, I did." His eyes never left her face as he took her hand. "I want everyone to know I'm only interested in one woman."

Amy's breath seized, and her pulse raced at his words. Her face grew warm again but for an entirely different reason this time. That's why he'd stared at her the whole time? He was letting everyone know he was interested in her?

He really did love her. His actions tonight showed that. More importantly, it proved to Amy she *was* lovable.

She itched to stand up and do a happy dance. Instead, she took a deep breath and grinned. "Well, it nearly backfired on you. Don't complain if you have to wait a month for your cake. I'm broke now, so I'm not sure I can afford the ingredients."

Ben laughed. "This whole auction was your idea, so it's only fair you feel the pinch a little."

"True. But it was meant to encourage Debbie to be generous."

"It worked. But poor Jake."

Amy grimaced. "Yeah, I feel bad about that—"

"Amy," Fanny Tucker, from the Festival committee, grabbed Amy's shoulder. "We made almost ten thousand dollars more than last year, thanks to the bachelor auction."

Amy gripped Ben's hand tighter—afraid he might pull away—before smiling at Fanny. "The women were very generous."

"Yes, they were. I'm going to go thank everyone." Her round figure bustled up to the stage.

Ben pulled Amy from her seat. "Come here." He looked back over his shoulder. "Paige, keep an eye on the girls, please."

BUTTERFLIES SWARMED in Amy's stomach as Ben led her from the gym and down the hall.

He opened the first door they came to. The janitor's closet.

"No, I can't do this here." He closed the door again.

"Do what?"

Tugging Amy's hand, he led her farther down the hall to the next door. Ben flipped the switch and fluorescent light illuminated rows of chairs with attached desks. He pulled Amy in and closed the door behind them. The scent of dust, pencil shavings, and paper reminded her of her high school days.

Ben drew Amy into his arms. "I can't kiss you in the janitor's closet."

Amy's heart raced. She'd waited two months for Ben to kiss her again. She didn't care where it happened. She wanted him to kiss her already. A smile teased her lips as she wrapped her arms around his neck. "What a shame. It looked kind of cozy."

"No. I'm going to do this right, this time." Ben stroked her cheek with his index finger. "I stole a kiss from my first girlfriend in that closet."

Amy's smile faltered.

"She dumped me two weeks later for Robert." He tilted her chin and pressed his lips to her temple. His voice dropped to a whisper. "I stole a kiss from you a couple months ago and I haven't stopped thinking about you since."

Amy's breath caught in her chest and her mouth went dry.

"I kissed Melanie for the first time in a janitor's closet. And she's gone too." Ben kissed the hollow below her ear. "I have to do it differently this time. I'll take my chances in my old English classroom."

Ben's warm breath against her ear sent a ripple of desire through her. He was definitely doing something right. Forcing herself to concentrate on his words, she pulled back. "Are you sure you're ready?"

"To kiss you again? I'm so ready, Amy."

Amy pushed against his chest as he leaned in to kiss her. "To move on, I mean. I don't want to rush you." She held her breath, waiting for his answer.

Ben cupped her cheek and gazed so deep into her eyes, she was certain he could see the very depths of her soul. Could he see how much she loved him?

"A part of my heart will always belong to Melanie, but since you came to Providence, my heart has grown, and my capacity to love has increased. I can't guarantee I won't still experience some grief on occasion, especially as Cassey grows up to look like her mother, but I'm ready to move on… as long as it's with you."

Amy leaned toward him, tipping her chin up. "Then kiss me already."

He slid his fingers into her hair and lowered his lips to hers.

A sigh escaped her as she welcomed this long-awaited kiss. Warmth seeped into her body as she responded to him the way she'd dreamed of doing ever since their first kiss.

The feel of his lips on hers erased any lingering doubts. Ben was the first man to come along after Lance, but he was the one she was meant to be with. The one who would commit to her, always protect her, and treat her right. And more importantly, without even knowing it, he'd taught her to love herself.

He moaned and tightened his arms around her, kissing her as though he'd never get another chance to do so again.

She returned his kiss with the same passion.

When he finally ended the kiss, he rested his forehead against hers. "Please don't ever leave me."

Amy struggled to catch her breath. "I love you, Ben Young. I don't care whether you're a mechanic or a lawyer. I love you. More than I ever thought it possible to love another person. But I can't promise nothing will ever happen to me."

Ben pulled back enough to look at her. "I know, but you've been talking about moving out. I couldn't bear it if you left and took Kallie with you." His voice grew ragged as he spoke, "I love that little angel like my own, and if you left, it would leave a hole in my heart that could never be filled." When Amy opened her mouth to speak, he hurried on, "and I'm afraid if you leave, Cassey would be heartbro—."

Amy pressed her lips against his to quiet him. Ben quickly overcame his surprise and deepened the kiss. She placed her hand behind his neck to prevent him from ending the connection before she was ready. She loved the taste of him. She couldn't seem to get enough.

She finally loosened her hold and broke the kiss. "I thought if I moved out it might make it easier for you to bond with Cassey. But, don't worry, after tonight, I can't afford to move out. Besides, I love Cassey too much to leave her."

He smiled. "Good."

She touched his dimple with her index finger.

Ben wrapped her in a tight embrace, sweeping the air from her lungs. "Thank you."

She pulled back. "For what?"

"For rescuing me." Tears filled his eyes. "You've told me more than once I rescued you when you broke down, but the truth is, you rescued me. When you and Kallie came to Providence, you brought a ray of sunshine with you. It took me a while, but I finally figured out how to let go of some of my grief and allow myself to be happy. I thought I'd never be able to love another woman. Then you and Kallie showed up, and I found myself feeling things I never thought I'd feel again."

Ben caressed her cheek, then let his thumb linger for a moment on her lips before his fingers traced her jaw and the length of her throat, leaving a trail of fire in their wake.

She stopped breathing in anticipation of another kiss. Her pulse throbbed as he slipped his fingers to the back of her neck and lowered his lips to hers again in another passionate kiss.

Warmth filled Amy's body, and she had a sense of coming home. She'd found what she'd searched for her entire life. A man who would love and cherish her.

When his lips finally left hers, she sucked in a shaky breath. "Wow. I'm definitely getting my money's worth and we haven't even gone on our date yet."

Ben chuckled and held her close.

Amy leaned her head against his chest. His racing heartbeat brought a smile to her face. She wasn't the only one affected by their kissing.

"Seeing as we haven't even gone out, it's probably too early to ask you to marry me. So, maybe you were right—one of us should move out. I'll move back to the apartment tomorrow."

Amy lifted her head. "Ben, no. That'll be hard on the girls."

He groaned. "It'll be hard on me to live in such close proximity to you without doing something horribly inappropriate with you in my parent's house." He wiggled his eyebrows, eliciting a chuckle from her.

His expression sobered. "Besides, people in small towns can be pretty judgmental. When word gets out that we are in a relationship, it won't look good for your reputation if we are living under the same roof."

Amy bit back a laugh. Ben was concerned about her reputation? The woman, who had a child out of wedlock with a wannabe rock star. Oh, how she loved this man, and the gentleman he was.

"It's your home. I should be the one to go."

"No, it's my parent's house. My home is next door being inhabited by a relentless widow."

"I've been told I'm pretty good widow repellent. Do we need to stage a PDA in the front yard?"

"Hmm... sounds tempting, but it won't be necessary. I told Debbie I'm ready to move back into my home. She's supposed to be out by the end of the month." Relief filled his voice. "Do you think you can handle living there? In the future, of course, after we're married?" He rushed to make his intentions clear.

"I don't know." She pretended to contemplate the dilemma. "It's such a big house, probably bigger than all the apartments I've ever lived in combined. It'll be hard to get used to living in such comfort." She smiled to make sure he knew she was teasing.

"I meant, will it bother you to live in a home I shared with Melanie?"

"Melanie is as much a part of your life as Lance is mine. Of course, Melanie was a higher quality part than Lance," she said with a wry smile. "I would never ask you to give up or turn away from that part of your life. You can always talk to me about Melanie, and when she's old enough to understand, I want you to tell Cassey all about her mom."

He captured her lips again. The intensity of this kiss told her he'd held back in their previous kisses. Electricity shot through Amy and her heart raced as one kiss turned into many.

~

By the time Ben and Amy returned to the gym, the clean-up was well under way. Having signed up for clean-up duty, Amy jumped in while Hope and James took the girls home to put them to bed. Ten minutes later, with arms full of centerpieces, Amy ran into a scowling Debbie.

"There's our heroine now." The venom in Debbie's voice made her usually attractive features not so pretty. "Look at you. You're such a do-gooder."

"Give it a rest, Debbie. I know you don't like me, and I can't say I care much for you either, but stop blaming me for Ben, Robert, and Jake's rejection of you."

Debbie sneered. "You may have won the date with Ben, but don't think you're going to get anything more than that. Don't forget I'm the one living in his house."

Not for much longer. Leaning closer to Debbie, Amy dropped her voice. "And I'm the one living *with* him. Did you know he sleeps shirtless?"

Stooping to Debbie's level was petty, but Amy was tired of her better-than-you attitude. Ben was in love with her, and she refused to let Debbie put a damper on her joy.

Debbie's eyes narrowed. "Well, I guess you really are the slut we all thought you were." She spun on her heels and walked away.

A gasp behind Amy made her turn around.

Paige, wide-eyed and rosy-cheeked, gaped after Debbie. "I can't believe she said that to you."

Amy shrugged. "She doesn't like me, I get it. I think she sees me as a threat. Kind of ironic, don't you think? With all the money she has, she's jealous of poor, little me."

Paige put her arm around Amy. "My grandpa used to say, you're never poor if you've got love."

Amy's gaze drifted to where Ben worked, dismantling the makeshift stage. Despite blowing her savings, Amy felt wealthy indeed.

"Your grandpa sounds pretty wise."

CHAPTER 30

SIX WEEKS LATER

*A*my pushed the massive centerpiece of two dozen red roses aside in order to gaze into the eyes of the man she loved. They sat at the dining table in Ben's house, and Amy dreamed of many more nights like this.

Ben never ceased to amaze her. They'd just returned from a magical Christmas Eve sleigh ride at the ranch to find a fancy Italian dinner—laid out for them by Paige, if her and Ben's whispered conversations were anything to go by—complete with candlelight and romantic music.

Finished eating, Amy pulled a rose from the arrangement and fingered the petals. Splendid, smooth, and vibrant. Just like Ben. She couldn't help comparing the man who sat across from her to the tortured man, who, four months ago, stood in the shadows of his parents' front porch and told her about his wife's death and his daughter's kidnapping.

She raised the rose to her nose and inhaled. Closing her eyes, she savored its sweet scent, like she savored each day that Ben made her feel like the most-loved woman in the world. The past six weeks since the bachelor auction had been the happiest of her life.

"Gorgeous," Ben murmured.

She opened her eyes to find him staring at her. Warmth filled her cheeks, and she gave him her most dazzling smile. "Thank you. For everything."

"Come here." Ben rose from the table and took her hand, leading her to the family room, where a glowing fire welcomed them.

Amy sank onto the sofa she'd helped him choose a couple weeks ago. "That was nice, Ben. Everything was perfect."

Instead of sitting beside her, he dropped to one knee in front of her and took her hand. "When Melanie died, I thought I'd never love another woman again. I knew I would never feel that way about anyone else, ever again. But then you showed up and managed to poke holes in my armor. Before I knew it, you'd worked your way under my skin, so deep you became a part of me. I probably don't deserve a second chance at love and happiness, but I'm taking it. Will you marry me, Amy?"

He pulled a ring box from his pocket and opened it to reveal a modest solitaire diamond flanked by a figure-eight design, cradling two tiny sapphires, in a white-gold band. The matching band had the same design with three tiny sapphires across it.

Amy gasped. "It's beautiful. Yes. Yes, I'll marry you!" The words came out a squeal. The excitement bubbling in her made her feel light and tingly.

Ben slipped the ring onto her finger, then sitting beside her, he pulled her into his arms and lowered his lips to hers.

A low moan escaped Amy when Ben's lips met hers. He never failed to take her breath away and set her pulse racing. How she loved this man. Despite their lingering kisses, lengthy embraces, and Ben's frequent declarations of what a temptation she was, he'd been a perfect gentleman, and Amy loved him all the more for it. He made her feel safe and comfortable; respected and cherished.

"Wow! Merry Christmas!" Ben's breath came in ragged puffs when he finally pulled away. "Please say we can have a short engagement."

Amy laughed. "I don't want a long engagement either, but I'd like to wait until Spring, because, where I would like to go for our honeymoon, would be better after the snow is gone."

He wrapped a lock of her hair around his finger. "I thought I was supposed to plan the honeymoon."

"You can plan it, but I have a request of where I'd like to go."

"Where?"

"Well, taking the girls into consideration—"

"Wait!" Ben said, "the girls don't get to go on the honeymoon with us."

"I know that." Amy poked his stomach. "But I think we'll both agree we don't want to be too far away from them." At his nod, Amy said, "I'd like you to take me to your mother's family's cabin."

Ben's smile faded, and the arm around her shoulders loosened.

"I know you spent some of the darkest months of your life at that cabin, but I also know some of your happiest childhood memories were from time spent there. I want to fill the cabin with happiness again. I want you to be able to take our daughters there so they can experience all the wonderful things you did as a child. Things, I never experienced."

"Happy memories, huh?" Ben said, warming to the idea. His eyebrows rose and desire filled his eyes. "Honeymoon kind of happy memories?"

"Exactly." Amy pressed her lips to his, releasing some of the passion she'd kept bottled up the past six weeks.

When the kiss finally ended, Ben smiled. "You know if we honeymoon at the cabin while there's snow it'll be more romantic. There won't be anything to do except make *happy memories*." Amy giggled and pushed him away as he leaned in for another kiss. *Talk about temptation.*

Ben pulled a large manila envelope off the end table. "I've got another present for you."

Amy opened the envelope and pulled out several papers held together by a paper clip. She looked to Ben for an explanation.

"I made a trip to Portland yesterday. You're holding papers signed by Lance, releasing total custody of Kallie to you. I need to file them with the state, but after we're married, I can adopt Kallie."

Amy's chest swelled, taking her breath away as effectively as Ben's kisses did. She, Ben, Kallie, and Cassey were going to be a family. "How did you get him to sign them? I know he wants nothing to do with Kallie, but I didn't expect him to sign over his rights so easily. Knowing Lance, I expected him to try to get money from you."

"He did, and I reminded him that was illegal. I told him if he wanted to bring up money, I would draw up child support papers outlining exactly what he needed to pay you each month for Kallie's support. He signed the papers without argument after that."

Amy hugged him. "Thank you, Ben. There's nothing I want more than for you to adopt Kallie."

"I have one more present for you." He stood and pulled her up with him.

"But I haven't given you any of yours."

She wanted to give Ben something extra special, but he already had everything.

In fact, he'd spent a lot of money refurnishing his spacious house after Debbie moved out. Amy had told him the furniture was fine— much nicer than any she had ever owned, but he'd insisted it needed to be replaced.

She suspected there were too many memories linked to the furniture he'd shared with Melanie. She'd never asked, and he hadn't said as much, but she'd selected an entirely different style when he insisted she help choose the new furniture. Even so, Amy wasn't sure he'd slept at the house yet.

"I'll open my presents in a minute." Ben pulled her toward the kitchen. He paused at the door to the garage. "You'll think I'm crazy, but I want you to know how much I love you and the girls, and how important your safety is to me." He opened the garage door and turned on the light. "Merry Christmas!"

Amy gasped. There in his garage was a shiny red Ford Expedition. Her stomach dropped.

"I understand your desire to keep us safe, Ben, but this..." She waved her hand at the SUV. "It's so expensive, and on top of my ring and the furniture and... and everything." Nausea swamped her as she thought about how much money Ben had spent lately.

She'd finally paid off the credit card Lance had maxed out.

"Relax." Ben put both hands on her shoulders. "I made decent money at the garage, with few expenses, and things are picking up at the law office since Uncle Brent has decided to retire. Besides, Debbie has been paying double the mortgage for the past year. Even though I've spent a lot of money recently, I want you to know I'm nothing like Lance. I'm actually very good with money. Everything is paid for, and I still have a little nest egg in savings."

"How? I mean, you've spent a lot of money."

"Remember the reward money you refused to accept?"

Amy thought about their first argument. Three days after she found Cassey. Ben had insisted she'd earned the ten-thousand-dollar reward with everything she'd gone through, which made her angry. Robert had helped Ben see that by insisting she take the money, Ben had belittled the whole reason Amy put herself in danger to find Cassey.

Amy nodded, and he continued, "I tried to give my parent's portion back to them, but they refused to take it. They told me to find a way to give it to you that you couldn't refuse." He picked up Amy's hand and touched the ring on her finger. "What I didn't use for your ring, went toward the SUV, which is used, not new, so it didn't cost as much as you think."

She smiled. "You're sneaky. I could never refuse this ring, nor will I refuse the SUV, because I know how important this is to you."

She turned to step into the garage, but Ben stopped her. "Amy, being a small-town lawyer, I'll never be able to give you the kind of life I could if I worked for a large firm in the city, but I promise to take care of our family. Even if it means working at the garage as well as the law office."

"I know you will. And I'm content to continue working at the diner for now. In fact, Charity has asked me to be the afternoon manager. She wants me to help redesign the menus, adding in some new recipes."

"Faith finally convinced her to slow down, huh?"

"I'm not sure she's ready to slow down, but I'm hoping I can convince her to ease up a little."

"Will your chocolate cake be on the menu?"

"Faith insisted."

"Hmm..." Ben pulled her into his arms. "Promise me you'll make me my own cake occasionally, so we can have a frosting fight."

Amy giggled and promised, sealing it with a kiss.

Ben pulled her into the garage, and they climbed in the SUV. He showed her all the features that sold him on the vehicle.

When they returned to the house, Amy grabbed the bag with Ben's gifts and waited for him to sit beside her. "It's your turn to open presents."

Her gifts for Ben, consisting of a silver tie with tiny blue diamonds in the pattern, that reminded Amy of his eyes, and a fancy, gold, monogrammed pen set for his office, felt inconsequential compared to the gifts he'd given her.

She'd wanted to give him something meaningful, but she hadn't been able to think of anything until two weeks ago. She'd enlisted Robert's and Paige's help to make it happen.

Ben opened the tie and pens first. "I love them. Thanks." He gave her a kiss after opening each present.

Amy moved away to the other end of the sofa as he grabbed the third gift.

Ben's eyebrows raised.

"Go ahead." She chewed on her bottom lip, her eyes glued to his face, as he opened the flat rectangular package.

His brow furrowed as he unwrapped the book and read the front cover, "Our Little Princess." He shot her a quick glance, then his eyes returned to the book.

He studied the pictures on each page. Pictures of him and Melanie holding their newborn daughter. Pictures of them at home with their new baby. More and more pictures showing Cassey getting progressively older. She'd included the picture from Ben's phone of Cassey wearing the pink coat that had ultimately led Amy to find Cassey. The next several pages were filled with Cassey learning to crawl, learning to feed herself, learning to walk, playing in the bathtub. Amy had been sure to include Cassey's first birthday and was careful to crop out Eddie and Clara. These pictures were of only Cassey.

Amy's eyes filled with tears as Ben repeatedly swiped at his. He continued turning pages, finding pictures taken the night Cassey was rescued and additional pictures of Cassey with him, with Amy, with Kallie, and her grandparents.

"How...?" Ben asked, looking up from the book.

"Anything to do with Cassey was removed from the house as evidence, so I asked Robert to go to Klickitat County to go through the evidence to find pictures of Cassey. He found a camera with these digital photos. He got permission to download them onto his laptop. Paige helped me go through the pictures and organize them. She also collected the earlier pictures from your scrapbooks."

"How did you find out all these things about Cassey?"

Amy looked down at her clasped hands, then back up to meet his eyes. "I asked Robert to get me permission to talk to Clara over the phone."

Ben sucked in a sharp breath. "That must have been difficult for you."

Amy shrugged. "She was never a threat to me. I never actually saw her until after the police had her in custody."

"I don't know how you could avoid reliving the whole ordeal while doing this for me." Ben's voice was tight.

Amy lowered her gaze again. It had been hard the past couple of weeks to separate pictures of Cassey in that house—with Eddie and Clara—from what happened in the barn.

Ben must have seen her struggle because he pulled her into his arms.

In the security of his embrace, Amy tried to let go of her fears. "Enough of this melancholy," she said, after a few long moments. "You have one more present to open." She handed him another gift, the same shape and size as the last one he'd opened.

She snuggled against him as he opened the second book with the words "Our Little Angel" written on the front. This book was the same as Cassey's but with pictures of Kallie. Amy wanted Ben to not only have the parts he'd missed of Cassey's life, but also the parts he'd missed of Kallie's.

Side by side, they looked through Kallie's book, then through Cassey's again, because Ben had a hard time seeing through the tears the first time.

Ben held Amy tight and pressed his lips to her forehead. "I don't know what I did to deserve a woman like you."

Amy thought the same thing. Of all the things she'd done wrong in her life, somewhere, somehow, she must have done something right to deserve a man as wonderful as Ben, and their two beautiful little girls.

THE END

< < < < > > > >

SNEAK PEEK OF JAKE'S STORY

CHAPTER 1

*J*ake Winters was convinced paperwork would be the death of him. It couldn't be today though because the ranch hands expected to be paid.

He hit submit on the first phase of paperwork for the government solar project and stretched. This was only the first of many phases and already he regretted his decision to install solar on his land. Not because he didn't think it would be worthwhile but because of the virtual mountain of paperwork it required.

He couldn't think of anything else to do with the large section of land that was too sandy for growing crops. This ranch was his life, and the solar project was his way of adding to the legacy he'd been left.

He pulled a checkbook from his desk.

"Ah, the dreaded paperwork!" Lottie stepped through the open office door.

Jake flinched, both welcoming and dreading the distraction. He hated being cooped up indoors, and interruptions prolonged the torture.

"Need something?" He set the completed paychecks on the corner of his desk.

Lottie Hamilton—his cook and housekeeper—was like a second mother to him. She and Zane, his ranch foreman, had both been with the ranch since before Jake was born.

"I'm headed to town. Do you need anything?" When Jake shook his head, she asked, "Do you want to look over the menu and grocery list?"

Jake tossed his pen onto his father's old mahogany desk. A desk whose rich, dark color belied its age. Of course, Blake Winters had hated paperwork as much as Jake did.

Man. It had been three years since his father died, but his absence still hit Jake hard sometimes.

He scowled. "Why would I want to do that?"

Lottie propped her hand on her hip. "To see if you want to change or add anything."

"Have I ever changed the menu?" Jake bit back a sigh. "Your cooking is amazing, and you anticipate my needs better than I do."

"Too well, I'm afraid." Despite Lottie's stern expression, the laugh lines around her eyes softened her features. She had her jet-black hair pulled back into a ponytail, an obvious sign of her no-nonsense-get-things-done mood.

"What's that supposed to mean?"

"It means, Jake Winters, you're spoiled. You're too comfortable. You need something, better yet, *someone* to shake you up a bit. I may not always be around, you know. What would you do then?"

Here we go again.

"This ranch is your home, you can't leave. And if you ever did, you'd have to go without Zane, because there's no way I'd ever let him go." Zane had held this ranch together after Jake's father's first stroke five years ago. At twenty-four, Jake hadn't been ready to assume the magnitude of responsibility thrust upon him.

Lottie rolled her eyes. "Whatever."

She enjoyed reminding Jake what a pitiful bachelor he was. And she'd grown more persistent in recent months—since his cousin, Ben, got remarried.

His usual response of, "I'm too busy for a wife," always earned him a scowl. Today, he kept his mouth shut. He learned a long time ago not to mess with Lottie when she had her hair in a ponytail.

"Well, I'm leaving. If you're lucky, I'll come back. If not... good luck." She laughed as she walked away.

Finally, some peace and quiet. Now there was no chance of interruption. Unless the phone rang. His mom knew he spent Friday afternoons doing paperwork and frequently called to chat. He'd better be careful, or he'd jinx himself.

He opened the window beside his desk, needing the fresh air like crops needed sunlight. As usual, his office had grown claustrophobic. Of course, the breeze blowing through the window wasn't exactly *fresh*. It carried the unmistakable scent of the manure they had hauled to the grazing pastures on the outer reaches of the ranch earlier in the week. The alfalfa fields that took priority were fertilized weeks ago.

A grin pulled at Jake's lips. Lottie would chew him out when she came home for *"stinking up the whole house."*

Focus.

The occasional low of cattle, clang of a metal gate, and drone of a tractor pulled at his attention. He wanted to be out there, not in here. But running a successful ranch required paying the bills and ordering supplies.

Jake's head snapped up at the screech of rubber on asphalt followed by the crunch of crumpling metal. A chill raced down his spine. He surged to his feet, heart in his throat, and bolted out the back door of the house. *Had one of his men been injured?*

A cool breeze hit him as he scanned the closest pastures where half a dozen horses grazed, followed by the stables, and what he could see of the stockyards. He saw nothing amiss. The green pastures and distant rolling hills looked as serene as always. *So where did the sound come from?*

He jogged to the paved lane beside the house, his gaze darting to the highway. Every muscle in his body tensed as he took in the black car wrapped around the steel beam encased in brick and concrete that supported the Double Diamond name and brand.

Jake fished the cell phone from his pocket as he sprinted toward the accident. He punched in 911 as he skidded to a stop at the wreckage. Wrenching open the front passenger door of the crumpled black sedan, he sucked in a sharp nitrogen-tainted breath. He scanned the interior of the car—the blown airbag, the shattered driver's side window, and the unconscious, bleeding driver.

"911. What is the address of your emergency?"

Recognizing the operator's voice, Jake turned away and swallowed hard, fighting the nausea threatening to overwhelm him. "Janice, this is Jake Winters. Send an ambulance to the Double Diamond Ranch. A car crashed into my front gate."

"I'm dispatching one now. Stay on the phone with me, Jake. I need you to tell me how many people are injured and how severely."

He glanced at the empty back seat. "Only one." He turned back to the unconscious driver sandwiched between the door and the center console. Blood flowed from a gaping wound on his head.

Jake pressed his fingers to the warm, sticky blood on the man's neck. A faint, slow pulse pushed back. A low gurgling sound confirmed the man still breathed. *He's alive.* Barely.

"He's in bad shape. Tell them to hurry, Janice!"

A low moan from the back seat drew Jake's attention. He inspected the area he'd previously thought empty. His stomach dropped at the sight of a woman crumpled on the floor.

Another low moan rose as he opened the back door.

A slender figure with a mass of auburn hair lay in a heap. Blood oozed from a gash above her left temple. She groaned and shifted.

"Easy... Don't move." He put his hand on her shoulder to calm her.

She turned her head, and the greenest eyes he'd ever seen stared at him.

"Help me. Don't let them kill me."

Jake's brow creased. *Kill her? Them?* Had she hit her head so hard she'd become delusional? "You're going to be okay. Help is on the way."

"Please, don't leave me." Her pleading eyes closed, and her face scrunched in pain as she rolled forward.

His gaze ran down the length of her arm, tucked behind her back at an awkward angle, to her bound wrists.

"What the..." Jake's lungs seized. He tightened his grip on the cell phone. "Janice, send another ambulance and get the sheriff out here! Quick!"

∿

Read Jake's story,
Refuge
Finding Providence Book 2,
Free on Kindle Unlimited, or from Amazon.

If you enjoyed Rescued, please consider leaving a review on Amazon.

ACKNOWLEDGMENTS

THANK YOU to my sisters and brother-in-law who read this book before I'd learned anything about writing. Thank you for telling me it was good even when it wasn't. A huge thank you to my critique group for your patience in helping me figuring out this writing thing. I won't list names because there have been so many of you and I don't want to forget anyone, but I especially want to thank Daniel Martin for challenging me and pushing me to be a better writer.

A special thanks to my beta-readers Lynda, Marie, Andria, Britney and Jenessa. Marie and Lynda, you taught me so much, and your steady encouragement has kept me going through this series.

Thank you to my editor, Michelle Henrie, for putting the finishing touches on this book. And thank you to Brenda at Blue Valley Author Services for her patience with me as she created this incredible cover. Thank you Tia for the chapter heading art.

And finally, thank you to my amazing husband who has been so supportive of me and my dreams. Thanks for making me take classes and pushing me outside my comfort zone. Thanks for holding down the fort. And thank you to my patient children who have stepped in and taken up the slack when Mom needed to write.

ABOUT THE AUTHOR

JILL HAS always been an avid reader, and romance has always been her favorite genre. If she's not writing or folding laundry her head is usually in a book.

When her father told her, "I've got a story I want you to write," she didn't think she'd ever actually do it.

But after twenty years of being a stay-at-home mom with seven children, the idea of writing and publishing a book sounded less terrifying than entering the workforce again. Boy, was she wrong!

Keep in touch with Jill Burrell
www.jillburrell.com
facebook.com/authorjillburrell

Printed in Great Britain
by Amazon

68396557R00183